INDIAN ECHOES
By Nicolas Kane

Dedicated to John, Frances, Linnette and Bardot.

Table of Contents

1

The body lay buried in the gully. Neil Adams shifted his weight on his haunches and fingered the dry earth beneath him, the sound of gravel grinding under the balls of his feet traveled like fresh blood on concrete. It broke a cradled stillness and brought him back into time.

There was a slight wind, hawks above him glided on thermals. He squinted and caught sight of one as it emerged from the sun. Neil pulled his attention from the sky and looked down at his chapped fingers and studied a wad of dirt he held between his right thumb and forefinger. He rolled and pressed the inert matter as if it were tealeaves, and prayed for some sort of answer.

"My God, what have I done?" he whispered.

It had taken a better part of an hour to bury the man, and the task had drained Neil both mentally and physically. A trickle of sweat rolled down the back of his neck. He felt it pass through his wet collar and come to a stop midway down his spine. He could feel his thirst, the intensity of it growing under the dry desert sun that pulled moisture from the midmorning air.

His eyes rested on his *Chippewa* boots. Dirty, dusty and scuffed, they were a far cry from their original condition when he had purchased them back East so many years ago. He nearly choked - to think of the contrast between that wintery day and his present situation. What he'd give to be there now - turn back the hands of time.

"Get up and run you idiot!" a voice screamed inside his head. "Get up, move - away from the body in case someone catches you here!"

Neil heard the voice, but didn't move. He felt dizzy, disconnected. Inside his mind dendrites were firing off electrical pulses, causing his thoughts to snap and move - some catching like windblown debris against a chain link fence. They moved from that East Coast memory to other things, neither settling on the thing of greatest concern nor immediate attention, but instead, swirled and danced about like undisciplined children. There was Sarah, his girlfriend - his mother and father. The man he had buried was about the same age as his father, maybe a little older. There was the police who were sure to arrive any minute and how he'd ever survive in prison. He thought of the money in the brown paper bag that lay next to him, crumbled and ominous - the one he'd taken from the dead man, and all the times he couldn't afford the things he wanted or needed, too many times to count. His eyes tightened. And he shook his head, bit his lower lip and pitied himself.

He turned and looked over at the shovel he had used to bury the man, its wooden handle worn and faded, ashen color from time and sun like an old bone. His eyes moved again, this time to the bag of money. The answer was obvious. He'd take the money and go to Vegas - bright lights, show girls, a roulette wheel; no more than five, maybe six hours from where he squatted. But the voice came again,

'You're ridiculous, pathetic.'

"Damn it!" he said. Going to Vegas with the bag of money wasn't in him. He was smaller than that. And he knew it. Vegas? Who was he fooling? He took a deep breath in and let it out. "God help me," he chastised himself. This wasn't some well polished, action film where the criminals and outlaws look so cool and appealing. This was reality, his reality, which was far from cool or well polished. He could feel his body beginning to tighten. He barely knew the man. Why had he done it - why? He threw the dirt he held between his fingers to the ground. He looked back again to the shovel lying still and at the lifeless mound in the gully and then gazed beyond them both, to the vast, desolate Arizona horizon - khaki colored sand, small parched brush, a ravine that cut through the land like a deep

6

wound, which led to reddish brown plateaus, and far beyond, big sky. There would've been Indians living out here, long ago: the Lakota, the Sioux and Apache. Some probably buried beneath his very feet. He could see them around their dwellings, smoke from their fires rising in the air, women cooking, dogs barking, children playing.......

'Time to leave - now!' the voice rang again in his head. 'Get away from the body - you're wasting time - move!'

His knees and upper back were beginning to ache. He stood up and stretched his back; he reached his arms high above and behind his head and then folded his body at the waist, touched his toes with his knees slightly bent, stayed there for a short while and slowly, rolled back up. He stood with his arms folded, cupping each elbow in the opposite hand. His lips had pressed together ever so slightly to accommodate a soft, odd smile formed by the onset of a summer that now flowed through his mind; scattered bits of shell from an acorn that had busted open, taking him back to a dead sparrow, a BB gun, running in fields that surrounded his home, shucking corn on a front porch, catching fireflies under starlit purple skies, searching for far off voices in solitary late night ham radio sessions, and playing Marco Polo in the neighbor's pool – memories - pockets of them, he hadn't realized were still in him, including these Indians he now imagined out here in this desert, which brought him back to the attic of his childhood home where he first discovered their histories through three books that had once belonged to his grandfather. Even in the dim light of that attic, the eyes that stared through the rugged and torn exteriors of these human beings shone sharp and pure with an undeniable kind of brilliant veracity. There were to be hours spent, pages spread, a sun soaked livingroom carpet, and time measured by a solitary grandfather clock that stood ticking in the corner.

Although he didn't look it, Neil Adams had just turned forty years old, and yet, in truth, he still felt more connected to that little boy on the rug than to any projected image of an adult. Had he changed since that summer in any real significant way? He couldn't tell.

Now here he was out in a desert with a bag of money and a dead man buried only a few feet from where he stood. His eyes, as restless as his mind, continued to move across the Arizona land. Behind him, resting on its center stand, was a nineteen seventy-four BMW R90/6 motorcycle that had brought him out here. It was an older two valve twin air cooled model that was much more simplistic and less sophisticated by the standards of today, but Neil found comfort in that. He had bought the motorcycle from an elderly widow several years earlier and it'd been reliable and predictable each time he rode it. He turned his attention to the motorcycle's tank that now glimmered in the late morning sun and tried to imagine at what level the gasoline lined the inside. He had passed a gas station about thirteen miles back along the sparse highway so, maybe, he'd be alright.

"Fucking choices," he said with a snicker. He hadn't stopped at the gas station on the way out here, and now, he - not only had to concern himself with the act he had just committed – but, also with the possibility of running out of fuel. 'It is all about choices, isn't it?' his mind continued. He was thinking on a much broader scale. His mind ran and jumped to seemingly disconnected thoughts. The image of his girlfriend, Sarah flashed in him again. A caustic mix of both pain and disgust filled his stomach. He began to play back the choice they had made to terminate her pregnancy. He quickly tried to wash this thought from his mind and replace it with the idea of getting on his motorcycle and riding back to the gas station, but the "choices" remark had yet to be finished and fully digested inside his head. Suddenly, words from that same voice that had earlier prodded him to get up and leave, popped back into his head, this time saying, 'It's the small choices that determine the larger'- Neil couldn't think of a word that fell naturally into place there; 'larger..... uhmmm, larger scheme of things, larger picture, larger scope, breadth...' larger picture, seemed right.

Words continued from this voice that had become more pronounced since the abortion. It was the kind of voice that never hesitated or second-guessed itself, but was direct and to the point like a headmaster or instructor reminding students what homework assignment was due. He had hoped the voice would simply go away, but it hadn't - and in fact, had only grown louder over time.

'This is what determines our future; the small choices we make today.' This imaginary instructor really bothered Neil because he knew, in some strange way, this annoying fuck might be right. There was no use fighting it, Neil was off and running, engaged with this voice inside his head.

'What about all those sorry souls who jump onto an ordinary commercial airliner, only to have it crash into a tower killing all on board, what determined their future?' Neil countered.

The Instructor didn't seem to have an answer here because the response, 'The choice to buy the airline ticket.' didn't seem to satisfy Neil.

Neil looked at the mound in the gully. He could feel himself beginning to shake. The wind pushed again and in it he thought he heard the sound of a siren. He listened more intently, but heard nothing. He slapped his hands together, and then rubbed the thighs of his jeans. Grabbing the brown paper bag, he strode up the small embankment. He fell backwards, got up and grabbed hold of the bag again. He went to his motorcycle and stuffed the bag into one of his saddlebags. He pulled out a canteen of water and gulped down the last few ounzes of warm liquid. He shook the empty canteen, screwed the cap on tight and tossed it back into the saddlebag. He closed the lid then walked over to the shovel and, picking it up, threw it with all his might out into the desert away from the body. He went back to his motorcycle and grabbed his black leather jacket lying across the seat and swung the heavy garment over his back and pulled his arms through the sleeves. He found the keys in the right side pocket and saddled the motorcycle. He turned the fuel petcocks, started the engine, and with his clear, plastic eyewear in place, Neil clicked the bike into first gear, held his left foot on the ground, slowly released the clutch, and leaned the bike into a U turn. He was in third gear by the time he adjusted his left side mirror and watched as the reflected, vibrating gully receded, becoming just a small point against a limitless sky.

2

His motorcycle liberated Neil, especially on long open roads. A rhythm evolved, connection between rider, machine and the surroundings – be it a stretch of land, a distant cloud or the passing of a blurred fence post. He had first heard of this 'rhythm' from older, experienced riders at a repair shop, *Dillards* he would visit mostly on the weekends. The place served, not only to facilitate mechanical fixes, but also as a hangout for a bunch of hardened, no nonsense men - the kind who didn't go much for mocha lattes or Pottery Barn catalogues. One of them, a recovering alcoholic named Bill, was a permanent fixture at the shop and would be pivotal in Neil's development and understanding of his motorcycle. Rumor had it, Bill worked as a machinist somewhere else, but no matter what time, day or night – one could always find him at *Dillards*, cigarette and coffee mug in hand.

"It's *not* about the motocycle," Bill had said when they first met. "It's about you and the motocycle, to yourself. It's a rhythm, a crazy, underwater dream seed rhythm."

Neil remembered laughing at those words. "A bunch of old-timer malarkey; nothing more than a romanticized view of motorcycle travel," he had told himself.

It wasn't until much later - when Neil had learned his bike's mannerisms, extinguished unnecessary fears, and began to relax with his motorcycle - that the meaning of this rhythm was personally discovered, a beatific numbness; his thoughts were allowed to wander in the playground of this created rhythm, thoughts, which had been deeply submerged within his brain, bubbled to the surface as he droned on down a lengthy stretch of road. It didn't happen each and every time he rode, but when it did happen, it came without effort like a baseball pitcher suddenly finding a zone. It was akin to cutting his parents' lawn when he was a kid; the stifling, thick heat of a humid Connecticut summer and the loud, steady buzz of a Briggs&Stratton 3.5 hp engine strapped to a lawnmower pushed into an endless expanse of grass, inducing a trance, which allowed his thoughts to float without self supervision.

Now, as he rode down the Arizona highway away from the buried body, the motorcycle engine hummed, the valves (which he always adjusted slightly loose) ticked, the air rushed, and the scenery moved; all the elements were in play to create the rhythm. But, his mind wasn't receptive; it was far from open. It felt tight, squeezed, strained - almost wounded. He wanted to stop, pull over, go to the police and get it over with. But how? What direction? Where to find them out here in the middle of nowhere - was anybody's guess.

"To hell with it," he said.

He opened the throttle. The engine sputtered, sucking the last remnants of fuel from the toaster tank. Unflinchingly, Neil leaned to each side, just as Bill had taught him, and switched the petcocks to their 'reserve' settings. There was a slight delay, the engine caught, the bike steadied and sped down flat. He focused on the immediate need for fuel, hoping to make the gas station before his reserves ran dry.

It was ten fifty six when Neil slowed and leaned his motorcycle into the filling station he had passed earlier in the day. A bell clanged as his two wheels rolled over a rubber hose that stretched between the pumps and station. A lean elderly man in denim coveralls and a baseball cap stood on a small, sturdy ladder pulling a wet rubber squeegee across the large picture window of the front office. He turned and nodded as Neil drove the bike to one of the two pumps. There were no other customers. The station had a beautiful simplicity to it, like that of a Cape Cod structure - small, white, and practical. Below the window, which the man was cleaning, lay a long wooden trough filled with geranium flowers. The building was a two bay facility, one of which was empty, allowing Neil a clear view of the clean, orderly workspace inside. Black hoses and belts hung on the back wall above a workbench that ran the entire width of the garage. Above the middle of the bench a set of wrenches hung on the wall like xylophone keys. The concrete floor looked freshly swept. Close to Neil, the chrome gas pump handles sparkled as though they'd been recently polished. The pump housing's fire engine red paint shimmered like a fresh coat of nail polish. At the top of these housings black bold numbers on a white faceplate rotated, displaying the amount of gas sold. Inside the garage, and just beyond the opened door of the office, lay the hind half of a sleeping dog. The man climbed off the ladder, leaned on the squeegee handle, silently watching.

Neil got off his bike and reached for the gas cap. It wouldn't open, so he forced it hard. He dropped his keys and lost his balance, causing him to nearly dump the bike. He caught it just in time. "Christ!" He centered the bike, grabbed the gas nozzle and jammed it into his tank. He watched as the pump hummed and the black numbers turned. Soon, the pump's handle clicked and kicked back at a little over twelve dollars. The man released the squeegee into a bucket of soapy water and ambled towards Neil.

"Having trouble balancing your bike?" the man asked with a grin.

"No, I'm fine." Neil said, picking his keys up off the ground.

"If you say so." The man chuckled. "How much ya got there?"

"A little over twelve, twelve thirty five to be exact."

"Exactly, twelve thirty five then."

Neil wanted to hit him. He took a moment, told himself he was just being hypersensitive. There was no malice here. He let it go.

'Be a man,' The Instructor barked inside his head.

Neil pulled a twenty dollar bill from his wallet and extended it towards the man who hadn't yet reached the pump. The man walked with a limp, the rubber sole of his left shoe built up seven or eight inches. He took the bill and turned toward the office.

"I'll get your change." He stopped and turned around. "Not much for counting?"

"Excuse me?" Neil answered.

The man held out the bill. "I said you're not much for counting, are ya?"

Neil looked at the one dollar bill pinched between the man's fingers. "Is that the bill I gave you?"

"Sure is, but it won't pay for what you put in your tank."

'Slight of hand trick- punch his ugly mug already and let's get outta here,' The Instructor said.

"I thought-" Neil looked at the bill again. "Sorry about that."

"Happens."

Neil reached into his pocket and found the twenty he'd been looking for. The man exchanged bills, gave Neil a hard look and walked towards the office.

Neil snapped shut the gas cap atop his motorcycle's freshly filled fuel tank and waited for the man to return. He kicked the toe of his right boot into the ground. A small cloud of dirt rose into the air and drifted north. Neil's eyes followed it, then moved across the empty two-lane highway, and farther still, to Auburn colored rock formations that stood in the distance against light pale blue sky. A Santa Fe train, with its iconic red and yellow markings, cut through the scene and lumbered westward. His eyes held on it and his mind moved.

Begun in 1863, and rivaled only by the construction of the Panama Canal several decades earlier, The Transcontinental Railroad was the most grandiose engineering feat America had ever accomplished. The railroad had been built with the hands of roughly twenty five thousand Chinese, Irish, German, South American immigrants and men who had served in the Civil war. Financed by wealthy Wall Street business tycoons, and of course, with the cooperation from the U.S. government, it was built when no white men lived west of Omaha, and the Indians, who did occupy that western land, were never asked permission for the laying of the tracks.

'What had the Cheyenne thought when they first saw this metal machine snake cross their hunting grounds?' Neil asked

14

himself, as he watched the Santa Fe train rumble westward. He imagined a search party, several bare chested Cheyenne warriors sitting silently on their horses from atop a high, rocky vantage point looking down on the construction below, and, seeing spikes being driven into their heartland like the harpooning of a whale, had probably felt helpless as their lives began to change forever. The railroad was like a cancerous cell - seeking new, virgin territory for nutrients, and once it started, wouldn't stop. It was the beginning of the end. The iron arteries spread south to where Neil now stood.

"Here you are." The man was back with Neil's change.

Neil hadn't heard him coming. "Oh, th - thanks."

"Didn't mean to startle you," the man said. "You okay?"

"No. Yes. I mean, yes. Just admiring the view, old West and all."

"Nice, huh? First time out here?"

"First time.... you mean first time here?" Neil asked.

"That's what I mean."

"Me? Not really."

"Not really?"

"Not - just sightseeing, know the area through...hearsay."

"Humm," the man's head jerked back a little. He paused for a moment, then motioned towards Neil's bike. "That gonna do it for ya then?"

"Yup. That's it," Neil answered. He caught a glimpse of the eyes staring at him from beneath the brim of the baseball cap: Husky steel blue eyes - clear, cool and piercing. He scrambled for something to say. "Any place to eat around here?"

"Hungry are ya?"

"A diner, restaurant, anything at all?"

"Well..." the man began.

'Ahh shit, here we go,' The Instuctor's voice broke loud and clear, 'country bumpkin bullshit - city slicker rolling into a small town without any sense of direction and here comes JimmyBob to the rescue, in all his glory, relishing the power.'

Neil indulged the man, giving him free rein. True, the only thing missing, and what Neil almost expected, was for this man to spit tobacco juice on the dusty ground. But so what? He had much bigger problems.

"Umm," The man thought for a second, "well...let's see, there's The Honey Dew Diner, that's more than a few miles up..... you need direction, that's what you're asking me for?"

'Jackass,' The Instructor interjected.

"Yeah, direction," Neil confirmed.

"Direction....if you stay on this road, about another seven miles or so up along the way, you'll find Mabeline's - great prime rib and rich, black coffee - a little fancier, mind you, but worth it."

"That sounds like a plan, Mabeline's."

"Everyone needs a plan," the man smiled.

Neil heard the man's words, but he wasn't listening. His arms felt weak and his head was about to collapse.

"Mind if I pull my bike over to the side of your garage and clean the air filter?" Neil asked. "These roads sure can kick up some dust."

"Not at all, as a matter of fact, if you'd like there's air and water on the side there too. You alright?"

"Fine. Thanks," Neil said and pushed the motorcycle from its center stand and rolled it towards the appointed side. He could feel the man's eyes hanging on him. He sat down with his head between his knees.

'Can I get you a diaper?'

'Leave me alone.'

'Maybe a little pacifier? You better toughen the fuck up, boy.'

It took a few minutes, but Neil rose to his feet. He looked around. The man had disappeared.

'Probably back in that office making phone calls.'

Neil reached for the seat and swung it open. Beneath the motorcycle seat was a plastic tray that provided just enough space for a black canvas tool pouch that held four screwdrivers, a set of Allen wrenches, a feeler gauge, several open ended wrenches, two pliers, and a tiny flashlight - that was all. The simplicity of the motorcycle meant that minor maintenance required few tools. It was another reason he had chosen this motorcycle - self-sufficiency.

Neil grabbed some of these tools and began work on the bike. He would take this time to settle himself, his mind. It was quiet and ideal for such a thing. Traffic was extremely light along the hot, dry highway, and as Neil worked on the motorcycle, he could hear every so often (without bothering to lift his head from the job at hand) the swish of a passing car. Not many stopped at the station, but almost all that did stop had been here before. Neil knew this because he could hear bits of familiar conversation and pockets of laughter pass between the attendant and his customers. He listened for the crackle of a patrol car's radio.

'He didn't have to die that way - you could have stopped it,' The Instructor said.

Neil's fingers slipped on the screwdriver he was using. His knuckles scrapped across the metal frame. There wasn't much blood, but his hands were shaking.

"Shit!"

'Ya killed him, plain and simple.'

'Didn't!'

Neil squeezed tight the screwdriver's handle and tried again, but his hands wouldn't have it.

"Just focus," he said, wiping tears from his eyes.

He took a breath in and closed his eyes. He needed to go to the proper authorities and confess all before it was too late.

'You're weak!' The Instructor said.

Neil didn't argue. If only he'd been born with a stronger constitution and thicker, impartial skin; the kind out on battlefields with men, soldiers who did what they were told without hesitation, without feeling or any second-guessing. What would he be like today, he wondered, had he served in the military - would he be less sensitive, emotional, about situations, including the one he was presently in?

When the sun had fallen well past its zenith, Neil's work with the motorcycle was practically finished.

"There's an authenticity in the selection of your motorcycle, member when these bikes first came out." The attendant was

17

standing over Neil with two bottles of soda. "Not the first of their bikes, mind you. I'm not that old," he laughed, "but this style." He motioned towards Neil's motorcycle with the two lower fingers of his right hand, which held one of the bottles.

"Nineteen seventy-four," Neil said, looking up while cupping his eyes from the sun.

"I guess it was seventy four," the man said, "don't see too many people working on this kinda bike. All chips and electronics now...thought you might be thirsty, here's a Coke."

'Guy's creepy, poison in that bottle, a molester perhaps or a sedative and is on to you, has called the authorities - holding you here until they arrive,' The Instructor's words skipped through Neil's head like a flat rock across water.

A wet, warm plug suddenly jabbed Neil's left ear as he knelt trying to make his way up on his feet. He fell back down.

"Chloe, off a him, come on girl!"

Wiping his ear, and immediately looking to his right, Neil saw the wagging tail of a slightly overweight Golden Retriever retreating behind her owner.

"She's harmless, I promise," the attendant reassured Neil.

Neil laughed. He was disappointed not to have one of his own and had it not been for the ridiculous, restrictive rental conditions he found himself under, would've owned one in a heartbeat.

He got up on his feet, took the cold wet bottle of Coke, twisted the cap off, and took a large gulp. The carbonated liquid hit his dry throat. He immediately coughed. He patted his chest then wiped his mouth with his forearm. He struggled to get a word out,

"Thanks."

"No problem."

Neil took a moment to let his throat settle.

"I know what you mean though with the newer bikes, at least I can work on this one myself, have an understanding of what I'm riding." He thought of Bill and was thankful.

The man walked around to the other side of the bike and looked the machine over.

"Know the mule you're riding. Well, it's same for cars too. Truth is, besides basic repair, there's less and less I can do for my customers when they bring newer cars in. Now only emergencies, someone stuck up on the highway, flat tire, over heating......
Listen, if you're up for it, my wife will be coming by soon with a late lunch, there's more than enough food, so if you're still hungry, you're more than welcome to join us."

"Thanks," Neil said, "But I can't -"

"She's coming by, it's really no trouble."

"I don't know."

"Well, the offer's out there, I mean, if you're not in a rush."

"No, no – I'm not in a rush, but, well ya know, I..."

The man said nothing, just looked at Neil.

Neil was hungry and after asking the man for directions to a place to eat, he knew the man knew this too.

"I mean, if it's really no problem, I suppose so..." said Neil.

'Dummy!'

"Don't even think twice about it, she often brings lunch, dinner sometimes - no problem at all." The attendant shifted his attention to the bike. "How did things work out here?"

"Fine," Neil responded. "A procedure that would have taken anyone else half the time, but I like taking my time with things like this."

"The old carpenter's adage, 'measure twice, cut once' or 'If you don't have time to do it right, when will you have time to do it over?'" He walked to the back of Neil's motorcycle and stopped. "Noticed your plates earlier, is that where you're coming from - California?"

"Yes," Neil said. He began to wipe down his scattered tools and place them back into the pouch.

'Tell him about the body.'

"Where in California?" the man asked.

"Long Beach."

"Oh, Long Beach, yup. Been there-nice area. Hadn't been there since I was in the Navy then a few years back the wife and I visited the Aquarium, and a terrific night spot. Saw a swing band." The man paused and looked up at the sky, "The name, the

19

name...... I can't remember, but a great spot, blue something or other, near the waterfront. He looked directly at Neil and said, "Quite a long way, Long Beach."

Neil occupied himself with his tools and avoided the man's eyes as best he could.

"I'm out here on a camping trip to Prescott National Forest, took a few days off from work."

"Couldn't have picked nicer weather for it," the man said. He extended his hand towards Neil, "Name's John, by the way."

Neil thought of his dirty hands and bloody knuckles, and the calluses formed by the shovel's handle. But, he didn't want to draw too much attention to himself. He extended his right hand and clasped John's hand,

"Neil. Nice to meet you," Neil said.

"Nice to meet you, too, Neil."

Even though he had just turned forty, there were still times when Neil felt like that insecure child being introduced to an adult for the first time. Somehow or another the term 'adult' just didn't seem to belong to him, wasn't something he considered himself to be. An 'adult' was someone who had a mortgage, participated in CNN polls, wore ironed shirts, read the business section of the morning paper, and constituted the faceless glue that held society together. And, now, having just left a man to rot in the desert, this feeling of inadequecy hit him especially hard. He had the urge to get on his motorcycle and run from this situation all together, but it seemed too late for that now.

There was still time before the wife arrived and Neil did his best to be cool. He and John talked weather, the present scenery, and fished for topics of mutual interest. Relief came in the way of a customer or two that diverted John's attention away from Neil. But it wasn't enough, and would have been completely intolerable, save for the fact that John did most of the talking.

Neil learned John had bought the station back in nineteen sixty three and enjoyed both the surrounding area and the people who lived here. He was content with his work and the more they talked, Neil could see there was a reassurance to John that reflected this contentment. He had the quality of those individuals who have, through fortune or troubled times, come to rest on solid rock; to have found their position in life and act in accordance with it. They possess a steadfast quality of calm stability drawn from the same breath as a ticking clock, changing seasons and Southwest rock formations, infusing hope and peace and less anxiety in the hearts of those who are around them. Neil felt this from John, reminding him of times when he had visited his grandparents; it was as though time slowed, hardly moved at all. It was a dance, the way these older people moved with time, the rotation of the earth, the rhythm of the world - there was no rush in their being, anymore than there's a rush in the moon, the tides or setting sun. All will be well, everything is eternal. These things and people serve as a nucleus, around which the dizzy, ever changing world of electrons swim.

Neil knew and had come to accept, of course, that nothing lasts forever, that things do change, but even if they had changed around John, he seemed to defy this concept. You could see it in the way he interacted with the customers who visited the station and was probably the reason they returned; to be rejuvenated, filled, and in some way reconnected each and every visit to a never ending, never yielding source - always leaving in better spirits than when they had arrived.

It was when the two men had moved into the office and Neil was helping to stock quarts of oil that had been delivered earlier in the day, that the sound of a car's horn stopped and pulled him from his work. Looking up, he saw a 1957 Chevy Nomad station wagon glide into the station. White and teal in color, the car's appearance betrayed its age; it looked as though it had just come off the showroom floor. Behind the wheel of the car was a woman who wore a blue paisley bandanna pulled back over her head, exposing just a few gray strands of hair that rested on each side of her temples; an invigorated Katharine Hepburn, making her way on a back country road to a fruit stand somewhere in Connecticut. She beamed, her skin looked tight and healthy. She parked and got out of the car.

John greeted her with a great smile, a kiss on the cheek.

"Ahhh," she said, "so sorry I'm late, you must be starving."

21

"Don't be ridiculous," John said. "Honey this is Neil. Neil this is my wife, Mary."

"Hello, Neil," Mary said. She was all smiles. "Glad you could join us for lunch." Her handshake was joyful, vibrant.

"Thanks," Neil replied. He looked for an answer in her eyes. Why did they invite a perfect stranger to lunch- it just didn't make sense. Were they purposefully stalling him here until the police arrived? He searched for an excuse to get over to his motorcycle. But, he wouldn't have time to find it; Mary began to unloaded items from the back of the station wagon that included: a wicker picnic basket, a blanket, a checkered tablecloth and a large glass jar of iced tea. She handed these off to John and Neil, who carried the items to a grassy spot partially shaded on the right side of the gas station. Everything seemed fine and Neil told himself to calm down and relax. Chloe, the Golden retriever, followed all the doings with happiness and anticipation. Neil bent to pet her and she licked his face.

'What is this, Norman fucking Rockwell?' The Instructor asked. 'Let's not forget -'

It wasn't Norman Rockwell. It was really happening. The reality of it was beautiful and Neil fought hard not to give into any cynical force that would try and have him think otherwise, but neither the dead man nor The Instructor would let go. Neil took a full breath and held on as best he could.

Soon, all three had settled down to the feast that Mary had provided: roasted chicken, fish cakes, coleslaw, corn on the cob, oranges, raspberry ice cream, and iced tea. Pulled from a leaning position against the side of the building, was an old canvas folding chair, which John sat in. An upright tree trunk served as a table. Neil sat with Mary on a blanket that covered a large patch of ground. The day was peaceful and beautiful. The reluctance that originally pulled Neil from eating lunch with strangers had begun to subside, replaced with a comfortable and effortless ease. It was as though he had known John and Mary his whole life and today's lunch was just one of many they had enjoyed together. Chloe sat next to John with attentive eyes and focused on the food, which he had begun to eat. The conversation was light and unforced. The only interruption came when John excused himself to attend to the few customers. After servicing a Jeep and talking briefly with the driver, John came back with a serious look on his face.

"Daryl says old man Williams has disappeared, Betty's beside herself."

"Not again," Mary said, "don't those people at that home know. They haven't seen him?"

"An orderly says he was in last night, checked on him, lights out at 9 sharp. This morning his bed was empty."

"Should be more oversight in that facility. Didn't this happen last month, found him out wandering near Eagle Trail in nothing but his underwear and shoes?"

"Yeah...... this time it's different. Betty's got a gut feeling he's been murdered."

"Oh please," Mary laughed. "Murdered? Here?"

"That's what she's telling everybody."

"Poor thing. Terrible. No fun getting old......she needs her family." She asked Neil about his family.

"Do have family in California?"

He told her about Connecticut, his brothers and sisters and the recent death of his father.

"I'm sorry," she said. "That's hard." She paused. "Must have a lot of nice memories, though, New England snow covered Christmas dinners and Thanksgiving family get togethers." She looked down at the blanket, and gently twisted a stray strand of fabric. "Must have been nice."

Eventually, all three had satisfied their hunger and the mood softened and slowed. Neil sipped his iced tea, Mary began packing the remains and John, sitting in his chair, pulled a pipe from his side pocket and, tapping it on one of the chair legs, knocked out the few remnants from its last use. He then dipped the empty bowl into a pouch of tobacco and softly packed it. Leaning back, he struck a match and held the flame over the pipe and drew on the worn and bitten black stem. The flame hit the tobacco. Smoke rose from his mouth. The tobacco held a heavy, musty smell, like old canvas- reminding Neil of the pages from his grandfather's large desktop dictionary and the books about the Indians.

"Neil, are you sure you wouldn't like any more food, plenty left?" Mary asked.

"No. I'm good, thanks. That was great."

"John?"

"Are you kidding? No thanks."

"I'm sure Chloe wouldn't mind a nibble or two," Neil said.

"Oh, she'll eat almost anything," Mary said.

"Including rocks," John added with a chuckle, inducing a shared memory on the lips of Mary.

Neil had not felt this comfortable in a very long time. He held an orange and began to peel it. There was no desire or need to speak. A lone bird chirped high in the tree above them. The beauty of the day seemed eternal.

Facing the back of the station, and looking to his right, Neil saw the large trunk of a tree. He guessed an Elm or Maple, its upper branches responsible for the shade that protected them from the glaring sun. He found it remarkable and odd that this type of tree could exist in this part of the country. The environment seemed too hostile and arid to allow anything more than sagebrush and cactus to grow. As Neil studied the trunk of the tree he caught sight of something a few feet from its other side. A black metal railing formed a squared off area of about 200 feet. The fenced in area was partly shaded, but in one of the sunlit spots stood a small white marker, a gravestone of some sort.

Following Neil's silent interest, and withdrawing the pipe from his mouth, John calmly spoke,

"It's a grave marker."

Mary, who'd been unaware of the interaction between the two men, now stopped and looked at John. She hesitated only briefly then lifted the iced tea jar and said in a quiet, yet layered tone, "I think I'll start packing the car."

Neil, sensing the shift in her behavior, offered to help her pack up the remaining items. She kindly refused and began walking back to the station wagon, parked a short distance away. John sat still in the chair, puffed his pipe, and looked beyond Neil to the parked car and Mary. And then, as if addressed to the shaded air around him, he said in an empty voice, "We lost our child many, too many years ago, when we were both young......... she - we don't talk much about it." His words were direct, simple and strong like the ancient land that surrounded them, delivered with no pretense and no other intention than to reveal what was hidden from Neil.

"I'm sorry," Neil said.

A few moments of silence passed. A long lean yellow Cadillac pulled into the station and life began again. John tapped his pipe against the side of the tree trunk table, dispensing the used tobacco, and placed the pipe into his pocket. He then pushed himself from the folding chair and walked to the gas pump where the Cadillac waited.

Neil looked again to the spot where the small gravestone was planted. Was this a terrible coincidence or some godawful reminder of what he'd done to that man out in the desert? How could this be happening? Did they know? How could they? The gravestone was there - and had been before his arrival. It wasn't about him. He took a bite of the orange and sipped his iced tea. He looked at John who was leaning on the driver's side of the car, sharing a funny story with the man inside. Neil looked at Mary as she finished packing the station wagon. He turned back to the tree and looked at the grave and thought of their loss. He wondered when it happened, how it happened, boy or girl? He thought of Sarah, what she might be doing at this moment back in L.A., and then, of course, Neil thought of the child, the life they had aborted. The weight of what he and Sarah had done now filled him with a sordid heaviness. Sitting beneath this tree every rational reason they had used to justify the choice they had made together seemed, empty, feeble, and in this moment, even pathetic. It occurred to him now, the cost for that act to his life, Sarah's life, might be greater than they could have anticipated. He knew too, that it was an act he couldn't take back, one that would last a lifetime and the ugliness of it sank in his stomach. He saw the pain caused by the unintentional death of a child that still affected John and Mary. They had lost something dear to them. Nothing lasts. Preservation is a myth. We are born, live so very briefly and die. We know not when or how. What right had he to throw away something so precious, thee most precious thing that this world had to offer?

But, as if stepping into a quagmire and realizing it at the last second, Neil quickly stepped back from this mental inquisition. This was neither the time nor the place for such a thought. The bird above him sang out again, drawing Neil's sight and mind to loftier things.

"Still some things left here." Mary was back from the station wagon.

Cut from his thoughts, Neil responded, "Here, Mary let me help."

"That's kind, Neil, but no," she said.

When all the items were loaded back into the station wagon, (including Chloe who sat panting in the front seat) Mary kissed John, shook Neil's hand, gave a kind, yet, lugubrious smile and said goodbye. She was off.

By now the air had cooled and the earth gave the first gentle signs of shedding another day. Neil began to think of the road, how many miles he'd ride, maybe late into the night or stop somewhere and rest early, that way, starting fresh in the morning.

John motioned him into the office. Maps lay on the counter top.

"Thought you might need these," John stated. "Go ahead, take your pick."

"How'd you know?"

"Don't know anyone who doesn't need a map, direction-" He read Neil's hesitation. "Go on n' choose any you'd like," John laughed, "they're free." He then disappeared into the workspace of the garage.

"Thanks, John, I will," Neil called out after him.

With the maps before him, Neil carefully considered each state he might be traveling through- 'Arizona, Texas, or was it- New Mexico before Texas, Louisiana....ummm Mississippi?' He looked up from the selection of maps, searching in the air for recollection of 4th grade geography; trying to remember the names of those blank states, which had been outlined on Xeroxed pieces of paper Ms. Rinaldi had handed out...- 'embarrassing, really not being able to know where all fifty states are located in this small country of ours, it's no wonder the rest of the world laughs at us for -' hanging on the wall behind the counter - next to a large, white face clock with black dials and a smooth red running second hand was a large road map of the entire United States. He laughed at the clock, and map. "Just like the ones in Ms. Rinaldi's class."

John's voice rang from somewhere inside the garage, "Not going back to California just yet?"

"No, not yet, going East. How'd ya know I wasn't going back to California?"

Through the work sounds that now came from the garage Neil thought he heard John's voice say, "East is nice, especially this time of year."

Neil felt a slight pang, an almost painful impulse, to tell John why he was really going East, and how Mary and John had, unwittingly, helped in that decision; their lives served as an example of a kind of debt being paid by the living to the dead. But, now, as the afternoon wore on, Neil was beginning to feel he had overstayed his welcome, and, too, feared if he didn't get underway soon, he might change his mind entirely. He checked his watch- time had gotten away from him. It was so much later than he thought. He quickly collected the maps he needed and prepared to leave. Outside, he packed his bike, and before departing, ducked his head into the garage one last time to say goodbye.

"Well, I just wanted to let you know I'm taking off and thank you."

John stood working on a carburetor. He looked up and wiped his hands on a clean rag. "Thank me, nothing. Thank you for the company today." He walked over to Neil, and looking him right in the eye, shook his hand. "Appreciate it."

"Your hospitality is a rare thing, thank you," Neil said. He was caught off guard by his own words, and immediately regretted the corny way they had come off. But, he also couldn't remember the last time he had been so direct and close with another stranger and he felt something starting to well up inside of him. He looked away and coughed.

"I don't know," John said, "and this may sound a bit heavy handed, but so be it. I believe one thing is certain, any hospitality you might have felt here today is abundant everywhere, if you open yourself up to it-remember, you get what you give and that ain't no lie. You be careful out there and enjoy New York. Take care, Neil."

"I will." Neil walked out to his motorcycle and grabbed his helmet, hanging from from the left side mirror, and fastened its strap beneath his chin. As he swung his right leg over the seat and straddled the bike, the last few words John had spoke hung in Neil's ears. Granted, he had been through a lot that day, but he hadn't remembered mentioning New York to John.

3

The sun was seriously low, just a wisp of pink sky. Neil had studied the maps and headed north. He was glad to be back on the road. The engine hummed beneath his thighs. The air moved around him and he could smell the pleasing, faint, cool sage. Behind him, tied to the seat and packed in the fiberglass saddlebags, were his belongings-clothing, tent, sleeping bag, all of which he had packed for his original camping trip out in the desert, and the newly acquired note and money. He was complete and a feeling of independence filled his being. Here was everything he needed. There wasn't much and it caused him to wonder how little was needed in his everyday life. It wasn't as though Neil had a lot of material possessions, he didn't, but now, as he rode along this early evening road with the first arrival of twinkling, faint stars shining above, he began to ruminate on the nature of material goods. The Buddha came to his mind; born a wealthy prince with all his material wants satisfied, but lacking spiritual truth, he left the confines of his opulent palace and set out on a quest to find spiritual enlightenment. At a crossing stream, he disrobed, cast off his extravagant garments, cut his hair and clothed himself in the traditional poor monk's attire of a saffron robe and sandals. After years and years of extreme searching, enlightenment finally came to The Buddha in the form of Nirvana beneath a bodhi-tree. Neil thought of this story and the material distractions in his own life. He certainly wasn't a prince with jades and unimaginable wealth, and spiritual enlightenment wasn't on his 'bucket list', but how much was enough? And, it wasn't only The Buddha who spoke about the pitfalls of material wealth; all the great spiritual teachings shared this commonality.

Neil could feel himself being lured into a mindful presence. The motorcycle was performing flawlessly, and the road stretched forever and emptied into a layered horizon of pinks, blues and blacks. The cool evening sky swayed like a speakeasy lounge. There was time to think. He took a mental tour of his studio apartment back in Long Beach; the desktop computer, was it *really* necessary? Some pots and pans in his overcrowded kitchen cupboard didn't get enough use to justify owning them, some of his clothing he hadn't worn in years, those he thought, could be easily donated to a charity center, other items, too, he found in his mental inventory could be given away. He contemplated the difference between need and want.

'Once these material distractions disappeared, I'd be left only with the necessities, and could possibly live a much more, simple, productive life.'

'Oh please-these material possessions you own define you – define who you are as an individual,' The Instructor said.

'Umm, not really- way out of line there.'

'Why did you choose *this* motorcycle? Why not another, say a Yamaha or a Kawasaki? And what about that fancy sleeping bag you own- why that one and not another?'

'But they're just items, things - dispensable products, used to make life a little easier, not define an individual,' Neil said.

'You naive fool, production is the hallmark of industry. These so-called, 'dispensable items' you speak of are a reflection of mankind's intellectual progress. By denying them is to deny reality, the fruits of our labor. And it does define us.'

'Artificially inseminated bastard!' Neil threw back, without knowing the exact meaning of these words or why he had chosen them, which caused him to pause, and at the same moment he laughed, a crazy wild man, mangy cat laugh that rolled and bounced around in his stomach before escaping. He laughed and laughed hard, realizing no one was here to judge him or his words. It made no difference if he was 'right' or 'wrong'. Those only mattered outside of his head. He screamed into the

30

darkness and laughed again. It didn't matter; an unrestricted license to say anything he wanted, whether it made sense or none at all. 'You'd love nothing more than to live in a machine driven, manufactured environment devoid of any real conceptual birth.' Again, he didn't understand the exact meaning of these words, but it didn't matter. It felt good to move and speak in a spontaneous flow uninterrupted by judgment. At first, there was no response to his comment. But he felt like one was coming, and it did.

'Talking crazy, so what is it, you want to hide from reality and become a monk?'

'That's not the point, and besides, reality is what you make of it.'

'Okay, Grasshopper. Is part of that reality being fired from your job, an aborted child, and a man left to rot out in the desert?'

'Shut up.'

'You make no sense. You have lost your bearings. I am right and you are wrong. What you'd like to get away from –'

'What?' Neil asked.

'You tell me.'

'Tell you what?'

'Keep on running.'

Tired of this game, this voice, these words which acted as talons tearing into him. Neil needed to end it.

'It is what it is,' he said.

'Not much in the way of intelligence tonight are we?'

'Yup. It is what it is.'

'Cutting a little too close to the bone?'

'Let me - it go.'

Neil shook this distracting, combative figure and words from his mind, and instead, focused his attention on the present moment and physical surroundings.

Glancing at the road far ahead, Neil could see the silhouetted horizon was quickly losing definition, and stars had multiplied in the darkening sky. There was something serene about it and in it he saw rest and completion, death and unity, darkness and eternity, and it was good and complete, with no fear. And what it held was conscionable, tender, warm and true and all there for the taking, if only he could plug into it and listen; a place where any question he had, or would ever have, could be answered, so they'd never be the need or desire to ask another. He was feeling the hum of the cable, but had not yet touched its current.

'There is no way..this Instructor or ....I will ruin this moment.' Light from the instrument panel was now visible in the darkness and Neil glanced at the steady seventy mile per hour speedometer needle, not because he needed to at this moment, but, because the lit instrument panel comforted him; it was a sign that things were working as they ought, all was well. It was fascinating to look at that speedometer needle; knowing that several hundred people whom he had never met, in a far off country, which he had never visited, had produced - not only that speedometer needle - but, also, those lit numbers, the headlight, the gas tank, the entire bike just to culminate in him riding here tonight. And it truly amazed him; to think of production lines all over the world and how something, such as a simple plastic laundry basket produced in Thailand, could find its way to a shelf at his local supermarket in Long Beach California was remarkable. This modern day economic commerce was mind-boggling.

From studying the maps earlier in the day, Neil knew a campground was not far away. He planned on camping there tonight and heading off early in the morning.

It was nearly eight O'clock when he approached a small clapboard shack at the entrance to the campground. As he got closer he saw the shack had a small, sliding glass window. Light shone through the window as if from the cockpit of an aircraft on a red eye, transatlantic flight, casting a lonesome glow out into the dark night. Looking through the glass window, Neil could see the lone pilot, a campground attendant standing inside. A calendar hung on a wall, along with various clipboards, and an assortment of keys. Nailed to the outside of the shack was a large white sign with red letters that read; **Welcome, No fireworks, No firearms, Pets must be on leash, Check out time**

11am, Only registered guests permitted after 10pm, Camp only in designated sites. There were a few others, but he hadn't time to read through them all.

"Howdy," the attendant had slid the glass window open. He was an older man with short cropped hair who gave the appearance of a retired Air Force general.

Neil caught the strong aroma of freshly brewed coffee.

"Reservation?" the man asked.

"No," Neil replied, "hoping to stay one night."

"Just yourself?"

"Yes, only one."

The man turned around and grabbed one of the clipboards from the wall. "Let's see..." he looked down at the clipboard and scanned it with his index finger, "Number seventeen, open."

Neil cut his engine. "Sounds good."

Although the man was friendly, disarming and affable enough, Neil still felt uneasy, as though he'd just knocked on a stranger's door and was asking to spend the night. Hat in hand, he waited while being scrutinized and judged from a man whom he felt was sure to see something in him that indicated what had happened out in the desert.

Neil distracted himself by looking again to the large white sign with the campground rules. What got him was the **No Firearms** posting; how many people had actually broken this common sense rule that a sign was needed to advise otherwise? Had some new numbnut arrival fired off live rounds above the heads of unsuspecting fellow campers as they toasted marshmallows around a campfire? He was getting farther away from home. Sure, he owned a gun, and occasionally he went to the indoor shooting range, but couldn't imagine himself shooting his firearm here.

"That'll be $13.75."

Neil fished in his pocket and withdrew a crumpled ten and five-dollar bill, which he ironed out as best he could and gave to the man. The man took the money and as he turned back inside the shack, an official looking patch sewn on the short sleeve of the man's green shirt caught Neil's attention. He wasn't that crazy about badges, uniforms or anything else that represented authority over the general public, especially now after what he'd done to that man out in the desert. But, even excluding that, it wasn't as though Neil thought himself a rebel who resisted authority, like those young kids he'd seen along Hollywood Boulevard or Venice Beach, with mohawks, piercings, or dressed in the anarchist all black, tattered, trademark clothes, always looking a little spooked, jumpy, teetering…like they had shattered something deep inside themselves and resisted the idea of ever coming back - back to that thing that had originally broken them, be it a relationship, a parent, a school system and, somehow, saw it as a mission to play out their unhappiness as a general hatred for society and, any form within society which represented authority. That was too simplistic and juvenile a view. In fact, Neil respected uniformed men and women, the ones who risked their lives for the protection and good of society- no, instead, it was those uniformed officials who took advantage of their authority and misused it against those who had no voice that he felt anger, resentment towards.

Misuse of authority was something he understood. It was why he'd been fired only days before from his job moving a forklift around, stocking items and filling orders inside a hanger at the Long Beach Airport.

'Sonofabitch deserved what he got.'

'You overreacted and now you're out a job and paycheck,' The Instructor stated the obvious.

'Everyone hated him - if it wasn't me it'd been someone else who'd done it.'

'Not like that,' The Instructor said.

'Always pushing, acting better than everyone else, degrading people the way he did. He shouldn't have grabbed me.'

'He was only trying to get your attention.'

'God, he pissed me off.' Neil remembered the way those fingers dug into his shoulder and then the yelping, like a wounded animal, eyes widened with fear, the supervisor dropping to his knees and Neil, hearing the snapping of bone while holding on to the bastard's broken wrist - and yelling above

34

his bent head, "If you EVER FUCK with me again, I'll take your God forsaken soul!"

"Now that's site number seventeen," the man inside the campground shack had returned, and with his head out the window, handed Neil $1.25 and a small variety of paperwork that included a receipt, rules, and map of the campground. Apparently, Neil had passed inspection. "Straight up here," the man said, pointing with his entire hand in the direction where he wanted Neil to go. "And when the road forks, make a left, your spot will be on the right."

"Straight, left, right-got it."

"Camp store closes at nine," the man said as he began to slide the window closed.

"Thanks," Neil got in just before the window clicked shut. In acknowledgement of hearing Neil's words, the man, with a halfhearted gesture, raised his hand.

Neil started his motorcycle and turned the key an extra notch, switching on the headlight. Riding at a slow pace, he took in the complete darkness that now surrounded him. All was black with the exception of the light beaming from his headlamp and a deep blue, almost purplish glow rising up from beyond the distant horizon. It was completely quiet and still, his engine the only sound. Looking up towards the sky, he could make out the dark outline of tall rocks and trees that ran along both sides of the road. There were large, massive formations that took on monstrous, intimidating shapes against the black sky and a bluish hue. It was Orson Wells, WAR OF THE WORLDS. And he was sure that at this very moment in some house just beyond those trees or maybe even a little farther, perhaps in middle America, surrounded by woods or cornfields, there sat a young kid tonight picking up short wave radio signals on a homemade radio kit just as Neil had done when he was a boy. And maybe, just maybe, that boy would be picking up one of those old broadcast signals from Leadbelly and Chesterfield cigarettes, which like a pin ball of old America, echoed and bounced against the infinite galaxies - a regal hobo tugging on somebody, anybody's sleeve asking if they'd like to hear a story, a story that should never be forgotten. He approached the first left and turning, could see, off in the distance through moving spaces of trees and cactus, campfires with shadowed figures of small darting children and fire lit faced adults who sat in chairs with tents behind them partially wrapped in darkness. Up ahead, a few hundred feet from Neil, lay a dirt road, which veered off to the right with a posted wooden sign in the shape of an arrow indicating Campsites 12-23.

'This must be it,' he thought - and so turned onto the road and within a minute he reached campsite, number seventeen. There wasn't much to it, just a parking spot with a tree and a wooden picnic table beside it. Off to the right of the picnic table was a small, dark, lifeless fire pit. Neil pulled into the parking spot, turned off his engine, and grabbed the key from the ignition. He dismounted the motorcycle, lifted the seat and dug out a small flashlight from the plastic compartment.

"Bobby, give it back, that's mine!" the shrill of a little voice shot through the marshmallow burnt air.

Neil looked up and saw a young girl about sixty feet away with brown hair running around a lit fire pit after something that had already slipped from the fire light. The girl, no older than nine, wearing an oversized hooded sweatshirt, and brandishing an empty marshmallow stick, continued her pursuit and quickly disappeared into the dark.

Around the fire pit, from which the girl had run, were larger figures, several of them in chairs, others stood talking, drinking from cups or cans. Behind them was pitched an enormous tent. Other sounds, besides that of the little girl, could be heard in the night air: every few seconds the air popped and crackled from burning wood, Frank Sinatra's melodic voice drifted from a distant campsite, an AM transistor blurted talk radio, and from inside an RV, where light flickered off its interior walls, there spat canned sitcom laughter from a portable television set. This whole scene seemed to be repeated in every direction Neil looked.

He began to unload and carry his camping gear to the spot he had selected to sleep for the night, under the tree close to the picnic bench. The spot looked used and very worn, the hard dirt packed from years of use, but he figured on laying down a ground cloth first, setting the tent on top and using his thin air mattress to help soften his sleep from the ground below. His tent was something he prided himself for having selected. Made to highest of standards, it was a solo tent, measuring only three feet high by three feet wide, and eight feet long. This provided Neil with less space than a normal two-person tent, but the advantages were its lightweight, and small, compact size. His sleeping bag was filled with premium down and made of the highest quality too. All of this was something Neil's girlfriend, Sarah had chided him about, calling it a 'guy thing', him spending weeks, sometimes months researching and choosing the perfect camping gear.

Having set up his tent, Neil began blowing air into his thin inflatable mattress when the little girl, who had earlier called out for 'Bobby', tentatively approached. In front of her, extending the full length of its leash and sniffing at Neil, was a vibrating beagle whose collar jingled with metal identification tags.

"Suzy!" the panicked voice of a protective mother blasted towards Neil.

Reminiscent of a dramatic film scene from the 1950's, the starring actress - wielding a metal flashlight - marched towards her sinking in the swamp daughter. Both head of beagle and Suzy turned back in the direction of this figure who was now fast approaching. Just before she reached her daughter, the woman stopped, and seeing the situation clearly - and sensing no immediate threat, dropped her voice, and in a soft, almost apologetic tone aimed at Neil, but spoken to Suzy, she said,

"Can't you see the man is busy? ...We shouldn't bother others."

Neil, still on his knees and holding the air mattress nozzle inches from his mouth, was about to speak, but the woman had already grabbed Suzy's wrist and all three headed briskly back to their fire- tugged along by mother hen, leading lady, "I'm ready for my close-up, Mister DeMille."

And, in what seemed like a last ditch effort for any possible respite, the little girl took a final moment and looked over her shoulder back at Neil. There was nothing he could do. An innocent encounter halted by a stranger's suspicions. Maybe the woman had sensed what he'd done out in the desert, kicking her maternal instinct into overdrive. Whatever the reason, it angered him. He wasn't here to hurt anyone.

'She'll be calling the police, gather those men, come back and string your ass up high,' The Instructor warned.

So what am I then? Neil thought, some kind of lone weirdo, child molester, murderer riding in here on my metal dragon under the darkness of night to snatch children of unsuspecting parents. Let's all post: **Wanted, Dead or Alive** posters of my sketched face with darkened five O'clock shadow and menacing scowl throughout the entire campground. Jesus, what have we become? Trust in one another has been shot to shit. Every stranger is suspect. So Goddamn fearful of one another or....who knows, maybe it's always been this way- Neanderthal mom rushing out of the cave to protect and recover her young. Even animals the behavior is the same, innate, a mother's protection; willing to sacrifice herself for the life of her offspring. But there's real danger and the perception of danger. Plato's shadows on the wall sometimes it's hard to tell the difference between reality and what is perceived as reality. She doesn't know me, what if I did have evil intentions? Those sick bastards you read about, surface in the news from time to time - the quiet next door neighbor who, "always seemed nice enough," eyewitnesses attest, and then comes the excavation of the backyard only to find remains of young boys and girls half eaten, cut up, tortured, mangled, hellish....... or the ever increasing occurrence of a pharmaceutically drugged teenager's shooting spree.

Neil had read some of these stories and knew how they clung to the brain like lint to Velcro. But then again, Neil had never, knowingly, met a serial killer, child molester, or ax murderer. This wasn't to suggest that these people didn't exist, of course they did, but the way the stories broke when these psychotic people were discovered, would have the news audience believe these wackos were everywhere. Neil had never been locked in his bathroom while an intruder's fingernails scrapped on the other side of the door, he'd never been thrown violently from a darkened waterfront pier or chased down a street at midnight by a mask wearing, chuckling, chain saw revving man with parked cars exploding and tear dropped balls of fire shooting towards a blood soaked moon. Maybe he'd just been lucky. Evil did exist, of that, Neil was certain. But he also knew evil often took much less dramatic, but often more insidious forms of expression; it was a wife cheating on her dutiful husband, it was a CEO stealing from hard working investors, it was an adult slapping back a child's open heart, it was a man in uniform killing another and knowing not the reason, why.

He blamed the press for much of what he saw as an unfounded mistrust in each other. So far apart and sparse were these ghoulish stories that when they did actually happen, became dinnertime slabs of meat for the press to feast on - much more juicy and appetizing than a mere traffic jam, weather report or any local government scandal. The name of the game was ratings, and executives knowing the more grotesque, bizarre, or chilling a story, the more an audience would become drawn to that story - almost as an escape from their own lives, like sitting on a bar stool and downing a shot of whiskey. And if the story didn't meet the thrill of some murderous rampage, and appeared a bit too prosaic, then you could bet the execs would put a spin on it just to push it as much as possible in that direction. There was so much of this sensationalism given to most stories, that news in general had become like Novacane for the brain, numbing the reader or consumer into a wash of drama, other people's problems, dilemmas; and served more as a distraction than useful information. It was as if the news organizations were taking away the realities of everyday life and with a kind of wink of the eye could be felt saying, "you think you have it bad, let's show you just how miserable life can be." - and then focusing the spotlight on some poor soul or tragic event. Of course, it worked the other way too, the fabulous celebrity or young, CEO internet sensation who has it all could shrink a reader or viewer into a sense of apathy.

He had come to understand that those who control the news, control the perception of the world, and therefore, the world itself. He'd read somewhere that America had, at one time, many different independent news sources. But, no more. Conglomerations had changed that. They had come along and bought up or forced these smaller agencies out. Acting with little or no sense of responsibility other than a bottom line for shareholders, these conglomerations had swept across the land like meth fueled fishing trawlers raging across the high seas; sucking up smaller, independent news organizations as if they were fish - irrespective of the species or damage to the eco-system, or what imperfect colorful stripes they bore. So all that remained after the mergers and greedy acquisitions had ended, was a country where only six corporations were dictating ninety percent of what anyone heard, watched or read. And, although every news organization totes unbiased reporting, behind every story there's a reporter, an organization, and an agenda. Independent investigative reporting? Ha!

This was why, in part, a few years back, Neil had given away his television set to a friend. The television; the bending of truth, acceptance of a truth not entirely one's own, filled with sensational news stories that seemed to propagate and prey on the universal hidden fears of the masses. He had heard people refer to television as the 'boob tube'- too cute and innocent a term, he thought. For him, television was plastic sitcoms, nonsensical, crapola advertising, and inconsequential, unrealistic violence. He felt this 'innocent' box was less about entertainment and education, and more about corporate mind control - that *the way things ought to be* was subconsciously taken in by the viewer, and *the way things ought to be* was really another way of saying *the way **corporations** want things to be*. *The way things ought to be,* included dress, behavior, what car to drive, cleaning products to use, and what type of look defines a lovable boy or girl, a sexy man or woman. If the violence and sensational news stories weren't enough of a reason to rid himself of this mind-numbing box, and corporate mind control seemed too farfetched, then just the single idea of wasting irretrievable hours watching a glass screen that shaped one's consciousness, cognitive reality, justified its disposal.

Now, after having finished the last few steps of setting up camp, Neil began walking to the restrooms located clear across the campground. As he walked, he could see large groups of families gathered inside enormous canopied tents lit by battery operated lanterns or by portable generators that hummed continuously. Inside these mosquito protective netted tents adults sat at plastic tables playing cards and children, who - either sat on the ground playing games of their own or - were still outside, gleefully immersed in this uncomplicated setting. Almost all the campsites had day campers or RV's. The RV's varied in size, but all had names like ADVENTURER, EXPLORER, FREEDOM TRAIL or NOMAD. These steel monsters had replaced the covered wagons and now somehow dared to proclaim the same lineage. Steps to an RV unfolded and retracted with the flick of switch. Neil thought of all those poor souls back in the 1800's who had made the covered wagon trek West in search of some golden promise, an elusive dream, a better life and he knew it hadn't been all that glamorous. Many died along the way, never to have completed the trek. Eyeing the RV's that littered the campground, Neil could bet that the word, 'adventure' held a different meaning back then; it wasn't some amusement park attribute or packaged vacation tour selling point, no, for the first people to head West the word, 'adventure' held life and death consequences, and the choice to enter such an enterprise, roused many sleepless worrisome days and a soldier's mother life for kith and kin. And because of this, it was, therefore hard to make any connection between those covered wagons and these RV's, especially when having a broken cup holder in one of these bad boys now constituted as a hardship.

By the time Neil had walked back from the restrooms to his campsite, things had begun to quiet down. The marshmallow fires had already lost much of their hot glow, gasping embers drizzled wisps of white smoke. He unzipped his tent and slid into his sleeping bag. With his head close to the mesh nylon tent door, he laid on his back, and looked up at the stars and thought of the day's beginning: the dying man, the words he had spoken, the money, the note and the promise.

41

Still the stars shone, and Neil's thoughts turned to the age of the universe, how long had these exact same stars twinkled across the American landscape, shone upon all those who had come before him? He shuddered to think of it because it made him feel small, smaller than small, insignificant even. The light, faint white trails of the Milky Way wafted above and beyond-uncharted specks of light, bioluminescent phytoplankton amidst a sea of blackness without end.

"Without end," he whispered. How was that even possible? A cavernous well, emitting no sound and no light and so deep that a pebble thrown into it would fall forever. And it troubled him, down right saddened him in fact, to consider amongst these infinite stars why he should matter at all. All that he would or wouldn't do in his life meant nothing, literally nothing against this infinite backdrop of creation. Kepler and Copernicus........Galieo. He thought of this, he thought of America, sleep came upon the Indians.

4

When Neil awoke it was still dark and the ground was slightly damp beneath him. Rising early when camping was not unusual for him. Even as a boy his normal inclination to sleep late had been absent when immersed in the "great outdoors."

With a hazy gauze of sleep still remaining in his eyes, he lumbered out of the tent and headed across the campground to the restrooms. All was quiet and he was careful in making as little noise as possible. When he returned to his site he clambered atop the picnic table and drank water from a stainless steel canteen. He spread a map of Arizona out before him and, keeping in mind his final East Coast destination, thought it best if he were to head in a northeasterly direction from his current position.

A sliver of orange was creeping over the horizon and only a few campers were stirring by the time Neil finished packing his gear back onto his motorcycle. He pushed the choke down, turned the engine over and returned to the picnic bench while the engine idled and warmed. A slight, but appreciable, chill had developed overnight and dampness hung in the air. He rubbed his hands together and brought his knees up close to his body. He craved a hot cup of coffee. He made one last sweep of the site, cleaning up the area before returning the choke to its off position. He got on his motorcycle and, making his way through the sleepy campground, kept a slow, steady pace until he reached the main road whereupon he exited the campground and opened the throttle to a respectable speed. Although he was somewhat groggy, it felt good to be riding with purpose again.

Headlights from perfumed cars and talk radio pickup trucks dotted the road and cut through the early morning darkness. Neil knew that all across America this scene had, or would be taking place today; the worker bees of America waking and commuting to build the nation's economic honeycomb. But, unlike actual bees, these worker bees, Neil believed, worked neither for the good of the hive, nor were they motivated by any lofty theories provided by Keynes, Kant, Marx, Engles or Gailbraith - instead, he felt, they worked out of an individual selfish desire and need to survive. These bees arrived at the honeycomb to pay off a mortgage, car payment, medical bills, groceries and children's clothes. Neil viewed all these workers not just as bees, but as gerbils stuck in a cage on a running wheel built on fragmented bones of the human condition and disgruntled necessity - running to work, to get a paycheck, to pay the bills, to buy more things, so as to run to work, to get a paycheck... an endless cycle, the gerbils ran and ran and ran on this stationary wheel in a effort that led nowhere.

Neil figured on making New Mexico today and farther east tomorrow. On the road this early morning, he was glad for his thick leather jacket, which provided warmth and protection. It was only a short ride, and just after he'd passed a large handmade sign advertising a swap meet, when a roadside diner came into view - a yellow, plain jane rectangular structure with white painted trim and two sets of stairs made of unfinished wood, running parallel to the diner and meeting at its front entrance. He slowed and pulled into the gravel parking lot and came to a stop in front of one of the two half buried wagon wheels anchored at each corner of the diner. Neil wasn't the only early bird.

Parked outside the diner was an ATV and a variety of utility vans and pickup trucks of all makes, models, and years. Most were dirty, dented and banged up, and looked as though they'd been used for what they were truly intended: work. The trucks around him weren't some sort of expensive fashion accessory, the kind of thing he'd seen in Los Angeles and New York City. Walking past a mud splattered Ford with plumbing equipment in the bed, Neil climbed the short steps to the diner's entrance and pulled opened the door. Smack dab in front of him was an older style cigarette machine, the kind that dispensed packs with the depositing of coins, the pulling of knobs and a no apology accessibility - it was old enough to burp up a vague recollection of a Howard Johnson's restaurant somewhere back East he had visited with his parents when he was just a child. To the right of the cigarette machine, and beyond this short entrance way, was the actual diner. There were long sets of red vinyl booths with white and grey speckled Formica tabletops. Each booth butted up against the window and, on the aisle side, had tall, dark wooden posts with coat hooks. Across from the row of booths, running the entire length of the diner, was a white counter with round, red vinyl covered stools that spun. Some had patches of grey or green where duck tape had been used to cover rips or tears. Neil felt a few eyes on him and a trickle of self-consciousness dripped into his veins. He sat down quickly on a stool at the counter where there was plenty of room on each side. He could still feel eyes on him. He directed his focus directly in front of him to an apparent workstation just behind the counter where there were coffee urns, napkins, and a grey plastic tub divided into sections for silverware.

"Coffee?" A heavyset woman in her mid-fifties, with drugstore colored red hair held in a bun by a couple of pencils, stood behind the counter looking at Neil. With the exception of a green apron tied around her waist, she had no uniform to really speak of. Wearing baby blue nylon stretch pants, a flannel shirt and a pair of reading glasses, which hung from around her neck, she asked this 'coffee' question as though it were rhetorical. She had the air of one who'd seen it all and now numb, no longer had the capacity to be inconvenienced. Her dreams had died and a hardness had replaced them.

"Sure, coffee," Neil answered.

The woman dropped a thick ceramic mug with voluptuous rounded edges on the counter, turned, grabbed a steaming pot of coffee and filled the mug. She then placed a worn laminated menu with curled and slightly peeled corners on the countertop,

45

slapped down a paper napkin, with fork, knife and spoon to Neil's right, and walked away.

Neil laughed inside from an imaginary response to her 'coffee' question: "Decaf latte, skim milk, 2% if you please."

But the next words inside his head swung him in a 180 degree direction, 'Better not screw around in here.' Looking around, he noticed the customers matched their vehicles that were parked outside - large, small, varying in age - but all rugged, worn, use to hard work and tough as nails.

"Know what ya want, sweetie?" The waitress was back. Her tone had softened and Neil seconded guessed his initial reading of her. Again, he caught himself laughing inside from another imaginary response that shot up inside him, 'Sure, Toots- how 'bout you plant your sweet little ass on the back of my bike and we'll make our way cross country together?' But the actual words he spoke differed, "Ah, I'll take the number three special, white toast, bacon, over easy."

She took the menu and was off.

A slight grin hung on his face as he peeled an Arizona State map from his side pocket. He sipped the bitter coffee, wished for cream but dared not ask, and laid the partly folded map out on the counter top.

"Looks like yer yer travel'in there," came the words from a character that could've been pulled from an old mule train. He sat two stools away. Neil took a quick inventory of the elderly man: nothing but skin and bones with a nose like a dried up huckleberry potato. He wore a beat up grease stained, suede cowboy hat with a tattered feather on one side. Gray, brittle hair stuck out from the sides of his hat like forgotten straw after having slept the night in a barn. He had on an unkempt, button down shirt with a crumpled collar partly tucked under a leather vest and smelled of stale tobacco and day old coffee. His eyes smiled, continuously blinking.

"Yea, traveling northeast into New Mexico," Neil was quick and to the point.

"What route route ya tak tak'in?" the man jabbered back.

"Not sure yet, but thinking of route 89 to the 160." Neil caught the old man's eyes and suddenly felt like a soft spoiled college kid, inadequately versed in the hard ways of real life and wrought iron men. He had a quick impulse to try and act like the company of those that now surrounded him, but knew it was of no use.

"If you don't mind me ask'in," the few brown teeth left in the man's mouth appeared briefly, "where ya com'in from?"

"Spent the night in Prescott National Forest, camping, but came from California."

"Caleefornia, land of milk and honey-used to be anyways- I could tell ya stories about the the groves, aveecado groves where's I use to work, all up and down Caleefornia. Course, that was a ways a ways back." The old man shook his head and drifted ever so slightly, then continued, "east ya say?"

"Well, northeast, into New Mexico."

"Construction on the 160, best bet up route 40, up through Holbrook, high mountain- Navajo country. That would put ya right right right into Gallup in a few hours time."

'Great, just what you need,' The Instructor said. Out of the woodwork they come. Look at this old fart, you follow this wack job's advice, you'll end up in Timbuktu, They-'

Neil cut away like an ice boat across a frozen windblown lake - "Oh, okay, I appreciate that," Neil responded.

The Instructor had been wrong about John yesterday.

Neil leaned over with an outstretched hand, "Name's Neil by the way."

The old man appeared caught off guard, "Oh, hey, hey Neil," the man twinkled, "Clint. Clint McGee. Proud ta meet ya."

"Proud to meet you too," Neil replied. He could feel the weight of Clint's hand - heavy and solid, with blackened creases and nicotine stains fused around small, tortoise shell nails.

"Here you go." The waitress was back with Neil's breakfast. Neil quickly folded up the map. She placed the plate down in front of him.

Neil looked up at her, "That was fast."

Her response was flat and dry, "Any ketchup, jam with that?"

"Sure."

47

"Well, which one?"

"Both."

She pulled the condiments from below the counter, and placed them next to the plate and then turned away.

The old man returned to his coffee, leaning into it by wrapping his fingers around the cup and blowing lightly across the top.

Neil hesitated. "Say Clint, I don't know if you've already eaten, but would you allow me to buy you breakfast, it's the least I can do for shaving a couple of hours off my traveling time."

"That's not necess necessary."

"Please, it'd be my pleasure, it's the least I can do, please."

"Well, I suppose some corned beef hash and scrambled eggs and a side a biscuits would do nicely."

Neil chuckled, "Alright, then." He motioned for the waitress, but immediately regretted it; like a Bird dog that had spotted prey, she stopped, pointed her nose and came directly at him. The look on her face and the manner in her approach, not only suggested she had sensed trouble, but that she was also more than willing to do battle.

Neil didn't flinch, "I'd like to order some corned beef hash and scrambled eggs," he plainly stated.

She stood with hand on hip, "Something wrong with that dish?"

"No not at all, just buying some breakfast for my friend here."

"It's your dime, sweetie. Toast with that?"

Neil looked to Clint for an answer. Clint's eyes barely left the rim of his cup, "White'll be fine, course pumpernickel would be better if they's got it or bis-"

"We got both," she snorted.

"Ohh Pump Pumpernickel it is then."

She turned without a word.

"A real humdinger - think we we was robbing a bank or someth'in. Ah, what's the use, all try trying to wear pants in a man's world-she needs a little grease in her sprocket is all, and bydangit if I'm not the one to give it to her too. A time was when when when a woman was a woman and a a man was a man,

48

now.... hehehe." The old man then turned to Neil and pointed at the stools between them, "Mind if I scoo scootch over a bit?"

"Oh, no – go ahead, wherever you'd like." Neil had become a little embolden, under the temporary liberation from The Instructor's judgment, and feeling good about it, was determined to ride its wave.

"Problem is," Clint continued, "ain't no nobody satisfied with their their lives no more, everybody try'in to be somebody else, all all of em chas'in an image, mirage, a ghost – hell, even the Holy ghost like myself.... they's looking in in in them girly fashion magazines, big t.v. and silver silverscreen. Time was you was yourself cause cause of yer work, yer faith, yer fam family.....hell in a hand basket now. No matter, everything equal in death. Find that that out, soon enough."

Neil wasn't sure what to say or even if it was his 'turn' to talk, but did anyway, "Well, I'd have to admit, sounds like you know what you're talking about." He reached for a more concrete subject. "This place looks like it must be doing something right," he said, looking over his shoulder as if to confirm his observation.

"Grub ain't too ba bad neither," Clint threw to his side.

"You from around these parts?" Neil asked.

'Parts?, Parts!' exclaimed the Instructor. 'When was the last time you used that phrase - might as well just stick your thumbs under your armpits and say, Howdy, Partna, or Puttie tharrr, while tipping your ten gallon hat for cry'in out loud!'

The image of the dead man left to die out in the desert suddenly jumped into Neil's mind , why now, and for what reason, was anyone's guess. It was just a fraction of a second - and along with it came The Instructor's presence, not complete and whole, but flickering, like a dorsal fin rippling beneath the water. As quickly as it all had started it disappeared and submerged back into the abyss.

'Simmer down, just enjoy the experience,' Neil tried calming himself.

"Been here last twen twen twenty years, before that, all over," the old timer was still at it, rattl'in on.

49

Neil tried to anchor himself, "Oh?" he replied. His eyes swam around the diner. His body was screaming to get up and run. Inside he was slipping and he was scared, scared of what was happening to him. He wondered if he was going mad; if what had happened out in the desert had pushed him over the edge and snapped something deep inside his mind – too far down to even fix.

Clint had stopped talking and his eyes narrowed. He looked Neil squarely in the eyes. Neil tried cracking a smile, but could feel his lips begin to quiver, so he pressed them tight together. Clint had sensed his fear and even, too, knew what had happened out in the desert and could read the madness in Neil's unstable eyes. Neil got up to use the restroom.

He ran cold water from the sink over his hands and splashed his face. He took a good, hard look at himself in the mirror, diving deep into his own eyes. When he managed to salvage a piece of himself he returned to the counter and sat back down. The waitress had delivered Clint's breakfast and the old man was hunched over his plate working on some eggs. Little was said for the next several minutes and small talk barely peppered their interaction. All seemed lost and Neil was ready to leave. He'd finish his cup of coffee and go.

It was only after Clint had shoveled down most of his food that a new sense of energy drew up in his veins and talk came a little easier. With bits of breakfast clinging to his beard, he started in again;

"See, thing is, you's young and a bit untamed, things ain't predictable as yet... you you wouldn't know it je jes by looking at me, but I'm well over eighty years old, and and that ain't no accident neither - breath that's the secret, plain ole brea breathing, know how to control that, know how to control everything."

Neil felt an enormous relief just to have him talking again, regardless of the subject matter. "I see."

"I also got this mag magnetical bracelet," Clint said, bending his arm to show his right wrist where a thin metal bracelet was clasped. "Thing works, don't need no doc doctor, tell you that, no siree. That and stand'in on my head twice a a day, helps to keep things mov moving to the joints and proper organs hehehe, strange strange, I know, but damned if it don't work."

"Never heard that before," Neil stated, "but if it works, it works."

"Damned too toot'in it works, keep me able to do do what I do."

"How's that? You mean with work?"

"With work, with liv'in, with with everything - lead in the pen pencil, even."

"What kind of work you involved with?" Neil asked, sidestepping the other item.

Clint grinned, and with a shoulder shaking laugh, said, "You name it, I've done it, one time nother' in my life-noth'in I ain't done. Oil fields mostly, had a leather shop there for awhile, fore' rig work and the like, s'matter fact one of them's camps up only few miles on this road here where's I use ta work."

"Wish I had time to take a look at it."

"No matter, not much left of it now no how, sorta like myself hehehe." Clint drew the coffee cup to his lips.

"Still be interesting, if I had t-"

"Time. I know," Clint interrupted, having withdrawn the cup from his lips, which he now held with a cocked arm. He looked disappointed, hurt - downright saddened in fact, so much so that it made Neil want to apologize, but the old man had more to say,

"Ain't nobody got *time* for anything anymore no how, much less the past. Time......community is what we had here," he continued with an almost angry tone, "even before I's born- no nonsense, real connection with the Earth and community, real community - miner's, Mexicans, Spanish Mormons, missionaries-Franciscan, I think they was, course Indians, Pueblo and the like. That was community, and they ALL had time, same time we's got, jest used it different."

"Well speaking of time...," Neil checked his watch. Clint said nothing. Neil pushed his plate to the side, and flipped over the check the waitress had earlier placed down.

51

Seeing this Clint spoke up, "I wish wish you the best wherever yer head'in."

"Thanks." Neil started up from his stool, reached in his pocket and placed money on top of the check.

"Pre preciate the breakfast, and happy trails," Clint said as he swiveled around on his stool and extended his hand up to Neil's.

Neil grabbed hold, "Thanks - you, too. Take care."

It was still early enough that when Neil started out of the diner parking lot and onto route 40 he felt no need to push. So why had he rushed out of there? Had he been rude to Clint? He hoped not. Maybe he should have spent more time with the old man, but, no —there was the money, letter and promise pulling him East.

Neil cranked the throttle open, heard the guttural sound of the carburetors, and gave himself to the road. The air rushed and his mind began to clear. The late September sun inched higher into the sky. It beamed on his face and hands, inducing a warm sense of reflection. He felt in sync with the season. Fall was inside him; reassessing memories. Some sad. Some regretful. Some painful, a faint whisper fluttering around scorched edges. Regrouping and letting go, old giving way to new and pray God without resentment or bitterness, but instead with dignity and purpose, like leaves that had given nourishment through sunlit spring and summer months, holding the sounds of children at play, picnics with fresh lemonade, swimming, laughter, bronzed bodies, and first loves........all to fade with the changing season. The leaves, which once frolicked high in the branches, fell in autumn like sobering thoughts upon the Earth. It was as though the Earth paused, actually took a breath, and allowed reflection for all. Eternal bliss, the mother's womb, God's embrace. Neil felt this, all of it, condensed into the air he now inhaled and the warmth drawn from the fire so far away.

It was a glorious ride, too - all John Wayne country with scenery that was big, flat and wide, including plateaus on the horizon where The Duke and Indians were sure to have shot it out. The road was straight and easy and mostly barren, but at a few points surprised Neil by taking him through swatches of green land with trees and vegetation and parts, too, where the road slightly rose, twisted, and gently turned. The Sun continued to warm his hands and face as it passed between a broken conveyor belt of clouds that sped on light winds from above, perfect conditions that might compel anyone to first get on a motorcycle.

He had weighed his options concerning a route back East and decided that, it being September, it would be best if he were to maintain a Southern route until reaching the coast and then head north, minimizing his chances of being exposed to cold weather.

Three effortless hours had passed when he made his way east, into Gallup, New Mexico. It was here he stopped for gas and a blended drink made from fresh bananas, strawberries, oranges and a whole raw egg, sold from a small Mexican woman in a fruit stand painted a vibrant mixture of yellow and orange. He continued on towards Albuquerque. The land was raw and unremarkable.

Just west of Albuquerque stood a small sign, *Los Alamos 63 miles Next exit*. 'Los Alamos,' Neil thought, 'the birthplace of the atomic bomb.' Images he'd collected his entire life from news clips, still photographs, and film documentaries congealed into a mental blip: steel tower in the desert, E=MC2, Fatboy, Enola Gay, Hiroshima, Nagasaki, Cuba, Kennedy, Gorbachev, Reagan, flash of light, mushroom cloud, burned skin and flesh hanging from x-rayed skeletons. His thoughts flattened and then concluded into one sad, yet logical question, 'Why?, why?'

'Building a strong defense is the best deterrent against aggression,' The Instructor, like a Pentagon spokesman, popped up. 'Mutual annihilation is what held the balance during the Cold War, and it worked.'

Neil was familiar with this cliché rhetoric and the questions surrounding Nuclear weapons, and he'd managed to keep it just that: rhetoric. Because to take it too personally, closely would be enough to drive anyone mad. Was it really possible that someone would push a button to annihilate, not only an entire country, but, all mankind? He had lived through the tension brought about between the Soviet Union and United States during the

1980's, reported in the news stories, which could only be viewed as an elaborate chess match with no king and no queen, just a Mad Hatter jumping from square to square, startling all remaining players with a pack of matches and a jug of kerosene. But it wasn't a game and the stakes were real and the threat tangible. And when he was younger it frightened and worried him terribly. But, at what point does one become tired while waiting for the first punch to be thrown? And in the end what had he to say or do about the development or proliferation of these weapons? It was futile. What could he do? He was a lone individual who had no control of how these weapons were used. So, somewhere and somehow the issue had slipped away; he'd gotten use to or become desensitized to the whole idea of these horrific tools of destruction. And like a girl who had broken his heart, sooner or later she'd fade and over the course of time become less real to him until eventually she'd no longer hold any sway in his daily life. But, here she was again, fifty- seven years later and only 63 miles away from where a Geiger counter would crackle like Jiffy Pop Popcorn over a hot flame. He had heard it said many times before, that the people who know war, have seen, tasted, smelled war, are the same ones, without exception, who pray to the Almighty never, never, ever to see, feel, taste, hear, or smell it again. They tell us the horrors of war are such, that the human mind is incapable of comprehending them. The stunned, zombied men on the beaches of Normandy or in the trenches of France or the jungles of Vietnam realize they have entered into Satan's garden, such elements of hell are truly reserved for the afterlife, but, come war, are vigorously ripped from the darkened bowels of their inferno birthplace, shedding skin over vomit crusted eyes on the lighted sphere of Earth.

'This country would not have been born without war,' The Instructor smugly noted.

'True, but no right minded person wants war,' Neil responded.

'Alright, cupcake, so war is NEVER necessary?'

'Of course war is sometimes necessary-

'When?'

'I'm not that naive.'

'Of course you are, you little peacenik. Deep down you'd love to see the whole world join hands and sing a happy little song together.'

'What the hell's wrong with that?'

'But, at the same time, you know the world doesn't operate that way, does it? The Instructor continued, 'there are people out there who want to destroy America-have it crash and burn.'

'I guess so,' Neil replied

'You guess so? Towers weren't enough for you, huh? So, it's okay – if say, another country wants to come in and take us over, you're willing to give up the very freedoms, way of life you currently have? Or how about change your religion like a pair of underwear?

'I don't need a lecture. I know this kind of life needs defending.'

'But you don't want to be the one to do it - or think about what that means or costs. You've become complacent with your life.'

He knew it came with a price, always a price -one that he sometimes felt was too steep and misaligned. He remembered that sometime in January of 1961 Dwight D. Eisenhower had given his farewell speech to the nation. It was a speech where he had spoken about the dangers of a government military industrial complex.

"...America is today the strongest, the most influential, and most productive nation in the world. Understandably proud of this Pre-eminence, we yet realize that America's leadership and prestige depend, not merely upon our unmatched material progress, riches and military strength, but on how we use our power in the interests of world peace and human betterment."..... "We face a hostile ideology global in scope, atheistic in character, ruthless in purpose and insidious in method."....."In the councils of government, we must guard against the acquisition of unwarranted influence, whether sought or unsought, by the military-industrial complex. The potential for the disastrous rise of misplaced power exists and will persist. We must never let the weight of this combination endanger our liberties or democratic processes. We should take

nothing for granted. Only an alert and knowledgeable citizenry can compel the proper meshing of the huge industrial and military machinery of defense with our peaceful methods and goals, so that security and liberty may prosper together."

Black birds flew overhead in a northerly direction. Neil thought of Ghandi who had transformed a country by peaceful means-wrestling India's independence back from the hands of British rule. There was a lesson in that somewhere. His mind skipped to the *Lao Tsu* book of the **Toa,** a book he had read over and over again. A book whose words seemed to have purpose, strength and, yet, also, the same ones he couldn't quite grasp. It was a paradox, the words flowed, seemed to make sense, but, on an analytical level, alluded him - the way dreams do after waking from sleep; the harder one tried, the fuzzier the dreams became. It was like trying to catch fish in a stream with bare hands, the fish slip and slide, ever present, but elusive. In fact, after reading through the book many times, Neil gave up his desire of comprehending it through analytical thought and, instead, just read it with no thought, hoping the words and their meaning would penetrate his mind subconsciously.

'*Yield and Overcome.*'

He blasted down route 40, heading east, making pretty good headway. Nothing interrupted him. Soon, it was time to get a bite to eat, top off his gas tank, look over maps, and decide where to stop when night eventually fell. He hadn't many options when he pulled off an exit. There was a small, no name gas station and a MISTER FROSTY- an eatery that had plastic tables outside and umbrellas with colorful advertisements printed on their edges. Neil got off his motorcycle and stretched. He was hungry. With his helmet under his right arm, he approached the order window and quickly scanned the menu board that hung outside. It was the usual greasy, processed stuff you'd expect to find at a place like this, in the middle of nowhere.

Peering inside, he could see a handful of teenagers milling around, preparing food, making loud remarks, and working over the metal frialator baskets. They all wore blue vests with white name tags and oval shaped paper hats. There was a large radio (with a broken antenna wrapped in aluminum foil) that pumped out top 40 music. A lanky kid with acne came to the window, his name tag read: *Ray*.

"Help ya, mister?"

Neil winced. He wasn't sure if he should slap this kid or get back on his bike. Instead he began to order and did so quickly because he could already feel a heavy scrutiny of *know it all* teenage judgment beaming from the eyes of 'Ray'.

"Yea, I'll have a cheeseburger," Neil said. "And curly fries and a FROSTY vanilla shake."

"Anything else?"

"Nope, that's it."

Ray had been scribbling on a pad, "That'll be $7.85." He drummed the eraser of the pencil he'd been writing with on the order pad while Neil scrounged for the correct change. "That your bike over there?" Ray pointed the eraser, out to where Neil had parked. Something in the way he asked this question made Neil feel sorry for him; there was an almost imperceptible yearning, not only in his voice, but also in his eyes.

"Yeah, that's my bike," Neil answered.

If Neil expected another comment or question from this kid, Ray, it wouldn't come. Instead, Ray gave a quick nod and then turned back inside the kitchen and shouted out the order.

Neil paid and sat at one of the outside tables to wait for his food and look over maps. The only other customer was a mother wearing a yellow tank top with the image of Tweety Bird on the front. She sipped at a soda while smoking a menthol cigarette and held on her lap her crewcut young boy, who, with ketchup coated fingers, was licking the remnants from a curly fries paper box. A mixture of yellow mustard and ketchup circled the boy's mouth evoking an image of a Dorthea Lange photograph from the dustbowl of the 1930's.

The synthetic music continued to blast from the kitchen and only served to heighten the fact these kids longed to be anywhere else but here, to be part of that cool Hip Hop world that they'd seen on T.V., heard in the music or imagined - all manipulated or passing through the mass media gatekeepers. Every teenager wants to be cool, every teenager's hometown 'sucks' and every music video corporate sponsor knows this, makes use of it, by selling coolness that exists far from any hometown. They sell kids this coolness in the form of commerce; Hey, buy this pair of jeans, sneakers, skateboard or latest cell phone and it will get you closer to that elusive cool world and everyone will want to be you.

Neil found the music had aged him - he knew none of it. To him, it all sounded the same and felt, like the food he was about to eat, without substance, was extremely processed, and devoid of much value. Maybe he was a bit hard about it all, and he told himself that older adults had probably felt the same about the music he had listened to when he was a teenager. But, that assumption, as he thought more about it, didn't exactly hold up. The music he had listened to as a teenager had withstood the test of time. He had grown up listening to the likes of The Beatles, Johnny Cash, Son House, The Grateful Dead, Led Zeppelin, Miles Davis, Dave Brubeck, Neil Young, Van Morrison, and Bob Dylan. All of these artists were storytellers, all held their own and, had cultivated their talent and their music, which stimulated the listener's mind to go places. In truth, Neil knew there to be a handful of contemporary artists that possessed these same truths and criteria and who deserved recognition, but - having reached the age of forty - he was also more easily apt in detecting bullshit when he saw or heard it; words to music which these so called 'artists' had no connection with and who, without the protection of technical studio gadgets, lipped synched songs in live venues. These 'artists' Neil saw as a disgrace - born more from a product of public relations, advertising campaigns, savvy executives and glossy music videos than from any real talent, heart or soul. Neil lost all hope for the music industry when the only magazine that had once stood for innovation and original thought succumbed to placing a winner of the *American Idol* television show on its cover. That rebellious magazine, once respected, fell into the corporate sponsored bullshit bin. The entire industry had become like an empty mass of cotton candy molded into the shape of an 18lb roasted turkey, with the consumer being asked if they wanted a breast or thigh.

Neil's food was ready and 'Ray' - who, only hours before, had the whole world figured out - was there to slide it through the window. Neil ate the cheeseburger, picked at the fries, and sipped half his shake. He opened the map and fingered his route. Staying on route 40 would put him in Texas by nightfall. His mind, again, went back to the dying man, the money, and his destination. He topped off his tank at a tiny no name station, got back on the road, and throttled onward.

He was anxious to make up time, and truly set- ready to ballin' the jack- make a good go of it. He was settled and in a good stride when after only forty minutes, he spotted orange colored cones, and soon, the road narrowed to just a one lane passage. It was a construction zone with florescent vested highway workers jack hammering, working backhoes, and surveying the terrain with tripod-mounted instruments. There was a sign that read: **Reduce Speed Fines Doubled**. Neil shifted down into third gear and kept his rpm's low. At first, the reduction in speed frustrated him, but like the political world he had earlier contemplated, he knew there was nothing he could do to change the situation. He resigned himself to the fact that it was out of his control and all he could do was make the best of it. He'd use the slower speed to give himself time to relax and enjoy the countryside, but, in fact, there really wasn't much to enjoy; the land around him was nothing more than brown earth, flat and dry.... After twelve miles riding in this slower paced work zone, Neil looked ahead and saw that the line of cars, which stretched far ahead, was coming to a gradual halt. He wanted to get out of his leather jacket, he could feel the heat from a stagnant sun that was unrelenting. Eventually, Neil came to a rest, too, with cars ahead and behind. He could feel the heat from his engine and the heavy sweat beneath his leather jacket and trapped under his jeans. He thought of racing ahead in the narrow strip that ran between the cars and edge of the road, but the pain of being pulled over and ticketed, discovered and arrested prevented him from acting on this idea. He didn't want the law anywhere near him. It was just too dangerous.

The line of cars began to move and he inched along with it. He stood on the foot pegs and pulled his body up far enough so as to see about a half mile ahead. From this vantage point he spotted flashing lights and some sort of emergency vehicles. With resignation, he sat back down and continued along this production line of automobiles. As traffic moved even farther along, he could make out a few police cars and two Government type vans with metal cages inside, separating driver from passengers. It was stop and go traffic. Two state police officers stood signaling traffic in order to hasten the looky-loos. The traffic again inched forward, and then came to a stop all together. He was right on top of the scene.

Neil straddled his motorcycle, planting both feet on the ground, shifted in to neutral and let the engine idle. He looked to his right and saw a handful of people - woman, young men, and older men, too, laying face down on the dirty embankment, all with hands clasped behind their backs held together with white plastic ties. Standing over them were several officers in brown uniforms, wearing thick leather gun belts, batons, radios and handcuffs. They were methodically writing on notepads. All was calm. All was orderly.

The traffic moved ahead several feet. Again, looking right, Neil noticed only a few feet away, and parked on the side of the road, a brown van with an official looking round emblem on the driver's side door that read: **U.S. Border Patrol and Customs**. There was another van with an emblem that read: **Department of Homeland Security**. One of the vans was filled with passengers, none seemed to be talking, all appeared to be immersed in silent thought. They sat as hollowed gourds. He could see a thick black ponytail, a set of grey hair held in a white knitted mesh hairnet, a young boy in a soiled tee shirt and red baseball cap. Then turning his head farther, with his chin almost touching his shoulder, Neil met a pair of dark, wood stained eyes. The eyes peered directly at him through the vans' window. Neil, quickly, looked away, took a moment as though to excuse himself, then looked back. The eyes still held their silent gaze. There was no expression in them. They lacked any trace of humanity, like a man on death row who has completely given up, accepted his fate and no longer struggles with the natural, human instinct to survive. All was loss. Neil took in the tightly woven straw cowboy hat, the white sideburns, plaid shirt with snap metal buttons, and the smooth sagging brown skin of the old man, who was staring at him. The eyes where forever directed on Neil and in them sat the sad fact that this was to be the last journey North for this old man. He had missed the boat and the only promised land that he'd ever hope to reach would now come only through death. Unsettled, Neil looked away again just as the traffic moved slowly forward. He looked down at the green neutral light on his instrument panel, pulled the clutch in, and clicked the motorcycle into first gear. Releasing the clutch, Neil for the last time, and for just an instant, looked to his right - time now slowed and each moment stretched - with his brown eyes still looking directly at Neil, the old man raised his palm and gently rested his fingertips to the window. The man's face remained unchanged. The traffic moved and Neil moved with it. The moment was gone, vanished and time bumped ahead, but the haunting image remained. Why had the man done this, why at Neil? It didn't make sense.

Odd, too, was to see this type of situation so far north of the border. It seemed too far north for Boarder Patrol agents to be chasing illegal immigrants. Having lived in California for the past three years, Neil was very aware of how often many people South of the U.S. border paid large sums of money to be surreptitiously escorted across the border into the United States by men and women known as 'coyotes'. It was big business with big risks, and therefore, big money too. Even the drug cartels had a piece of the action.

The construction zone ended and traffic opened up.

'Illegals - have no right coming into this country,' The Instructor was back. 'Come here, have children, filthy, pay no taxes, live off our welfare system.'

61

'It's known as public assistance and it's not just illegals who use it,' Neil interjected, 'and filthy is an ugly description.'

'But it's true, and you know it-that family that lives next to you in Long Beach, the children throwing used corn on the cob on the sidewalk, gum wrappers, soda cans, old mattresses. And it's annoyed you, don't lie-seen you mutter, seen you curse'

'It may not be typical of all immigrants.'

'You're so good, Neil. Who are you fighting to impress? I know who you are.'

'Look, public assistance is for everyone in need.'

'You're so righteous, Poppi Chulo,' The Instructor said. 'But let me ask you - do they come for a country or do they come for a land?'

'It's for everyone.'

'But do they come for a country or do they come for a land?'

'Regardless,' Neil stated, 'it's for everyone.'

'Even illegals?'

'I.....'

'My point exactly, they laugh behind your back. It's theft-illegal - abuses the rights and privileges of those who have worked to develop the system, namely, citizens of these United States.'

'Funny, the illegals I've met - cooks, cleaning ladies, gardeners - all work very hard, just want to better themselves and their families,' Neil retorted.

'Then become a legal citizen, your grandparents did. Besides, not ALL come here with your rosy little picture, you know one third of our prison population is comprised of illegals.'

He did know the stats, that one third of the U.S. prison population were illegal aliens and American tax payers were footing the bill for their incarceration. He knew, too, what every American knew that to solve the illegal immigration problem fairly and honestly was to fine the employers who hired illegals. It was so simple. If there was no work the illegals wouldn't come. He had heard the proposal to fine companies, penalties, large amounts of money, for each illegal they'd hired with part of the collected fine going to the whistleblower. Why it hadn't been

62

done was like so many other issues. There had to be politics and money. Anything that seemed too simple and wasn't done was always because it was mired in politics. Politicians were either too scared to follow the will of the American people or had been paid off by contrary sources with different agendas. Neil understood the solution, but he had a soft spot.

'I know, and in a certain sense, it's wrong what they do - sneaking across the border - but, I'd probably do the same thing if given their circumstances.'

They steal our jobs,' The Instructor said.

'Steal our jobs? They do the jobs most of us wouldn't do. Tell me the California Agriculture business would survive without these workers, Ceasar Chavez ring a bell?'

'Sounding now like liberal talk radio.'

'This whole country is a land of immigrants!,' Neil exclaimed. 'These railroads connecting our great nation were built by the Chinese, Irish, and other cheap immigrant labor, before that, slavery in the South, sweatshops with children in the North, and when American corporations couldn't compete on a level playing field, they tipped the scales by moving jobs overseas to underdeveloped countries to exploit the 15 cent a day workers there.'

'It's called Capitalism.'

'Capitalism, my ass - how 'bout a living wage?'

'Do you understand the tariffs other countries place on our goods?' The Instructor asked. 'Tell me what would happen if the shoe were on the other foot and Americans illegally migrated south, do you think the Mexican Government and its people would be so tolerant of little ol Gringo? No other country in the world tolerates such nonsense as America. It's illegal what they do, they know it too, and as hard as they might, cannot justify or change that fact. They're stealing not just our jobs, but our sovereignty too. Your grandparents had come for a new and better life here in America and embraced this young land and its customs, by coming to America they had made the choice to take on a new identity and assimilated themselves. They had come to America to become Americans.'

'Are you saying that these people don't?'

'Look around you, do they come for a country or do they come for a land? You know what to be true. Why do I have to "press 1" if I want to speak English in my own country, isn't that still the official language here? Or what about stepping outside my door and seeing the figure of death, Darth Vader himself, sweeping down the street in the form of a full on burka?'

'Maybe America is changing.'

'Or disappearing.'

Neil's eyelids closed, maybe The Instructor did have a point, but it didn't make sense. It was all too much. He was losing his mind, of that he was certain. How else could he explain such a thing to be happening and at this point, truthfully, it didn't even seem to matter to him - he was just too tired to care. If madness were to come, then he felt better to let it happen sooner than later, there was no point in postponing the inevitable. It would just prolong the pain of trying to fight it off, and at this moment he didn't have the energy. He had never been much for winning for winning sake, this idea of being number one when he had no fight left in him. He was weak that way. During his time as a high school student he had been on the wrestling team and was considered a natural. He was physically strong, agile and fast, but when he got tired, he always gave into his opponent. He would be far ahead in points and could still remember the look of surprised delight, and disbelief when he'd allow his opponent to pin him down for a win. Coach hated him for it. He just didn't care enough because he knew and recognized on an existential level that it didn't really matter who won, who lost. 'I mean in the REAL scheme of things,' he would think, 'in a tiny auditorium in the middle of nowhere on a blue ball floating in space, does it really matter?'-it would only matter if he cared, and he never had that kind of strong investment, not when it came to wrestling anyway. The old man's gentle hand and empty stare returned.

Neil tried forging ahead, but his mind phlinged flanged like a trumpeter fluttering between keys, grappling for the next note. He needed to pull off somewhere and take a short break; being on his motorcycle wasn't safe, not now. A large rest stop offered him what he needed, a cul-de-sac for the distractions in his head. For 65 cents, a machine dispensed a cup of coffee and gave him solace. Neil inhaled the aroma of the hot black liquid and held the cup with both hands while walking the green grounds. There was something in him that needed figuring out, a pain in him he couldn't remove. He could feel, had a sense of this thing that bothered him, but hadn't or wasn't able to put his finger on it, like trying to place a name with a face of someone he had met long ago, vague, but gnawing and real. He felt a need to do something, not necessarily at this moment, but something overall with his life. He wasn't sure. He sat down on a bench and watched as a father placed his two young daughters in the back of a car, gently buckled them in, said a few reassuring words and was off. Neil got back on his bike and continued on.

He had to make up for lost time. For the next few hours nothing distracted Neil, he rode, just rode. He rode the rest of the day and into the early evening. Just after sunset, too road weary to look anywhere else, he opted for the lure of a small, neon lit 'Motel' sign just outside Adrian, Texas.

The motel, ordinary and unremarkable, looked as if it was struggling to make it through another day without the owner suffering any extra expenditures. Weeds sprung from cracks between the parking lot pavement and the concrete walkway where the rooms stood in line like abandoned barracks. Checking in at the lobby was like being admitted into a cancer ward; a heavy dose of gloom and sadness quietly filled the room. It was as if a cat had curled up in a corner and died. Everything looked tired and worn, including the carpet at the entrance, which had been beaten down to raw floor. There were a couple of cushioned chairs spotted with stains and throw pillows embroidered with Land of Nod child like themes. Small tables, chipped at their corners exposed particleboard beneath their laminate finish. On top were lamps with mismatched shades. A reading rack held outdated pamphlets and brochures. A strong smell of curry permeated the air. Neil immediately regretted his decision, but was too tired to do anything about it.

"Good day, sir." A man from India, who had the ominous presence of an insomnia afflicted, funeral home director, stood behind the check in counter. "Checking in?"

This had to be the owner. "Yes. Checking in," Neil said.

"Any bags you'd like carried?"

Neil had to do 'a double take' over his shoulder, "Bag- no bags, just, just what I can manage myself."

"Very well, then," the man said.

The phone rang and the man answered it. He spoke in his native tongue and Neil understood none of it except the phrase 'American Express'. The man hung up the phone. He was agitated. He turned to a curtain behind him and threw it open. There was a room where Neil could see a woman sitting on the floor around a pot that simmered on a hotplate. A small girl of about six or seven years in age knelt beside her with a coloring book and abacus. She reminded Neil of Dora the Explorer. The man said a few harsh words to them and let the curtain fall back in place. The woman then said something through the curtain, which made the man pull it back again. She kept her head down and said nothing. Satisfied, the man let the curtain fall for a second time and returned to Neil.

It pained Neil to be here and further still, to even look at the man, who looked as if he were literally working himself to death: a short sleeve button down shirt reeking from layers of old sweat and eyes, tired and grey, sunk deep inside purplish black, fig colored skin that clung to a face as though it were an unnecessary annoyance. The man's hair had thinned to the point that only a few strands remained and those were pasted back with sweat and oil. He turned a thick logbook around on the counter for Neil to sign.

Despite all that surrounded him, it was obvious the owner was trying his best to present a more profitable, respectable and upscale establishment, which only caused in Neil a deeper sense of anguish.

"If there's anything you should need," the man said as he handed over the room key, "don't hesitate to ask. You are welcome to all the amenities. Check out is at 12 noon. Enjoy your stay."

Whatever euphoria Neil may have carried in from the road or from anything else in general had dried up, been sucked away. There was such sadness. And as he turned to leave he felt an urge to cry, not for this man, and this man alone, but for all mankind. For in this man he saw every man; the fragility of life, a man struggling against unbeatable odds and against a world that cared nothing for him or his situation, a world that had somehow forgotten to roll his dice. And, yet, here he was and still fighting to put a better face on what he understood the underlying reality to be.

Neil unloaded his motorcycle and walked to his room. He unlocked and opened the door. If he was looking for something to lift his spirits, he wouldn't find it here. The room was empty of surprises and predictably drab - typical motif consisting of cheap curtains, institutional carpet, dubious sheets, last night's odors, and an old television set. The room was stale and lifeless with a kind of sickness that hung in the air like a draped coffin. The idea that maybe he should make the effort to get the hell out of here and look for a campsite occurred to him, but here he had already paid the money, had unloaded his bags and the very notion of requesting a refund from the hotel owner was just too terrible and tragic a thought.

'Stupid idiot,' he said as he took his boots off and threw them under a chair. 'Never a carcinogenic motel room again!'

He undressed, showered and laid in bed. Although he was tired from the road, it was still an uneasy sleep. He was angry and the stale smell of the motel room wouldn't leave his nostrils. There were thumps against the walls, tires in the parking lot, bits of talk, doors closing and the soda machine, just outside his room, constantly hummed - broken every so often with the sound of clinking coins and the slamming birth of an aluminum can. The place felt sterile, foreign, and for the first time, in a long time, Neil felt afraid - not because of the surroundings per se, but because these conditions provided soil for the uncertainty which now flowered in his mind. What was he doing here? Not just in

67

this room, but here in Texas, without a friend, no one knowing he was here, no one. He felt out of sorts and fearfully alone. All he amounted to, his total sum at this moment, was a name in a front desk logbook and a room number.

'Maybe if I had a drink, grab a few beers somewhere,' he thought. but, no - he knew it would only make matters worse and the morning that much more unwelcome. He was in the thick mire of banality, pointlessness, when a flickering moment of time present is swallowed and made trivial by the vast universe of time past and future.

'How meaningless it all is,' he said, laying on his back in the strange darkness of this temporary setting.

Red digital numbers glowed from an alarm clock bolted to the nightstand. He looked at the pragmatic numbers and clock and laughed.

'The ridiculous nature of it all,' he thought. 'Man's attempt to somehow control even time.'

It hit him hard. The precise and methodical nature of it seemed ludicrous, and miserable at the same time; the lit numbers, unblinking and unswerving in their impassiveness for life, moving ahead with no contention or compassion for the human condition,

'An indifference,' It came to him now. 'That's what it is, an indifference.' He knew it was just an instrument, but, yet he couldn't help it.

'For once it would be nice to see a a a..... mistake or some human quality.'

He looked again at the clock, but still the continuous, predictable nature of this device remained unmoved and it bothered him and caused him to question its very purpose.

'What time?' he wondered. 'Man's feeble attempt to harness, control, make sense of, and stabilize it. Trying to control the universe.'

And now in his mind, it was all a lie. There was no such thing as time...it was an invention. He looked up at the ceiling and rolled on to his side.

He was sinking, becoming smaller, a small round marble imploding in on itself like a dying star compressed and squeezed from its own weight. His personal life and efforts now appeared to him as being insignificant. An entire lifetime, his history, at this point added up to nothing, producing not even the slightest of ripples in the infinite universal pool of time and space. His thoughts were thick and oddly sublime. 'The hundred and thousands of millions of people who have lived before me and I knew them not. They lived their lives, had their troubles, fought their battles and now are gone, dead. Where is the connection, what is the purpose, where am I going in this universal story, am I even playing a part? Oh God, you are laughing.'

'If only you had stayed in college-made something of yourself,' The Instructor chimed in. But the night was too heavy, solemn, in fact, for such a voice. Hands in pockets, he disappeared back into a deep darkness.

Neil's thoughts then turned to words from his prep school graduation where the headmaster had spoken to the graduating class, saying, "To those whom much is given, much will be expected." It was funny he should even have remembered such a thing, never had he given those words much thought, but tonight his mind was running, running down dark alleys and forgotten places. The weight of those words and this entire night was squeezing him. His body felt far from sleep. There was the man he'd buried in the desert. What had he done? His mind had much more to say. His eyes ran snippets of a movie in which he had played a part; summer days as a young child growing up along the coastline of Connecticut, sitting in the neighbor's kitchen with lobster pots and buoys and having his first hair cut, wanting it to be over, his attention drawn to a small wooden box mounted on the wall which held lollipops of assorted colors, orange being his favorite. The smell of canvas and marline from the ship builder's basement as the grey bearded man sucked at a cigar and spoke of Hemingway things with Neil's father. Heading out on wicker seats in early wet morning fog off Long Island Sound, paddling Old Towne wooden canoe. Tide bands of seaweed planted far below swirling in whirlpool strokes, navigating snowy tundra of wind swept golf course while pulling Flexible Flyer sled and tiny Neil bundled in butterball one piece snowsuit sniffling red runny nose.

Adolescent cricket summer nights with first beer and cigarette and innocent girls who wanted dreams to come true. Young boys wanting everything, promising anything, and ready to burn it all for nothing. Rock n' roll, no need to learn what I already know, cocky statements made from his ignorant, naive mouth came back now, washed over him with shame and embarrassment and deep regret. First bitter taste of deadlines and responsibilities with college and experimentation, dorm rooms, scrounging coins, comrades, laughing, drinking, girls, always girls, paint is art, rebellious, stubborn and yet black and white must yield to grey, differences, beliefs, values, I am I, who am I.....

It was impossible for him to sleep. The images kept coming and he turned from side to side trying to find a comfortable position that would help lull him away.

Sarah appeared from one Saturday morning several months back when she had risen early to make breakfast. He had woken from a deep satisfying sleep a few minutes later and had followed her to the kitchen. The warmth of the bed still clung to their bodies. He remembered leaning his shoulder and head against the kitchen doorway, simply staring at her as she stood at the stove making him breakfast. Neither spoke. It was early, early enough that he felt as though they had somehow cheated the day of a few precious moments. The sun had barely broken the horizon and the first strands of light, which had wrestled free, shone through the kitchen window and touched Sarah's face and figure. She was suffused with a soft amber glow that accented her growing belly and radiant complexion; here was Egypt, Cleopatra, black waves rolling off the Red Sea, and the fertile banks of the Nile. His eyes welling up with a sense of boundlessness, limitless possibilities, not only of an entire weekend, but of a lifetime. There was no then, now or when.

So kind, so giving Sarah was, and how little he had actually given of himself to her - now hit Neil in this lonely hotel room with regret and sadness. He felt sorry for her, shuddered at his own inadequacies, and questioned her intelligence. She was always trying to make things work; making him coffee before he woke in the morning, making a bigger deal of his birthday than he ever would, and the delight she got in seeing him happy - the way only a woman can. He wished to God he could hold her now, kiss her hips, inhale her hair, and whisper things he wanted to say, things she needed to hear. And, then of course, he thought of the abortion. To think back on that rain soaked windy day - a day, which seemed to ache and cry from the protest of a voiceless child when they had entered the abortion clinic - made him numb.

5

The earth had turned, the morning had come and the hydrogen burned. Neil awoke late and began packing his items back on his bike as if he were going off to work; it felt obligatory, mundane and nothing about it had much appeal. He was irritable; bothered by something that he had neither the desire nor ability to define. A scratching, squealing hyena, biting at a cage - had found its way inside his head. The night in the motel had not been a restful one. A hardy breakfast might improve things, but a diner was out of the question. He wasn't ready to interact with anyone. He'd have to settle for something far less than what he wanted.

In the town of Amarillo, he grabbed a cup of watery coffee and a stale Danish at a convenience store. Looking down its prepackaged aisles, he noticed that the gerbils had begun to spin their wheels again. One, even at this early morning hour, made for the artificially bright colors of a spinning slush machine. Another filled an oversized plastic cup with diet soda and crushed ice. Neil moved towards the check out counter where a few people stood in line. Rows and rows of colorful wrappers formed a fortified wall of modified corn syrup and chemical compounds, separating customer from cashier. Next to the counter was a newsstand with newspapers and magazines. He walked over to have a look. Every subject under the sun seemed to be represented. There was a magazine on running, photography, cooking, hotrods and hot babes. There were celebrity magazines with catchy headlines about divorce, weight loss and Hollywood dating gossip. At eye level, was a magazine about art galleries and auction houses. Neil took hold of it. The front of the magazine was a name he thought he recognized. He flipped it opened and found a small article on someone he knew, or rather had known back when he had lived in New York. He didn't have the heart to read it all, but caught the gist of it- here was someone who had garnered some attention in the art world, was making a splash and the critics had begun to take notice. Neil squinted his eyes and then raised his eyebrows, "Man. Wow." Why wasn't it him?- he should have been on the cover. But, why should it matter, why did he even care? "Ah, good for him," Neil said to himself and pushed the magazine back on to the shelf and got in line.

'Go back and stock shelves at the hanger,' The Instructor said.

Neil didn't respond.

'You're the one who didn't want to paint anymore- it's a win win for all of us.' And then in a sing songy way The Instructor said, 'Oh what have you done with your life today, what have you done with your life I say?'

There were only two people ahead of Neil, but the line seemed to be taking forever. He thought about going back and grabbing the magazine, but someone stepped up behind him and he didn't want to lose his place. He let out a sigh. Bags of chips were clipped to racks and hung like Christmas tree ornaments. Neil swatted at the bags. Behind the counter a hotdog machine slowly spun three overworked reminders from the night before on hot metal rollers. The smell took him back to linoleum floors, hairnets, plastic gloves and a noisy fifth grade lunchroom cafeteria.

'Even back then you could have made better choices,' said The Instructor, 'it's always about the choices.'

He was next in line when he happened to glance at a clock hanging on the wall above the cashier and noticed the difference in time between his watch and the clock. Immediately he knew-

"Shit, I've lost an hour!" Neil said.

The man ahead of him half turned then turned back to the cashier and smirked.

"Fucker," Neil muttered under his breath.

73

The man immediately straightened up and turned around, "What did you say?"

'Take him out and bury him, just like ya did the old man,' said The Instructor.

Neil held the man squarely with his cold eyes, "I wasn't talking to you."

The man's eyes darted across Neil's face searching for an answer or an excuse. Neil didn't blinked, didn't look away, but instead held his stare. Neither one said a word. The man turned back to pay. After his transaction he grabbed his things and gave Neil a final challenging look before hitting the door.

Neil plopped his Danish and coffee down on the counter and searched his pockets. His hands were shaking.

"Close one, huh?" said the cashier. He was a young kid with curly hair and wild eyes.

Neil kept his eyes on the counter. "I guess."

"Want a ticket with that?"

Neil was at a loss. "A what?"

"Yeah, a ticket, a quickpick - ya know for the lottery? It's up to hundred and twenty million."

'The new opium of the masses, masses, masses, new opium of the masses,' The Instructor raged.

"No thanks, just the coffee and Danish and I'll take one of those prepaid phone cards hanging behind you," Neil said.

Outside Neil scanned the parking lot for the man who had accosted him. He was nowhere in sight.

'Yellowbelly,' The Instructor said.

'Just what I need,' Neil responded, 'draw attention to myself, have the cops come and put me away.'

He went to adjust his watch, but his hands were still unsure, his mind jittery. He looked up again to make sure the man wasn't around.

"This is all I need after getting a late start this morning and losing an hour," Neil said and took a bite of his Danish and sat down on the curb to calm himself. He took a sip of his coffee. He must've entered the Central Standard time zone sometime last night while crossing the Texas border. He set the coffee and

Danish down and gave his watch another try. He unscrewed the crown and turned the hands forward.

'Time, units of time -so made up in a certain way..' he thought. Like a hair stuck on his tongue, remnants from last night's inner monologue hadn't completely been spat out.

'Why twenty four hours? Who had decided on twenty four, or even the concept of an hour, sixty minutes? Why a week, a month?' Parceling of time, the fabrication of units called hours and minutes was something he had read about once, but now couldn't remember.

He guessed that a month most likely had something to do with the cycles of the moon and minutes into hours had something to do with ancient mariners. Kicking around his head was something about the Chinese being the first to invent the clock, but again, he wasn't sure and spent no more effort trying to figure it out. Instead, he screwed the crown back into its socket of his Swiss Army watch given to him as a gift from Sarah when they first began dating, an anniversary present of some kind. With the tip of his thumbnail, he flicked the edge of the coffee cup's plastic lid up and down in a repetitive pattern, thinking of nothing, looking nowhere and stretched his back.

On the right side of the convenience store was a pay phone. He walked over, placed his Styrofoam cup on top of it and picked up the receiver. He was surprised to hear a dial tone. It seemed the whole world had gone cellular. Squeezing the receiver between his right shoulder and ear, he punched in the numbers of the prepaid phone card and a telephone number. A voice picked up on the other end, "Dillards."

Neil recognized the voice. "Hey Steve, this is Neil- is Bill there?"

There was a slight pause. "Oh hey, Neil a you- haven't you heard?

"Heard? No what?"

"Bill is gone, man."

"What a mean gone?"

"Well, gone, sorta disappeared. Hasn't been here for a while, weeks. Nobody's seen him."

"Shit."

"Thought you knew already."

"No."

"Snack's wife, Karen said she'd seen 'em with his ex and then went off drinking again, but I don't know. Nobody's sure."

"Alright."

"Who knows? Could show up today or tomorrow for all that matters."

"Thanks, I'll check in later."

"Okay. Sorry man."

"Thanks."

Neil hung up the phone and sat down on the curb. He sat there for a while and then raised himself up, picked the phone up again and dialed. The phone rang and on the other end an answering machine picked up;

"Hi this is Sarah, please leave your name, number and a brief message after the beep." A sharp beep sounded and a surge of anxiety shot through Neil - an actor who'd forgotten his lines, yet still thrust on stage, naked, alone.

"Hey Sarah, how are you? Neil." He heard his voice break a little. "I just wanted to call, see how you're doing, say hello. I'm still out here, in Texas, actually. Decided to head East a bit, but still coming back in a week, about a week. Dealing with a lot. Bill from the shop isn't doing too well and other stuff besides, but no need for concern. Alright, well, hope you're doing well. Take care. I - I miss you. Bye." Neil hung up feeling incomplete, disappointed with himself, his words - words that never seemed to match the perfect ones he had formulated and conjured up in his mind, but never made it to his tongue.

In what felt like the final dying spasms of a dream, Sarah and Neil had been going through the motions of a relationship. The abortion had caused a sad and silent rift between them. They had been together long enough for marriage to be a consideration, but he'd only brought the topic up after she'd become pregnant. He had meant it then, but why he had avoided the topic of marriage up until her pregnancy was something of a mystery; after all, she had all the attributes Neil could want in a woman-she was smart and funny, unbelievably sexy with a beautiful heart and soft soul. It shouldn't have taken a pregnancy for him to see this. Why was it so hard then for him to allow this girl a permanent place in his life, in his being? Yes, he cherished the freedom and possibilities each day presented when he woke up alone. He didn't *have* to pick his clothes up off the floor. He didn't *have* to go grocery shopping with a list. He didn't *have* to wait for someone else to get ready before leaving the house, and his shower wouldn't be overrun with mysterious products. But, these reasons were all bullshit and he knew it; they were superficial, empty and made especially irrelevant when just her smile alone gave his existence purpose.

Neil finished the Danish and threw the half filled coffee cup into the trash. He got on his motorcycle and headed east. Riding through the rushing air, a voice with a familiar tone barely broke, making but one pronouncement,

'Marriage is an institution, sacred, holy forged with commitment and children in which only real men need apply.'

Wichita Falls was a place Neil had only known in name. He was hoping to change that today. All he had to do was stay on route 287. He fell behind a string of traffic and tried to analyze the news of Bill by figuring out what it all meant. He wondered where he'd gone and what kind of shape he was in. If only he was back there and could do something useful to help find him. But, here was this trip. He looked over the passing landscape and felt empty. There'd be no beauty around him. And if the road had anything to offer today it would have to lay by the wayside.

Just as he began to wonder why he had even started this trip in the first place, he caught sight of a highway patrol car in his side view mirror. The patrol car moved from the fast lane and came up close behind him.

"Sonofabitch!" Neil said. "Perfect."

'Hey, Cool hand-looks like we got ourselves a smokyyyyy,' The Instructor pointed out. 'Bad boy, bad boy - whatcha gonna do when they come for you? I can hear it now, 'Dead man in the desert, officer? What Dead man? Why I was jest hav'in meself a couple a beers....you are wearing a wife beater under that jacket a yours, aren't ya, Neil?'

Neil did his best to keep calm, but the patrol car was holding a steady bead from behind. Neil could feel the state trooper's authoritative fingers typing in his motorcycle's license plate number into an onboard computer.

'What we have here is failure to communicate,' The Instructor said.

Neil kept silent and fought to hold a straight line and perfect speed limit. He braced himself for the flashing lights, siren and voice through the bullhorn instructing him to pull over when suddenly the patrol car broke rank, zoomed ahead and was lost in traffic.

"Oh, thank God," Neil said.
He wondered if it was all worth it.

"What the hell am I doing out here?" he asked himself. New York seemed so far away and everything about this ordeal appeared as a dreadful mistake, which he now regretted, and yet, still, he continued to ride. The wind picked up and he battled against it. He could feel the vulnerability of his motorcycle against the elements and the fast moving traffic. He felt ridiculous now on this stupid machine, exposed and child-like.

'It would be so much nicer if Sarah were here,' he thought. 'If we could cruise along together in the plush, protective interior of a car like we had two years ago...' He was remembering the time they had driven up the California coast for a wine tasting weekend in Sonoma county.... driving through the rugged, sometimes rocky, always twisting road of Big Sur lined with enormous Pine trees and a jagged coast, munching on snacks, laughing, listening to music, and sharing their dreams.

He remembered her tiny smooth bare feet propped up on the hot dashboard and the bliss they had felt together as they drove along that Summer day. They stopped for the night in Big Sur at a rustic cabin motel. Despite its rugged appearance, their cabin had all the comforts of a well appointed home, including a Jacuzzi that was accessed through French doors of the master bedroom and on a deck surrounded by trees that reached far into the sky. With the fireplace ablaze inside their cabin, they sat together in the Jacuzzi drinking Heffenweissen beer with slices of lemon and looked up through the tunnel of trees into the dream driven night sky. Neil remembered playing a game that night, pretending to be a lumberjack who had just returned from a day spent deep within the nearby woods, and now was lost-asking Sarah for directions, what her name was, her favorite color and whether or not she liked the look of rough, untamed men. Sarah just smiled from across the bubbling water and played along. A beautiful weekend it had been.

Now out here on his motorcycle, it was dry, plain and the memory of that weekend with Sarah only intensified his misery. Neil slugged onward along route 287. There was little enthusiasm in him. It was boring, flat and all of it so goddamn uninteresting that it had become like an unwanted chore; just needing to get from point A to point B. He rode hard and constant, not letting up, all grit and grime - riding straight through to Wichita Falls. The sun hadn't quite set by the time he reached the town, but the wind, let alone the approaching darkness, was enough for him to call it quits. There was no fight left in him.

Keeping the promise he made to himself from the night before, of staying away from motels, he putted along side streets until he found a campground on the outskirts of town. It was a large facility that accommodated RVs, but had no sites for tents. He was told there was another campground where he could pitch his tent, but after more than twenty minutes of trying to find it he gave up. He was angry and tired. And soon he was lost on back roads with small, single story ranch houses with pickup trucks and quiet little yards. Dogs barked from backyards and through front windows as he passed by on his motorcycle. He could see no need in a rural town like this to pay for a campsite, so when he came across a park that looked large enough for him to go unnoticed, he turned into the entrance. He rode past a series of small ponds connected by quaint little Japanese styled arched bridges used by pedestrians. Riding farther into the interior, the park opened up into expansive fields that stretched wide and far and looked more like several golf courses linked together than any city park. There were clusters of trees and even a public swimming pool with a clubhouse. The swimming pool had been drained and the clubhouse stood empty. The season had ended and the summer was gone: vacant seashells, resting like memories on a dry ocean floor. It gave Neil an eerie feeling to think of all the children, scented sunscreen, splashing water and life here, including the playful screams, a life guard's whistle, muscle car cowboys, parking lot angels and now there was nothing. It didn't seem possible.

He moved into a more secluded back section of the park and found a perfect spot beneath two large pines to conceal his motorcycle and tent away from view of the road. He'd come back later. Maybe just after dark when he was sure no one would see him and unload his gear. For now, he decided it was a good time to head into town and find a Laundromat.

Parts of the small city reminded him of a community college; it was laid out flat, concrete and functional with one square industrial no nonsense building after another. A yellow school bus with flashing lights stopped ahead of him and released a soccer team of girls in blue and white jerseys. A few blocks later he passed a young boy walking alone on the side of the road carrying a beat up trombone case. A few men in polyester shirts and department store ties drove by in square ubiquitous cars. The town had an Orwellian, utilitarian feel to it. It had taken on a tone from the kind of day when the world seems frighteningly real, dull, and devoid of ethereal qualities and words like, 'hope' or 'promise' don't come so easily to the tongue without sounding hollow and hypocritical, luxurious toys reserved for fools and children. After turning several blocks, and zigzagging bland city streets, Neil spotted a Laundromat. The front of the building was made largely of glass with the words "Laun" and "M" painted in gold and black -the rest of the letters had worn off, gone with age so only their outlines remained. He pulled up right in front and threw a few nickels in the parking meter.

He gathered his clothes from his saddlebags and stepped up on to the sidewalk and pushed open the glass door. Inside were iconic markings of depression: there was florescent lighting, spilled detergent, cracked floor tiles and grave marked welfare mothers. The somberness of the place seemed to have added weight to his boots. As he made his way to a top loader and searched his pockets for quarters, he looked at some of the people around him and saw they all shared the lowest rungs of the economic ladder. He placed almost all his clothes, including the t-shirt he was wearing, inside the washer. He was left wearing only shorts, a leather jacket and boots- but he didn't care - it mattered little in a place like this.

No one was talking inside the Laundromat. All were strangers. A tangible air of mistrust had mixed with fabric softener and Neil imagined that this is what prison must be like; everyone keeping to themselves, trusting no one under impersonal institutional conditions. Of course, here you were free to leave at any time, not forced to join a gang, and rape was as much a possibility as seeing a dancing bear scrub socks.

Across the way, sitting on one of the folding tables, was a girl - a hip young chick who was wearing a faded baby blue colored nineteen seventies retro "Big Wheels" t-shirt over a long sleeve white thermal top. The top was a size too small, small enough to expose a belly button piercing. She had on low, waist hugging jeans and high top canvas sneakers. Her black hair was short, spiky with red and purple highlights. She wore black lipstick that helped to accent a nose ring. She was too cool to take notice of anyone around her, including Neil.

A short lady in her mid-fifties with a faint moustache on her upper lip waddled past Neil and then folded laundry on top of some washers next to him. She had thick arms, tree trunk legs and wore pink, plastic sandals. A delicate bracelet on her right ankle held on for dear life. The lower part of her gut poked through the bottom half of a white fishnet shirt, exposing tributaries of stretch marks etched like a river transporting third world workers to a 99 cent store or 24 hour bodega. It pained him to be here and he could feel his whole mindset sinking into a thick porridge of depression and hopelessness. After feeding several bills into the 'Insert bill face up as shown' change machine, and collecting the quarters that dropped into the curved metal slot, Neil deposited the coins into the soap dispenser. The soap dispenser reflected the age of this place, an older machine with an odd looking metal bar that had to be moved to one of the soap boxes displayed behind a small, clear plastic window. It was more an arcade game under this sad circus tent than any soap dispenser he'd ever seen. With soap and quarters now in his hand, he went back to his washing machines and poured in the soap, deposited the quarters, and sat back in a plastic chair while the machines started their cycles.

He hadn't sat very long when the front door opened and a man wearing tattered clothing, rags really, with plastic bags for shoes, electrical tape for a belt, and hair so matted it'd make a Rasta man cry, came into the Laundromat muttering to himself or an invisible counterpart. A putrid, rotting meat odor hit Neil's nostrils. A slap in the face followed by an immediate gag reflex forced him to cover his mouth with his knuckles while he held his breath and made a dash for the door. Once outside, Neil let go of his lungs and sucked in massive gobs of fresh air. He looked back through the window and saw the man making his way down the row of washers, opening some of the lids, looking in, muttering, closing the lids and moving on. This process continued until he had gotten to the end of the line of washers and then disappeared out a back exit and into an alley. Still no one said anything or seemed to react to what had just happened.

After what seemed like a sufficient amount of time, Neil went back inside, and sat down. The foul smell still lingered, but paled in comparison to the earlier stench. A few minutes remained before his clothes would finish washing. He looked around for reading material, but found none. There was nothing to do but wait. A few feet away from him stood a young Guatemalan girl with thick, shiny raven hair worn in a ponytail that extended down to her waist. She pulled clothes from a dryer. A sad resignation hung on her like a veil of missed novenas. An older woman who must have been her mother stood quietly beside her in a, shy-like, tentative manner. She held a newborn swaddled in blankets with the baby's pink, turnip face and tiny wet lips exposed. You could feel their heritage, old country ways that they'd carried across the border; cornmeal being ground against stone and hearth with fire blazing and a smack, smack, smack sound from tamales between this older woman's hands before fetching water from the town's only well.

Hanging on the bleak walls above the machines were signs that read, "NO WASHERS STARTED AFTER 8PM" and "LIMIT TWO DRYERS PER CUSTOMER", "ABSOLUTELY NO TINTING OR DYEING - VIOLATORS WILL BE PROSECUTED FOR DAMAGE" and almost as a cruel afterthought, another sign read, "SORRY, NOT RESPONSIBLE FOR LOST, DAMAGED OR STOLEN ARTICLES". It gave Neil a chill to think of the do-gooder men who first put up these signs, and even sadder still, to think of anyone here who might lose a simple article of clothing and made the investment to recover it.

As Neil tossed his washed clothes into two large **Speed Queen** dryers, a cell phone rang. It was for Ms. Hipster and she answered it, not only in a voice that made you feel like this was her living room, but also, with a kind of 'Fuck you' attitude to anyone who'd dare bend their ears to listen. Somehow she had gotten lost in here with these losers, maybe taken a wrong turn between Coolsville and the town of selectavision. Maybe it was the President calling or a Paris fashion designer, her record promoter, her backstage pass, her happen'in party, her unkempt boyfriend, her self-righteous girlfriend, her runaway daddy, her pill popping mommy, herself, finally, herself.

The **Speed Queen** continued to turn and Neil watched as the glass door steamed, and his clothes eventually dried. He gathered the clothes from the dryer and brought a few items to his nose. The clothes smelled clean, fresh. He put on a warm grey t-shirt, socks, and a pair of worn jeans. He folded the rest of the clothes and brought them out to his motorcycle, and tucked them into a saddlebag.

He returned to the park. There was no one in sight. He set up his tent and unloaded some gear. He looked at his watch. It was only six O'clock.

Way too early to go to bed, he thought.

There was still time to kill. He'd go back into town. Maybe grab a bite to eat, maybe even see a movie.

He rode towards town and, again, headed for its meek center. Turning on to Main Street, he looked up. An orange and white angular sign shot high into the air. It had the shape of an upside down slice of pizza, an elongated triangle - its tip closest to the ground. As if freshly pulled from a 1950's Vegas casino, the sign was lit with large, retro styled bulbs, a flashing mix of red, white and orange that ran from top to bottom spelling out the word, 'Bowl'. The last letter, 'L' had next to it an image of two pins knocking together in high dramatic fashion.

Neil turned into the bowling alley parking lot, parked his motorcycle and walked towards the bowling alley entrance. He stopped to get a better look at the sign that had pulled him in here. He hadn't seen anything like it except on vintage postcards from the 1950's. The sign fascinated, tugged at him in an unexpected way that caught him off guard. He wondered how it must have been: The 1950's, large, heavy cars, a Saturday night, girls in poodle dresses, young men, ducktail hairdos and a new fangled sound called, "Rock n' roll" pumping through a meshed cloth dashboard speaker. But, the music didn't drown out everything; there was the hard reality of Sputnik, Kruchev, the cold war, 'duck and cover', segregation, union strikes. Yet, even among all these menaces, lay a tinge of innocence too. World War II had ended and the entire country cheered, celebrated the idealism of the American dream; owning a home, raising a family, a nine to five job, peace and prosperity. Wives dreamt of Frigidaire, cocktail parties, and Tupperware. Men thought of barbeques, big cars, and television sets and chilled martinis with big fat olives. The war that had taken so much, had also given a new appreciation for life, family, God and country.

This bowling alley served as a conduit to that era. Inside, Neil took note of the orange and red low pile carpet and a smell of filterless cigarettes and Aqua Velva aftershave that seemed to have been circulating through its air conditioning ducts since 1954. The place was a wormhole, transporting its occupants back to another generation. The only reminder of modern times was a television set hanging in the corner of a bar. But, even that, with its black and white screen, looked old enough to have broadcast the first moon landing, the war in Vietnam and President Nixon's resignation speech from the oval office. That same television now served to display a game of Keno.

Off to the side of the bar were two restrooms. And looking more part Vegas cocktail lounge than bowling alley, there hung above each entrance a small brass sign lit with corresponding white letters that read either, "men" or "women".

Neil felt out of place walking in with his helmet, leather jacket and motorcycle boots. He could feel his face flush with the sudden stupidity of owning his damn motorcycle. Along a section of wall closest to the building's entrance was a batch of small lockers. He walked over and deposited some coins into two lockers and pulled a key with a plastic number attached from each after stuffing his jacket into one and his helmet into the other.

The bowling alley was split into two levels, separated by just a few steps. The lower half held about twenty lanes from where the sound of pins and balls broke the air. Each lane had a booth where players recorded their scores and waited their turn. On the upper level, ran a railing with tables and chairs. Opposite them were vending machines with chips, snacks and soda and a machine that polished bowling balls.

In addition to AMF banners that hung above the lanes, there were other signs that announced nightly specials for each day of the week. And as Neil walked along the upper level and looked down on the lanes, it was apparent tonight was dedicated to senior citizens. Most lanes, with the exception of only one or two, held bowlers who were elderly, retired looking. Almost as proof of their age was a large folding table that had been set up on the upper level to accommodate pink, cardboard boxes lined with wax paper and filled with donuts. Towering above the boxes was an enormous stainless steel coffee urn with an indicator light and water level tube. Next to the urn and at the ready were an upside down stack of white Styrofoam cups, a bundle of red plastic stirrers, powdered creamer, and a variety of sweeteners.

As Neil watched the bowlers a little more closely, it was easy to see they were taking advantage of the night. They were like children who had been let out of school early; they hobbled around, made gestures, and were just plain giddy with excitement. The one big difference he noticed though, between these bowlers and any child, happened only when it came time to bowl, actually toe the line and knock down pins; these elders took their time, funneling their concentration and energies with utmost sincerity. None of the players seemed rushed or hurried by things outside their control, but instead methodically steadied themselves, seemingly turning inward before releasing the ball, which often landed with a loud thud, followed by a slow, deliberate roll down the lane.

But it was funny to see as soon as the ball got down to the other end of the lane and did whatever it was going to do, these bowlers turned, lightened, and resumed their lives with child like energies and a 'let the chips fall where they may' kind of attitude. This was true down every lane he looked. Other similarities shared between them included not only bowling edict, but dress too-most of the women had short puffed up hair with a look of being freshly blowed dryed, curled, heavily sprayed or maybe all three. Somewhere in town a hair salon was doing one heck of a business. As for the men, they all had a simple, conservative look.

Not all the bowlers were senior citizens. Two of the lanes held bowlers that constituted parts of younger families, and there was one lane where a bunch of surly teenagers roistered about. It unnerved Neil, made him uneasy, to look at these kids who threw curse words in the air like circus knives, showing no respect for anything or anyone, including the elders around them. The boys wore baggy pants low enough to partially expose their underwear, and with no method, or apparent desire to play the game by any set of rules, were not here to bowl, but instead seemed bent on proving something to themselves or their friends. There was an insidious undercurrent to everything they did, which teetered on the verge of becoming something truly dangerous and uncontrollable. It gave Neil a sense of relief to see that the older bowlers didn't seem to notice the teenagers or, if they did, had chosen to ignore them.

Inside the bowling alley was an old fashioned coffee shop with sharp, clean lines and lots of chrome. Things sold and served, not only included eggs, coffee and cheeseburgers, but, also bowling shirts, pins, ashtrays and a mish-mash of mementos. Neil walked inside and rotated a tall, wobbly, metal rack filled with postcards. The postcards came in different sizes and had everything from pictures of grizzly bears to a cartoon showing a man with an enormous beer gut fishing from a small boat with the caption: 'A bad day fishing is still better than a good day at the office.' It was funny to see that most of the postcards had nothing to do with the town at all. A light layer of dust had gathered on some of the cards and there were a few that had even begun to yellow on their back corners. One postcard had an artist's sketching of the bowling alley done in an art deco style. Neil bought several of these cards and a cup of chicken noodle soup and carried them back to a small table on the upper level overlooking the bowling lanes. He pulled a pen from his pocket and laid the small stack of postcards out in front of him.

He tore open the cellophane package of saltine crackers, crushed and emptied them into his soup. With his spoon, he pushed the crackers down, submerging them beneath the piping hot surface and looked out to the lane directly below him. It was lane number 14 and there were two elderly couples bowling. They looked so neat and clean. The sound of Elvis Presley's', "Never been to Spain" came through the bowling alley sound system.

Neil felt comfortable and relaxed, as if he were at home soaking in a hot bath. He melted down into the lanes and became part of what he saw. All the years and life experiences compiled here amongst these bowlers washed over him; he felt all their heartache, tragedies, unexpected moments of joy, and something inside him, a good part of him anyway, wanted to go down and talk with them, be with them, laugh and hug them because, in part, he recognized these older people were heroes, champions to a certain degree - they had made it through the hoops and obstacle course of life. And what amazed him, what he found beauty in, was he could see that they had a relative sense of this accomplishment too. Like an athlete after a race, they appeared relaxed, patting one another's backs. Gone were any pre-race jitters or hard ego-driven desire to win, all now replaced with a joy of the present moment where nothing is past, nothing is hurried, and where there is no preoccupation of future races.

He blew across the top of his spoon filled with the hot soup, allowing it to cool slightly before taking in the delicious liquid. It was perfect and looking out across the lanes, Neil thought of all the combined history here in this place tonight. He began to marvel at how much could be learned from these individuals. And what he knew, understood deeply in this moment, was, that life is defined by acts an individual performs between birth and death- the bookends of one's time on earth. That's it - nothing more. He thought of his life and with it came the sourness of regret. There was so much he regretted and the painful, awful choices he had made in life and time he'd wasted. Choices could be healed, he knew that, but time, time was something he'd never get back. He took a heavy breath and held still the empty spoon above the bowl. He became lost in the thought, contemplating the choice he and Sarah had made to terminate a life and then, of course, it was inevitable that his mind should turn to image of the man whom he had buried out in the desert only a few days earlier. He could see the old man's face and hear his words. He felt ashamed to be here, in the company of these older good and decent people who had a grace and dignity about them, which had been earned over time, of lessons learned from personal wars they had fought, battles they had lost, won- principles gained through it all. He eased his shame as best he could with the idea that wisdom can clearly, only, come through experience, and, experience requires time. And, then there was redemption; his life wasn't over yet.

He looked at the postcards and turned one of them over. The thought of scribbling down the words; 'No job, Dead man, money, note – on the lam, may kill self before reaching N.Y.' was funny in a morbid sort of way for about a second, but the truth pushed his mind to the respectful presence of the here and now.

The older couples on lane 14 had the women chatting medicine, children, and other women. The men didn't say too much but talked a little of the coffee, college football, and local news stories. Each of the four individuals bowled and meticulously recorded their scores. The women squeaked and squawked while the men bowled, sat, and bowled again. The women continued on, commenting on one another's hair and the latest storewide sale at such and such department store. It was amazing to Neil to think that most women, until they lay resting in their graves, would always concern themselves with makeup, hair, and shoes- didn't matter how young or how old, it was built deep within their genetic structure. It also seemed part of their genetic code to master a household, to direct, bark out orders, and eventually run things-little birds fixing their nests. A hard and rocky road it would be for any man not to learn this early. Some men learned through trial and error during the first few years of marriage, others might hold out a bit longer, but like a tired Mustang heaving and snorting inside a fenced corral, eventually allowed the fighting sweat to cool, resigning themselves to the rope handler with the pretty little boots.

Often, it was a sweet resignation, though, and with it came the man's realization that it was in his best interests, because a woman more often than not, seemed to be right about most things. He'd learn this in small passing, consistent examples, which if he didn't get the first time around, would surely get and understand after repeated universal laws to which only woman were privy; "Don't eat that second portion, honey, you don't want to upset your stomach." But sure enough, the man wanting to retain a small token of his independence, even if it does merely involve his intake of food, indulges in that scrumptious second helping and like gravity, discovers within minutes the dire digestive consequences for engaging in such an act. Other sayings, which involve those same principled laws, might also include, "Shouldn't a plumber being doing that?", "Do you want me to call to see what time they open?", "Should we stop for directions?"

So, here in the bowling alley, Neil observed the two men who sat smiling, laughing and happily took their turns bowling free from the burdens of responsibilities long ago abdicated by a wife who would remind them when it was time to leave, what errands needed to be run, what bills needed paying, and the scheduling of important events of next week, next month, next year. He didn't feel sorry for them though, because he knew these men hadn't given themselves, completely. They still secretly harbored independent boyhood dreams of yesteryear - a trip to the Outback, or the Yukon Territory, sport fishing off the Caymans, live aboard a sailboat, or horse ranch somewhere in Wyoming. And in appeasement of such fantasies, the wife sensing all, wisely loosened the reins and doled out Cliffnote, abbreviated, piecemeal versions, of independence, allowing the husband to play poker once a week, go to a baseball or basketball game with fellow male companions. And, yet so masterful were the horse handler's skills, that upon the man's return from such events, and with plans for still greater things to expand his independence for which he might express such adventurous desires, would only be met by a loving wife who, never argued against said proclamations, but instead calmed the playful horse with soothing words like, "That's good, honey." Knowing all the while how such plans would never materialize

Somehow it worked. These older couples had stayed married through thick and thin and now lived under the terms of a mutual contract developed over time based on a deep concern, and love for one another. The proof of that was down every lane Neil looked. Marriage. My God, he wondered - what did it take to keep such a thing together? It wasn't a perfect thing, he knew that. He supposed that it depended on recognizing the strengths, and weaknesses not just in oneself, but one's partner as well. It was in this recognition that allowed for the shifting weight, like the balancing of a seesaw. The weights would be in constant flux, needing constant, daily attention and adjustment. It would be this daily exercise in attention, or lack of, that would keep the marriage sails trimmed and full, or slack and in irons.

"They're out there now." Neil heard one woman say to the other.

"Now, doing what, for the love of God?" the other asked as she waited for her ball to return from a spare.

"Roping off the entire sign," the first one responded.

"Won't be long now," one husband said then folded his arms and pinched his nose.

The first woman continued, "I saw 'em on the way back from the ladies room just now, out there getting started. They got yellow tape around it, a couple of workers buzzing like bees."

"Can't say they didn't warn us," the second husband threw in.

"Still."

"It's just the beginning, by next month they say this'll all be gone."

"Just a month?"

"Harriet says her daughter, Joan has already filled out an application for one of the mall's stores."

"Hump."

"Don't understand it though, say what you will, it's not for lack of business here-just look around."

"It's the money, of course, always the money."

"Out with the old, my dear, in with the new."

"Took thirty years here to get my score where it is now," one of the men lamented.

"Still another thirty to match mine, though," the other quipped.

They all laughed, but it dwindled abruptly, like an awkward beat in a well-measured song. And, since they had already finished the last frame, they silently tallied their scores, sipped their cold, stale coffee, and unlaced their shoes.

Neil finished writing out his postcards, collected his helmet and jacket, and walked out into the parking lot. He looked skyward, up at the large bowling sign that had first drawn him here. Although it was night the sign's bulbs were dark. A crane lift was parked below the sign and had hoisted two men in its bucket. The men now stood unscrewing the large bulbs from their sockets and were dropping them into an unseen, but audible metal container. A gentle gust of night air blew, and for a moment, just a moment, Neil, with his head tilted back towards distant Orion, caught a fifty year old smell of chili fries and chocolate malts.

It was a slow, soft subdued ride back to the park. Nothing stirred, the only tent in the desolate darkness belonged to the rider of an old motorcycle.

6

A sound, satisfying sleep had found Neil during the night and he awoke with a renewed sense of purpose and a better sense of self. He would move onward today, east towards the promise of fulfilling the pact between himself and a dead man. He lay awake in his warm goose down sleeping bag that had formed a caressing mold around his body and looked up through the dew misted translucent fabric of his tent and giggled inside from an unrestrained feeling of freedom; it was jumping off a high rocky cliff and knowing he could fly. Soon, he would get up and start his day, but not before allowing himself a small grace period to bathe in this delightful feeling. With his hands clasped under his head, he lay on his back and relished the thought of stolen time, and appreciated the fact he was not harnessed to any work schedule. No one knew his whereabouts, he was floating free from the entanglements of everyday life; there were no pestering phone calls, traffic reports, or hurried morning preparations. With no petty accountability, and not a single person to whom he had to answer, meant he could do anything, anything he wanted, which also meant he could do nothing at all. The tent's nylon fabric diffused the sun's rays, creating a soft blue glow. He floated in it and within a mindful presence. His body tingled as he imagined warm pockets of healing plasma, moving, like globs in lava lamp, from one area to another inside his body. This was where he belonged. Minutes passed and his thoughts undulated........what symphonies in silence. The deepest and most awesome thoughts and moods rush in. Like music. Rushing

melodies and movements. Le grand solitude. C'est "La Mer"-
C'est le bon Dieu. C'est vrai - SHwwwwwixxxzzzzzzzz

The monstrous sound of a motorized nylon cord ripping
through grass and weeds tore through the air. It ripped through
his tent into his ears and shredded his thoughts. The sound
threw Neil into the present and, with it, the desire to get his day
moving and underway. A park, like many other things, required
regular maintenance and the gerbils had risen and were keeping
on schedule. With bent back, Neil squeezed through the tent
door. There, about a hundred yards away, was a man wearing a
hardhat, safety goggles, and a set of orange earmuffs, resembling
headphones from the nineteen seventies. He was trimming,
slicing and manicuring the grounds with a loud weed whacker
that threw out, not only a caustic sound, but also a noxious
exhaust similar to the leaf blowers Neil had seen used by
Mexican gardeners in Long Beach.

"Christ Almighty," he hissed, "bad enough to hear them back
home, but here too!"

He hated the machines, especially early in the morning, and
worst still on weekends. And the men starting them up – what
the hell were they thinking? Conscious of the early morning
hour, they could only perpetrate such an act as part of a passive
aggressive response directed at the slumbering lazy gringo, who
had too much time and money to appreciate the working poor,
manual labor or reparation. The effect on the dozing inhabitants
was one, which could turn any sane, NAFTA loving supporter,
into a raving maniac, inciting an absolute compulsion to tear a
shotgun off the wall and charge out the door screaming,
"Remember the Alamo!!!!"

He stretched, gathered his belongings, disassembled the tent
and packed everything onto the motorcycle. He didn't care if the
groundskeeper saw him. "Screw it," he said. The sun shone
through clear blue sky, promising a perfect day for motorcycle
riding and he'd be damned if he'd allow anyone to ruin it.

Neil left the park and headed east down route 82. The harsh,
dirty wind that had plagued him yesterday was gone. Brilliant
sunshine shot through crystal clear air. Wanderlust was in his

heart, calling and fusing with heat vapors wavering above the
black pavement like an oasis or mirage. And in it was everything
and anything that meant life; an ever need of blood pumping,
moving, sweating, expecting, and thrilling, ejaculating and
conceiving, giving birth to new ideas and outer limits to things
new and wonderful with a never ending connection to all things,
living, dead into the universe to connect it all and then releasing,
expanding and contracting like a heart and all the while knowing
there was something out there better and meaningful fulfilling a
needed destiny or purpose fertilized in the womb and manifested
in the road. And because of all this and more, he leaned into the
handlebars with an enthusiasm usually reserved for the start of a
trip where unexpected things wait to be discovered. Hours
hummed by and he cut through the air and all was good. He
stopped only for a quick lunch then continued on. Everything
came easy; today was his day and his mind rested, Zen like, in a
well-worn catcher's mitt of right thought, right action, right
speech. The sparse brown, dry landscape that had dominated
much of his trip faded behind his rear wheel. Greens popped up -
richer and more abundant - as he made his way to the eastern
edge of Texas, and closer to the Arkansas border. Neil knew
nothing about Arkansas other than it had been the birthplace of a
president who did not know the meaning of the word, "is" and
had asked a grand jury, "What is, is?" Neil cared little for politics,
but certain political moments were inescapable. So disinterested
in politics was Neil, that he rarely voted. He saw the choice
between the two major parties as ineffectual; was there any real
difference between them? Money and lobbyists seemed to win
out no matter who sat in office. The American people were
secondary, an after thought, used or amused in order to keep the
cash cow called America oiled and giving. All that mattered were
corporate interests protected by The Pentagon, The State
Department and Federal Reserve.

By mid-afternoon, the weariness of the road began catching
up with Neil. His body had tired, and he was stiff between his
shoulder blades with a sharp biting pain up around his neck. His
fingers had tightened and become slightly numb and his reaction

time had slowed. It was always best to stop when one felt this way, not to stop when signs of fatigue began to set in, was an invitation for serious trouble and he wasn't about to push his luck. The closest town now was El Dorado. He made his way from austere lane changes into the town, passing fast food restaurants, car dealerships, an electrical supply store and city parks and signs. He passed a large Confederate statue, an ode to some past and forgotten southern gallantry. But, from what Neil could make of it - The Civil War hadn't completely been dispelled here. Whatever flavor remained had been sprinkled and fused with some Wild West outpost to create a very distinctive pedigree.

He found it odd that for such a small town there was an awful lot of traffic. He didn't make sense of it until he saw in the distance the top portion of a Ferris wheel. As he came into the center of town, and pitter putted along side the parking meter lined sidewalks of main street, he witnessed clusters of people - families, friends, teenagers, and small children yanking on the arms of mothers - all heading in the Ferris wheel's direction. Neil quickly came upon the spider web like center of interest. It was a festival with white tents, booths, rides, and games. He took a quick moment and considered where he was in terms of mileage and overall progress and decided that these factors, combined with his fatigue, along with the addition of this local festival, made El Dorado an ideal place to stop for today.

What he needed first, and foremost, was a place to camp for the night. He knew it wouldn't be in the center of town, so he turned back around until he found a large gas station farther out along the outskirts of El Dorado. Killing two birds with one stone, he filled his tank and got directions to a local campsite from a mechanic whose belt line lay hidden beneath a teardrop belly, and, who Neil was certain, owned a dog named Duke. The mechanic spoke with a twang saying "Got alittle ways to go there, imagine not many people out there this timea year." He had a greasemonkey friend and two teenage girls beside him who just stared at Neil. Neil knew better than to stare back or even give them a second glance.

Neil got on his motorcycle and rode out to where the man had directed him. He planned on setting up camp and then return to town and check out the festival. The ride to the campground was longer than he anticipated. But it was an easy, flat two lane highway and he gunned it.

'Leaving a man to die in a ditch and now we're going to the circus, isn't life grand,' The Instructor said.

Neil knew better than to respond, but couldn't resist, 'I'm making this trip because of him, you know that, so shut the hell up.'

'Could have spared his life.'

'Please, the man is dead- no way I could have done anything differently. I have no regrets.'

'But, to leave him in a ditch!' The Instructor drummed.

'A shallow grave, it's not what I wanted, look, I had no choice.'

"Choices?, I can tell you about choi-'

Neil was weary and had neither the time nor the energy for any kind of argument. His concentration was to be spent on other things, such as the sign he was approaching, posted by the side of the road having something to do with a campground. He came upon it quickly and took in the words; *Entering Felsenthal National Wildlife Refuge*. Soon after came another sign with several stick figures, and symbols indicating which facilities the campground had to offer, including an upside down letter, "V" to represent tent camping. He knew he was heading in the right direction. And a minute later was still, yet, another sign that read something about a visitors center, then one more sign and then Neil noticed the beginnings of the wildlife refuge; there were low hanging trees, and thick dense vegetation. He pushed farther inside until, after a few miles, he reached the campground. Although he was a good twenty miles or more from town, it hadn't taken long to get here and he figured for the peace of mind a campsite provided, it had been worth the effort. He pulled his bike slowly on to a hard dirt road and looked around and wondered where, exactly, he should go; there was no gate, no ranger booth or any formal entrance what so ever. He knew it to be the campsite, but only because of the sign he had passed. Now the road forked and, looking down the one that veered to his right, he could make out off in the distance what appeared to be a single tent and two R.V.'s. The other road, the one to his left, was empty. Shrugging it off, Neil gunned his engine and headed deeper down the dirt road that led toward the two R.V.'s and tent until he found a remote spot set way back, close to a small lake with lily pads and cracked and broken trees and naked stumps sticking out of the water like Halloween caricatures. A small sign close to the waters edge warned of alligators. Minnows flashed silver in the shallows of the water, darting close to the muddy bank. For a millisecond they are like diamonds, ripples on the surface, sparkling underwater sequins, which disappear in the shadows. With his engine off, there was an almost eerie silence that surrounded him. A mosquito buzzed and insects hummed. A few birds somewhere in the trees let out intermittent cries. There was something prehistoric about it, lending itself to an expectation that at any moment a monstrous raptor would come screeching down from the sky. But more earthbound concerns Neil needed tending. He pitched his tent far back on slightly higher ground, and then, armed with a bar of soap and a small bottle of shampoo, he walked in his flip-flops to an outdoor shower, which consisted of nothing more than a concrete slab, a water pipe and a showerhead that was connected to a frayed rope. He bit the bullet, pulled the rope, and jumped under the cold water - a tight shock at first, but so refreshing that he stayed long enough to wash his entire body, shampoo his hair and rinse off.

After he had dressed, Neil took whatever food he had, placed it in a bag and strung it high between two trees. What he wanted more than anything was to find somewhere to sit down and enjoy a hot meal. He got on his bike and headed out of the refuge and back towards the Ferris wheel. Although he had stocked up on a variety of camping food before leaving Long Beach, and as much as he would have liked to think himself a camping purist and self sufficient, when it came right down to it, the idea of munching on packaged, dehydrated and canned food for days on end, wasn't something that appealed to him. He didn't care much for a

Bunsen burner meal unless it was an absolute necessity. Tonight was no different.

Out of the refuge, and on a stretch of road close to town, he came up behind a pickup truck and through the back window of its cab could see three men in tee shirts with sunburned dirty arms, their faces shining red in the late afternoon sun. Around the next bend the road widened and an immense baseball field with a gravel parking lot appeared on his right. The truck ahead, slowed, almost coming to a complete stop, then turned into it. Parked in the lot were a couple of cars and several pickup trucks. On the field itself, men had gathered after work to play on uniformed teams. Two men wearing cleats sat on the tailgate of one of the pickup trucks, dangling their legs off the back probably talking strategy or reliving parts of a game. Behind the men, inside the bed of the truck, were baseball bats, gloves, an empty plastic milk crate and a large, blue ice chest with its white top opened. A handful of other men stood around the truck drinking beer, laughing and talking with one another. One man opened a tin of tobacco, withdrew a pinch and then placed it between his lip and lower gum. He spat and took a quick swig of beer. This same scene repeated itself in one form or another throughout the parking lot; men standing around the bed of pickups shooting the bull and enjoying themselves.

To see these men was like a fractured bone, a painful reminder that he didn't belong, not here, not back home, not anywhere. He felt ostracized, especially now, but didn't argue with the feeling, since he thought it justified, a price paid for the sin he'd committed out in the desert. If only he, too, could be in the company of slap happy friends, to forget about life's worries and troubles. How nice it would be to be drinking beer and laughing with these men after a hard day of work. He remembered now that it was Friday, and the weekend had arrived.

He opened the throttle, picked up speed and headed into town. The knowledge of the weekend's arrival put him in better spirits, and seemed to match the hour of the day, when things begin to slow and the anticipation of night draws out the plausibility of dreams.

He passed beneath a water tower that marked the edge of town, crossed a set of railroad tracks, and came to a street that bustled with cars and people and searched for a place to park his bike. All the parking spots were taken. He could park on the sidewalk, but didn't want to risk a ticket or impoundment. Instead, he continued to search. Having lived in Long Beach, he was well acquainted with the juggling and jostling that often comes in finding a metered parking spot in a city and knew the value of both luck and patience. He circled a second time and caught sight of backup lights from a stationary car. He flicked on his blinker, the car left, and he slid into the spot. A silly sense of joy and relief tickled him. It was a ridiculous, childish reaction, for such a small accomplishment, but it was honest. He took his helmet off and stowed it away inside one of his saddlebags and dragged his fingers through his damp hair.

The sidewalks were filled with people and the young night had a wildness about it. He could see the lights and hear the distant sounds of the festival. He stood at the curb near his motorcycle, allowing pedestrians to move past, and looked first to his left in the direction of the festival and then to his right down a long row of lit storefronts. He walked in the direction most were moving - towards the festival. Three small children brushed past his knee, chasing one another with an abandon, reckless pace. Just in front of him, a group of high school boys rustled along- one punched another in the arm and, then laughing, ducked ahead and disappeared inside the thick crowd. Cigar smoke fell behind the bald head of a heavy set man. The whole mass moved with the energy of salmon swimming upstream to spawn after having traveled hundreds of miles and, here, only a few steps away, was their final destination and nothing would stop them. The atmosphere was loud, mindless, buzzing with frenetic, unfocused energy. The sidewalk ended and the crowd spilled out on to a street that still held traffic; the cars inched along and seemed almost swallowed amidst the swarms of people- where were John, Paul, Ringo and George? Up ahead, under the red and blue flashing lights of a patrol car, police officers had blocked the street and were rerouting traffic. Wearing reflective vests, each stood facing the on coming traffic, and swung an orange cone flashlight with one hand while directing the traffic to a side street with the other.

On the right side of the street was the festival itself, occupying a field so large that the end disappeared, couldn't be seen, and seemed to drop like a cliff - leaving nothing but black sky. Entering the park was like coming into a wide gauntlet; rows of white booths formed walls on both sides, forcing its patrons to funnel between them. The booths hawked food, games and, cheap, useless, plastic, dust collecting trinkets whose only rightful place was exclusively here. Long strings of naked lights hung above the booths. Bells rang, balloons popped, and excited voices bounced in the air. Cotton candy, fried dough, grilled sausages - all drawn into Neil's nostrils as he walked along.

A brightly lit booth was selling Italian sausages. He ordered one with onions and peppers and ate while he stood and watched heavyset couples, and single big-bellied men place their orders. There were a bevy of overweight people in this crowd, but if there had been any thought of dieting it would have to wait until tomorrow.

Neil finished the sausage, wiped his mouth and greasy fingers with a handful of paper napkins, and looked to quench his thirst. He was feeling the mood of the place. A small pack of gussied up, lipstick teenage girls passed him by and giggled. He ordered a large draft beer served icy cold in an oversized waxed paper cup. A meniscus hung above the rim. It was challenge not to spill any of its contents. He tilted the cup just enough to shift the white foam away from the edge and brought it to his mouth. The foam bristled on his upper lip as he drew in the crisp, light golden liquid.

'Life's small pleasures,' he said to himself and wiped his upper lip with the back of his wrist. A simple happiness filled him.

Across the way was a row of bent backs of squinting and squirming game players who squeezed the triggers of water filled pistols aimed at the mouths of balloon capped cartoon figures. There was a pop, a bell rang and an immediate chorus of laughter, praise and disgust swam around the one who had taken the prize.

Off in the distance Neil could see where the booths ended, and a wide space opened up that held rides like the *spider* and *wildcat,* all emitting the ebbing and flowing waves of their screaming occupants.

Neil took it all in; standing here, on this early October night, in the middle of Arkansas sipping a cold beer, watching the carnival scene unfold before him - the simplicity of the moment, the sense of comfort, beauty and awe was complete - anything he needed or would ever need was here now and had been forever. He drew in the night, released his worries, felt his shoulders drop and allowed a slight smile to cross his lips.

He thought of a story he had heard sometime back about two bulls, one young and one old who are looking down from a hill on a group of lovely female cows grazing below. The young bull is intent on charging down the hill and get with the beauties, but the old bull simply chews cud, knowing, that given time, the cows will come to them. Odd Neil should think of that now, but maybe not- he was feeling the need for more moments like this, enjoy what's around, not having to go out and search for something that is right before us; to trust in having been given what he needed, all will be provided.

He walked in the direction of the rides, holding the night like a warm sphere in his hand. The lights of the *Round Up* twirled and swirled, mixing terror, laughter and unkempt hair. He passed a ring toss, a baseball throw, small rubber ducks floating on water. Ping-Pong balls clinked against rims of goldfish bowls. He was coming to the end of the row of booths and closer to the open area with more rides. A bell rang. Someone had won at the strongman. It was a rickety, wooden contraption shaped as a totem pole with an impassive Indian head at its top in full war bonnet holding a never changing, mountain like expression hewn from the center of the earth. Every bit of it: bell, pole and Indian head - looked old enough to have been around since the days of Wild Bill Hickok. People danced and laughed below the Indian.

Money exchanged hands and someone else stepped up to try their luck and test their strength.

Neil kept walking. The crowd thinned a little bit. He was close to the very last booth when something caught his eye. Off to the side was a small folding card table. Covering the table, and hanging over its edges, was an exotic looking purple colored silk cloth. From the center of the table glowed a large round candle. In addition to the candle, a few other items littered the table: stones, crystals, small carved figures and some burning incense. An older woman with deep set eyes, pale skin, and peroxide blonde hair, flickered above the candle – she wore a white tank top and was gypsy to the core, not Hollywood, but real - European, Romanian refugee. A small sign rested on the table's front edge with the words, "Fortunes read $5". There was a plain, empty folding wooden chair to the woman's left. She flipped through a stack of large cards with colorful images painted on them. Neil could see the large silver rings the woman wore and heard the rattle from her metal bracelets.

As he approached closer to the woman, an uncomfortable feeling overtook him. His instinct, something - told him he should turn around, but it was too late. She had sensed his presence and he, hers. It wouldn't be a problem, he told himself; he would ignore this. He would pass unnoticed and invisible. He directed his walk with false purpose, as if to avoid a panhandler's eyes on an empty street. But, just as he was passing right in front of the table, his resolution slipped - a moment, only for a moment, and his eyes yielded to the table - the deep set eyes, once dark, now caught the candle's flame, and the fingerling potato fingers froze, stopped with a single painted card flipped on the deck's top. The card held a shrouded figure. Neil, like a puppeteer pulling strings, jerked his eyes back, but he hadn't been quick enough, "Young man you sit. Sit. Fortune read. Love, money, all in cards." Neil would have nothing to do with her. She stopped and seemed finished. And then it hit. The carnival stopped. He could hear nothing; the bracelets were still, the laughter was gone, the music had faded. He felt vulnerable, stripped naked. All that connected him now to his life was the soft, numb ground below his feet. Then he felt the moist words kiss his ears, "Dead men see, Dead men know."

Neil stared straight ahead, trying his best, pretending not to have heard the words, and was almost out of her grasp, but the gypsy wasn't through with him yet: she spoke again and this time louder still,

"The dead man knows, the dead man sees!"

Tears filled his eyes. He bent forward and staggered through a wall of people who'd just been dispensed from one of the carnival rides, and then continued on until he was out, away and completely free from the gypsy's reach.

"Bitch, how dare she-," he said aloud. There was a sharp laugh, and looking up with a scowl, expecting to confront those who had heard his remark, Neil was met only by a drunk couple smashing cotton candy into one another's mouth.

'Don't let people notice, you freak-move farther away towards the rides,' The Instructor directed his wounded patient with a detectable hint of enjoyment.

Neil moved closer to the rides and began a measured intake of air. He took a breath, then another until he began to regain his body. He righted himself as best he could and felt a cold sensation in his right hand, he had forgotten about the beer. He took a large gulp and looked up into the dark twinkling horizon. Held atop the highest outstretched arm of the Ferris wheel, a father and son gently rocked in the night sky.

A sense of calm grew, and with his body held in check, Neil began to access what had happened.

'Wow, where did all that emotion come from?' he thought. 'One minute I'm having a great time and the next minute some old bag enrages me.'

More than anything else, he was surprised at his involuntary reaction to the woman and her words; how they had violated something deep within him. He needed time to reflect and understand it all.

'Maybe these were words, just words, words she threw out at everyone who passed by....it seemed so specific, though.'

Neil watched the Ferris wheel start again; it begin to slowly turn, stop, then turn again, releasing riders from each of its buckets as they paused at the bottom. The father and son were next in line.

'There's no way she could know what happened in Arizona.' But her words had cut his bones and slashed his brain, 'There's nothing to fear or be ashamed of, I'm heading East with the note and money and not hiding from that fact, but embracing it.'

Suddenly, it occurred to him that, rather than accusatory, maybe her words were in praise of his act. 'Maybe the dead man sees, the dead man knows and the dead man is happy,' he thought, shining new light on these dark words.

'Maybe the dead man wants you to hurry up and get to New York already,' The Instructor said.

'Maybe you should shut the hell up,' Neil lashed back.

'Maybe that's not the smartest of responses.'

'Maybe-' Neil stopped and laughed. Here he was arguing with 'The Instructor' half way across the country and in the middle of a festival. It was laughable, alright, but it wasn't funny and his laugh was only the manifestation of a temporary lie.

Before disappearing, The Instructor put on sunglasses and a movie role saying, 'I'll be back.'

'Like a bad case of herpes.'

Now, finally alone, Neil felt safe again and much better, except for the small pinprick of an idea that maybe The Instructor was right, certainly not with all he had said, but with one small part - maybe the dead man did want Neil to hasten his journey, maybe.

But, this night had become filled with just too many maybes. His mind had become cluttered with so many doubts, and questions concerning the stability of his thinking, his sanity, his self - too much to figure out tonight.

He needed to let it go. He took a breath, complete and full, and felt his feet connected to the ground. He took another breath and then continued walking. There was a sense of relief and he felt light as though he had just finished an argument and all had been settled, like the kind he had with Sarah, which always seemed to conclude with resolution, sex and a sprinkling of kind and tender understanding. He wished she could be with him tonight.

He walked, slowly, sipping his beer, taking in the joys of the festival that surrounded him. He thought of joy, the very nature of it, how temporary a thing it was - like the carnival itself, never permanently planting itself anywhere, but moving impetuously from one place to another leaving nothing behind but an empty space and butterfly memories susceptible to winter winds.

Neil crossed to the other side of the park, opposite the rows of booths. Here a crowd had gathered in front of a darkened platform, part of a large flatbed truck with wheels. It was a makeshift stage with colored overhead spotlights that had just turned on. There were several men and a redheaded woman tinkering around on stage. Each worked at separate tasks of plugging in amps, adjusting cords, or tuning instruments. Above the stage hung a large, white banner with blue letters that read, *BLUEGRASS MUSIC FESTIVAL.*

A man in a yellow polo shirt and pressed khakis walked up on stage and conversed with one of the men who held a fiddle. The man in the khakis and polo shirt then went to one of the three microphones and spoke into it. There was no sound. His mouth moved, but no words could be heard, instead, only an electrical hum of feedback filled the stage and the area around it. Realizing the situation, the man turned back over his left shoulder and pointed at something, then turning back, tapped the microphone. There were several crackles, the humming stopped, and the man's voice broke through with a friendly, "Good evening." The audience applauded, not for the man or his message, but for the fact that a remedy for the feedback had been found; they were glad, happy to have the show underway.

"Thank you, thank you very much," he went on, "welcome all to the 23rd annual bluegrass music fest. I'd like to start by first introducing the band that'll kick it all off for us this year, won't you please give a warm welcome to John King and the Tennessee Morning Glories!" - and with this - the man stepped away from the microphone, swung his right arm back to introduce the band then scooted offstage. More applause from the audience sounded.

Five members of the band came forward: three older men, a middle aged man with a bald head and a handlebar mustache and, finally, the woman with the red hair. The bald man held a guitar, another a mandolin, another a banjo, and the last man an upright bass. The woman had no traditional instrument to speak of, but instead held a washboard. The oldest of the men, with bowed legs and pants worn high, approached the microphone. He held a fiddle in one hand and a bow, hanging, in the other.

Looking closer, Neil noticed the man had somewhat of a puckered mouth, which he imagined held very few teeth and supposed, too, that this was probably John King.

The man spoke softly and unhurried as though he had just sat down in his living room and was now discussing Sunday morning yard work that needed tending. "Thanks, folks. We always enjoy playing here and I know this time's no different. I've always said bluegrass music is America- it's where we come from, who we are and what we share....,anywho, don't wanna take too much time gumflapp'in and all."

A few feet from Neil stood a young kid wearing an oversized basketball jersey, a gold chain necklace, and a baseball cap cocked sideways. "Look at this old geezer, fucker scratch some hip hop," the kid snickered to his empty stonewashed girlfriend, who was bent at the waist, pulling at a strand of chewing gum from between her giggling teeth.

Mr. King turned back to the band as though making a last minute check, but immediately came back to the microphone. Years of travel and woeful things were in his voice. "As some of you already know, this past year my wife of forty plus years passed on. Thank you all for all your prayers and kind thoughts. I'd like to play for her tonight. Here's a well known song called, 'I'll fly away', goes something like this-"

The band started in and after a few notes, John King began to sing. It was a surprise really, because it wasn't a soft or worn voice, which he'd used when talking, but instead the voice he sang with was loud, strained, and painfully earnest. It was like being introduced to someone that had no time or care for small talk, manners or contrived politeness, but instead hit you smack dab blunt in your gut with truth and directness - the kind that would catch you off guard, make you stumble for a second or two. It wasn't polished in any conventional way, but, instead, held such a kind of serious consequence, and contriteness in its search for truth that it made Neil feel both embarrassed and connected at the same time. The beauty was in the fact that his voice opened up private thoughts, feelings, which you alone thought had been exclusively yours, and that this man had somehow stolen and now shared with the crowd. The redheaded woman sang too, layering the song with such a sweet melodic ring that it was if she were tenderly rocking a cradle; her voice floated on the thin air then fell softly where it was supposed to fall, and rose where it was supposed to rise, like a humming bird collecting nectar. Neil couldn't help but fall in love with her and in a short time imagined her wrapped in his arms out in the dark field beyond the rides. The music filled the park and plucked at Neil's musical sensibilities. He could feel himself in the music and moved with its rhythm. Looking around, he could see the effect was the same for most everyone. This had been an event for which many around him had prepared; scattered across the grounds in the dark were pockets of lawn chairs and ice chests. Most who'd come were older folks, some middle-aged and others even younger, who held babies. The majority of the people in the park were engaged in other activities, but Neil and the people around him felt they were privy to something scarce, sacred.

John King, this old thin man on stage, stretched his neck so far and taut, that it appeared as if, at any moment, his head might pop off: an old turkey clucking out his last swan song. His clothes hung from his bony scarecrow body like donations from an Oklahoma Goodwill store. Dark purple veins ran over his hands and down to his long, lean fingers pumping a tempo of blood. It was all energy. Some people close to the stage clapped their hands. A woman stood bobbing a wrapped infant up and down in her arms, moving with the music. The young couple who had earlier made the "old geezer" comment now stood silently transfixed as though their deceased grandparents were calling them home for dinner. It all went on like this until finally the music came to an end. There was hardly enough time to clap before the band jumped into another tune. It was a lively number and, this time, in addition to all the toe-tapping and foot stomping, a few couples up front, linked arms and actually began swinging one another round n' round. The spirit of the music throbbed, banged, plucked and spoke in an effortless, completely unconscious way.

Neil took a beat, and, looking around, saw the tenderness of the night - people, families coming together and for a moment, letting go of any earthly concerns; the love between that mother and helpless child seemed infinite, an older couple sat beside one another in lawn chairs and held hands. It was as if the universal bosom of God's eternal bliss had opened up, provided sustenance for all his children. And, now, Neil didn't see gerbils, but, instead, people, human beings trying to survive, striving to do their best, hoping to find a small island of happiness in a torrent of strife and distress, and dreaming in a dream no different than his own. There was no pretension, no judgment, no ego.

'Beautiful, how beautiful it all is..' His eyes burned with a dancing, wet emotional layer.

The music rang through the night air and Neil began to drift. It was as if the music was seeping into his pores and waking ancient cells. The music sank deep within the tissues of his body unlocking old ancestral memories, taking his mind down overgrown rivers in white birch canoes to fire lit, bank side encampments where padded moccasins and the rustle of whippoorwill calls echoed deep inside misty woods.

This music had roots born and spawned in the backcountry of Appalachia. It had thrived for decades. It cried out for President Johnson's war on poverty, an empty promise, which had changed nothing other than providing paved roads for large companies to tear down lumber and extract coal and minerals by means of strip mining-leaving barren ground, black lung, poverty and death. The people who had started this music were mountain people and had survived on only the most basic resources.

Listening to the music here on this night in Arkansas was for Neil, like opening up a forgotten history book. He felt the isolation, could see the dirt roads, worn shacks, shoeless feet and gaunt faces. There was a lack of modern conveniences such as phones, washing machines, and newspapers. The rugged, impenetrable mountain terrain created a culture dependent only upon its own resources and ingenuity for survival. His toes now tapped on dilapidated planks of a rotting porch, his hands felt the hard brittle crumbling lead paint, and his eyes could see the backyard clutter, clothesline, washtub, and vegetable garden. His nose took in the boiling cabbage, tobacco, and corn mash. But, it was the music that told all this and more: the metal lunch pails, the black coal faces, the company store, the union, the strike breakers, the worn creaky springs below a feeble mattress, wrinkled hands peeling potatoes, a tied ribcage dog barking in the dirty yard, a fifteen year old mother, the birth of a sickly baby, the early death of malnourished men and women too young to be so old. The music passed this entire story down from one generation to the next.

The songs went through the musician's hands like a set of old nets cast into the sea, the bounty of which wasn't released until their set had come to an end and other bands began setting up. With the music stopped and the stage dark, Neil looked at his watch and knew it was time for him to start back to camp. He was sorry to go. He bought an iced tea and walked towards the open gates. Many people and families were doing the same, deciding it was time to leave. He walked past the gates and crossed behind the police and onto the sidewalk. A young girl sat on the curb crying, both hands covering her fallen head with her long hair touching her knees. Another girl squatted next to her, resting a hand on the sobbing girl's shaking back in an effort to console her.

"He's not worth it, never liked him to begin with......"

Neil didn't, and wouldn't, catch the rest of what she said; he passed quickly behind them recognizing the universal carnage of teenage heartache. He thought of Sarah and what she might be doing tonight.

Sipping his iced tea, Neil walked on and took in the small shops along the street. Most were dark, with a desk lamp or small Christmas like glow in a display window. He knew it would be lonesome back at camp and wasn't quite ready to head back there. He walked past the storefronts and continued until the sidewalks darkened into a residential area. A lone nightingale sang from somewhere in the distance. He found himself alone. The lights of the Ferris wheel had disappeared and the night took on an isolated quality. Still, he walked. Then, looking through the darkness off to his right and across an immense lawn, he saw a white colonial like structure with two large pillars, which stood square and heavy. A single lantern burned near its entrance. There was something Gothic about the building that betrayed all other facilities in town. The single lantern attached to the building gave an austere, plain, and for no apparent reason, haunting quality. The black street address numbers, 322 were lit by the lantern's light. A quick, cold chill, lasting just a fragment of a second, ran up through Neil's torso and into the top of his shoulders causing a slight shudder. The building held a fearful quality as though eyes belonging to hidden faces were peering from behind its windows and dark interior, studying Neil's every move. Nefarious, evil, uneasy like someone in a parked car beneath an underpass at midnight. He couldn't see it, but could feel it. He wanted to explode, run from where he now stood, but to do so would only give him away, and expose his awareness to those who were watching him. He needed to control his fear and find a way to leave without letting on he knew of the unseen presence that resided within this house. He found an imaginary spot on his left shoe and bent down to dust it off, then came slowly back up, and taking one last quick glance towards the building, saw the stone engraved words, ***Masonic Temple*** above its doorway. He then put his hands in his pockets looked up at the sky, turned on his heels and strode casually back towards town. His eyes held the sidewalk, but his mind turned murky corners and tiny pathways searching to uncover pockets of information.

'Someone's behind you!'

Neil jumped, turned around, but the sidewalk was as empty as The Instructor's false warning. He cursed himself for having listened to this voice in the first place. He unclenched his fists and resumed his walk. Street lights from above illuminated his steps, casting shadows against the sidewalk.

'Why did I even listen to that voice?' He again reprimanded himself. His ruminations continued, 'Masonic Temple?, Masons, freemasonry big in the 1700's- a secret society of men, an order of men. Going back hundreds of years... they thought themselves descendents from knights of Templars. No one really gets this stuff, understands it, other than its members what exactly the order is about, so strange a bewitching thing, really. These men built thousands of structures all over the world in honor of, and to serve their order.'

Stranger still, was the fact that The United States of America was constructed by members of Freemasonry; Benjamin Franklin, Paul Revere, Alexander Hamilton and even George Washington, Founding Father, were all free masons. This secret society had symbols, signs, ceremonies of initiation, and death to any member who betrayed its secret oath. This group of men felt they were superior to all others and were determined, destined to control all societies in which they lived and, therefore, traded favors amongst themselves in government buildings, courthouses and banking institutions.

The principles that guided these men remain a mystery, but what is known, are the Gospel of Saint John, light and geometry all played a major part. Neil remembered the first time he really examined a dollar bill and wondered at the figure of a pyramid with an illuminated eye at its peak. It was a symbol used by the Freemasons.

One tradition of the Freemasons was to wear an apron once a year, representing the fig leaf originally worn by Adam and Eve after the fall from the Garden of Eden. On the front of the apron was a figure of skull and bones. 'Skull and Bones', an offshoot of the Freemasons, became the name of one very well known secret order. William H. Russell founded skull and Bones in the 1830's at Yale University. Since it's conception, it has fostered over 200

112

members who seek to ingratiate themselves, like the Freemasons, in the power controlling elements of free society. Among the fifteen Junior classman chosen each year at Yale have been prominent men such as George Bush senior, George Bush junior, Senator John Kerry, and men who ran the country, usurped its power and fed the gerbils. These men and others with names like Soros, Koch acted as single wires spun into a thick cable that held society, the world in check.

As he came back into town, the fading light and life of El Dorado's night had dwindled down to a close and drew up around Neil. He got to his motorcycle, fired it up and rode in solitary blackness back to his campsite. The refuge was still, removed and alone; a type of reclusive outpost composed of blackness and devoid of sound, deathly quiet. The trees rustled for a moment in the wind, but then fell silent. Slipping into his sleeping bag, and with only himself, his thoughts, he fell asleep thinking of the woman, the gypsy who had called out those words earlier in the evening about the dead man. He questioned his actions out in the desert. He could see now how it had only brought him angst and confusion. He told himself that he should have gone to the police in the first place, but he hadn't and now he was on the run, and knew somehow this whole mess would catch up with him. It made his stomach turn to think of what he had done to that man out in the desert. And then, of course, there was The Instructor's voice, which he had heard again inside his head tonight. He knew he was coming unraveled and it frightened him, how else could he explain such a thing, this voice? Was he really going insane, crazy or...? He knew it was wishful thinking, but maybe this was some sort of phase he was going through, he laughed at that idea, but then immediately questioned his laugh - was it the laugh of a sane person or someone who was falling apart, fingers slipping from a ledge, plunging into the abyss? He could feel something that needed to come out of him, fighting against him, vying for a voice - needing his attention, which Neil had somehow neglected. He considered heading back to Long Beach, but the reality of it seemed ridiculous, downright futile. And he knew that. He was too deeply entrenched, had made it too far, and ... somehow or another he knew that by getting to New York the gypsy's words and the men deep inside television sets would have a home. He was making that first drop into deep deep sleep when something momentarily broke the surface of the water near his tent; there was a silvery reptilian splash and then nothing, only ripples.

7

Neil woke early and began to pack his things with a newly acquired ritualistic familiarity. He then rode to town and ate breakfast in a sunny little restaurant with plastic plants and nautical themed trinkets decorating the walls.

His plan for the day was simple: to cut through Mississippi and into Alabama. He was hoping to make Birmingham by nightfall, six maybe seven hours of moderate riding in order to reach that destination. Heading east on route 82, he was thankful for yet, another beautiful day of fine weather and clear skies. The sun simmered low in the morning sky and Neil was determined to ride with it as long as possible. Many parts of the country were already beginning to feel the pinch of the approaching Winter. He dreaded the idea of riding anywhere near chilly winds or biting snow dust.

At 8:30 in the morning, Neil crossed into Mississippi and entered Greenville. Here he stopped, stretched, sipped bland, unremarkable coffee and not wanting to waste any time, quickly got back on his way. He moved with purpose, collecting miles. A fast and steady continuous stream of pavement flowed beneath his motorcycle. Signs for route 55 appeared, which if taken, would bring him into Memphis. A large, white truck thundered past him, the words, *Memphis Gallery* marked its side.

'I'm really in the south,' Neil thought, transfixed at the whole idea. Never before had he been this far South, and to be here for the first time gave him an odd and lonesome feeling. He was a long way from home - a stranger in a strange land. There was uneasiness in him from words, things and characters associated with The South. Granted, the world had changed a great deal, but having lived up North most of his life, the 'South' had connotations that just wouldn't die. There were rednecks, the Union Jack, old slave plantations, spiteful words over the rim of a Mint Julep, backwoods ways, and mean spirited acts. It was the kind of place where three college students, belonging to the Student Nonviolent Coordination Committee from up North, could disappear during a 1960's Civil Rights movement, and later be found dead - shot point blank by a bunch of local boys and a sheriff named Cecil Price who had little tolerance for nigger lovers. Just to think of it scared the hell out of Neil and maybe it was intended to do just that, but he didn't like it, not here, not now. He thought it best to keep his gas tank full and stick only to the main roads or he'd end up like Peter Fonda in *Easy Rider*.

But, what was he thinking? 'C'mon, man,' he told himself. 'Stop being paranoid.' 'After all,' he reasoned, 'these are modern times, not some hillbilly, moonshine, banjo play'in notion of yesteryear.'

Yet, what he could neither prevent, nor control were the scattered bits of history scratching the underside of his skull; small droplets of information planted inside his brain that had been dormant, now stirred, congealed and fed his fear. He remembered pieces from that brief paragraph in American history when a young black boy from Chicago named Emmett Till had traveled South in the summer of 1955 to visit his aunt in Mississippi. The boy had whistled at a white woman as she walked out of a general store. That whistle proved fatal. His body was found floating in a stream - so brutally beaten, disfigured - that his own mother could only identify the corpse by means of a ring the boy had worn.

Neil gripped tight the rubber throttle to his motorcycle and glanced at the eighty-five mile an hour speedometer and held it there. A minute later he backed off the throttle as an ugly scenario popped up in his mind of some tobacco chewing, potbellied, good ole boy, sheriff pulling over a two wheeled California Yankee transplant for violating the sanctity of the legal posted speed limit that reflected the respected laws by which all good citizens of the South abide. He could hear the conversation now,

'What's wrooong with youu boi, got no laws out there in California? Pam Anderson keep'in you busy?... or you jest some cleva Yankee type think he's smarter than our judicial system? - us poor ole dumb Southerners.'

His imagination ran and Neil tried his best to bring it under control. But, before he could fortify his mind, another voice slipped under the wire,

'These boys have fun with you.' Eyes of The Instructor gleamed brightly, 'Shouldn't come down here if you don't agree with their policies.'

It was a long ride to Birmingham.

'What policies?' Neil asked.

'What policies? The Instructor asked in disbelief, 'policies that govern any group or body of people.'

'Meaning what?'

'Meaning what works for them may not work for you.'

'I'm not just talking about speed limits,' Neil protested.

'Neither am I,' The Instructor smugly responded.

'You know about Emmitt Till, the injustices-'

'Yap yap yap, that was fifty years ago, Chief. Besides, that boy had no right whistling at a white lady like that.'

'You've got to be kidding me, the boy was tortured, murdered.'

'Should've known better.'

'You can't be serious.'

'Before you get all politically correct, high and mighty - why don't you just ask yourself if you've ever called someone a nigger or a tight wad Jew, a spic, a wetback, a Guinea.'

'Well, there's -'

'And I don't mean to their face, but even under your breath, in your mind, behind the wheel of a car after somebody's cut you off.'

'I'm no saint.'

'There's your answer.' The Instructor pointed out

'I may have faltered with those words, things I said, but it's not truly how I feel, or who I am- you know that.' Immediately

Neil sensed the futility and knew his protest was more to himself now than to anyone else, especially The Instructor.

The Instructor chuckled. 'Whatever you say,' he said now sipping bourbon, leaning back in a swivel chair, smoking a cigar and cleaning a disassembled rifle. '-want to believe is rigghhhht, make ya feelllll gooooodd.'

Neil needed this conversation to end.

'I'm not- this isn't about what's right, absolutely right based on human decency, not even human, but God's decency of given rights...not even 'right' or 'wrong', but just what IS.'

'That makes a hellava lot of sense,' The Instructor said.

'Besides, it's a long leap from a simple racial slur to murder!' Neil exclaimed.

'Is it really now, Neil?'

'Shut up, you fool!'

Neil continued on, slightly troubled, but - at the same time - feeling better about having engaged The Instructor. The road opened up and became wide with slow rolling hills surrounded by thick woods on both sides; Black Forest fairy tales with hidden evils dwelling just beyond those trees. Neil felt safe on this highway and dared not stray from its path. He pushed on.

The *Memphis Gallery* truck was up ahead and exiting onto route 55, probably on its way North to its Memphis home. A black and white frozen image of men leaning over a motel railing and pointing in the direction of shots fired had been a snapshot seared into Neil's mind. He couldn't even remember where and when he had first seen this iconic image. It was as if he had been born with it, part of his genetic makeup. Shots had been fired, a leader had died, and a nation reflected. Dr. Martin Luther King Jr. was a brave man, a man of principle, and a man who saw the power of faith not exclusively reserved for those whose knees knelt inside a church, but as an embodiment for change - a promised land he knew lived in each of us.

Neil thought too, of John Fitzgerald Kennedy and his brother, Bobby. He had always linked these three men together. Maybe it was because of the time in which they had lived, or maybe it was the way in which they all had died. But, for whatever reason, he saw a common denominator in these men whose sense of faith and truth had come at a cost - a cost, not only to a nation, but a cost to self and to the faceless name of righteousness.

What made their deaths so heartfelt and, especially tragic, was, that as leaders, these heroic figures were human, tender, kind, tough, calculating, and fallible, most importantly, fallible. Outwardly, they spoke of principles, overcoming obstacles, but at the same time, all three of these men were filled with self-doubt, personal weakness, and contradiction. And, wasn't this every man, every human being that ever lived? So, who better to lead than men, whose knowledge of personal struggle and personal pitfalls combined with a hungering sense for redemption, and strength would cast them on the shoulders of a God fearing nation?

These three leaders became so connected to the very soul of the nation, to one's self, because one saw in them what one saw in the better part of one's self: the part, which included a willingness, a struggle, to do what was right to overcome weakness. A nation was found inside these men. And inside these men a nation found itself.

'Justice', 'truth', and 'freedom' – words that had become overworked tools, beyond repair, so abused, recycled in the public domain that their meaning had lost much, if not all, relevance. Neil felt no connection to these words when he heard them spoken from the mouths of politicians or used in sound bites dictated for a press release. It was rare, so very rare, then, for any politician to care enough to possess the dire need and humble willingness to serve. Instead, public office had become a game of self-satisfying hubris, power and petty postures. Had it always been this way? He wondered. After all, politicians had been ever present, it seemed, not only in the infantile history of America, but throughout ancient times too. With so much of a past, why would things be any different now?

When he first heard the "I have a dream" and "Ask not what your country can do for you.." speeches, he dared to imagine maybe things could have been different. He knew these words could only have originated from men who played by a different

119

set of rules, dictated not by political motives alone, but, derived and spoken by men who longed for guidance from a higher providence. The statements were wishful aspirations, of course, and seemed to reflect not exactly what we were, but what we wanted to become - things maybe only foreseen in the kingdom of God; to lift the world of men up to the ideals of the divine. In the fallible, tragic and heroic hearts and souls of these three men were found the wishes and desires of a better nation. Their words and fates seemed to be scripted for the time in which they lived, and, for which, they profoundly died. They recognized that it is not in apathy that the will or character of a man or a nation is found, but rather, in the active struggle to obtain the highest principles to which it subscribes.

Neil's thoughts turned to Abraham Lincoln. For, here too, fate and time lent itself to the sweat on bent backs picking cotton and the pain of blood spilled from the fallen Civil war brethren in the locust-laden fields that currently passed him by. The sad, proud history of the South was all around him now, and able bodied or not, still seemed ready to stand defiant of what was expected from it by outsiders. It would be as it had always been, come hell or high water. Neil was a visitor riding through this land on a hundred and forty year old guest pass. He felt the presence of its Civil war ghosts, the credence placed on family names, flat-bottomed skiffs, Faulkner. It was a foreign land and the fragile favor given Neil was palpable.

"Well, I hope Neil Young will remember..." lyrics to a Lynard Skynard song played inside his head, "that a Southern man don't need him around anyhow.."

Just before noon, he entered the town of Starkville and knew the Alabama border was close. He pressed forward, passing just outside of Starkville and it was then, when he stopped for lunch, that he noticed the leak. He had pulled the bike onto its center stand in the blacktop parking lot of the restaurant, taken off his helmet, and was getting ready to unzip his motorcycle jacket when the shiny telltale sign of oil caught his eye. Looking down at his feet, he saw oil covered much of the toe of his left boot. He bent close to his motorcycle to find where the leak had started.

The shifting gear, which was held in place by an Allen head bolt, had come loose. The gear housing was dripping oil. Neil pulled the tool set from beneath his motorcycle seat and tightened the loose bolt with an Allen wrench. The flow of oil stopped. Neil replaced the tool bag, wiped his hands, and walked into the restaurant.

After riding nonstop for hours, it felt great to finally sit, relax and eat. When riding his motorcycle long distances, Neil tried to follow a policy of stopping every two to three hours, to stretch and rest. This policy worked in preventing the weariness of the road from affecting his awareness, helping to maintain a certain level of safety.

Sitting inside the air-conditioned restaurant, he pulled at the front of his shirt to cool himself and looked the menu over. Although a chain restaurant, it still offered homestyle cooking, including fried chicken and barbequed ribs. He went with the fried chicken, biscuit and gravy.

The mid-day hour had brought the business gerbils into feed. There were a few patrons who appeared to be no different than himself, road weary travelers, looking for a decent meal. But, the majority were small office workers and salesman who wore polyester shirts and wrinkle resistant chino pants with cell phones hanging from belts like old fashioned six shooters. He shivered at the idea of working a nine to five job in any office, small or large.

'That's because you don't have resposibilities, a family.'

'Thank God for that,' Neil thought.

'But, you're incomplete - missing something they have and you don't.'

'Headaches?'

'Something deeper, something a boy, man child wouldn't understand. Sixty years old and no family, child, lineage.'

'I'm not sixty!'

'Not yet.'

When he crossed into Alabama, he noted the land hadn't changed much.

'But why should it?' he thought, 'man's artificial borders don't control the contours or nature of the land.'

As he rode along route 82, he passed smaller arteries of roads that ran deeper into the belly of the land and to unseen destinations.

Somewhere close to Birmingham he shifted gears and heard the dry meshing sound of metal against metal. Looking down to his left side, he noticed the same heavy sheen of oil had reappeared, covering the same spot on his left boot as in the parking lot, but only this time, in a much greater amount. He needed to stop. He slowed his bike, pulling off the main road and on to a wooded secondary road. His bike, like a wounded animal, staggered forward. Gingerly working the shifter, he tried putting the bike into a lower gear, but the shifter fought him - pushing back with an ugly sound of grinding metal and a vibrating resistance that shot through his boot. He tried shifting again, but his bike wouldn't have it, yet again, he tried, then again, until finally after several frustrating attempts he was able to get the bike into first gear. He had slowed, crawling at a little over ten miles per hour. He looked behind him and again, in front of him. There was nothing, no vehicles in either direction. The slow road was empty and silent. He moved tentatively, crossing an iron railroad trestle and over wooden planks so broken up and in need of repair that, more than once, they threatened to throw him from his bike. Up ahead, on the side of the road, was a small, crescent shaped patch of dirt. He pulled the clutch in and coasted to it. He turned the engine off, dismounted the bike and examined the shifter. The gear oil had emptied out onto the shifter and frame. He looked past his front tire and ahead to the winding, sleepy road, that disappeared around a leafy green bend. He pondered the prospect of a repair shop being anywhere along it's route. He knew the possibility was slim, but the road had to lead somewhere and staying here certainly wouldn't solve the problem. He'd passed a small white sign just after the railroad trestle that he thought might hold some information. He ran back and turned to view the sign, but it offered nothing more than the amount fined for illegally dumping trash by the side of the road.

Not wanting to risk further damage to the motorcycle, and hoping the town had a suitable place for repair, Neil clicked the bike into neutral, and began pushing the motorcycle by the front handle bars, slowly walking beside it towards the direction of the town. The road was flat and at certain points even dipped, allowing Neil to intermittently jump on the coasting bike and let gravity do the work. The foliage that surrounded him glowed in the sun and it was easy to imagine barefooted school children carrying sticks and book satchels walking this same road. It reminded him of the walks he had taken as a child to the bus stop early in the morning on crisp Autumn days, kicking colored leaves and hoping the bully from atop the hill wouldn't be there and the pretty girl with the two older sisters would sit next to him. This road time took on a different beat, there was no need for frenzied or hurried cellular, digital concerns. Things were simple here - pristine clothes drying on a line and fresh baked pies cooling on a window's ledge kind of simple.

After a mile the road opened up to a large expansive, imperfect circle, causing the road to pause before moving ahead. A weathered mailbox at the foot of a dirt driveway belonging to a small, green single story house stood to his right. To his left, and across the street - only a stone's throw away, was a red and brown dilapidated filling station with a white triangular overhang that jutted out over the pumps. The station had seen better days and by its elegant lines must have been cutting edge for its time, offering something new and exciting out here in a rural area with few amenities. On one side of the station was a pile of old tires which had served their purpose long ago and been discarded. Next to the tires was an olive colored fuel truck that looked sad and worn with a shattered front window and weed covered rims that sank heavy in the earth. Rusted patches like hair torn from a dog marked its body.

Neil crossed the street and cautiously escorted his motorcycle into the station and parked on the hard dirt. A smell of thick grease and oil saturated the air. He could now see the fuel pumps were lifeless, relics of a bygone era, empty tin in need of a heart. The dialed numbers were frozen still, the metal was pockmarked, pitted with age and a cobweb had formed between one of the pump handles and the housing. Neil hung his helmet on his handle bar and walked into the shade beneath the triangular overhang, and closer to the pump island. At the front of the building was a wooden framed screen door, and book marking its sides, were two worn benches that butted up against the building.

Although the structure had some characteristics defining it as a place of business, it still lacked many of the telltale signs and qualities that one usually associates with such a place. Neil approached the door with trepidation. He was deciding if he should knock or go right in and only a few feet from the door when a child's face suddenly appeared from within the dark interior, eyes peering through the mesh screen portion of the door directly up at Neil. The face was that of a pudgy little black girl whose braided hair held brightly colored plastic balls. She immediately turned from the door and disappeared back into the dark where her voice sounded the alarm.

"Daddy, daddy," she cried. "There's a white boy at the door!"

Neil froze. He didn't know what to do. He felt targeted, in some way castigated. The last thing he wanted was for someone to think him a threat, call the police and uncover the crime committed in the desert. He focused his energy on trying to appear docile. He drew his attention to a Maxwell coffee can filled with sand and cigarette butts on the ground next to one of the benches and pushed his hands deep into his back pockets. He felt like a foreigner before a newfound village tribe. He waited to be sniffed out, inspected and, hopefully, approved.

Somewhere from inside the dark interior of the building a figure moved and Neil could hear the sound of hard boots shuffling across wooden floorboards towards the screen door. There wasn't much light and the figure was difficult to make out at first, but as it came into the sunlight, which fell through the screen door, there appeared a man wearing a loose fitting pair of jeans that hung on his waist without a belt. He had on, a once white, now grey t-shirt, and black boots, untied with the tongue flaps hanging loose. He was a black man with salt and pepper hair cut close like sandpaper, thick black-rimmed eyeglasses and preying mantis like fingers, which were presently occupied at the task of rolling a cigarette. Without lifting his eyes from the cigarette and speaking in a flat, indifferent tone, the man addressed Neil.

"Yes, sir?"

Neil, both hands still in his back pockets, twisted his torso to the left and pointed with his head and bent elbow in the direction of his motorcycle that was hidden from view behind the building's left wall.

"Got my motorcycle over here, just looking for a place to get it fixed, broke down on the highway, took this exit."

A small black boy with soft, excited eyes grabbed the leg of the man rolling the cigarette and took turns looking out at Neil and into the man's pant leg.

"From around here?" the man asked, eyes still downcast.

Neil felt a twinge of anxiety and chose carefully his next words,

"No sir, I'm actually from California, just passing through."

Another man's voice suddenly came from somewhere inside,

"California, now Dat's a ways. Nice place too, palm trees, pretty girls and plenty a sunthine."

The man in the door licked the rolling paper, spit a piece of tobacco from his lower lip then gently inspected his finished product.

"Don't specialize in motorcycles," he plainly stated.

"I figured that may be," Neil said. "But I think it's just a gasket."

The man turned his head back towards the interior. A pink scar with the texture of an earthworm ran from his neck to just below his cheek. He pulled up his jeans with a finger though an empty belt loop.

"Cecil, old McGregor's place up on 15, Yamaha, right?"

"Oh, I fink dey thpec- in in Honda or thome Jap brand or da like," came the response from the unseen man named Cecil.

125

"How far's this McGregor's place, can I walk it?" Neil asked.

"Ten, twelve miles up here."

Neil looked down and shook his head.

"Can't make it that far, besides it's not Japanese."

"Normally we service lawnmowers, chainsaws, dresser draws, radios-things of that nature," the man responded.

Neil took a split second to try and link those items together but instantly gave up.

"Oh, I see...." It was a hell of an awkward thing to do but Neil had no choice, "Is there a phone I can use?"

"A payphone, you mean a payphone?"

"Yeah, sure a payphone or..any phone."

"No payphone here."

"No payphone, well....."

The man, for the first time since being at the door, looked up at Neil, but only for a split second. He averted his eyes, yanked up his jeans and said,

"Phone inside here you can use." And with that, he begrudgingly pushed the screen door open a few inches with his right shoulder and turned back inside. Neil barely caught the door with his fingertips just as it was about to slam shut and pulled it open, wide. The little boy darted from the man and past Neil, out into the open, outdoor space. "Phone's on the counter. Jessie, don't go mess'in with that motorcycle, ya hear!"

Neil must have misjudged the last step because the tip of his right boot caught on something causing him to trip as he came inside. He stumbled, but didn't fall. He let go of the screen door and it slapped shut behind him. The man stopped for a moment, but didn't turn around to see what had happened and instead moved farther to the back of the room.

Neil stopped too, allowing his eyes to adjust to the dark surroundings. He felt the cooler temperature condense and chill the sweat he hadn't noticed until now on his upper back. There was a smell of damp wood and fresh tobacco. The floor, made of thin, dark wooden planks, gave ever so slightly, spongy like beneath his feet. The walls and ceiling were a pale blue, almost green color with patches of white shaped icebergs where paint was either missing or peeling. He noticed a ceiling fan, which was motionless - having sat long enough for barnacles of dust to grow on its blades. An amber colored fly strip, like withered beef jerky, hung in a corner peppered with black-speckled, fossilized remains.

The entire place had a haphazard look; there were stacks of boxes, loose wires, metal piping, and other odd items, all of which, formed a wall off to the right. To the left of Neil, and running half way across the room, was a vintage candy case with a wood frame and a display counter with a thick, glass top. On the glass top were scattered papers, receipts, an old piston, and a grease stained phone book. At the edge of the counter was an older style rotary phone with an extra long cord that had twisted around itself like two snakes fighting each other. Straight, at the end of the room, and up against the wall, was a matching set of sturdy chairs, which Neil guessed had come from a barbershop. They had large heavy metal railings, a grated footrest and thick red vinyl upholstery infused with tiny bits of glitter that sparkled. An older black man sat in the chair farthest left and next to a doorway that led to a back room.

Without turning around the man, who yanked at his jeans said,

"Phone's there." He barely moved his head towards the counter. He then walked and disappeared through the back doorway. The little girl, who had been first to spot Neil, stood behind the counter, her head barely extending over its top, allowing just her hair, forehead and eyes to be visible. She raised her arms straight up and then reached her hands, palms down on the glass top. The girl seemed to be reading Neil's mind,

"Who you calling?"

Neil fumbled at the point blank question,

"I'm, ah, I'm really not sure, need to find a BMW dealer or garage"

"BM who?" she asked.

"BMW," Neil repeated. "It's the make of my motorcycle."

"My name's Shawna, that's with an S. What's yours?" the little girl asked.

127

"Ne-"

"Shawna, leave that man be and go find your brother!" the man said as he returned through the doorway.

Her arms retreated like lazy snakes off the glass top,

"Probably not even here, went to the house," she protested. Then in an act only a child could reason, she bent her head and upper body, dropped both arms lifelessly inches from the floor and, lending a wide swagger to her steps, let out an elephant roar before hitting the screen door and popping outside.

Neil smiled after her, but returned straight faced to the phonebook, which he began to thumb through. He flipped through the B's, but there was nothing. He decided to try 800 information. There was a North American BMW information center that directed his call to a small shop in Birmingham. Once connected to the shop, he explained the situation and was told that the rubber gasket could be replaced for a small fee, but with no way of getting the motorcycle to Birmingham, the end result was to have Fed-ex deliver the part to his current location- it also meant Neil would have to wait a day.

"Man says he can Fedex the part here, is that okay with you?" Neil asked the apparent owner while cupping the phone's receiver.

"Suppose," the man answered from one of the chairs where he sat head down pressing a thumb into his other hand's upturned palm.

"Oh, Fedex, dey thip worldwide now, uh-huh, worldwide," came the comment from the man named Cecil who had lowered his newspaper and spoke with a lisp, "thip worldwide everyday."

Neil returned to the phone, made the necessary arrangements then hung up.

"Thanks for the use of your phone."

"Um," the owner barely got out.

Neil stood there a few moments. Nothing was said.

Cecil again lowered the newspaper, this time as if to observe a ping-pong match that had stopped, stalled or maybe delayed.

The owner sat silent.

Neil looked to the door and then back at the owner.

'Guy's a real son of a bitch,' The Instructor said, 'tell him to go to hell.'

The silence was building. Neil finally broke it,

"Well, I'll check on my bike and make the necessary arrang-"

The screen door suddenly popped open, and a man dressed in a suit of fine tailored clothes and donning a white fedora rustled in,

"Wettier than a whore on a Saturday night soon 'nough," he loudly proclaimed. He took a quick look at Neil and, in a courtly gesture, pinched the brim of his hat while giving his head a slight nod.

"Eh," he said.

Impulsively, Neil nodded back, "Hey."

The man moved on as though he'd just paid a small toll and was now free to continue uninterrupted with his journey. Although he looked to be seventy years old, his eyes had a much younger, playful quality that sparkled, lit up and tickled the room. In addition to his hat, he wore an impeccable brown suit, a perfectly thin tie, patent leather shoes, and carried a wooden cane that thumped on the floorboards with an irregular beat from its rubber tip as he walked, stopped, pivoted, took a step, moved again, and beebopped along. His energy was high and bright. And left in its wake was a feeling of both excitement and inadequacy.

"Yes indeedy, be raining fore' the days out." He thumped towards the two chairs.

"Confirmed here in the weather thection," Cecil said from behind the newspaper.

"Oh, is that what it says?" the suited man slyly asked, then with an enormous grin, winked at the owner, and added, "What else that paper say today?"

"A Liddle of dis a Liddle of dat." Having lowered the paper, it was plain to see the gap from Cecil's missing front teeth.

The man in the suit, standing just a few feet from Cecil, lifted his cane high and struck it on the floor and the balls of his cheeks glowed as the room rippled with his laughter,

"If I had a nickel everytime you said that, I'd be swimming in pootang and drinking gin out a cat's ass -Cecil, you know's yous can't read, boy, why you even bother with that paper!"

"Fings to look at," Cecil meekly pointed out

"How you go on." Then turning his attention to the owner, "Say, Willie what was the name of that sweet little thing down there at Minnies, one behind the counter?"

The owner rose from his seat and pointing to his left cheek said, "You mean the one with the small mark here?"

"That's the one."

"Name's Angie, best I remember."

"That sweet little thing, saw her this morning, in there for coffee. yes, sir pudd'in pie, pudd'in pie- like to get me some of that pudd'in pie."

The owner, Willie, sauntered towards the front door and the sharp dresser followed.

"Don't know if ya heard," the sharp dresser said. "But they say Lester's getting worse-probably gone by next month,'cord'in to the the doctors."

Willie opened the door and both men disappeared to take a seat on one of the outside benches.

"Damn shame." Came Willie's response through the screen door.

Cecil sat still as a log behind the paper.

Neil was left alone, awkwardly forgotten, but at the same time freed from any social pretense. He decided to walk outside to his motorcycle. White smoke rose from a freshly lit cigarette and ran across the outside of the screen door. Neil walked towards the door and placed his hand on its frame to push it open, but stopped. Across the street in the front yard of the green house was a heavyset woman thundering in Neil's direction. She wore a floral house dress and plastic flip flops that snapped sharp and quick. She had flabby arms that could threaten to knock down a freight train. Neil heard the voice of the sharp dresser,

"Uh, Willie, here she come."

"Don't you worry 'bout noth'in, Dexter," Willie said and whistled in a strange half song, half bird like call, which triggered a frantic rustling of newspaper and commotion from behind Neil. Cecil had jumped up and was hurriedly putting away the paper and, like a cornered mouse in a state of panic, began searching the room. Quicker than Neil thought this old timer could move, Cecil had found a broom and began sweeping the floor.

Turning back towards the door, Neil could see the woman was already half way across the road, heading right in his direction.

Neil heard the sharp dresser, Dexter, say in a real low voice, "You do noth'in this morn'in to upset her?"

"Shit, all's I got to do is breathe-you just simmer down, Dexter, I got it now," Willie answered.

The woman had crossed onto the repair shop's property and small puffs of dust could be seen from the backs of her flip-flops with each step she took. She was a rhino on the charge. Neil felt his neck tighten, his heart raced, and his knees wanted to move.

"Good morn'in, buttercup," Willie shot his first salvo.

There was no response.

"Beautiful morning, Mattie!" Neil heard Dexter shout out to the approaching woman.

Still there was no response, but she must have heard them because as she came within a few feet to where the men (who were now standing) she let go her first words,

"Morning me noth'in-near afternoon yet! Idle hands mak'in work for the devil. Miss Wilson call'in me up, ask'in for that mower a hers, I know you but out here smok'in, celebrat'in gett'in that job done."

"Now look here, Mattie, I'm the man of this household-"

"Don't tell me man, man huh!" she said sternly, "a man provides for his family, doesn't sit around daydreaming for a bag money fall from the sky, a man works."

Dexter had somehow mysteriously moved from the bench, and, seeming half the size from when he had first arrived, said, "Well, I best be getting along." He pinched the brim of his hat and slightly bowed, "Willie, Mattie."

"Best *BE* getting along," Mattie threw after him while still holding her gaze on Willie who had begun to put out his half smoked cigarette against the inside wall of the coffee can. Mattie

131

wasn't through with him yet, "That mower done or not?" she demanded.

"Sure it's done, just finishing it up out back," Willie said while adjusting his jeans.

Neil could see little Shawna skipping across the road coming towards her parents who had both turned to watch her. Mattie turned back to Willie,

"Shawna tells me a white boy done broke his motorscooter here."

"That's right," Willie confirmed, "inside now."

Neil moved silently back from the screen door, then loudly shuffled his feet, walked forward and pushed the screen door opened and paused in the doorway just above the outside steps.

Mattie was first to speak, looking up at Neil and with the voice of a fragile debutant, she said, "Willie, why don't you make the introductions."

It was plain to see Willie wanted nothing more than to avoid more trouble, but was at a loss for words. He tried awfully hard to squeeze something out,

"Ahh this, here is the man who broke down and Mattie, my wife."

Mattie's face flickered hard for a moment then burned with an angelic shine. A dry white residue of baking soda or talcum powder could be seen in the pit of her arm as she extended her hand up to Neil. Her words took on a honey coated tone, "A pleasure, what's your name chil?"

Neil gently shook the solid hand offered, "Neil, Neil Adams."

"Such a strong name - Neil. It's a real pleasure, Neil."

"Pleasure's all mine, Mattie."

"Where you from, Neil?"

"California, ma'am."

"Um um um, you come all the way from California on a motorscooter?"

Neil was feeling incredibly formal, "yes ma'am, indeed I did."

"Chil, you done lost your head," she said in a very lighthearted tone. "All the way from California. Then looking over at Willie, she asked, "Willie, You known this, California?"

Willie, who sat fingering his teeth, barely nodded, "Uh-huh."

Mattie hung on Willie a few seconds and then looked back at Neil,

"And now you done broke down here?"

"Just waiting on a part to arrive from Birmingham."

"Lord, oh Lord, *But now in Christ Jesus Ye who sometimes were far off are made nigh by the blood of Christ* when's that part coming in?"

"Tomorrow morning."

"Tomorrow morning?- Willie, you-" she paused then dismissed the reason causing her upset, "no use. All the way from California and here stuck waiting for a part?"

"That's correct, ma'am," Neil confirmed.

"Mighty Christian Willie, you is. Christian as Christian git, ain't you-knowing this boy stuck here and you ain't got the common decency to provide for a stranger in need?" Mattie stood over Willie as though she really expected an answer to her question.

Shawna stood silently behind her mother holding a small, soft, grey guinea pig, which she gently petted and held close to her body. Neil, still at the door's threshold, absently picked at the hard plastic part of his motorcycle's ignition key. As a courtesy to Willie and as dictated by the unwritten brotherhood law never to infringe or witness another man's belittlement by a woman, Neil started through the door and began down the steps.

"Beg your pardon, but if you'll excuse me, Mattie, I'd just like to make a quick check on my motorcycle."

"You go do that, Neil - and bring it here in the shade if you'd like."

Walking backwards in the direction of the building's corner, Neil said, "thanks I may just do that." When he turned the corner, he found his bike where he had left it. A heavy dark circle covered the ground below the shifter. Whatever little oil had remained in the motorcycle's gear box was now completely drained, gone.

"Brrrrrmmmmmmmm.." The little boy with the soft eyes who had earlier clutched his father's leg, now held a stick horizontal

133

between his two outstretched hands and was squatting next to Neil's motorcycle. The boy's imagination had him somewhere in the middle of a fast ride.

"Hi," Neil interrupted.

The little boy turned, stood up and stared at Neil.

"Oh, he don't talk. He's what they call, dumb," Shawna spoke from behind Neil, "he can hear though, not well 'nough, cord'in ta Momma -jest when he wants, ain't that right, Jessie?"

The little boy held his round eyes on Shawna as she spoke. He kept the stick upright in front of himself, slowly tapping it against his forehead.

"Do you like motorcycles?" Neil asked.

The boy continued to bump the stick against his head, but now slowed, and with his mouth slightly opened, shyly swung the stick to his right side with one hand as though it were hinged in the dirt and smiled.

Shawna came closer.

"He ain't never been on no motorcycle fore," she said. "Can Albert sit on it too?" She cupped the grey guinea pig and kissed the top of its head.

"Is that Albert?" Neil asked, looking at the Guinea pig.

"Sure is, and he likes motorcycles too, you wanna pet him? He don't bite."

"I'd love to pet Albert, but let's first see if we can put Jessie up on the seat."

"Kay."

Neil turned and squatted down in front of Jessie who had placed the stick back against his forehead and was looking down at the ground.

"Hey, Jessie, my name's Neil." Neil reached tenderly for Jessie's small right hand. Jessie's arm held no resistance. "Alright, now that we know each other, what do you say, would you like to sit on the motorcycle?"

The boy shook his head, 'yes'.

"I'll have to pick you up, is that okay?" Neil asked.

Again, a 'yes'.

134

"Alright," Neil said. "First, let me tell you the secret motorcycle rule, can you remember it, if I tell it to you?"

Another 'yes' from Jessie who had lifted his eyes.

"The one and only rule is, not to touch the engine or the tail pipes, because they can still be hot, can you remember that?"

This time, there was a serious 'yes' nod.

"Okay, here we go." Neil grabbed hold under Jessie's armpits. He could feel the small boy's arms tremble as he lifted him onto the seat.

Jessie's expression was one of uncontrolled excitement mixed with bewilderment. Neil explained the various controls and parts of the motorcycle and their function as Jessie stretched his torso over the fuel tank in order to grab hold of the handlebar. Shawna placed Albert on the back of the seat. They played like this for several minutes, until, Neil, feeling it was safe, let the children continue on their own and began to take a closer look at the problem that had caused him to stop here in the first place. He got his tools out and pulled off the shifter and pried out the torn rubber gasket. He rolled the remains of the rubber gasket (like half-mastecated grits) between his fingers. There was nothing he could do until the part arrived. The children, with the excitement from a newly found friend and experience, began heading back inside the building. Left alone, Neil began to organize his things and make preparations for the night ahead. He needed to find a campground, or at the very least, a place to set up his tent. Maybe he'd hike to a nearby field or- he didn't expect to find a cab around here, but there might be a car service to take him somewhere he could spend the night. He'd need to go back inside and look for information within the yellow pages. He walked around the building, towards the screen door and heard Mattie's voice come from inside,

"Jest telling you that's all, ain't no way, need to check yerself with the good graces of the Lord."

Neil knocked on the door.

Mattie opened it all smiles, "You c'mon in, Neil. How's that motorscooter a yours?"

"Not much to do except wait for that part. I'd like to use your phone if I might, see if there's a campground nearby." Neil stepped inside.

Cecil swept at a clean floor and the children fiddle faddeled around.

"Campground?" Mattie's face hardened.

Neil clarified his statement," See if there's one nearby, a place to spend the night - till morning when the part arrives."

"See you got this boy think'in?" She had turned to Willie who was rummaging through some old boxes, "Assume spend the night with serpents and vermin than goodhearted folk." She turned back to Neil and asked in a voice containing both disbelief and dismay, "Campground?"

Neil checked himself, then began again,

Yes, ma'am, a campground, a campsite," His statement was somehow turning into a question, but he couldn't control it, "set up a tent and sleep the night?"

"Now, Neil you know we can't allow such a thing."

"Ma'am?"

"Ain't that right, Willie?"

Willie held two metal parts, absorbed with putting them together,

"Uh-huh."

"Ain't much room in the house with children, their grandma as such, best you stay here, plenty a room. Cot's in the back there." She motioned towards the back door.

"That's very kind, something to think about," Neil said.

"Think nothing, I'll be bring'in down som clean sheets fo ya. Dinner'll be up at the house come five o'clock."

"Thank you, Mattie."

"I'll be back with those sheets soon 'nough now." She took a beat, then looked at Cecil, "You sand'in or sweep'in that floor?"

"Okay not thure," he said, head staying bent on the busy broom.

"Uhummmm," Mattie turned back to Neil, "Make yourself at home here, town's two mile's in, lemonade, sandwiches up at the house."

136

Her work done, and satisfied, she now made to leave, " Jessie, Shawna, come on y'all." with that, she stepped outside, the children filed behind, and walked happily back towards the house.

Cecil placed the broom against the wall, pulled the newspaper from his back pocket, and sat back down in one of the red chairs. Willie continued with the metal parts. Neither men spoke or paid attention to anything other than what interested themselves.

Neil cleared his throat, "Well, I think I'm going to take a walk into town, poke around a bit - need anything while I'm there?" this was directed in a general way to both men.

"I'm all set, Neil, fanks jes da thame." Cecil had pulled aside the paper and was grinning like a clam.

Willie just shook his head.

"Okay, then, enjoy the afternoon," Neil said and pushed opened the door.

"Will do," Cecil shot back.

Neil first went to his bike and changed into a tee shirt and long sleeve thermal, and stowed his leather jacket and helmet into a saddlebag. He then began his walk towards town on the small blacktop road that had retained much of the heat from the day. To his left, across the road, behind Willie's shop, and running a good distance parallel to the road, was an overgrown field. A gusty wind blew warm and moist across his face. The air had mass and it pushed and stirred the leaves of the hickory and oak trees that flanked the road. The leaves rustled and a brook running along the right side of the road gurgled. Despite the wind, the air still hadn't cooled much. Not a single car passed and the solitude lured him into a sense of freedom and relaxation. A rabbit jumped into the roadside thicket and disappeared. Dragonflies zipped by like tiny Spitfires off to enemy territory. It was a majestic day with an expansive sky, free running fields, rusted barbed wire fences, bouncing butterflies, and an abundance of moving air. It took him back when he was a child; roaming through woods with classmates after school in dark autumn hours before suppertime when the days were short and regimented. And again, through the twilight Summer months when the days stretched forever and time was endless. He was younger then and closer to immortality, to his beginning; every boy's beginning, with a strong connection to the earth, the woods and a pull towards the womb.

He was older now, which meant he no longer did many of the things he used to do as a child and to actually 'take a walk' felt odd. He couldn't remember any time recent when his sole purpose was to, 'take a walk'. A walk was always a necessary byproduct of somewhere he had to get. 'To take a walk' was reserved for English lords or some French countess. But, here he was, 'taking a walk' and it felt wonderful. It forced him to slow down and take in what was around him, giving him time to reflect and enjoy one of the simple pleasures which life had to offer.

He'd never have taken this walk had it not been for the simple fact that his motorcycle had broken down here and the choice he had made to stop at Willie's place. It was a series of events and choices that needed to have happened at an exact time, sequence, moment and place for him to be here, right now on this road with a cloud moving, bird flying and rabbit hopping; it was the same for the birth of a child, which is dependant on two people meeting, copulating at an exact moment - not just any moment because any other moment, even a fraction or two later or prior, and the child who'd be born would be one completely different- a different child unlike any other.

As he neared town, he passed a large weathered barn that leaned to one side. The doors were opened and he could see bales of hay stored inside. Behind a long wire fence that ran along the side of the road were a handful of chestnut colored horses. The sun glimmered, creating sheen on their necks and backs. One horse trotted beside the fence close to Neil then stopped and stuck it's soft black nose over the top. Its large nostrils like whiskered stove pipes, exhaled hot air. Neil stopped too and scratched the nose of the animal and, looking past the enormous lashes into the large eyes, thought of the connection between all living things. He thought of the owner, who then maybe had a daughter; a beautiful country girl whose firm milky breasts and

138

sex starved voluptuous body longed for contact. He imagined afternoon lovemaking on a plush blanket of hay and her tantalizing giggles as she pulled at a piece of straw between her wanting lips and drew her body up to his. The fantasy wouldn't last-

'Probably back there stripping your motorcycle,' The Instructor's voice clawed through Neil's consciousness, 'Sell off the parts. That Willie's a real sumbitch and all that woman's Christian gobbly gook.'

'Kind people,' Neil countered.

'Creepy make believe stuff. Enough to make your skin crawl.'

'Think what you want, I just want to enjoy the rest of this walk.'

The Instructor took on a British accent,

'Ohhhhhhh, enjoy the rest of this walk. Is that right?'

'Yeah that's right-'

'You sound like a faggot, all this touchy feely crap.'

Neil's tolerance for The Instructor's opinions was dying fast. He closed his eyes and drew in a deep calm breath and held it for a few seconds. He then expelled The Instructor from his nostrils, body and mind. He knew it was only a temporary measure, but it would suffice for now.

The town wasn't much; there was an insurance office, a car wash, and auto supply store and a small sandwich shop that served subs and offered a hot Chinese buffet. Along the main street, a few American flags hung from poles anchored to the pillars of small shops. At a hardware store Neil bought flowers for Mattie, a can of tobacco for Willie, and a few boxes of 'Good n' Plenty' candy for the children. He relished the idea of walking into a town and running errands; it seemed everyone he knew (including himself) drove everywhere to do whatever needed to get done - whether it was work, groceries, or picking up stamps at the post office. He bought a copy of the local newspaper and sat down on a curb outside an Aluminum shed storage company and scanned the articles. The few cars that passed slowed just enough to remind him that he was in a small town.

139

Neil started back along the road to the shop. He was glad for the walk and glad, too, he had brought his thermal top; the temperature had dropped. The wind had picked up, and massive billows of formidable thunderhead clouds lay low in the sky. Everything had changed since first he left the shop and this walk back was like a different trip all together from the one he had taken to get here. Although it was the same road, it didn't look it. There was a whole new feel and tone due to the change in the weather and light. It was amazing really, and Neil knew there had to be a lesson in that somewhere.

Upon returning to the shop, he found Cecil putting on a jacket and getting ready to leave.

"How's dat trip ta town, Neil?"

"Oh fine, Cecil - beautiful walk actually."

"Tends ta be dat way round here."

"Say, Willie around?"

"He's out back, through da door dere, jes finish'in up. I'm on my way out- maybe I thee you morrow."

"Okay, Cecil."

Cecil left through the front and Neil now stood alone. He pulled the can of tobacco from the brown paper bag and placed it on the glass counter. He was uncertain what to do next. To be alone with Willie wasn't something that thrilled him, but to leave might appear rude if Willie had heard him come in.

'Get out of here before that cold hearted, socially inept ingrate comes back. He's so full of hatred towards you, so obvious. No need to talk to him, and you should let him know how we feel too. Take the tobacco back, he'll think you're weak and just kissing his ass,' The Instructor coaxed.

"Willie?" Neil called out.

The Instructor, in a Sicilian alleyway, flicked his thumb from under his front teeth.

"Willie!" Neil called out again.

Still no answer. Neil poked his head through the back door. There was a small room with a cot, a makeshift coffee table made from two wooden apple crates and a plywood top. There was also a transistor radio, some cardboard boxes and a metal pail

140

beneath a window missing several panes of glass. On the other side of the small room was another opened doorway with wooden steps descending to a large outside work area with a dirt floor and covered by a slanted, green fiberglass roof.

The last thing he wanted was to be perceived as a trespasser, Neil turned back into the main room. He still held the bag containing the flowers and candy. He looked at the bag, then at the light blue can of tobacco on the countertop and suddenly there came the thought,

'I'm not to blame.'

This statement didn't make sense at first, but out of curiosity and in search of meaning, Neil allowed his mind to follow the thought upstream to its source.

'I am who I am, I'm not here to hurt anyone - I have nothing to hide, be ashamed of, or about. I'm not responsible for all things past or present that have hurt people, hurt Willie' - and that was the real point, 'the things that have hurt Willie.' Neil had somehow, unconsciously perhaps, felt responsible for Willie's reactions and attitude, part of the burden carried by another man. Sure, Willie was unreceptive, but now, at this moment, Neil refused to accept responsibility for Willie's behavior or the cause for it.

Willie's dislike for Neil wasn't about Neil; it was about the men who Neil vaguely resembled and the things associated with those men: a slur in the back of the bus, sour eyes at a lunch counter, a university in Birmingham, a slave ship, a plantation in 1840. Neil, of course, was none of those things, but in Willie's mind, and melded into his sinew, was a history of events that neither Willie, nor Neil, could escape.

The problem for Willie was that Neil was an individual free from other men, and, if any judgment were to take place, it would be based on the character of life present - not past. Neil left the tobacco on the counter and walked out of the shop.

The day had turned grey and the air was soft and wet. Clouds had formed a slow moving blanket that pillowed the entire sky. Neil looked across the street and to the simple house on the hill. It was square and plain and its paint a faded green. It looked too

141

small a house for an entire family. Two worn dirt tire tracks running along the right side of the house served as a driveway and ended where a plastic blue tarp covered a someday car. A broken up couch and an old bathroom sink lay a few feet back among a thicket of trees. On the opposite side of the car and attached to the house was a set of cracked concrete steps, which led up to an aluminum door and kitchen entrance. The house looked both vulnerable and isolated against the immense, darkening sky. Neil headed up to the house and spent the rest of the day pushing an old manual, rotary mower that had been left to rust by the side of the house. The grass had grown rich, green and high. He cut, raked and trimmed the yard. The work felt honest, and meaningful in a way he hadn't felt in a long time. It was great to be off his motorcycle and engaged in manual labor, moving, sweating and straining his body in the simple joy of work. The smell of cut grass married with the damp air, awakening him to a myriad of things forgotten. Crickets sang their comforting songs, chirping late summer melodies, reminders of Chinese wisdom and the invitation, the call to contemplation.

At one point the children brought out a pitcher of lemonade with small waxed paper cups, each with a silly riddle printed on the side and supplied with an answer on the bottom. Shawna laughed at Neil's intellectual inadequacies. The children helped out with the yard work for several minutes, but then quickly found interest in the clothes line, a tiny frog, a caterpillar, a bumblebee and an astronaut that had become stranded in a volcano. By five o'clock it had started to grow dark. Mattie called the children in the house to wash up for dinner. Neil spent time finishing up by putting away the mower and permanently attaching the rake head (which continuously wobbled and kept popping off) to the handle by tapping two nails through the head into the handle's base. With everyone up at the house, Neil walked down through the yard, across the street and back to the shop. There, out back in the work area, he showered using a garden hose, changed clothes and walked back up the yard to the house.

Light from the kitchen streamed through a dishrag curtain window. He walked to the side and up the concrete steps and knocked on the aluminum door.

"Neil we was just talking about you," Mattie announced as she opened the door. "Come right in."

"Thank you."

"Been a long time since anyone gave me flowers," then with a quick look over her shoulder, and directed to the room behind her she said it again, but even louder, "Yes sir, a LONG time."

As Neil crossed the entrance and came into the brightly lit kitchen illuminated by a donut shaped florescent light fixture that hung loose from the ceiling, he saw where the last part of her sentence had been aimed; across the kitchen and in the brown shag carpeted living room and slumped in a sagging armchair sat Willie watching television.

The children, having heard the knock at the door came rushing into the kitchen. They were filled with the energy of a holiday.

"Neil here, Neil, Neil, Neil!" Shawna shouted and Jessie mouthed, their little bodies shaking with excitement.

"Hey there, you two," Neil answered the children's calls and then turning back to Mattie, he said, "I'm glad you liked the flowers, Mattie."

"Beautiful they is, I put em' in a vase ova tha." She pointed to the kitchen table, where smack dap in the middle was a glass vase that held the flowers. Oval shaped with a white Formica top and yellow metal legs that had white tipped rubber ends, the table was reminiscent of the one Neil had crawled under as child at his uncle's place in the nineteen sixties. Running across the width, and in the middle of the table, was a crack, allowing the table to be divided in two sections so a third might be added. Although there were five chairs, only two matched. On the table were two liter sized plastic containers of 'Kola' and a pitcher of water and glasses with cartoon figures and fast food characters. There were ceramic bowls of different colors and sizes filled with spinach, grits, mashed potatoes, and peas. All the bowls had large wooden serving spoons or forks.

143

Mattie removed the glass vase with the flowers from the table and carefully placed it on the windowsill above the kitchen sink. Then holding a thick dishtowel and oven mitt, she pulled a tuna casserole from the oven.

"You can sit over tha, Neil," she said, nodding to a chair with its back to the livingroom and where the oval table formed one of its peaks.

"Alright, time for dinner, y'all."

The children came and sat in their chairs and fiddled with their silverware. Shawna swung her legs back and forth under the table. Willie was last to arrive, wearing leather slippers in place of his work boots and pajama bottoms had replaced his loose fitting jeans. He dumped his body down in the chair closest to the kitchen door and opposite Neil. Mattie hovered the casserole above the table then lowered it down in the center. Next, she sat in her chair and folded her hands. Everyone followed and bowed their heads. Mattie spoke,

"Lord, we thank you for all that is before us, provided by your good graces. We pray, in God's name that wherever we be at, our eyes never become blind to your light and kindness. We pray this in Jesus' name. Amen."

Everyone Amen'd, lifted their heads and began passing the food around.

"Now, Neil don't be bashful, eat what you feel," Mattie said as she placed a heap of mashed potatoes on her plate.

Neil was touched, felt honored by the generosity shown here at this simple table; a family with such meager means, yet willing to share all with a stranger. The conversation was polite, general and Neil was on his best behavior. Willie was silent the entire time, except when it came to the passing of the food. Mattie asked Neil if he was married.

"No, not just yet."

"Now, don't be telling me you a'int got nobody special."

"Well, there is a girl-"

"Always is, now what's her name?"

"Name's Sarah."

144

"You, see there, that's what I'm talking about. How long you seeing this girl, Sarah?"

"On and off for the last three years-"

Mattie nearly dropped her fork, "Three years at your *age* an you ain't married that girl? Getting that milk for free, you need to do right, make an honest woman a her. She too good to you Neil, too good, what I understand here. Far me up in anybody's b'sness- never have never will, but my own, love to sit that sweet l'ille girl down, though, tell you that right now, yes sir, give her a talk, get you changed right, um um ummm. She leave you too, find herself another man - you wait too long. Sun don't wait for the rooster to crow."

Neil could feel himself blush with guilt, feeling as though he'd just let slip a vile trait he had been concealing his entire life. It was a governor's pardon when the subject was changed and dinner moved on.

Mattie reminded the children that it wasn't polite to stare, but they couldn't help themselves, and so sneaked as many glances at Neil as they could without being caught. They asked questions too (Jessie using Shawna as a go between), questions that only a child dare ask, seemingly unconnected and illogical, but so innocent and beautiful, and free that it made Neil want to reach across the table and kiss their little cheeks. They asked if palm trees had any fingers, and if the ocean, really was blue, if he'd ever ridden a seahorse.

And so on it went until the meal had ended, and when the mint n' chip ice cream began being doled out with a big metal spoon and the children's sticky fingers, Mattie looked to her side, directly at Neil's forehead and said in a voice that tittered on the verge of shouting,

"Fix you up a plate, Momma?"

This so startled Neil that his mouth opened to scream but before he could formulate a response, there came a low, raspy voice from the living room,

"Umm, Not really interested much."

The voice passed over Neil's head and back to Mattie who responded,

"No need be, I'll bring a small plate in, just a little som'em."

"That'll do," the voice answered.

Neil burned to turn and see who was behind him, but was afraid if he did, it'd come off as rude. He found an excuse to do so a few seconds later when he rose from his chair to help clear the dishes (at which point he was given a hard, and only look all night from Willie). Upon rising, he was able to grab a quick sideways glance inside the dark living room. Seated on the couch was a slightly bent figure - that was it, not enough to make out any more detail.

"There's no need fo you to help with the dishes, why don't you jest sit yerself down now," Mattie said to Neil as she finished placing food on a small plate, nibbled off extra potato salad from her thumb and then carried the plate of food past Neil and into the living room. The children, meanwhile, had stepped outside and sat on the concrete steps eating spoonfuls of ice cream from ceramic cups.

Willie and Neil sat alone in the kitchen. And even with his revelation earlier in the day, the idea of spending any amount of time alone with Willie didn't hold much appeal for Neil -and from Willie's behavior the feeling seemed to be mutual. Both sat in uncomfortable silence.

"Bring that young man in here," the voice inside the livingroom rattled like tire chains up a snowy pass.

"You need to eat first, momma," Mattie responded.

"Set up the tray, I'll be fine -"

The rest of the words spoken were inaudible. Through the screen door and kitchen window came a brilliant flash of light and a tremendous crack. The blue children sitting on the steps reacted first; Shawna screamed, and Jessie jumped. The thunder that followed rumbled high above, shook the ground and commanded all. Focusing his attention through the screen door and to the outside, Neil could see the effect the wind had on a cluster of trees as a second bolt of lightning illuminated high swaying branches, exposing the underside of leaves that moved like frightened schools of fish.

146

The children scurried inside the kitchen just as another loud crack ripped through the air. The house shook and a hard rain began to pour.

Mattie came back into the kitchen with the authority of a ship's captain and said,

"Shawna, go close all the windows. See you do em' tight."

"Momma, I -"

"Go on now, noth'in gonna bite you, do it quick n' come back in here."

Shawna darted off and Jessie climbed into his daddy's lap. Willie spoke soft to the boy and stroked his hair. Mattie continued on as though no storm surrounded them. Lightning flickered on her face,

"Momma talk'in crazy gain tonight, say she been to California-"

CRACK!

"After I tell her that's where Neil's from."

The lights in the house flickered, Willie looked up at the ceiling fixture.

"Best be getting flashlight, candles ready," he said and started up from his chair. Jessie clung close to Willie as he crossed the kitchen and reached up high into one of the cabinets.

Neil put aside his paper napkin.

"Well, I guess I better make my way down to the shop and settle in for the night."

"Nonsense," Mattie answered, "not without a flashlight first, something, at least, to light your way. This here's serious business tonight."

And just like that another lightning bolt flashed and crackled loud.

Shawna came back to the kitchen, out of breath, and declared her battle with the windows had been victorious,

"Windows done, Momma."

"Good job, baby girl, now help your father find some matches."

"What can I do?" Neil asked Mattie.

"Don't be silly, now Neil. A'int noth'in to help with, jest you sit tight, relax, make yourself at home-washroom's through the living room, in the hallway if you need it."

"Thanks, I'll do that."

Neil stepped into the living room just as another flash of lightning filled the house. He took a few steps and the house went black, the lights had gone out. Thunder boomed.

He was half way through the darkened living room and groping for direction when a voice spoke.

"California, nice this time a year."

Neil stood frozen. It was the voice of a grandmother, wise and old, a voice that seemed to shed the night of its secrets for those who had ears to listen.

Neil stood where he was, but didn't yet answer, thinking of Mattie's 'crazy' comment just a few minutes earlier. Not sure if the 'California' statement was directed at him, or just an empty room, Neil again began trying to find his way to the hallway.

"Isn't that where you from, California?"

Neil stopped again and this time looked towards a dark outline seated on the couch and the vague shadow of a dinner tray.

The figure spoke again, "It's storm'in tonight. Come over here and sit with me a short while."

The sound of Willie's voice rose above the sound of crashing pots and pans from the kitchen.

"I know they's in here somewhere."

Neil turned towards the couch.

"Don't hesitate, child."

He was moving closer to the couch when suddenly he felt a delicate, bony leathery skinned, hand slip into his.

"Sit now and hear an old woman."

He did what he was told and sat beside the woman. Her hands sandwiched his left. He felt trapped.

"You're traveling too, aren't you?"

"Yes," Neil answered as if it were a confession.

He could feel a smile in the woman's voice as she spoke,

148

"I've traveled to California, been there- the orange groves, pink sunsets, palm trees and endless coastline."

"It's nice." Neil could see her words.

"Golden really," she said, "been all over this land and other lands too. All over and beyond. Fact is, I've traveled to many, many places and my steps are getting larger. Today, I had a cup of coffee on a mountainside in Brazil-"

Lightning lit the room, allowing Neil a glimpse of the steady white eyes, thinning hair, wrinkled face and all knowing lips of the blind woman who now held his hand. The thunder clapped loud and close.

She giggled like a little girl, "He he, old man's rag'in tonight, angry at someone. Nights like tonight can bring the truth a little closer, rises up who we was, who we are and who we'll become. No difference sometimes. Like no difference tween places I seen as a young girl so long ago or places I see now- all is mind-no difference, no difference t' all. As a traveler you must know that too, so I need not tell you some'em you knows yerself."

Here she let out another little giggle just as a bolt of lightning fired and the sky boomed. She squirmed even closer to Neil and placed one of her wrinkled hands gently on his face.

"Mind is free...travel anywhere, real is made real only in mind...free is free in mind too, slave to no one...only mind-"

Her hand stopped cold.

"Slave...ummm. Someone inside yoou?" she asked. "Looks like you not alone- got yerself a traveling companion. Let yourself be owned by master of your own choosing. Master is as master does, sometimes you ain't knowed the difference. He got you on the run....yes now slave master wich you, boy...run, run, run travel as much, but look behind hound dog of hell always on yer heels. You running from someone?, breath on yer steps...needs to slow, run never more..go up his house, where he live, befriend him, kill him, sacrifice him like a lamb or become him run never more........"

Mattie entered the living room with a lit candle.

"Momma look you doing here, keeping this boy, talk'in crazy I bet. Touched nothing on your plate. Sorry, Neil-"

"That's fine, Mattie."

"Find the bathroom okay?" Mattie asked.

"Not yet," Neil answered. "Through the door, in the hallway?"

"Uh-huh."

Neil rose, shakey kneed from the couch and went into the bathroom. The words of the old woman had flipped him sideways. He emptied his bowels and then took a moment to study his reflection in the mirror above the sink and compose himself. He didn't want to understand it all, not now. But, he knew they, the words the woman had spoken, were like gifts reserved for unwrapping at the appropriate time. Coming back into the kitchen, Neil found Willie had placed a flashlight and a large plastic garbage bag, which he had fashioned with duct tape as a makeshift poncho, on the table for Neil to take back to the shop. Neil thanked everyone and said goodnight.

He stepped out into the black night. The rain was still heavy and the wind was blowing strong. If he wanted to stay dry, he'd have to hurry to the shop. He ran down the hill and made for the shop's overhang, which he knew would protect him from the rain. With each swing of his arms he could feel himself gaining momentum from the downward sloping hill and his ears were penetrated by the sound made from the plastic poncho and pelting rain. He was careful not to slip on the wet grass, which was rain soaked and soggy, and he could feel the tentative nature of the soil beneath him. He came to the bottom of the hill and was just about to cross the road when he saw in front of him a large puddle, its surface quivered like black mercury. It was too late to stop, he pushed hard off his right foot and, in an attempt to jump the puddle, leapt high into the air, extending his left foot slightly out in front of him. He was in mid-air and directly above the pool of water when he heard the sound of laughter coming from the old woman in the dark house behind him and in that same exact moment with his head bent down, was startled to see staring up at him, reflected from the puddle below, the image of someone other than himself. There was no time to digest these things, or if he had really heard and seen them at all. He landed hard on the other side, coming to a halt on solid pavement. The

150

ribbon loosened like those two antique trunks he'd first opened with the Indians inside the attic of his childhood home. It was his mind, it had to be his mind; there was no other explanation for it. He tried pushing it away, off like a skintight wetsuit..... or straightjacket, but it wasn't easy.

Now would be a good time to admit himself into a psychiatric ward, a hospital, a place for the insane. He was losing this battle, didn't have the energy to fight. Before going into the shop, Neil pushed his bike from the pouring rain and parked it beneath the overhang. Using the beam of light from the flashlight to guide his way, he pushed opened the door to the shop and entered. It was a relief to be back in a dry, warm spot. He shook the rain from the makeshift poncho, toweled off his wet hair and undressed for bed. Laying down on the cot, he was surprised to find it to be so comfortable. He pulled the blankets over him, laid his head down on the pillow, took a deep breath and let go his shaking body. Rain beat the roof and with each flash of lighting he could see a fine mist blowing across the missing windowpanes, but it didn't worry him. He was warm and the day was through. But he would not be alone tonight; the old woman would be with him - her words, her face, her history.

And here, surrounded by overgrown cotton fields, and drops that continued to fall, Neil Adams closed his eyes and listened; and what he heard was rain, a hopeful rain: powerful enough to wash blood from calloused fingertips, erode the bitter reminder of yesteryear and filled with just enough hope- that within each falling drop - lay the power of a faint promise, a fragile promise, perhaps, but a promise nevertheless to someday yield a different, more tender, forgiving fruit from seeds hidden deep beneath a thick soil.

8

The storm had passed sometime during the night and a new day broke. The sky was clear, crisp and bright. Neil woke early and felt as fresh as the earth around him.

Mattie brought down coffee and biscuits to the shop. A short time later the same crew from the day before had gathered once again. Just after ten O'clock the Fed Ex truck arrived and Neil installed the new part with some help from Willie, who supplied and filled the gear oil. After a short test ride, and satisfied that the new part was in working order, Neil packed his things and got ready to leave. Shawna held Albert and kissed the top of his head. Jessie dreamily watched Neil and his motorcycle. Mattie recited words from the Bible. Dexter pinched his hat. Willie stuffed his hands into his pockets, looked down and shuffled his feet. Cecil toothlessly smiled. And from a house on a hill, a blind woman watched.

He was on his way again, riding along route 20, heading north through Birmingham, onward towards Atlanta. And at a point in the trip when he should have been happy, happy because of the kindness shown him by a family he'd just met, happy that the repair had gone so smoothly, happy to be safe, happy to be free and not in prison...he wasn't happy. There was a malaise in leaving this family behind. Between the asphalt, hard metal, and painted highway lines came a touch of sadness. He wondered about Shawna and Jessie, what kind of life lay ahead for them both; whether or not they'd ever travel far from home, what they'd be like when they got to be older, what jobs they'd hold, families they'd raise? More than that he thought about his own life: time, possibilities, regrets. He'd been a child same as Jessie and Shawna. Forty years later and what had he done? Where had the time gone and what had he to show for its passing? He had wasted time. That was easy to see. And, in hindsight, he knew it was because he hadn't recognized the value of a day, an hour or even a moment, especially a moment. Time had gotten away from him....or maybe he'd let it go....there was always tomorrow....but his tomorrows were shrinking, getting smaller and he knew it. He felt closer to the end than the beginning-just like the old man out in the desert.

It was plain to him what he had overlooked; that life is NOW-at this moment, not something that waits to begin when you're ready or when all your ducks are in a row or when some goal is achieved or stipulation met. And in that acknowledgement was the fact that years were composed of months, and months were composed of weeks, and weeks composed of days, and days of hours, and hours of minutes, and minutes of seconds and seconds from the present moment. He thought of his own family, and the simple message written on a placard that his father had hung on the wall near the refrigerator, the one that had hung for years without much notice.

"SALUTATION OF THE DAWN"

Look to this day, for it is life, the very life of life for in its brief course lie all the challenges and meaning of your existence: The bliss of growth, splendor of beauty, glory of action. Look well, then, to this day, For yesterday is but a dream and tomorrow only a vision. But, today well lived makes every yesterday a dream of happiness, Every tomorrow a vision of hope. Look, therefore, to this day. Such is the salutation of the dawn.
(Kalidasa)

He moved sluggishly through traffic. He was just outside of Atlanta, when Neil decided to pass through Georgia's capital and head north on route 85, taking him in the direction of Charlotte, North Carolina, which put him in direct contact with his past.

Charlotte was close to a small Catholic college he had attended over fifteen years ago. He had to add it up in his head twice to confirm the number of years that had passed, and still he couldn't believe it.

153

'Fifteen years!' he wondered, "where did all that time go?'

College had been bittersweet for Neil. Why then revisit the college and part of his past? It was strange he should even entertain such an idea. Perhaps it was something, an unanswered question, or ....sentimental longings that pulled at him now as he rode along, prompting him to wonder, 'But why not; why not visit the college? It would be the first time back since leaving during that Junior year...'

After all, he was closest in proximity to the college than at any other time since leaving it and in all likelihood wouldn't pass this way again for a very long time – maybe never. If he were to go, it would have to be now.

He rolled his motorcycle north through the linking arms of Atlanta's intersecting highway systems and figured on making the college in four hours. He crossed the Tugaloo River and pulled into a rest stop. He found a picnic table and sat down. He peeled back an orange and watched as men who were dressed in fishing gear checked their poles, nets and lines in the back of a pickup truck. Neil thought of his freshman year at college and especially the young Irish kid, Andrew Murphy, who everyone knew as 'Murph'. Murph was the kind of kid everyone liked. He was short and stocky, red-faced with cherub cheeks and a gleam in his eye. His speech was often filled with quick- witted remarks both kind and foul, but always delivered with impeccable timing. He looked more pub owner than college student. His roots were from a respectable New England family whose grandfather had been the inventor of a small device used in the manufacture of telegraph insulators. Murph was also an alcoholic, but that would only come to light later.

Neil had been assigned a dorm room directly across from Murph's room and when, the first day was finished (having been spent unpacking and filling out class forms), and night fell, Murph's room erupted. Neil remembered sitting alone at his desk inside his sterile dorm room and hearing the bar room noises from across the hall. Neil went out to investigate and discovered Murph's door was wide opened and, through the cigarette haze and loud music, saw a drinking game was in full swing. When Neil poked his head timidly through Murph's doorway he was greeted by Murph who looked up with a glassy eyed smile, and yelled, "Heyyyyy!" It was said in a way as though they were the closest of friends, who'd lost contact and had finally been reconnected. A far cry from its original stark, cellblock character, the room had been transformed into a pub, complete with an Irish flag draping an entire wall, music, bar room chatter, clinking glasses, laughter, girls and, of course, beer. It had been a glorious, outrageous night. Neil remembered how his sides had literally ached the following morning from having laughed so much. That night would be the cornerstone upon which came the few close bonds of friendships he formed through his entire college experience.

Having finished eating the orange, and with the men in the fishing garb gone, Neil decided it was time for him to move along too. The land was beautiful and he was sorry to leave it behind. He was now in South Carolina, having crossed the border at the river and knew it'd only be a matter of a short ride through this state to reach his former college in North Carolina. Back on the road, Neil leaned into his handlebars, accelerated and felt the rush of air press against his cheeks. He was moving towards his past and felt anxious to get there, but as he began to steady the bike a ball of hesitation ballooned inside his stomach and suddenly the image of The Instructor, wearing a graduation cap, emerged.

'Going back, and what have we to show for all these years - expect a new campus building to have been erected in your honor?' he laughed. 'Oh what have you done with your life today, what have you done with your life I say?'

Neil wanted to push The Instructor away, but felt distracted and weakened from the increasing anxiety as the miles shortened between himself and his former college. His mind found no firm ground from which to fight. He took the blows.

'Didn't make it to any class reunions because you're embarrassing - Hey, stock boy, big plans you had, Mr. artist a regular Renoir you are,' The Instructor continued on in a slightly bombastic tone, 'you should have studied harder, joined some clubs, but maybe when all is said and done you're just not smart enough, plain and simple.'

The image of Murph and his party came back into Neil's head, but this time instead of happy memories, the image took on a disgusting, ugly tone with drunken, wasted time and connotations of failure.

'Maybe...Maybe if,' Neil began thinking, but realizing he was on the run from The Instructor's blows, and staging a defensive posture stopped himself. He tried to regain his footing. He didn't want to go into 'maybes' he knew better because it hadn't been a matter of studying harder or joining the right clubs. He could not have faked something he had no interest in-even back then. 'I am who I am, I was who I was. "...to thine own self be true." '

"Whoa, look who's quoting the bard, and at a fifth grade level nonetheless. My knees are shaking. That's not only the most overworked quote, but a cop-out to boot," The Instructor, still in the ring, moved on working another angle, 'You had interest in painting, what happened there, pretty boy?'

'Had,' Neil countered. 'I had it, maybe, but..lost it, I suppose.'
'So where's it, gone?'
"First college, now painting-what's your point?"
'Let me spell it out for you, L-O-S-E-R.'

Neil pressed on through the wind. Eight miles into North Carolina and only a few miles from the college, a distant, but familiar landscape began to appear around him and suddenly, Neil found himself smiling. With the exception of a new Mexican restaurant and a few stores, not much seemed to have changed since he was here last. it was exactly as he remembered, a snapshot memory which now came alive. He rode until he came to the bottom of a large hill upon which stood the campus. At the bottom of the hill lay the town's center: a nondescript supermarket, a small gas station, post office, bookstore & coffee house, pizza joint, and barbershop. Just outside the center, and hidden from view behind well-groomed hedges, and accessed only through a formidable gated entrance and up a gravel road, was an enormous inn, beautiful, elegant in nature. The lavish inn

156

seemed somewhat out of place in a small town like this, but the college attracted money and the inn fed from this runoff.

It was close to dinnertime when Neil pulled into the town's center and he was happy to see a pizzeria was opened. The pizzeria had been a private house at one point, which was easy to tell from the large, thick wooden steps that led up to the front door entrance, and natural rocks of all shapes and sizes that made up the foundation. The front, with its white clapboard siding, had two large bay windows through which could be seen booths and tables. A small cowbell hung on the inside of the thick front door and clanged as Neil walked inside. Red and white checker plastic tablecloths covered tables amid a sea of red-globed candles.

The place was empty. There were no customers. A lone waitress stood at the back counter flipping through a magazine. The smell of garlic and marinara sauce came from the kitchen. She left her magazine and walked to the "PLEASE WAIT TO BE SEATED" sign - which Neil, foolishly stood next to like a driver stopped at a red light in a one car town. The waitress gave a mechanical 'part of the job' smile then dipped her hand quickly behind the hostess stand and pulled out a menu.

Neil couldn't resist the temptation. "I'd like a quiet table, if you have one."

His joke seemed to have missed its mark,

"A booth okay?" she asked.

"Oh, that's fine, I was just kidding."

'You babbling fool,' a familiar voice muttered inside Neil's head.

The girl walked ahead, sashaying between the empty tables towards a booth, Neil followed behind, taking note of her beautiful white shorts, and soft young legs. She wore a pair of delicate canvas shoes with short running socks, exposing her bare, clean ankles. She half turned and extended one of her arms indicating the booth where Neil was to sit.

He dropped into the booth feeling slightly flush, eyes to the floor, as he took the menu she offered. He could feel her stare,

"Anything to start you off with, something to drink?"

"A coke'll be fine," Neil said and looked up just as she turned away. He intentionally drew his attention down to the menu and let go a breath he hadn't realized he had been holding.

'Pervert, she's half your age,' The Instructor drummed the obvious.

Neil steadied himself as he caught sight of the returning girl from the corner of his eye. She was Beautiful. If only he could go back in time. She placed a red plastic soda glass with a half wrapped straw on the table. He pretended not to notice, and acted surprised by her return.

"Oh, thank you," he focused his eyes on the glass she had placed on the table.

'And the Oscar goes to....' The Instructor announced above a drum roll.

"Are you ready to order?" Her voice was pure and sweet.

He looked up at her for just a moment then returned to his menu.

'This is ridiculous,' he thought, 'get a hold of yourself man!'

"Ahhh, yes- I guess I'll have a small regular pizza." He looked at her soft, short, blonde hair and angelic skin and for a moment thought he could smell her neck. She wore a red tee shirt with small white lettering, '*Rizzi's Pizza*' placed slightly above her perfectly firm breasts. Around her little sunshine wrist was a thin bracelet made of multi colored strings, which brushed against his arm when she reached in front of him to take his menu. He smiled up at her, she smiled back and for a fraction of a second he felt they had looked beyond themselves and the cosmos flickered. His attraction for her was maddening; it was a desire with which his entire body bubbled, but his stalemate mind fought.

She turned to leave, and with a slowed mind Neil felt his nose rake through her hair, his cheek glide across her flat stomach, and his fingers run under her panties and cascade down along her pelvic dip and to the soft spot of creation. He was left alone at the table and looked for something to occupy his time while he waited for his food. He got up and walked to the front of the restaurant where there was a stack of free newspapers. He grabbed one and went back to his table. He'd thumbed through a few pages when the waitress returned.

"Another coke?" Her lips looked freshly glossed and her hair brushed.

"No thanks, good for now." Neil took a quick look around, "Not too busy in here, am I missing a holiday?"

"Not a holiday," she smiled brightly, "but there's a big game up on campus, and it's still a little early yet."

"Busy later on then?" Neil asked.

"Lots of delivery."

"That's what I remember." Neil felt his upper lip gathering sweat. He wanted to wipe it, but didn't.

"Oh, you went to school here?"

"Yep, a few years ago, just wanted to come back and visit."

'A few years, my ass!'

"Wow, that's cool. Where are you coming from?" She bent her left knee and pointed the toe of her shoe into the floor.

"Believe it or not, California, but I'm on my way to New York."

"On a motorcycle?" her tender voice rose, and, in its melodic pitch, came the awful, undeniable truth of the disparity between them; she was too young and he too old. And in this disparity, Neil found a kind of sadness because he knew he'd never again be as young and innocent as this girl that stood before him and, in some strange way too, something cruel and unforgiving told him that some vague, yet real opportunity had been missed, lost and would never ever come again. He wondered what happened to all that time, the time, which had passed since he had been her age. It was hard to believe he had gotten this old. Forty? God. Yet, somehow it had happened. And this girl was here to confirm it.

"I know- crazy, right?" Neil said.

"No. It sounds amazing."

A bell dinged and the girl looked back to the kitchen and then again at Neil.

"Your pizza must be up," she said and began back towards the kitchen.

He gently rocked the prongs of his fork, pressing them into the table with his index finger, and watched as the handle sprang up and down. A girl he had dated back in high school flashed inside him. She had been the first in their class to get a driver's license. He remembered driving with her, how daring and adventurous it felt to cross over to a neighboring town or down to the public beach or just to drive anywhere at all- without any supervision. They were so cool, so free: the cigarettes and clothing, and music that was uniquely theirs with lyrics that understood their teenage frustration, angst and isolation. He felt the embarrassment from the memory and pushed it away with a sip of his coke.

The girl returned holding a hot, round metal tray of pizza, supported by an oven mitt on one hand, and, a metal wire stand in her other. She placed the stand on the table and put the round tray on top.

"Be careful, it's hot," she said, removing the oven mitt from her hand.

"I will. Thanks," Neil could smell her candy perfume, which floated through the steaming pizza. They both looked to the front door as the cowbell banged and a girl with dark red hair and freckles walked in carrying a folded apron.

"Hey, Jen," the girl at Neil's table said.

"Hi, Christy," the redhead called back, as she walked past tables in the direction of the kitchen.

"How was practice?"

"Ah - don't ask," said the redhead with a lazy dismissal of her hand.

Christy turned her head towards Neil and straightened her body, "Crushed pepper, grated cheese?"

"No," he said, "this is fine."

"Enjoy."

"Thanks."

Christy walked back towards the redhead, who had drawn herself a coke from the soda machine, placed her apron on the counter, and sat with one leg bent under her on a stool and sipped at a straw.

Neil pulled his first slice. The pizza was thick and incredibly hot. The cheese slid like tectonic plates. He struggled to let it cool while taking small bites. The redhead got up from her stool and the two girls disappeared into the back. Neil was on his fourth and final slice when the two girls finally emerged. The redhead tied an apron around her waist and tossed small glances in Neil's direction. He felt as though a silent secret had passed between the two girls, or maybe he was imaging things, being paranoid, or worse yet, self-centered.

Christy came back over to Neil's table and ripped a check from her order pad and gently pushed it on the tabletop.

"Here's the check, there's no rush- it's just that I have to leave- Jen will help you now."

Neil pushed his legs under the table, arched his back and reached inside his front jean pocket to produce a crisp twenty-dollar bill, which he placed on top of the check.

"You can take this now, I was pretty much finished."

"Thanks."

She took the money and check, went to the register, and returned with his change. He thought of all the cheap, raucous late night stoner college kids this girl Christy probably had to deal with.

"Keep the change," he said.

"Oh - okay. Thanks."

'Mr. Big shot,' The Instructor quipped.

"By the way," Christy said. "If you're not doing anything tonight there's a theater production of *The Seagull* up on campus. It starts at eight o'clock - I'm in the cast, I've got to go back and get ready."

"Yeah, sure. I-

"I mean if you don't have anything else –"

"No. I don't have. Not tonight."

"It's not a big deal if you do," Christy said. "It's just a small part, no big deal."

"No no no. I'd love to make it."

"Okay then, oh - what's your name?"

"Neil."

161

Her smile revealed perfect little teeth. Neil thought of her parents and the dental bills they must have paid. They shook hands.

"Christy," she said and turned to the front door and waved goodbye to Jen. "Bye, Jen."

Jen smiled from behind the counter. "Good luck tonight!" she shouted.

"You mean, break a leg," Christy replied.

"That's right, break a leg."

Christy exited.

Neil sat and enjoyed the moment. He wiped his hands, finished off his coke, and gathered his things. Jen was already consumed by a steady flow of phone orders as he left.

With little or nothing to do until the theater production began, he decided while there was still daylight he'd find a campsite and get setup for the night. He rode towards a nearby campsite he had visited a few times during his college days. He had often camped and hiked around this entire area, sometimes with a small group of friends where they'd drink, laugh and carouse late into the night around a roaring campfire. But, often times, too, on more solitary, reflective sojourns when he wasn't in the mood for company and would venture off alone, starting off from the campus with nothing more than a sleeping bag, bivy sack, and a backpack filled with paints, brushes and a scant provisions. He would hike along trails and back woods, through meadows and streams in search of some picturesque spot where the light was just right and he would sit and paint.

To be here in the same area after so many years brought back memories and a strange sense of betrayal; under his present circumstances, it all felt out of context, almost surreal as though he were jumping back into an old photograph and trying to rearrange it, and too, he felt that if his friends, had by chance, come upon him now, might question this odd behavior, just as as one might a grave robber caught red handed.

He came to the bottom of a familiar mountain range that he had hiked countless times. He stopped and let his bike idle. A thick rusted chain stretched across the campground entrance

162

that prevented cars from passing – but maybe just enough space for a motorcycle. He gave it a shot. After barely squeezing past the chained entrance, he rode along a walking trail until he found a remote spot - not designated for camping - but it being so late in the season, he knew no one would care. It was long after Labor day and the park was empty. He set his tent up, unpacked his belongings and, there, under a late afternoon sun, Neil napped. By the time he woke, it was already dark and his face was puffy and clammy from sleep. He fumbled through the tent door to the outside darkness and stretched. He felt a little stiff, but well rested- the nap had done him good. He was reminded by the chill in the air that the Fall season had arrived. He packed a new change of clothes and a shaving kit, started his motorcycle and rode out back towards the college.

Once he had passed through the main gates of the college he moved slowly along a roadway that formed a loop around the entire campus. It was fairly quiet. The grounds were just as he remembered, impeccably groomed like that of a golf course. A small number of students in groups of two or three walked along paths and over the green grounds. He rode past the massive library, light from its high arched windows lit the ground below. Neil looked though the windows and saw the bent heads of students as they studied at tables.

'The gerbils are in training, the gerbils are in training!' an excited voice erupted somewhere inside his head.

Years had passed since last he'd been here and it felt as if he were putting on an old blazer, which he'd long outgrown. The very fact he was on the campus, refueled much of the anxiety, which had plagued him earlier in the day. Flames of uncertainty fed speculative scenarios, which were not only possible, but also probable. His heart raced. It was easy to imagine him bumping into his former English lit teacher, Mrs. Haines around the next corner "So, Neil, what have you been doing since leaving college?" He heard her ask, and his fumbling, inadequate response. He saw his wrestling coach, his college counselor, even his former girlfriend. 'Oh what have you done with your life today, what have done with your life I say?' Then his mind ran to the one thought he had successfully managed to avoid for some time... to the desert and the man he had buried out there and it twisted his brain tighter with knots of anxiety, doubts and misgivings. His grip on the motorcycle's throttle weakened and his palms became sweaty. He wondered, again, whether or not he was in control of himself, if his mind was slipping, truly slipping. Had he made a horrendous mistake in coming back to this college? Had he lost the capacity to reason?

He banked left into the first bend of the large oval loop. Soon, he was at the lower, farthest end of the campus, down around the playing fields. He stopped outside a field clubhouse used by the college sports teams and parked his bike next to a team van that was squeezed between two small cars. Bicycles leaned against the building. He entered the clubhouse, minus his motorcycle jacket and helmet, and tried as best he could to fit in. A few remaining college jocks were finishing up from an earlier football game, and by all the laughing and wisecracks, Neil guessed it must have been a triumphant day. The air was heavy with shower steam and hard cologne. Despite his age, no one paid Neil much mind. He certainly didn't look as young as these kids, as a matter of fact, he couldn't remember anyone looking as young as these students when he attended this college. At the end of a long row of lockers he sat on the edge of a plastic bench and undressed. He walked into the empty shower room and turned the water up high. The water hit his body hard. It was plentiful and hot, and he relished in its rejuvenating stream. His road tightened muscles loosened and his entire body and mind softened. He then shaved, put on a fresh set of clothes and was ready to go. He wondered if what he had been doing was all for Christy, but didn't force himself to answer.

He left his motorcycle at the clubhouse, and began to walk across the campus in the direction of the theater. Memories of his former college experience accompanied him, nights like this when he had taken walks with girls down here by the playing fields to drink cheap wine or a six pack of beer, watch stars and explore. He remembered too, now with shame, the open, candid talks they had shared and naive dreams fermented in this youthful environment, not yet aware of any cynical effects cast by realities outside the confines of these campus grounds and touched neither by the gears of the banker's impossible timepiece nor the hollow sound of compromised dreams.

He remembered Patricia, a girl with whom he'd taken such nighttime sojourns. They had met in a drawing and perspective class during his freshman year. Her name was hard for him to recall at first, but her face was still with him. It was long, Elizabethan and damn near royal save for a nose that had been broken and hooked slightly to the left. Neil adored her. She was from Kentucky and had a frank and whimsical charm about her without the conventional collegiate prattle. She seemed to have little to no sense for lipstick, dresses or eyeliner and if she had, showed no interest in proving it. She was an open book. She and Neil hit it off, and thought themselves quite different and special. Unlike the rest of the students who had taken the class as a means of acquiring an easy credit, they saw themselves as artists and were intent on living their lives as such. They were passionate about what they shared as their life's mission. They became close. He shared himself with her in a way he'd never done with anyone else before. With his guy friends he might have talked about his ambitions but with this girl he was as honest as he had been when alone in a room. He told her everything- his inner, most private thoughts and feelings. He was comfortable in being vulnerable, and trusted her like no one else he had ever met. She felt the same and shared with Neil stories of her childhood, growing up with an abusive father, alcoholic mother and neglected household. She told Neil about the uncle who had molested her at age nine. She spoke about her attempted suicide and recovery.

He stopped, stood still and paused for a moment and allowed the nighttime campus to settle around him. It was quiet and still. The only sound he heard was his own breath and he became very calm and his breath slowed. He felt connected to everything around him; it was as if he had actually managed to reach through the purple night and somehow expand his consciousness. His ears, now wolf like, picked up excited voices, snapping through the Fall air from the hill of the main campus. From miles above came the faint sound of an airliner moving through the remote night sky. His eyes, like those of a nocturnal feline, grasped pinpoint white stars, which dotted the inkwell bubble. He stood transfixed. And in the moment all made sense, he understood, he felt right, in tune and complete. In a very primordial sense he was connected to everything eternal. He had had this feeling before, and familiar with its pattern, knew it wouldn't last. He savored it as best he knew how. He took another slow inhale of the crisp, night air and exhaled it through his nose.

His thoughts again turned to Patricia and the secrets they had shared, 'What happened to those dreams and wishes, those plans?' he wondered. He remembered all of it, but wished he hadn't. He had failed, fallen short of those expectations.

"God, so damn embarrassing," he said aloud. "Those dreams, so confident, self assured." And here he laughed as if to excuse himself from his youth, but the insincerity of the laugh was inescapable - the kind of laugh heard at a cocktail party where words like 'fabulous' and 'darling' flow. He recognized the falseness in it, but dared not stop and question or fault himself, instead he continued and reflected on the aspirations he had here as a student at this college so many years ago, aspirations of greatness for which he felt himself entitled and justified because of the talent he knew to be in him, which he possessed, had been confirmed by his peers, teachers.

'I really could have shown the world something,' Neil thought. He was somber and sincere 'I, it's, damn it, I was a good painter, an incredible painter on par with the best.' He was thinking of his opening show at the student union and how everyone -

'Shit, they're only students what the hell did they know, no one knows anything, even the teachers. They teach. If I'm to judge myself by the opinion garnered by faculty and students, I'm in deep trouble,' He chastised himself

A voice began to sing again, 'Oh, what have you done with your life today, what have you done with your life I say?'

166

Neil moved down a campus path to the theater where students circulated around its main entrance. Some were smoking, talking -a boy with a black crow on his shoulder walked by. Another came to an abrupt stop from a loud and fast skateboard that he flipped up into his hand. A girl screeched then laughed from an unexpected pinch. Among it all was an ever so slight, yet tangible insecurity that danced in the air with the agility of a humming bird; everyone seemed in one way or another to be checking out everyone else. The girls were eyeing each other's outfits, shoes, hairstyles and companions.

Inside the lit ticket booth sat a heavyset girl sipping from a plastic water bottle. She was either unaware of all the social goggling, or, simply, didn't give a damn. She wasn't here to impress anybody. She pressed her eyeglasses with her index finger against the bridge of her nose and serenely looked at Neil through the booth's glass partition.

"How many?"

"Just one."

"Faculty?"

"No," Neil replied

"Twelve dollars."

Neil handed her the money and took his ticket and looked one last time at the girl inside the booth. She had already gone on to help someone else and, suddenly, deep inside him, came an overwhelming urge to hug this girl. He knew her. Understood her. Could see her later on that night after her shift was over, how she'd be getting off the bus, just as she'd done a hundred times or more before, alone to an empty apartment where she'd watch T.V., read a book, feed the cat and make the phone call to her mother - the one with small lies before going off to bed. This girl was living a plain life filled with simple kind acts without any false hopes, but knowing, perhaps in some small way she might someday make a difference in someone else's life. And here she was going unnoticed by self-centered children who were lacking any real, universal knowledge and who, worse still, were ungrateful for the things that had been given them and that life had offered. She wasn't concerned about the transitory nature of

167

college fashion, politics or popularity – the always striving, competing, and for what? Life is inside you, not somewhere else. She was grounded, eternal.

'See, she's got it together,' he said to himself, 'not filled with any false expectations and deserves something good and kind.'

He took the blue ticket and walked inside the theater's lobby. The old, musty decrepit theater building he remembered as having been here when he was student had been remodeled, and replaced with plush red carpet, blonde wood walls and elegant halogen lighting. The place had a sophisticated, clean feel to it and Neil felt pampered as he made his way across the lobby and toward the darkened doors to the theatre auditorium. In the doorway of the theater were two students working as ushers, denoted by the word, "STAFF" printed in bold white letters on the back of the black tee shirts each one wore. One of them, with an abundance of styling gel in his short spiky hair and a permanent smirk pasted above his clenched jaw, took Neil's ticket and ripped it in half and gave him back the stub. At the same moment, a young girl beside this boy handed Neil a program. Both students looked a little too perfect, a boxed set of Ken and Barbie dolls displayed on a department store's shelf waiting to be sold.

"Here you are sir," the girl said, smiling as if posing for a picture.

These two kids who screamed 'actors' were high school students or had lied about their age on the college entrance exam. They looked too young to be here. Neil had seen these kids before in Los Angeles, the boys with the squush and push hairdos, or frohawks, and the girls with the, 'I'm gonna make it' vapid countenance behind injured eyes. And, always on a cell phone as though nothing so immediate and real around them could match the importance or meaning of some distant cellular voice. They just didn't seem sincere and authentic enough to posses an artistic calling, too empty, nothing inside – and what had they to offer? It was one thing to have a dream, but one filled with ignorance, from a bunch of posers with no sense of history or self caused Neil to feel both sad and sick. He actually felt bitterness towards these kids, and downright disgust. But, what bothered him most about it all, and what he fought to admit; was that in some strange way what he felt about these two actors had more to do with the cynical feeling he had about his own shortcomings, self and disillusionment than from the reality that was before him.

With both scorn and petulance, Neil walked with his ticket stub and program about halfway down the center aisle, found a seat in the dimly lit theater and dropped into it. To distract himself he began to look over the program. On the front, was a drawing of a dead seagull and below that, the play's title and playwrights name, **_The Seagull_** by Anton Chekhov. He started to open the program, but the lights went down, the curtain opened and the play began.

What appeared first was an elaborate set with a large painted mural in the background, which depicted a rural setting of a wooded landscape, including a lake. On stage were a few actors on a pathway in front of a small stage with benches. It was evident by the scenery, costumes, and makeup that all these kids had put a great deal of time and effort into the production. A strong odor of papier-mache' props and watercolors gave proof that a rushed deadline had nearly been missed. The actors were already in place and wore costumes from the 1800's. Young college students played some of the older characters. Christy came in early during the first act, playing the part of Nina. She radiated. Her beauty, sparkling and undeniable under the glow of the stage lights, caused a palpable stir in the audience. Unspoken thoughts and desires rippled through the auditorium.

The production, overall, was mediocre, lacking spontaneity and vitality; too many moments, Neil thought, were stark and stiff and a little too calculated. It seemed a bit too mechanical as though each actor had some predisposed idea of what they needed to play and worked on imitating it. This included enunciation, tempo, and where in the text premeditated, emotional responses were to be placed. Nina did this too, but it didn't matter- she was too beautiful for anyone to care (except, perhaps, for the jealous wrangling of her female cohorts).

Whatever level of skill these actors displayed, the fact that they had gotten out on stage and performed, in and of itself, was admirable to Neil. He respected the art and the bravery; he knew it took guts and a strong constitution just to stand in front of an audience and it was something that awed him. At the same time, however, he didn't go much for acting and actors. Having lived so close to Hollywood, and the movie industry, he'd met enough jackals and aspiring actors to form his own opinion. He didn't bother with it much - Hollywood, the movies and actors. On top of all that, how was one supposed to have respect for acting when models, porn stars, and hotel baron daughters were calling themselves actors? And in a world where digitally pasted, CGI, reality TV shows, publicists, cut up scenes, press agent packets, and celebrity gossip muddled through the airwaves how was anyone expected to make sense of this overload? In the end, it all seemed to blend together, pressed out from some homogenized tube of goo called The Hollywood industry onto a plate for the sterilized gerbils to eat. And eat they did.

It was refreshing, then, for Neil to sit in a theater and watch a story in real time, with real people unfold before him. Regardless of the talent displayed, it was exciting and real with no second takes, dubbed laughter, or special effects and in this environment he felt the potential for magic, fantasy and wanderlust.

And, so it happened: indian eyes from the attic shot through one of the actors, who stood oddly apart and, who, grabbed Neil by the lapels and shook him good. When the actor (playing the part of Treplev) first appeared, it seemed someone, a stagehand perhaps, had accidentally stumbled on stage, the way in which he appeared so real and in tune. Instead of stiff, prefabricated emotions, it was apparent that this actor's behavior stemmed from a unique set of rules; there was a sense of intimacy, fragility and truth.....teetering on a tightrope. And when juxtaposed with the other actors on stage, their inadequacies were painfully evident. Neil knew all these kids had studied in the same acting classes offered at the college, all were around the same age, but there was something entirely different about this actor. This actor believed so strongly in what he said and did, that for a few moments, it felt as if the walls of the theater had melted away. The blind woman's words of travel came back into Neil's mind, the thin membrane between reality and fantasy.

Neil felt an affinity with this actor. And anger began to rise inside him. He saw something, a part of himself in this student on stage that sparked in him both wonderful and painful memories of time he had spent in the art department here at the college. Why wasn't he on stage-not here of course, but overall, doing something that would showcase, express who he truly was.

The curtain fell and a fifteen-minute intermission was announced. Neil remained in his seat and flipped through the program. His eyes might have been fixed on the program, but his mind was held on the idea of talent. He contemplated the difference in talent among people, artists and the very nature of talent itself. Having attended many art classes, he knew first hand that no amount of training could or would produce a great artist. A class could definitely help improve skills, but great talent could not be taught. It was easy for him to see that those who reached legendary status, based on their talent, had an innate sensibility that given the right environment would flourish. He'd been touched by the great, great talents such as Da Vinci, Mozart, Rimbaud, Dylan, Plato and other geniuses and his conclusion was always the same; that their talents so extraordinary, uncomprehendable and impossible were there to point us in the direction of truth, closer to God.

As Neil sat with these thoughts about talent, there came, deep inside him, a twinge of remorse.

'I really need to start painting again,' he heard himself thinking. He was surprised by this thought. It was the kind of thought he'd long ago neutered, a thought connected to a history of disappointment and pain, a thought that shouldn't be allowed.

When he'd been a student here at this college he excelled in his art classes. He'd never before felt so passionate about anything in his life as he had with painting. He spent all of his time between the studio, local galleries, and outdoor excursions where he'd set up his easel and paint. He was consumed with painting, form and light and transmuting ideas. But things weren't perfect. Shortly after his second semester his overall grades slipped. He'd been waking up late, going on hikes, painting, sketching and neglecting his other requirements. He'd been skipping his classes. It was sad, then, at that at the same time he'd found an overwhelming sense of purpose in his life, his college enrollment was in jeopardy.

"If I'm going to paint for a living, why do I need these other classes?" He remembered asking the advisor. It was a hard reality check when the advisor answered,

"You should have thought about that before applying to a liberal arts college. Here, you need to satisfy all the humanities instead of just one."

He wanted to comply and fulfill his other requirements, but his heart, entire body, wasn't in it and remembered how, with quiet reservation, he just never returned mid way through his Junior year. His parents were more understanding than he expected. They didn't yell or shout, scream or get angry. But, what hurt was the disappointment they tried to hide- especially Neil's father who never had the opportunity to attend college.

The lights in the theater rose, then lowered, rose again, and lowered once more, accompanied with a soft melodic chime, which indicated the intermission had ended and the play would continue.

"Oh I'm different now, I'm a real actress. I enjoy acting. I adore it. I get madly excited on stage, I feel I'm beautiful and since I've been here, I've kept going for walks, walking around and thinking - thinking and feeling my morale improving everyday. Constatine, I know now, I've come to see, that in our work - no matter whether we're actors or writers - the great thing isn't fame or glory, it isn't what I used to dream of, but simply stamina. You must know how to bear your cross and have faith. I have faith and things don't hurt me so much now. And when I think of my vocation, I'm not afraid of life."

Christy spoke her dialogue and Chekhov's stomping cane echoed through the aisles. The play soon ended and the curtain closed. The lights went down and then back up, the curtain

172

opened again, and riding high on the wave of applause, each of the actors took their bows.

Neil remained in his seat as the actors disappeared back stage and the audience headed for the lobby exits. Eventually, he got up too and filed out one of the exits. In the plush lobby was Christy, still in costume surrounded by a small group of friends. She was smiling, talking and excitedly mad with a performer's afterglow. Her limitless energy was infectious, the lobby was buzzing with talk and possibility. With his program rolled tightly in both hands, Neil tentatively approached her group. She immediately jumped at his arrival,

"Neil, oh Neil, you made it," she said, and then turned to the group, "everyone, this is Neil. He attended college here, and came to support me tonight." She looked and smiled at Neil, who laughed. Introductions were made followed by a few awkward handshakes.

"There's a cast party up at McClain's, you're invited, if you'd like to come," she said sweetly to Neil.

"That sounds fine."

"I've got to get changed - if you want to, you can wait here, we're all going over there together."

"Okay."

"Wait here, I'll be back in a couple minutes," she said and then fled like a princess from a castle.

Her absence left a hole filled with small talk. The rest of the group seemed to know one another and Neil felt out of place. Her return was a relief and gave purpose to the entire group.

"Okay everyone, onward!" Christy corralled the group out of the theater and led them towards the pub only a short walking distance away. The campus watering hole, McClain's pub was located beneath the student union. And it was just as Neil remembered; the walls were adorned with all the typical college paraphernalia manufactured by a marketing department from all the major beer and liquor companies. There were posters with scantily clad buxom girls with perfectly airbrushed skin, wearing tight half skirts or shorts, all in provocative poses-one holding a garden hose, another in a swimsuit made with the beer makers

173

logo and, still, another dressed as a sexy ski bunny - a beer bottle or two in hand, all white, bright smiles and slogans written around them like, "This is the one for you," "Wet your whistle," "Give in to your thirst." or, "It's good to be bad."

Along with the posters were college pennants hanging on the dark walls, a glowing neon clock shaped as a liquor bottle, a pool table in the corner, a pinball machine, jukebox, and dartboard with a beer logo across its top. The sterilization had really grabbed hold here.

It was obvious this group of kids had been here before. They waved and called out to their fellow classmates by name who were working the bar and beer taps. The group made themselves at home, pulling a few tables together to form one large block. Pitchers of beer were ordered, along with wine coolers for two of the girls. Christy drank beer and sat next to Neil.

At first it was small talk chatter with everyone contributing a point about this teacher or that teacher or what new policy the administration had considered imposing, where to find good skiing and, of course, tonight's performance. But as the night rolled on, Neil found he and Christy were talking more to one another and less to the rest of the group. They were in a glass cocoon. They joked, played, listened and really connected; they hoarded a secret which only they, and, they alone, understood. She was close to him and, there was nothing – only a beginning.

'What the hell are you doing here?' The Instructor asked. 'AARP is calling, wants to renew your membership.'

"Shots!" a voice rang out somewhere in the group. No one fought the idea and within minutes shot glasses filled with a dark liquid were lined on top of the table.

"What are we drinking?" Neil heard someone ask, knowing of course, the answer wouldn't matter much.

"It's called a mindblower," another answered, "101 proof of something delicious. Just drink up."

The shots were doled out, clinked together in a communal toast. Suddenly, there came the sound of shattered glass.

174

"Your mother!" exclaimed a girl, while pushing her chair back like a crab and looking down between her feet. "I just paid for these fucking sneakers!"

The shot was replaced. Everyone drank, and slammed their empty glasses on the table in a sign of comradeship.

Neil had too many experiences mixing beer and shots and knew the result wouldn't be pleasing come morning, but this knowledge had arrived only with age and experience. More importantly, was his rule to never drink more than a beer when riding his motorcycle - a bit prudish to some, but he didn't care. He wasn't out to prove anything to anybody just to satisfy some macho image. He'd seen the missing or tangled limbs come in to *Dillards* and heard the horrible death stories. His untouched shot glass sat on the table in front of him.

"What's wrong, you don't like it?" Christy asked.

"No it looks great, but I'll be driving my motorcycle tonight, and the two don't mix."

"You don't have to, you know," Christy smiled and looked at him with a theatrical set of pursed lips.

"Have to what?" Neil asked, already sensing the answer.

"You know...drive."

"Stay -"

"In my room," Christy said. "My roommate's out of town. There's an extra bed."

Neil took a moment. "In that case," he said, "as part of my gratitude I offer you my shot." He slid the shot glass in Christy's direction.

"I'll gladly accept," she said and kissed his cheek and drank.

Neil ordered another beer.

The Instructor threw in his two cents,

'Tell her about the dead man, see how much she likes you then.'

A few hours and many more shots later, last call was announced and everyone piled out of the pub. Remnants of conversations were tied up and loud laughing goodbyes exchanged. Christy had clasped Neil's arm and they began to walk the campus. She teetered a little.

"I can't believe we're here together, isn't that weird?" She stumbled slightly but Neil caught her.

"Take it easy there. Are you alright?"

'Like taking candy from a baby, Sickko,' The Instructor chimed in.

"Yes, of course. I'm fine." She reassured him.

She dropped her head for a second; Neil caught her embarrassment and asked about her acting,

"How long have you been acting?"

"Oh, ever since I got here, but I've always been interested in it. It's what I'll be doing for a living."

"Who are some of your favorites?"

"Favorites?" she replied.

"Yeah, you know, favorite actors, actresses, ones you admire."

"No, I get what you mean," Christy said. "It's just that I'm not sure- I mean, I like Katie Holmes."

"What about Meryl Streep, Diane Keaton, Ellen Burstyn?

"Oh sure I love Meryl Streep, she's old, but good."

"The older ones are great, though, look at Marlon Brando, Montgomery Clift, Paul Newman, Pacino."

"Speaking of old-how old are you?" she asked.

"Oh my God." Neil lifted his head back towards the sky and smiled.

"No no no," Christy laughed, "I - I didn't mean it that way. I was just curious that's all."

"Old enough to be your father," Neil said.

'A'int that the truth,' The Instructor affirmed.

"Really?" Christy asked.

"Well, yeah. Kind of," Neil replied.

'Not *Kind of* - you *Are*,' The Instructor clenched his fists and bent his head, 'Ohhh, how I wish her old man was here tonight so he could kick your ass.'

"Ohh daddy." Christy teased.

"That's a little gross."

"It is, isn't it?" She noticed Neil wasn't laughing.

'No more tonight,' he said.

A smile crossed The Instructor's lips, 'Have it your way, but I'll see you again.'

"To be honest,' Christy said, 'I don't have much in common with guys my age. I've always dated older men."

"Can we get back to the subject?"

"A little sensitive?" Christy asked.

"Never mind."

"No, go ahead. I'm only kidding." Christy pulled at Neil's arm, "Okay, subject...which was......?"

"Which was Newman, Brando, Clift and other actors."

"I'm not sure?"

"Not sure-about ...their talent?" Neil asked.

"Nooo, just I, don't -"

"You know who they are though, right? Marlon Brando, Newman, Monty Clift."

"Of course I know Paul Newman, The Color of Money and Newman's Own. Duhhhh. But, we really don't, like watch old films or anything, theater history. It's more about acting and performing."

"What about the Group Theatre?

"Not really-"

"But, come on please tell me you've heard of Brando, you know with Elia Kazan..... Stella Adler?"

Christy hesitated, "I've heard his naaaammmee, but......."

Neil fished a little more, "Do you guys discuss anything about ....,

Christy just looked at Neil and smiled.

Neil laughed, "Christy, you're killing me here."

"Sorry, I really don't know-" She hugged her ears with her shoulders and through another smile, gave a cute, playful, but defensive wince.

He eased up. "It doesn't matter, but anyway that's what I think The Actor's Studio and most other places to study in New York came out of, all that stuff.

"That's where Jake's going, the one who played Treplev."

"Where? The Actor's Studio?"

"I think so. Somewhere in New York- or maybe The Acting Studio."

"What about you?" Neil asked. "Where are you going, New York too?"

"No, I'm going off to Hollywood, I'm more of a film actress, darling." She threw her hair back in a dramatic gesture. "That's what I've been told anyway."

It was easy to forgive Christy's lack of knowledge on account of her age, but the thought of not understanding history, the progression of one's interest - whether acting, painting, politics, or zebra hunting, had, in Neil's mind, dire consequences. History abhors a vacuum.

They moved down small walking paths until they came to a boulder next to a fountain. The fountain was dry. It was quiet and dark and they were alone. They sat together on the boulder and Christy leaned in close to Neil, hooked his arm with hers.

"And you?" she asked almost in a whisper.

"And me, what about me?" he responded.

"What are your dreams and aspirations?"

"What if I told you I have none."

"I'd say you're a liar," she half laughed.

"I'm telling you, I don't."

"Oh come on." She nudged him.

"You don't believe me?" Neil asked.

Christy turned and looked at him, "I'd say it's impossible to live life without them. Everyone has dreams."

"You really are young, aren't you?"

She hesitated and said, "What do you do besides work at the airport? Don't you have any hobbies, interests?"

"First of all, it's not an airport, not like I'm checking baggage or anything - and secondly, I don't have time for hobbies."

"Okay, so what if you had all the money in the world, what'd you do then, still work at the airport?"

"Maybe."

"You're so full of it. What did you study here at college? You haven't told me."

"Oh boy."

Christy's voice rose in excitement, "Seeeee."

"Please. That was a long time ago-ages in fact."

"But, you did study something?" Christy said, more as a statement of fact than a question.

"Yes."

"Well, what was it?"

"Art," said Neil. "Painting."

"Oh wow. I knew it."

"Knew what, that I studied art?"

"Something creative. What happened?"

"It fizzled," Neil said.

Christy's forehead furrowed. She shook her head and lifted both palms up, "Fizzled?"

Neil wasn't about to tell her about Patricia; how she left for Christmas break and never came back. He couldn't remember who told him, how he'd first learned of Patricia's suicide. Maybe it was her old roommate, maybe someone on his floor when he returned after a night drinking with Murph. It had been three months since they had talked. Her death had left an ambiguous hole.

"Yeah, you know, life goes on - things come up - bills need paying."

"You're an odd little chicken."

Neil didn't want to be harsh, but the tone was already in his voice by the time he spoke, "Things happen okay. You're here, in college you're young and full of dreams, ideas, ambition and that's cool, that's great. I get it- the way it's supposed to be but-" He slid off the boulder and looked away from Christy, out to the dark. "Then comes reality and reality isn't always kind." He turned and looked at her and then at the ground. "Look, you don't need a lecture and I'm not trying to be cruel, but-"

"But, what?"

"You get thrown down enough times, and sooner or later you don't get back up."

"You know how you sound when you talk like that?"

"No, How?"

"Bitter."

"Yeah, well."

"Very bitter. My parents divorced last year right after my mother was diagnosed with breast cancer, so I know about being thrown down. I barely made it back to college."

Neil didn't know where to look. "Sorry."

Christy hugged both her knees real tight and looked up at the stars, "My mother always said everybody's got a song to sing and to die with that song still inside them is a crime."

Neil pulled his head back up and looked at Christy. He had a smirk on his face. "Who am I to argue with your mother-especially if she's like you. You're feisty, you know that?"

"Three older brothers, had to be."

It was well past midnight when Christy and Neil walked hand in hand back to her dormitory. Christy opened her dorm room. She turned on the light and shut the door. Neil caught her waist. She pressed his body to hers, held his head between her hands and kissed his lips. He found her tongue. He needed her, all of her, to consume her, suck her in and never let go. She was life, energy, innocence, youth and eternity. They grappled with one another's clothes, fumbling. Only her panties remained and his jeans, one leg out and the other rising up out of the pant leg, balancing like an injured flamingo. He wanted her, was ready for her and he knew this was that moment, that point in his life, when he'd never again have someone so young and beautiful as Christy. He'd bet his life on it. Here she was sexy, young and gorgeous.

He couldn't believe himself. "Ahhhh shit-"

'You fucking idiot!' The Instructor screeched.

"What's wrong?" Christy asked.

'Wuss.'

"Nothing," Neil cupped his face with his hands, "It's just I, I'm sorry Christy- it's n', see I, I have Sarah and- I-"

"Seriously?"

"I know, crazy. I-you're so hot, and..."

"Thanks."

Neil had lied to Christy earlier at McLain's when she asked if he had a girlfriend, telling her he was going through a breakup. It

wasn't a flat out lie, exactly, but it wasn't completely true either-
He didn't know what was happening between him and Sarah.

"I'm sorry," Neil said.

Christy ran her hands down his shoulders. She turned and
grabbed her clothes and put them on. Neil did the same.

They talked a little more, but it felt estranged. He got ready to
leave. Christy spoke,

"You can still stay- if you want."

Neil did stay, but things were different and their conversation
was cautious. Christy turned off the light and got into her bed.
Neil lay in her roommate's bed on the other side of the room.
From somewhere in the dark came Christy's voice, "You're not
going to kill me in my sleep or anything are you?"

"Funny. No."

"Just checking. By the way, you're hot too. Goodnight."

"Goodnight," Neil responded. "Christy if I didn't have-"

"I know, Neil."

"Thanks for letting me spend the night."

"You're welcome."

"Sweet dreams."

"You too, Neil."

He woke early, and the darkened room caused him confusion;
it took him a few seconds to get his bearings. He felt about in the
darkness and found his watch by his head and looked down at
the glowing dial; just after six O'clock. He hadn't slept well, and,
under the present circumstances, knew he wouldn't fall back into
a solid sleep. He quietly got up. He thought he saw Christy move,
but was still again. He put his boots on and slipped into his heavy
leather jacket. He found a pencil and a blank sheet of paper on
Christy's desk.

*'Christy, couldn't sleep, decided to leave early and get back
on the road. Thanks for a great night of theater, a beautiful
memory and I wish you all the best. You're perfect. Take care, -
always, Neil'*

The handle clicked hard when he closed the door; the sound
bounced off glossy waxed floors and institutional cinder block
walls layered with as many coats of paint as the college was old.

He walked down the hallway towards the exit. He might as well been in a morgue or ghostly infirmary; it was empty, silent and nothing stirred. But, he knew behind each door he passed, there lay students who slumbered under the comfort of flannel sheets sent, or packed, by loving parents, a scene repeated throughout all these dorms on this Sunday morning. He felt like a criminal in this girl's dormitory. He silently cursed his boots, which clumped so loud, the sound amplified and echoed off the walls, making it seem as if he were Frankenstein in a ballet class. He was glad then when he finally reached the exit.

Outside, a thick, damp, white and grey fog had cloaked the entire campus, forcing Neil to recall its layout. It was familiar enough, but had he never been here, he would surely have lost his way in this grey abyss. It was cold, his hair was a mess, and his breath was stale. He sniffled, zipped his jacket up high and threw his hands into its pockets. His shoulders tightened as he bent his head and began to navigate through the moist air. Nothing stirred, but somewhere out there came the coo cooing sound of a lone morning dove.

The wet grass lay as testament to the day's virginity: the dark patches left behind by Neil's boots were the first of such markings. Then, in the distance, a dark hooded figure floated up out of the white fog. It was moving in Neil's direction. The backbone of the college was that of a Benedictine order. Christian monks had founded this Catholic college in the late 1800s and still served as a continuing presence. Neil wasn't in the mood to interact with anyone right now, especially anything holy. But, like two ships passing in a vast empty ocean, the possibility of not acknowledging one another would besmirch the human condition. He lifted his head and put on the best face he could manage, and readied himself to signal the oncoming figure whose eyes were only now beginning to appear from beneath the dark hood.

Neil was just opening his mouth to say good morning, but stopped himself at the recognition of a familiar memory.

"Father Matthews." Neil spoke with a 'surprised to see you' inflection.

182

The man behind the hood appeared much older than what Neil had actually remembered. The man held a wooden rosary clasped around frail hands that trembled slightly.

"Good morning!" Neil said.

"Good morning," came back the response from the man who blankly stared at Neil.

"I used to go to school here. I'm N -"

"Neil, yes, Neil, the painter, of course. How are you son?" The robed man spoke with a slight Irish accent.

"Fine."

"Still have your painting hanging in the rectory. Sorry. Took me a minute to recognize you, mind's not what it used to be," he laughed. "How have you been?"

"Good, Father."

"What brings you here, so early in the morning?"

"I'm just visiting, came in last night - heading out this morning."

"Oh, I see. Would you like to join me for a cup of tea, I'm on my way to prepare for service, do you have time?"

"Sure, I mean if you have the time, I don't want to impose - so early and-"

"Not t'all. Pleenty of time before Mass, would love the company."

The two walked together through the fog towards the small rectory adjacent a large Catholic church.

"So, what is it that you've been up to, son? Painting still - I hope."

"Well, not so much anymore." Neil hadn't picked up a brush in years, and it hurt to hear himself admit it. Back in California, no one knew of his interest in painting. It was a part of his life he hid.

Time had not paused or faltered since last he saw Father Matthews and it amazed Neil to see how fragile and aged this man had become. His steps were small, slow, and deliberate. There was a slight bend to his upper back, and his entire body seemed to have shrunk in size. No one eludes time, and Neil wondered at the changes in himself.

Father Matthews pushed opened the thick oak door to the rectory and both men entered. The inside was dark and smelled of frankincense. It was just as Neil had remembered: An office with thick burgundy colored carpet, the enormous desk, bookcases, and quiet, always quiet as though the office wasn't inside a building at all, but instead, set deep inside a cave. The only sound was a ticking grandfather clock with a rotating face painted with the moon, stars and sun. The ticking was something Neil had forgotten and it reminded him of his home in Connecticut. It was like flipping through an old yearbook, long forgotten and pulled from a dusty attic. To his right, was a bookshelf containing thick, leather bound volumes, and hanging from the wall behind the desk was a painted portrait of a Benedictine monk. The desk, with its ornately carved legs and worn, but sturdy mahogany top, looked older than the age of these two men combined. On the top of the desk were books, pens, paperclips and piles of paperwork held down by several paperweights (including a glass snow globe with a happy monk inside Mont Saint-Michel). One of the books lay upside down, pages spread, marking the spot the reader had left off. The entire office was small, cluttered as though too many things were trying to fit into too small a space, but at the same time, comfortable like a warm familiar blanket. On top of a small cabinet, behind the desk, was an electric hotplate with an empty glass kettle and mismatched ceramic cups.

"Earl Grey or Orange Peakoe?" Father Matthews asked, shuffling slowly behind the desk.

"Earl Grey, thanks," Neil replied.

Father Matthew's hand shook as he reached for the glass pot. Neil thought of offering help, but wasn't sure how the gesture might be interpreted, so held back.

"Go ahead, and have a seat if you'd like - this will only take a minute," said Father Matthews.

Neil studied his options; there were two small English country, 'tea for two' type chairs that faced one another and a thick rich leather armchair with small brass tacks which faced the desk. He sunk down in the armchair and looked over the walls.

"I'll be damned -"

"Not if I can help it," Father Matthews quickly responded with exaggerated concern.

Neil laughed, and although there was no need for an apology, he offered one just the same, "Sorry, Father. I only meant, I can't believe you still have my painting hanging here."

Father Matthews had been the highest bidder of Neil's painting at a silent auction, which was traditionally held each year in the school's gymnasium. It was how the two had met. The painting was based on the story of Icarus; in it a saddened sun watches as the boy's waxed wings melt. The dripping wax, painted as drops of blood, fall into sinister waves of a dark ocean that laps at each falling drop.

"What's that? Not believing me then when I told you it was here in my office, 'tis a shame casting doubt on a man of the cloth, and here I am making ya tea. Oh, how you hurt me boy - me sensibilities, lad." Father Matthews feebly made his way to a small bathroom, pulled a string, which turned on a bare light bulb that hung from the ceiling and began filling the kettle with water from the sink. "You wouldn't believe the number of people who comment on that painting, Neil, some right where you're sitting now, you wouldn't believe."

Neil viewed the painting as a painful reminder. As he looked at the painting his mind jetted back to his teacher, the airy sunlit studio, the smell of paint, the feel of a brush against canvas, the excitement of creating, and Patricia. He liked the painting, and felt proud and, as he sat in the armchair, he could feel the possibility of hope begin to rise inside him. But, he quickly punched it back down. Hope was a lie. It couldn't compete and sustain him. The lie of an artist; to live in an indifferent caustic world of commerce, and cold transactions that loom larger as a sterilization spreads - a place where dreams are reserved for children and dismissed under the hard soles of a rational workforce.

The kettle came to a boil and the tea prepared. Neil looked at Father Matthews and felt ashamed and a sense of guilt for the act he committed out in the desert. He wanted nothing more than to confess....or run, run from the confines of this office past himself, his painting, and the desert. He needed to confess to Father Matthews. If he couldn't forgive himself, perhaps God could.

'Tell him, go on tell him about the dead body, you little liar,' The Instructor prodded, 'go on, tell him!'

Instead, Neil sank with his tea bag into the depths of his cup. More than anything, he wanted Father Matthews not to ask him anything remotely personal, not now, not with how he felt about his life, this trip and himself.

'Please, don't ask me about what I do for a living, or the crappy little apartment I live in, or anything else about painting,' Neil prayed into his cup.

'Oh what have you done with your life today, what have you done with your life I say?'

Something, perhaps it was because of his age or his wisdom, compassion or maybe it was just plain luck that the questions Neil dreaded and feared most hearing from the lips of Father Matthews never were asked. Instead, what he offered most was silence and tidbits about his trip to Ireland he'd taken over the summer.

Neil sat and watched as the old man dilly-dallied around, moving papers, books, and notes on the desk in search of something he either had prepared, or had just thought of to use for this morning's service. Almost all of Father Matthew's sermons were from inspired thoughts extrapolated from small events or occurrences he had encountered that day, that morning, or afternoon. He wasn't one to follow a formatted script written and tailored by others. With the exception of Bible readings, nothing he spoke from the pulpit was scripted by others, but, instead, was born from the introspective life of a devoutly religious man. This method often raised eyebrows among fellow clergymen, who regarded Father Matthews as a slightly dangerous renegade, a loose canon. But, he paid little heed to them or the board of lawyers the college had hired whose job was to set the politically correct rules of do's and don'ts when it came to delivering church doctrine. The words he spoke were not stale and safe, but wild and true. And, because of that, there were some who thought he had lost part of his mind, as the sermons he delivered were often viewed with confusion - a senseless series of ramblings, with no connection to anything... like the Toa, until in a clear state, one could see purpose and meaning in what had been spoken. It was as if he took each listener by the hand and led them on a walk through a wild, fantastical garden pruned by God.

The time between Neil and Father Matthews was almost up, the service would begin in a few minutes. Father Matthews now stood in front of an opened small closet that held a variety of vestments.

"You know, I'll be retiring at the end of this year," he said while draping a wide ornate scarf around his neck and over his shoulders.

"Congratulations, Father. It's been a long time for you here at the college?"

"Long indeed - and wonderful, but things change and change.....change, is what makes life interesting."

"Life is full of change, that's for sure," Neil affirmed.

"Tis.'tis. As a favor to me, will you do me the honor and stay for the morning service?"

Neil had wanted to get on his way this morning, but would make this exception.

"I will, Father."

"As I have an appointment following the service, I'll have to say my goodbyes to you now," Father Matthews said. He shook Neil's hand, and with a happy secret glint, added, "God Bless you, my child. I'll see you again."

Neil exited the office, allowing Father Matthews to make the last few preparations in private. Neil then filed into the church along with a handful of students (far too few, he thought given the size of the church). Although it was a requirement for all students to attend daily Mass -whether a morning, afternoon or evening service, most chose the evening service. He found a

187

middle pew, bent one knee, crossed himself and took a seat. Two alter boys dressed in white gowns went about lighting candles and preparing the altar. Within a couple of minutes, Father Matthews entered. The congregation silently rose. The vows were said and the Mass proceeded: The Catholic creed recited, hymns sung (half heartedly by most) and a reading of Philippians 4:6-9. Father Matthews, like a chiseled marble figure sat so still and silent in a chair, it was as if he had melded with the stone bricks and pillars and become part of the church. When it came time for the sermon he rose slowly and carefully and made his way to the pulpit.

His face, unlike what Neil had seen in the office, held a perplexing combination of both a serious countenance and a quiet confidence. His hands shook no more. He looked out into the church pews as though he were slowly counting souls or the sins that each parishioner had committed. He took his time, and stood so long in silence that it seemed as if he'd forgotten the words, which he had prepared. It appeared he would go on like this forever and an uneasiness fell upon the parishioners, then, suddenly, like a window slamming shut in the middle of the night, his voice broke clear and loud, his words reverberating off the church walls.

"We find there is a darkness marching. And suffering throughout the world screams, "Christ!" louder than ever. Love screams out in everything. The agony in the universal garden. The more persecution, the more Christ is alive. Those who would kill him are confounded amid the proliferation of his will. The desert of Saint John the Baptisit is in our modern despair and the cacophony of noise, pleasure seeking and materialism. His church has moved into the world at last. The monasteries, seminaries, parochial schools, societies, religious orders have done their work and launched a million missiles of evolutionary destiny. The song goes on. A hymn of praise sung or screamed at the void. Everything is closing the circle within which love is defined as the enigmatic zero; the infinite hole in the donut. We see but don't see. And the lion sleeps tonight; blind and crying like the tears of Merton.

And so I say, there is a darkness marching..... from the East upon the Earth and from places unseen. To deny this is to deny the very purpose of God. This darkness has been and may be forever, flowing and ebbing with the infinite ticking of time. The clock ticks again and we find the tide is high and the drums of this marching darkness grow louder. This darkness, fed by the cynical fires burning in the doubting hearts of men, comes with many masks. It comes as deceit, greed - thirsting, not for righteousness, but instead bent on satisfying the hungry ego, which defiles not only the self, but all of mankind - trickling into our hearts. We read of war, rumors of war and the tragedies they incur. And what of it? A crusade appears, I say again, a crusade. The shameless, empty, hollow goals perpetuated by a weakened, deprived, infantile soul. To be steadfast in the principles of God's words and Christ's works is often obscured by senseless manifestations of our modern society. We are born, we live, we die, and we think why, for what purpose, for what end! Our mortal lives are temporary, but our choices eternal. What fate do you choose? And what kind of fight are you willing to bring to those who jeopardize that choice? What is it then, we do to shut tight this darkness against our hearts and souls? We are in the midst of a crusade. Life, simply a test, a testament to mine, our, YOUR values, a test of your character, a test of our dedication to an eternal God. It is our choice then, nay, our duty, to fight against any evil, darkness that opposes that test."

Here he took a pause as though he were allowing his words to settle to the very marrow of each person who had heard his message. He placed both hands firmly on each side of the pulpit.

"But how, how? That is the question I pose to you this morning. How do we combat this Evil? Do we band together and form an enormous army of men, women and children to take up arms and fight an enemy that has too many names, faces and invisible places to hide, or do we fight by the seemingly small, unseen, individual choices we make on a daily basis. Afterall, what is our life, except choices. We battle darkness by radiating light - the light of optimism, the light of love over anger, the light of inspiration over decadence, the light of fortitude over lethargy,

189

the light of will over indifference, the light of humility over hubris. God has given us all the power and ability to triumph over evil, but it is our choice whether or not we use what God has provided. Again, I ask how do we overcome darkness, evil? The answer; to take the gifts of and from God, our heavenly father and use them. And, by deeply utilizing the gifts of God, we shine all the power and light of God, shed the darkness and we, ourselves, move closer still to touching the very hand of God. It is in our words, faith and actions that we profess our connection to Christ, to God. Whatever gift The Almighty has given you, use it then to dispel this darkness. The gift you have, be it a gift of song, bricklaying or poetry, or swimming or mathematics, or...painting. Use *these* gifts for the betterment of all. This is our duty in the name and kingdom of God. Prepare the way for the Lord. On this we pray."

Father Matthews stepped down from the pulpit and returned to his seat. After the Eucharist, Neil rode back to his campsite, collected his things and got back on the road.

9

Neil rode north and crossed into Virginia. A thunderous group of bikers, leathered and tattooed, passed him and gave him the biker's nod. He thought of Bill, hoped he was okay and sent him a silent prayer. He stopped in the town of Danville and grabbed a hot breakfast, fueled up on coffee, filled his bike, checked his oil, used the restroom and was off again. He continued moving north. It was getting colder with each passing mile. The sun held less warmth and clouds covered much of the sky, shadowing the land in a bland, ashen colored blanket. The air, crisp and Fall like, was tolerable when he was stopped, but any speed above forty miles an hour and a cold wind with an icy edge began cutting at him. In Lynchburg, he changed into a thermal top and layered that with two tee shirts underneath his leather jacket. His bike benefited from the colder temperature, running smoother, with the cold air being sucked between the cylinder fins and cooling the hot engine oil. He patted the side of his fuel tank like a faithful horse.

He was now following the outline of the Blue Ridge Mountains, which rose up on his left - gorgeous, orange, yellow, and red foliage. A change was occurring, not only in the weather and topography, but also, in how he felt about this trip. He was closer to his goal, his destination and, was glad he had made the journey, but still wished for it to be over.

'Not gonna make it,' The Instructor's imitation of George Bush senior rocked inside his head, 'read my lips, son- not gonna make it.'

He crossed the Potomac River and stopped for lunch in Frederick, Maryland. He had succeeded thus far in avoiding the larger cities that lined the east coast such as D.C., Baltimore, and Philadelphia, but after examining his road map again, he recognized the need to start eastward through the more densely populated areas.

He missed the warmth the West had provided and wanted nothing more than to make New York and get out of this cold. It was hard to imagine the same sun that blazed above him only days before in the Western sky was the same one that now did little more than provide light, and soon, that would be gone too. The warmer temperature wasn't the only difference. The West seemed to have a certain looseness and freedom that the East lacked; here it felt tight and restricted, not only were the roads smaller, more narrow and confined, but the people, too, seemed different. There were hard cars with hard people dressed in practical clothes that passed him by, and in their eyes was something distant or.... impersonal. Perhaps it was a product of the land, cold and austere. He thought of the Puritan founding fathers, the Liberty Bell, Ben Franklin, Independence Hall and the colonies.

Off the highway a great parking lot with massive stadium lighting lit a shopping mall.

'There's your new colonies,' Neil thought, 'so many of them too.' All across the country they had dotted his route. Unlike the colonies of old, these newer ones originated, not from a religious or political nature, but from a corporate bottom line. They were spread out exactly the same way, duplicating like a virus in a Petri dish, serving as incubation outposts ready to destroy diversity. These colonies had familiar names, big box franchises. Sure, they made things convenient with one stop shopping under one roof, 'but at what cost?' Neil had wondered. He had thought about this on the longer stretches when he had time to think. 'And, not only with commerce, the things we buy,' but 'also with the information we receive; radio stations, the internet, newspapers, television conglomerates and film studios.' The end result would be to colonize us all into sameness supplied from a feeding tube filled with a homogenized paste squeezed by consumerism.

Consumerism, production, labor and commerce all had a deep history here in Pennsylvania. Even before it became a colony, Pennsylvania had been home to indian tribes - The Shawnee, Iroquois, Huron, and Lenape, all trading furs with the Europeans. There were the Swedes and Dutch laying claim to this land in order to expand power, control and increase trade revenue. Then in 1681, as means of paying a large monetary debt owed, King Charles II of England gave the land to William Penn.

After the American revolution, Pennsylvania and the rest of the United States were composed mostly of independent, self employed farmers and artisans; people, who grew their own crops, and lived on farms where they raised sheep, cattle, pigs and chickens. But, as early as 1791, a crucial debate raged as to what economic sysytem the United States would follow. Two opposing views reigned. One of the views, expressed by Secretary of treasury, Alexander Hamilton, was that this newly found country should follow the example of England and become an Industrial nation. The other view, held by Secretary of State, Thomas Jefferson was that these United States should remain an agricultural society.

Hamilton wanted the United States to be a country that was able to mass-produce goods and, therefore, become completely independent from any other country.

Jefferson had been to England and formed his opinion that the United States should be agriculturally based, in part, because of the abhorrent work and environmental conditions he saw when visiting England.

Hamilton's view won out. The United States would become an Industrial based society. And, so it began, spreading from the fastidious East to the virgin territory of the West - the Cotton Gin in 1793, poor factory girls in Lowell Massachusetts run ragged by the Merrimack Manufacturing Company, the steam engine, the sewing machine, the telegraph, Robert Fulton's steamboats, the telephone, electricity, Edison Central power plant, light bulbs turning night into day defying natural cycles of time, mass

193

production, The model T, roads, expansion, exploitation, mining, shipping, export, import, migration to cities, more factories, oil, steel, coal, building, expanding, processing plants, skyscrapers, neon, corporations, strikes, insurance companies, textiles, mutual funds, commerce, and the gerbils jumping, always jumping. It was an industrial age when commerce would ride over the broken backs and petty souls of ordinary men. John D. Rockefeller and Andrew Carnegie were there to shake and rattle the gerbil cages in an age of naked greed. And then in 1859 oil was struck in the same state Neil was now traversing and Rockefeller established a refinery to form Standard Oil Trust. Andrew Carnegie, first making money on the railroad, formed Carnegie Steel Company and in 1892 workers went on strike in Homestead, Pennsylvania. Industrial age, truckers, Unions, smokestacks, iron ore, strikes, broken people, sulfur, the bitterness of unemployment imbedded deep in haggard hardened lined faces. It was the beginning of sterilization and some of the gerbils did not go easily into their cages.

But what it was all about, really about and what controlled everything, of course, was oil. It was all about oil and this land, this very land Neil was traveling through, was the land where the infantile stages of sterilization had first sprouted and taken root. Everything had been about oil every since its discovery in Pennsylvania back in 1859 in the town of Titusville by a man named Colonel Edwin Drake. The entire world was controlled - neither by politicians nor by the common man - but by one word and one word alone - oil. Even back in the early days, so powerful was this commodity that President Calvin Coolidge had said,

"It is even probable that the supremacy of nations may be determined by the possession of available petroleum and its products."

Up until the discovery of oil the primary fuel in the United States had been whale oil and coal. After the discovery men from all over flocked to Pennsylvania in droves reminiscent of the ragtag minions who had migrated to California fourteen years earlier during the gold rush. They wanted to strike it rich. Oil was America's new gold parceled out, not in ounces or pounds, but in barrels consisting of forty-two U.S. gallons. And one man would monopolize it all. He emerged among many, but he, and he alone, would seize control of this gushing liquid. His name was John D. Rockefeller - And the name of his conglomerate enterprise? Standard Oil.

Just a few short years after its discovery, oil had become a substance America could not do without. The Western world had begun its love affair and addiction to oil and Rockefeller was there to supply this need. It wasn't long before he had expanded his control by purchasing refineries, giving him the powerful advantage to refine the crude oil himself rather than paying someone else to do it. The next step in killing off any competitors would come in secret backroom deals, where he was able to convince the railroad owners to give special rebates on the transportation of his oil and his oil *only*. Without transportation, oil, no matter how potentially valuable or how much of it was produced, would go nowhere, do nothing and become useless. His competitors simply couldn't compete and, over time, sold their interests to Rockefeller - his influence and power growing larger and larger with each purchase he made. By the late 1800's, and, again in secret deals, he had reached overseas and aboard to make Standard Oil one of the richest companies in the world. And, the consumption of oil only grew. By the end of the ninetieth century the combustion engine was widespread and growing with no end in sight. Even The United States Navy in 1904 decided to convert all naval ships from coal to oil. And the rest of the U.S. armed forces soon followed suit. It now meant oil had become a commodity of National interest upon which our sovereignty as a nation depended and the United States would stop at nothing to acquire it. It also meant that Rockefeller was becoming invincible. Oil production was no longer an independent enterprise comprised of a few ragtag men looking to strike it rich. As with Rockefeller, it was organized, deliberate and calculating with the intent to build profit and reap power. Unlike other commodities in a fair market, oil was not a luxury, but a necessity. Everything the country did, was dependent on oil; heating homes, lubricating machinery, running automobiles and paving roads. Everything was in some way or another connected to oil. And, if controlled by one person or just one company, with no competition, the price set for such a commodity would be absolute, irrespective of the principles that govern the classic economic supply and demand model. It would be the same as if one person controlled the very air needed to breathe and turned it into a commodity for sale. By the early 1900's Rockefeller's power had superseded that of the United States government and there seemed no limit to his monopoly and power. But, with such control and virtually no competition, Rockefeller became a very unpopular man, not only with a government that felt threatened, but also among the public who felt he had to be challenged. That challenge came in 1890 by a Republican senator named, John Sherman who grabbed hold of the anti-trust sentiment that had been building by the public and others against Rockefeller and Standard Oil. He proposed a bill named, the anti-trust act designed to make it unlawful to form a trust or conspiracy and for anyone that attempts to monopolize trade or commerce among states or nations. Standard oil was challenged in court. After several years of contests, it led to a United States Supreme Court decision in 1911 that upheld the Anti-trust law and forced the break up of Standard Oil.

Eventually, what developed and materialized out of the court's decision to break up Standard Oil would become known as the Seven Sisters; seven corporations worldwide that controlled virtually all oil production: Exxon, Shell, British Petroleum(BP), Gulf, Texaco, Mobil and Chevron, and all attached with names like Mellon, Rockefeller, Archbold, Moffets, Teagles, Samuel, D'Arcy and Deterding. These men - and other men like them in the oil business - controlled everything. They controlled a product that the world could no longer function without, and they knew it. Everything and anything from plastic buttons, keyboards, bicycle tires, vinyl upholstery, plastic wrap, fertilizer, cosmetics was and is, a product of oil. Everything known to sustain life in a modern world, makes the world go round - from the freight trains and 18 wheelers that move containers of goods

196

across the country to cargo ships and jetliners that move over and across vast oceans is dependent upon oil.

Not long after Standard Oil had broken up and the seven sisters had formed, oil had become an international game with high stakes in places like Russia, Mexico, Venezuela, The Ottoman empire, and central Asia. And both oil companies and governments wanted a share; they were in a bitter battle to own this commodity that controlled all world commerce. Oil was power. To quell such turmoil a meeting was called to divide the world into oil territories, fix pricing and stabilize the market.

Mobsters in a Brooklyn basement would have nothing on the seven sisters when they met in secret to carve up world oil. But, in lieu of a basement in Brooklyn, the meeting took place in the highlands of Scotland at the Achnacarry Castle where the bosses worked out a deal, to not only end fluctuated prices and fix pricing, but also, seal a deal among the seven sisters to divide markets and limit production and supply. They named it the "As is" policy. Despite the anti-trust law, the meeting was to put Rockefeller in a league of other men who would follow in his footsteps: Bill Gates, George Soros, Warren Buffet, the Koch brothers, Carlos Slim and Vladimir Putin.

As Neil headed into the very heart of Pennsylvania, the sky darkened and night approached. The brilliant fall foliage now took on sinister tones. Shadows lengthened and the sunlight disappeared, and color faded. The moon inched higher and hung above the treetops. Neil's entire being vibrated like a string tuned to the local history, which shaped the air around him. This was Ichabod Crane country, galloping hoofs deep in the dark hills that surrounded him. Thoughts of hayrides, apple orchids, and hot buttered rum helped little in lifting his spirits, everything felt ghoulish.

Clouds rolled in and it began to drizzle, Neil pushed on. He felt tired, disgusted and his mood had changed considerably since earlier in the day. He had been riding steady, continuously for over eight hours, without his usual breaks and he felt shaky, exhausted, causing lapses in his concentration, which manifested itself in second guessed images of road signs and traffic movement. It was a dangerous time to be driving; porous cracks in the pavement held thin layers of water, which had lifted oil to the surface. Darkness now fell and lights from the oncoming cars appeared as miniature searchlights diffracted through the highway night, snatching and highlighting bits of falling rain. Frustration fueled his desire to move closer to the finish line of this pointless trip. The motorcycle felt cumbersome, metal on metal, random pieces bolted together forming one bulky mass. Steamy side passenger windows of passing cars taunted him, and only served to heighten his awareness of his pathetic situation. Judgment and ridicule peered from the warm protected interiors. The Instructor sat amongst them,

"You're ridiculous - look at you. How old are you? Ha, like a teenager, no money, and immature decisions. The only fool within a five hundred mile radius stupid enough to be riding a motorcycle in these conditions. Motorcycle season is over, jackass!- you're pathetic, everyone is laughing at you." And then, of course, 'Oh what have you done with your life today, what have you done with your life I say?'

Neil tried washing this voice from his mind, but it was difficult. He, again, feared for his mental stability, prompting him to wonder if mental illness ran in his family. Maybe his parents hadn't told him about it as a means of protecting him from that terrible truth, or perhaps they were simply unaware of this defective gene. He fought within himself to ward off such negative ideas, but it was of little use. He rode at a steady slow, cautious pace keeping well below the posted speed limit. Still, the rain pelted his body and hands, striking his bare skin like tiny pinprick arrows. Cars swished by in the fast lane, throwing up a dirty mist. It was getting dangerous. He needed to pull over, get his bearings, and figure out where to stop for the night. He had traveled far and, with his hands numb and clothes soaked, he longed for a hot shower and soft bed. Through his dirty, water streaked goggles an exit ramp wavered up ahead. He took the exit and followed its dark path down to where it met a desolate secondary road. Here, he came to a stop and allowed the bike to idle while he studied his options to his left and right. Straddling the motorcycle, he felt the heaviness from his wet jeans that clung to his thighs and the pelting raindrops that popped against his helmet. His raw hands rested on the wet, dead rubber handgrips. He found it difficult to make a decision. His options looked rather bleak; in both directions the road was wooded, dark and held no clues as to where they led. Each was equally dismal. There was another option, however, and that was to get back on the highway.

'No way in hell,' he said to himself.

Instead, he took a gamble and turned right. His headlight meekly lit a path of a rolling, then slightly twisting road. The rain fell hard, but he hadn't much choice and so, pushed forward still. Soon small plain houses dotted the roadside. A sad matter of fact road sign leaned from a hillside that announced he was entering the township of East Hanover. Soon after, he accelerated to the top of a hill and began to ride quickly down the other side. He looked ahead and could see there was a four-way intersection at the bottom of the hill and so; he began to make preparations to stop. He tapped the back brake with his foot and his right hand reached for the front brake. The weariness of the day had taken its toll. There was confusion with this front brake, instead of pulling it in, Neil's hand slipped on the throttle causing the motorcycle to lurch forward at a fantastic speed. His left hand, numb from the cold rain, fumbled for the clutch, hesitated and pulled ineffectively. It was all too late, too fast. He wouldn't make the stop sign. Panic filled his chest and arms, he stomped his right boot down hard on the metal peg of the back brake, his boot was angled and slipped and he felt the peg tear into his leg. All happened in an instant - the handle bars turned hard to the left, he was off the bike tumbling, turning, then sliding, legs out, rolling then jolted upright into an almost seated position and watched on the hard wet road, as the riderless motorcycle, a headless horseman continued at an even faster pace, on its side at first, scraping, bits, things torn away, hitting a curbside, bouncing up striking a metal blue postal box, twirling gas tank, clothes, oil, noise and then, and then silence - nothing. The remaining hulk of machinery had come to rest on the other side of the curb in a flat stretch of grass; a thoroughbred down on a desolate track with empty stands, an absence of cheers, bets and bifocals. Neil sat in the middle of the dark, wet road. There was no light, save for a few street lamps at the bottom of the hill. The rain fell, but there was nothing, no sound, no feeling, nothing.

It was thirty, maybe even forty seconds later when a tip tip tap tip began to trickle into Neil's consciousness. Raindrops had continued to fall on his helmet.

"My helmet..." Neil placed his right palm on top of the round slick surface, "Thank God, my helmet."

In a numb, automated state, Neil pushed himself up from the road and stood in the empty darkness. The precarious nature of his situation; a dark road on a dark night, with diminished visibility, caused him to realize this, perhaps, wasn't the best place to be standing should a car come roaring over the hill. He walked to the roadside and began trudging slowly down the hill to examine what remained of his motorcycle. His left hand was bleeding. Exactly how that had happened he wasn't sure, but it bothered him little. He unsnapped his helmet and, taking it off his head, noticed his plastic eyewear had disappeared, thrown from the impact, or maybe he had already taken them off back in the road.

He walked through the intersection to where his motorcycle had hit the curb and been thrown into the air. The postal box leaned oddly to one side, dented and reshaped from the motorcycle's impact. Neil, without thought, mechanically began picking up articles of clothing: a few tee shirts, socks, a single shoe, a bungee cord, a bathroom kit, a metal spoon. Some of these were in the road, but across the intersection and up the hill in the direction he had come, was one of his saddlebags. The other saddlebag, which had also separated from the bike, lay off to his right, amazingly, still in one piece and unopened. More still, he saw parts of the motorcycle itself, strewn in a wide, but directed path; the horn, a carburetor, a chunk of a cylinder fin, a mirror, the battery side cover, a clear piece of plastic. He then walked to the hulk of motorcycle and stood over it. The trusty frame that had carried him so far looked awkward and unfamiliar, several spokes to the front wheel were bent or missing, and the cracked crankcase seeped oil and formed a puddle around the mangled mess like a pool of blood. He didn't know what to think.

"You okay?" something, somewhere spoke.

"You okay?" the voice repeated.

Neil turned from the wreck and stood facing a short, bald, Asian man, eyes squinting from the rain that fell and dripped on his head and face. He wore a *Members Only* jacket and his lips threw bits of rain as he spoke,

"I see whole thing, you okay?" he again asked, his figure outlined, book cased between two headlights from a white van that was parked behind him with engine idling, "Accident happen, but okay?"

"Yeah, yeah, I'm okay," Neil answered.

"Maybe not, your hand bleed."

"It's okay, I'm alright," Neil absently replied, then began gathering more of his strewn items, collecting them into a pile. Without another word, the man did the same until there were two piles. Both men, completely soaked from the falling rain, now stood between the piles.

"Thanks," Neil yelled to the man through the rain.

The man looked at Neil and thumbed towards the van with its steaming tailpipe, and slapping windshield wipers.

"What about all this stuff?" Neil added.

"Yeah yeah stuff too," the little man immediately shot back with an abundance of energy and, strangely enough, a slight smile too.

Neil ran his fingers through his wet hair and, looking at the piles seemed to be tallying the result of what had just happened,

"Jesus Christ. Man..." he muttered and then in a louder voice he added to no one in particular, "I don't know, know what the hell to do."

The man provided an answer where none was really expected, "Put things in van, you get dry, things work out." He then trotted over to the van, got in, and backed it up to the two piles.

201

He then jumped down from the drivers seat (which seemed an awfully long way for a man of his stature) and went to the back of the van and opened the two doors. After rearranging some things in the van, both he and Neil began carrying items from the rain soaked piles to the back of the van. For the very last item, the motorcycle frame and parts connected to it, the man brought out two planks of wood, leaning them against the edge of the van's back floor to provide a makeshift ramp, whereupon, the two of them pushed and pulled the heavy wreck into the van. With everything now in the van, the little man shut the back doors. Both he and Neil got in the front.

The van had the smell of brand new rubber and vinyl mixed with a slight hint of fresh cut wood and grass. The van was extra long-the kind used to transport school teams, prison inmates or state workers, except the rows of seats in back had been removed to make room for shovels, spades, a few bags of woodchips, fertilizer, and now, Neil's wreck. Lights of a high-tech instrument panel glowed brightly, displaying colors of blue indigo, red, orange and green. Neil shook out his wet hair and, grabbing his left wrist with his right hand, spread his left hand on his knee and examined it. The flowing blood had slowed and he could see bits of gravel that clung to the wound. He took his bandanna and wiped away blood and gravel. The exposed wound appeared to be nothing more than a severe case of road rash with a small gash between his pinky and ring finger. For the first time all night he felt lucky. He was pretty damn lucky, indeed, to have walked away with such relatively minor injuries. Nothing seemed to be broken. He tried bending his outstretched pinky, but couldn't - it was then he noticed there was a slight deformation to it. "Screw it," he muttered to himself. He knew there was nothing to be done about it now and so let it go as an afterthought.

With his feet barely touching the pedals, the little man, adjusted the wipers, threw the van into drive and leaned into the bleary night. The van shot up the hill to where Neil had crashed and popped out the other side and began retracing the route Neil had taken from the highway.

"Where you go now?" the man asked, keeping his eyes on the wet road ahead. "Friend home, your home?"

Neil sat staring numbly out at the, 'objects may be closer than they appear' warning on the passenger side mirror and offered a half hearted answer,

"No. No friend home, house. No friend. I'm from California, my home in California."

"Ohhhh -jeees, louiise, you long way, California very very far. You come long way," The man's cheeks beamed.

"Yeah, long way."

"You, you want hospital?"

Neil paused, he hated hospitals, and used them only as a last resort, but his finger was beginning to throb with pain. He wasn't a masochist.

"How far is the hospital?" he asked

"Maybe thirteen miles from here." Then sensing Neil's reluctance the man added, "You think hospital for hand?"

"No. yes, my finger -my finger, actually," Neil held up his left hand.

The man took it in with a quick glance then returned to the road, "Finger no problem, no other problem wiff you?"

"No."

"Okay we take care of finger, anything else, poowice?"

Neil was caught off guard by the quick dismissal of his finger but somehow trusted this man's strong opinion, and, so, focused on the shift in subject of the police. The whole idea of police entering his life right now was out of the question, but, on the other hand, not to file a report and run from the scene of this accident might somehow escalate things. He didn't want to give the police any excuse to track him down and trace his steps back to the incident in the desert. Besides, he knew his insurance company would need a report in order for him to file a claim. "Yes, police station. I need to file a report,"

"Okay," the man said then fell silent and seemed finished with questions for a while.

Neil slumped down in his seat and allowed the sad stark passing night to wash over him. Neither men talked.

The jostling of a speed bump in the police station parking lot pushed Neil to his present circumstances. He must have fallen asleep or passed out.

"I wait here, you go inside," The Asian man said as he pulled the van into an empty parking space. Then looking at Neil's left hand said, "Back in place?"

Neil's finger hurt, and the pain was beginning to pulse up through his wrist and forearm. "You mean my finger, I don't understand?"

"Back in place," the man repeated in a loud almost harsh tone. "Give me hand, look out there!" he urgently pointed to something outside Neil's side window.

Neil quickly turned and searched to find what he had pointed at - it happened in the space of a breath; the man had taken Neil's left hand and snapped the dislocated finger back into place, an exclamation had risen in his throat, but hadn't time to form on Neil's vocal chords. The pain was gone. Neil took his hand back with a mixture of insult, violation, gratitude and amazement. He still hadn't settled on one by the time he opened the passenger door and made for the police station entrance.

Now, his heart pounded and he felt slightly dizzy as he thought of the dead man in the desert. "A report here matching your description........" His fingers and stomach began to tingle with anguished anticipation of someone inside this station reciting this line to him. He thought of turning around and getting back into the van, but it would only add to their suspicion; there had to be surveillance cameras around here somewhere, somehow recording his every move. He'd have to go through with this now. Like a schoolboy, who whistles to compensate for having just stolen candy, Neil tried his best to display an air of innocence and tried, too, to remember exactly what that meant he should do in order to convey such a thing. His movements felt awkward, disconnected from himself and forced like some sort of remote controlled mechanical dummy.

When Neil walked into the station, anything he had ever done wrong or thought of doing wrong in his life flushed through his guilt ridden body. In the small hallway, which led to the front desk, were display cases lining the walls. Inside the cases were a wide assortment of metals, ribbons, plaques and rigid formatted department store pictures of uniformed police officers posed with a blue background and an American flag draped in the corner. Neil checked his eyes; for a second or two he thought he saw The Instructor smiling and even waving dressed as one of the men pictured.

Everything inside the building felt tight, institutional and reeked of conformity. There was no room for monkey business here. Under the stale florescent lights and with a matter of fact, almost sleepy, passive protocol, the desk sergeant filed the report. Neil got the feeling that had he entered the station completely naked with an arrow up his ass and possum hair stuck in his teeth, the reaction from the sergeant would've been the same.

"Name?"

"Neil Adams, sir."

"Address?"

"121 Cherry Ave, Long Beach, California"

Here the sergeant actually looked up from the paperwork, "What are you doing out here from California?"

'Yeah, what are you doing out here from California?' The Instructor asked, 'gonna tell him about the dead -'

Neil held on as best he could, "I'm on my way to New York, to visit, friends and family there."

"Hell of a time to be on a motorcycle."

"I know, it's just that I don't have alot of money and.." The man was peering hard at Neil, who was beginning to feel his throat tighten and conviction slip. "and well, it's the least expensive way I had of getting here, there, sir."

'Sir sir sir - like a Maitre d' looking to get greased on a Friday night - you blabbering idiot! Probably matching your face to a wanted poster they have hanging in the back.'

"Riding a motorcycle on a night like this. You in a hurry to get somewhere?"

"No, sir"- there it was again, 'sir'. Neil let out a small laugh, "Naw, I'm just trying to make decent time, I was actually looking for a place to spend the night when I got in this accident."

"You have anything to drink tonight?"

"No."

"Any witnesses?"

"Sure, he's outside in a van with my things, and my motorcycle, what remains of it, anyway."

"Wait right here." The man turned his back and went through a locked door that had to be buzzed open.

The Instructor cherished the alone time, 'You're so screwed now, and you deserve what you get.'

Neil heard a low murmur of voices from behind the locked door. One was the sergeant, the other was that of an unseen woman. The door buzzed again and the sergeant returned with a clipboard and a small Styrofoam cup of coffee. He handed Neil the clipboard and took a sip from the cup,

"Here, I need you to fill out this form with all your information and I'll need to see your drivers license and registration."

Neil did as he was told, heading out to the van to grab his registration where the Asian man still sat.

"Here already, check things."

Neil just smiled and brushed off this nonsensical statement - he didn't have time for it- not now. He went back into the station and finished the form. With the form completed, he handed the clipboard back to the sergeant, who sat typing behind the desk at a computer keyboard. The sergeant rose and looked over the information and seemingly satisfied with the results, said, "Okay then."

"Is that it, can I leave now?" Neil asked. "I mean, what about the postal box and witness?"

"You'll be held responsible for the box – USPS will file a claim, which your insurance will most likely cover, and I have your information here. We already sent someone out to take a look at your motorcycle while you were inside here. You still need to call to confirm the witness' name and contact information. Take this copy." He tore the top sheet from the form and handed it to Neil.

"Thank you, sergeant, sir."

He left feeling as if he'd just received clemency; liberation blew through his body and, with the report folded in his hand, he returned to the van happy and free.

"Violent man, die violent death," said his new friend after Neil had sat down and closed the passenger door.

"What are you Bruce Lee now?" Neil felt like asking, but didn't. He wasn't exactly sure where this fortune cookie saying had come from or what the hell had prompted it, but he wasn't about to take issue with it, not now, not with all his belongings in the back of this strange little man's van and the rain still falling. He thought about his next step.

"Hey, listen," said Neil, "thanks for helping me out here, can I at least give you a few bucks for your time, gas, whatever?" –

It was as though Neil had just delivered the funniest punch line; the man's head went back and his squinting eyes tightened, he let go an enormous gut-wrenching laugh that banged throughout the van's interior. He spoke while trying to catch his breath,

"You...you, funny guy...whew, what your name, funny guy?"

Neil thought of hitting him,

"Neil."

"Neil funny guy, you makea me laugh."

"What's so funny?"

"Ohh Neil...."

"I'm a real riot."

"Neil, real riot."

The Instructor was at a loss too. 'What's with this wack job repeating everything you say?'

"What's your name, wise guy?" Neil was surprised to hear himself ask.

"Mein, my name Mein," he said with sudden child-like sincerity.

Neil's anger softened, he was confused.

207

'Cuckoo...I'm telling you, this guy is out of his frigg'in mind, a wacko, weirdo,' The Instructor argued.

"Well, Mein, is there a hotel near by - someplace I can get to, stay the night?"

"Maybe," Mein's seemed indifferent as if he hadn't heard the question.

Feeling as though he hadn't been clear, Neil pressed harder, "I really don't know what to do now, I mean, with all this mess in back here," he gestured behind him at the remnants of his bike, which had filled the van with the smell of useless gasoline and oil.

Mein had already dislodged the van from the parking spot and held it with a blinker at the parking lot's exit. He looked right then left for oncoming traffic and, noticing there was none, pulled out onto the road.

"Okay." Mein clicked off the blinker and they pulled on ahead.

Neil was puzzled by this vague response; was 'okay' in reference to a hotel or the motorcycle wreckage, or both? He didn't bother with it too much, afterall, what did it matter anyway - he was alive and safe and out of the rain, and besides things would work out under Mein's direction. They didn't say anything for a while.

Mein broke the silence, "I'm a Yankee doodle dandy bown on da fouwth of July, a real wife ....." He sang this while tapping his fingers on the rim of the steering wheel.

'Nut job,' The Instructor pointed out.

Mein stopped singing, which Neil thought was because he must have gotten tired or forgotten the words to the song, but after rolling down his window, Mein inhaled deeply through his nose several times until he produced what sounded like a sizeable wad of Phlegm, and violently discarded the mass out into the rainy night.

'That's attractive,' The Instructor said.

Mein rolled his window back up and continued humming the song, not exactly in rhythm, but just something more in the way to fill a mood he was feeling. He kept his concentration and eyes fixed past the windshield wipers and on the road ahead. It was,

what seemed like, a long while before he spoke again and it
surprised Neil, not only because it broke a comfortable silence,
but, also because Mein's words picked up part of a conversation
which should have been left behind,

"Many hotels, stop first, then hotel."

They pulled off into a brightly lit twenty four hour gas station
with a large convenience store where Mein got out and, dwarfed
amidst rows of high tech pumps, filled the tank. He came back
inside the van saying,

"Now Neil spend money on gas for Mein. Pay for gas, make
you feel good. Go on. Go inside. Pay." It was said so plainly and
abruptly that it almost fit the pattern of a demanding insult, but
at the same time the statement fell like a dropped rag with little
or no pretense attached to it, so that Neil had a difficult time
deciding how to react. But, with all that had already happened
tonight, there was little use in spending much energy or thought
on this. Neil got out of the van to pay.

The physical effects from the accident were beginning to creep
up on him; he was still wet and now the outside cold air chilled
his damp clothes, causing him to shiver. His entire body felt
slightly stiff and any movement brought an awareness of a
general ache that permeated throughout his tissues and muscles.

It was now late, close to midnight and Neil was exhausted. If
only he could soak in a hot bathtub- with a beer in hand just as
he had done with Sarah in Big Sur. 'No -better yet,' came the
amendment, 'a snifter of good cognac.' He got back in the van
with the dwindling effects of warm cognac burning against the
back of his throat.

"How far to the hotel, Mein?"

"Not far, first one stop."

'How many stops can this son of a bitch make tonight?' Neil,
thought. He had unzipped his leather jacket, turned it around,
and using it as a blanket, covered his shoulders and upper torso.
The van like a single white blood cell made it's way through the
pitch dark arteries of a wooded countryside, up winding roads,
bumping around corners, careening onward, upward, bending
against the night. They traveled far, deep, and high into the

ancient Pennsylvania mountains. Mein sat behind the wheel as though behind an ox - pushing, urging it ahead. The higher they rose, the greater became The Instructor's anxiety and increasing warnings, 'This lunatic will kill and violate us in these evil woods!'

Finally, they came to a break in the road and after making a right turn, Mein leveled the van, but soon they began to climb again. This new climb took them on a narrow road and had forced the van to slow considerably; Neil could hear and feel crunching gravel beneath the van's tires. Peering out to where the headlights ended, he could see the small gravel road, the woods on the side and a large ornate red and white archway, under which the van was about to pass.

'You stupid idiot, he's going to kill us out here in the middle of nowhere, get out of the van, now, get out!'

As tiring and exhausting as the day had been, Neil still held the growing, budding knowledge that this pestilent voice was becoming, not only annoying, but perhaps, completely unnecessary. It, therefore, filled him with a certain amount of satisfaction to see this spineless voice so anguished under the present circumstances.

Passing under the decorative arch, the trees disappeared and the space around them opened up onto wide, empty grounds. Sets of reflective eyes hinted at wildlife that now freely roamed in this nocturnal setting. Next, the headlights fell upon an enormous white building with gold and red trim. Mein pulled close to the building, parked the van and turned the engine off. He began opening his door.

"Must be quiet, all asleep now."

"Should I get out too?" Neil asked.

"Yeah, yeah, you get out," Mein answered and jumped out of the van.

Neil grabbed his jacket and got out of the van. The rain was still falling and using his jacket as an umbrella, held it above his head, bent forward and ran to catch up with Mein who was now walking ahead with a no-nonsense gait.

"Where are we, what about all my stuff back there?" Neil asked.

Mein continued walking, "No need worry," he said and began climbing a set of stairs built from large blocks of stone.

Feeling as though he were a small pestering child, Neil fell silent and continued to follow behind Mein. None of this seemed right, but it was late, the day had been trying, and his will was spent. Having climbed two more sets of stone stairs, they now walked along a rainlicked stone pathway that led past two small ponds filled with fat fish that mouthed at the rippled surface. The stone pathway split and they took the one to the right, which brought them to a large red wooden door. Mein clicked its handle and both men entered the structure.

They had entered into a large square room where the only light came from two candles attached to the wall. There was a large, elaborate rug that covered much of the floor. Neil guessed it was from India, Pakistan, or some other exotic land. There were more rugs and tapestries of the same sort that hung from the walls, and another that hung from the ceiling, bowed so much at its center that it resembled an enormous pillow. The room appeared to be an entrance hall of some kind. Close to the door, and off the rug, was a long row of shoes and sandals that were lined up against the wall. The musty remains of incense lay low and heavy and cushioned the air around them.

Mein took off his shoes and motioned for Neil to do the same. He then led Neil through a series of hallways, a dining area, and back through more hallways. There, in a large washroom Neil was able to clean and dress his wound. With no time to waste, Mein led Neil down more hallways and opened another door. Nothing much could be seen until Mein struck a match and lit a candle. It was a small room that consisted of nothing more than a small, plain bed, a throw rug, a cedar chest, a writing desk, chair and a fireplace with a mantle piece. Mein placed the candle with its holder on the mantle piece and began to light a prepared pile of wood that lay neatly stacked in the fireplace. The wood, which had been split several times, in order to make kindling, was stacked meticulously in a pattern that resembled a miniature

211

Lincoln log cabin. In no time at all, Mein had started a small fire, which quickly grew larger. He then pushed himself up from his knees, put back the screen in front of the hearth, and motioned for Neil to put on a robe that was hanging from a peg on the side wall.

"Hotel too late, put on robe, you make home. I return with tea soon," He darted out of the room and disappeared back into the dark hallway, closing the door behind him.

Neil stood in the empty room and took a second or two to study his firelit reflection from a window at the foot of the bed. He wasn't alone,

'Time to make a dash for it. Tea, yeah sure - tea for two in the nude maybe - these Japs are into some pretty kinky, perverse shit.'

Mein was probably Chinese, but that made little difference to The Instructor, 'Time to leave, run, damn it, run!'

Neil sat down on the edge of the bed and slowly began to undress. His body felt tight and his movements were calculated. He laughed at his body as he discovered new pockets of pain while undressing. His socks were the hardest to remove; wet and gripping to his feet like octopus, they stretched out twice their original size before finally relinquishing their hold, and only after he had pulled at them using all the strength his bruised arms and sore fingers could possibly muster. With each item of clothing removed, he felt an increasing amount of panic from The Instructor. Completely naked, Neil reached for the terry cloth robe and slid into the cushioned comfort. Looking at the window again, he saw a whimpering figure jump between the red glowing flames between two logs and vanish.

There was a gentle rap on the door and then it swung open. Mein entered holding a tray with a cup of steaming tea, and black mission figs. He placed the tray on the cedar chest by the foot of the bed, then clasped both hands together close to his chest, and with a quick nod said, "See you the morningtime." and left.

Neil was now beginning to feel the effects from the fire; he was warm, relaxed and his eyes became heavy. He sat, sipped the tea and ate part of a fig. He dropped the top portion of his robe and let the warmth of the fire thaw his waterlogged body. He held the steaming teacup and stared into the fire. His thoughts were heavy, round, and slow. He tried accessing all that had happened today, but it would have to wait. He returned the half filled cup to the tray, laid his body down and fell into a deep, deep slumber.

10

Sunlight from the window filled the room. Ashes, like remnants of a dream, lay lifeless and still in the cold fireplace. Neil rustled, tossed, and eventually flipped himself in the morning light. He blinked, squeezed his eyes open and shut several times, and began to remember the where's and why's of his present circumstances. He pulled himself up, and in a blurry state, placed both bare feet on the floor and sat at the edge of the bed. The spelunker traveled back up to the light of day, and somewhere in his brain a factory whistle blew; night workers punched out and day workers begrudgingly punched in. He grabbed his jeans, which had dried and become stiff from the heat of the fire, and pushed his feet slowly through each cardboard pant leg. It was difficult. He moved with a stiffness comparable to the one he'd found the morning after his first wrestling practice. His body had developed new aches during the night and also a tremendous thirst.

He put on his tee shirt and walked to the window. Looking outside and to his left, he saw what appeared to be part of the backside of the building. Straight ahead were large, exacting rows of trees. Some still held a few leaves, but most were stark with dark leafless branches, stripped bare from the cold weather, reminding him of a Van Gogh charcoal sketching. The rows went on forever, extending off a long distance before finally disappearing below the mountaintop horizon. Peeking up in the far distance were hills, valleys and other mountaintops. He finished dressing and wrapped his watch around his wrist. Ten thirty.

He combed his fingers through his hair and rubbed the back of his neck, "You've got to be kidding me."

He hadn't slept this late in a long time. Damn it. Where the hell was Mein? He opened the door and walked down the hallway, trying to retrace his steps from the night before. There were hushed voices coming from the dining area, which he had passed through the evening prior with Mein. He leaned in and saw two monks with shaved heads, wearing saffron robes sitting on long benches talking to one another. Neither one looked up, taking no notice of Neil as he entered and passed through the room. Had he died in the accident and become a ghost?

He continued on, into another hallway, and looking to his right through a doorway, saw a large airy kitchen with tall windows. A woman wearing thin wire rim glasses, overalls and red knee high socks stood leaning against the sink, munching on a carrot and conversing in German to a man who sat opposite her on one of the counter tops. Neil continued on down the hallway until he reached the entranceway where he had first taken off his boots. A guy in his mid-twenties with a beard, torn jeans and a thick wool sweater sat on a pile of throw pillows reading a book, his fingers twirling his long unkempt hair. The atmosphere of the entire place was that of an enormous youth hostel.

Neil found his boots where he had left them the night before, and put them on, laced them up and headed outside to look for Mein. He went to the van, but Mein wasn't there. He decided to search the property. There was a lawn, a great lawn - so grand and magnificent and meticulously kept that it harkened back to the grounds and gardens of French palaces and chateaux - the kind seen inside posh coffee table books - the kind with Kings and queens. The lawn was truly impressive and Neil marveled at the lines of symmetry, the sense of balance and 'natural' flow. On the lawn, tied to tall stakes that were planted in the ground, were a series of colored flags and ribbons that fluttered in the light wind. Looking back towards the door he had come out, Neil saw a terrace built from stones with a flat patio extending off from the kitchen. With a better sense of perspective, he could now see that this large monastery had several wings, attachments, and additions. The roof of the entire structure was covered with red clay terra cotta shingles All along the building, and built either into the stones or the building's awnings, were exquisitely carved figures of lions and serpents. For all he knew Mein could be anywhere. The wind blew cold, and Neil wished he had put on something more than just a tee-shirt.

He walked to the back of the main building where there stood the row of trees he had first seen from his window. There, among the row of trees, was a single diminutive figure bent over a burlap bag with a wheelbarrow resting nearby filled with gardening tools.

Neil made his way quickly down the row of trees, towards the distant figure. He could see his own breath and his fingers, ears and nose burned. He crossed his arms and tucked his hands beneath his armpits. When he got closer to the figure he saw it was Mein, who was taking a gooey mixture from a small paper bucket and was slapping it with a wooden tongue depressor onto a small tree that had just been grafted. He wore a plaid thick wool coat, rubber boots, a pair of green khakis and a black colored beanie with a 'John Deere' logo. A piece of string hung from both corners of his mouth.

Neil approached, "Hey Mein."

Mein took the string from his mouth and began tying it around the gooey spot of the tree, "Hey Neil," he said without looking up.

"Hell of a night, last night. Thanks for allowing me to stay here."

Mein continued, silently focused on his task.

A few seconds passed, and still, Neil waited. Seeing, Mein wasn't responding, Neil tried again, "Well, I guess I'll go around to the van and see what's what with my bike and gear..............see what's of use anymore."

Mein withdrew a knife from a leather pouch attached to his belt and cut the string, "Okay."

Neil stood above Mein and waited for more....... eye contact maybe, there was none. Neil turned and walked back through the sleeping trees.

The Instructor was indignant, 'This motherf-'

'Oh shut up!' Neil wouldn't allow room for insults. True, this man seemed...not exactly rude, but..indifferent. It was such a contrast to the happy go lucky guy he had seen last night, darting here and there, wearing a constant smile, and even singing-but who knew, maybe he just had something on his mind or was even Bipolar. Still, it troubled Neil and he wondered if he had done or said something to upset this man. Walking back to the van, he retraced the previous night's events inside his head, but could find nothing that would account for Mein's strange behavior.

He got to the van and collected all his belongings and brought them inside the room. He separated everything - wet from dry, clean from dirty and then went back outside again, this time to gather his tools and other items stored beneath the motorcycle seat. Once that was done, all that remained were parts of the motorcycle and the larger wrecked mass including, the frame, tires, and engine. Back inside the van, he knelt up close to what was left of his motorcycle. He placed his palms and then entire hands on the cold aluminum crankcase and slid them slowly across the lifeless shell, feeling all the small dimpled imperfections in the aluminum skin and it made him sad. A silly thing, really- a simple collection of metal, but it had carried him far and had served without complaint. He knew better to think such an inanimate object could have a soul, but somehow..somehow – he had damn near felt the glee this machine experienced when the oil pumped, the gas flowed, the sparkplugs fired, and the pistons shouted. He knew better, but somehow it didn't matter. He was saying goodbye to an old friend.

He thought of the elderly man he had buried in the Arizona desert only a few days before. He had to keep moving and finish what he had started. Or did he? 'I mean look at this motorcycle...,' he thought. 'What's the point? All the resources, workers, lives it took to build it, bring it to life, transport it across an ocean. I bought the thing, took all that time in finding it, dealing with the DMV, getting my license, taking care of it, changing the tires, washing it, waxing it, doing the upkeep, tune ups, the tools I bought for its well being, even involving the life of other people, Bill at *Dillards,* repairing it with Mattie and Willie, all the work, effort, and for what - to have it finally come back and return where it began, as a hunk of useless metal? What's the point of having even started with it?

It would be easy to throw in the towel, forget this whole mess.

'Wouldn't be the first time.'

'Mind your own damn business.' Neil warned The Instructor.

'Hey, you gave it your best shot - and - like always, fallen short.'

'Tried harder than most.'

'Try try try,' The Instructor openly laughed, 'everybody tries, not many do. Why not head back to California?'

'Another failure.'

'Hey hey,' The Instructor said. 'So what? You -we go back. No harm, no foul.'

'And do what?' Neil asked.

'Life goes on, just as before.'

'Love that wouldn't you? Coward, liar, thief. I made a promise. Gotta make a change!'

'Change is overrated.'

"You talk with ghost?"

Mein had finished with his work and had come around to the back of the van.

"Oh, no," Neil said, "just talking to myself, I guess."

Mein looked at the wreck. "Motorcycle, no more - loss, all changes."

'Tell Mr. Miyagi, we're all set here,' The Instructor said.

Neil wasn't exactly in the mood for any ancient Chinese secret wisdom right now, especially after having been snubbed earlier. He sketched Mein's profile from the corner of his eye.

"Yeah, well it's still a damn shame - a great bike."

"You count lucky stars, you not in van too."

"No, I know." Neil said.

"What you know?"

This question seemed offensive to Neil and he felt a jolt of anger flash through his body. He hid the emotion behind a chuckle,

"What I know? I know, I know that, such a waste it now is. Look at it," Neil said, nodding to the lifeless motorcycle. "See, such a waste, all the effort to get it here and for what? A great bike and now nothing - it's gone."

Mein was smiling, "Same motorcycle, same man, being, life, why you cry at life?"

"Cry? What do you mean, cry? I'm not crying."

"Maybe inside?"

"You better watch it."

"Watch what?" Mein asked.

"You gotta give me a hard time about it?"

"Hard time?" Mein laughed.

Neil looked at Mein, clenched his fist and looked away. "Forget it."

"Hard time?" Mein repeated. "Ohhh hard time? Life hard time, all hard time. All straw dogs. Happiness is rooted in misery. Misery lurks beneath happiness. Who knows what the future holds?"

Neil recognized these words from somewhere, but his mind was still too preoccupied with the 'cry' comment and everything else to remember the source.

"Getting to New York is in my future, Mein," Neil directly pointed out.

"Big Apple?"

"Yes, the Big Apple!"

"Ummm, okay. Big Apple soon, lunch now." Mein motioned for Neil to get out of the van. Neil hesitated, but jumped out. Mein closed the doors and both walked up to the monastery in silence.

Inside an eclectic group of people had gathered and mingled around the dining and kitchen area. Some sat eating at the large table, while others fussed about in the kitchen, moving plates, seasoning their food, or just taking time to catch up with one another. Neil found a spot at the large table next to Mein who ate his food with big slurping noises, dismissing any pretense of manner or etiquette; he bent his head down close to his bowl and shoveled the food into his mouth as though it were just another chore such as washing or sleeping. Neil sat and ate too. The dish was some sort of stew with chunks of tofu, carrots, potato, and rice, and served with thick slices of homemade brown bread that was rustic and hardy. The food tasted a bit over seasoned for his taste, with a pronounced flavor of curry and cayenne, but still it was good and it warmed his body. Mein lifted his thigh, leaned to one side and released a loud flatulent. "Good stuff," he said.

When the meal had ended, Neil approached Mein,

"I was thinking of taking a bus or-"

"No worry, Neil think too much for self and me," Mein laughed at his own words, and still smiling said, "train station, tomorrow night, I bring you there for big apple."

"Train station, you mean, like Amtrak?"

"Amtrak, yes like Amtrak." His eyes twinkled with unusual delight. "You no need worry, why so worry - you need worry and busy, you worry busy with dishes, clean kitchen." He patted Neil's shoulder and turned away.

Again, Neil felt pushed aside by Mein and his words. Feeling agitated, he walked into the kitchen and began cleaning up. There were four other people already cleaning inside the kitchen. One was the young kid with the hipster beard who Neil had seen reading earlier in the day, and the other three were bald silent women wearing saffron robes. Neil introduced himself to them and was met with the same cold indifference given by Mein.

'What's with these freaks, everyone seems half asleep,' The Instructor noted.

As it turned out, not everyone was uncommunicative. The kid, whose name was Mark, had been at the monastery for just over a week now. He was from Oregon and this was his third time visiting the monastery. He explained to Neil that the monastery was a place of retreat open to all. The way that it worked was, you either paid for your stay as in a group, or you worked in exchange for room and board. And, even if you did pay, you were still expected to help out with a number of assorted chores. The kind of chores varied and depended upon the things in need of repair, but always included cooking, cleaning, yard work, carpentry, moving dirt, washing dishes – whatever upkeep needed to be done. Mark also explained that many groups from all over the country visited the monastery as part of silent weekend retreats where none of the participants was supposed to talk. He even gave Neil the run down as to where things were located in, and around, this enormous complex; he spoke of the hiking trails, meditation hall, the steam hut, the hot springs, the library, and annual festival.

It was a relief for Neil to finally find someone who spoke fluent English. But, it also seemed, Mark wouldn't have offered up this information had Neil not pressed him for it. Everyone in the monastery kept to him or herself and seemed to be doing their own thing. The entire place seemed to lack focus, with a laissez faire type of feel to it; no one seemed driven or hurried, but rather bumped around with a non directed, 'whatever' attitude. It reminded Neil of those types he had met while living in California, especially among the surfer crowd, that finished every other sentence with, "whatever, dude." This type of response had always pissed Neil off because it seemed such a cop out to him, as though these individuals were cowering from strong opinions, and lacking any kind of backbone, offered this 'whatever' response as a way of shrinking from any form of responsibility or accountability. There was no affirmation for life felt in these responses. It was as if they had been given a heavy dose of lithium and just drifted with the current.

He could see it here now in the monastery; there appeared to be no formatted organization, structure or accountability to anyone or anything. He didn't care if it wasn't being done out of spite or malice, it irked him. And, at the same time it perplexed him, too, because everything that needed to get done, did get done - whether it was the cooking, painting or feeding the fish. It all got done despite this general 'whatever' attitude.

After helping clean up in the kitchen, Neil, still feeling a mixture of disgust and mild confusion, decided to go back to his room and lie down for a while. He got back to his room, and out of habit looked at his watch, but remembered the instrument had no purpose here. He thought of his motorcycle, the desert, and why he was even here in the first place. He wanted to call the insurance company, but knew that would have to wait until he could reach a phone. He figured he'd leave the wreckage here and let a regional insurance adjuster come and take a look. He was glad now to have filled out the police report - it was one less thing to worry about. Maybe Mein had a point; he did worry a lot. He was always checking, double checking, worrying about things such as a map, the road, a clock and always with a need to go, move on to the next thing to do. Now there was nothing for him to do until tomorrow night when he'd catch a train to New York.

He sat on the bed and stared out the window. The stark black trees stood hauntingly against a light blue sun and the thought of painting, again, came to Neil. The loss of his motorcycle, combined with an increasing shift of something inside him, panged at his sensibilities. He longed for a brush, canvas, some oils - there was a growing need to release part of himself into something, and his head talked in colored brush strokes. He continued, just staring and, for no apparent reason, a slow moving ground swell engulfed him entirely, infusing a heavy layered mix of melancholy and vague frustration beneath his skin. He thought of the dead man out in the desert and what he'd done to him, he thought of Sarah and the abortion. He thought of Patricia. He thought of his father. And then he felt it coming. He didn't try to stop it. Why should he? He was alone. He wept.

When he awoke it was late in the afternoon. He dressed and went outside. He walked along some of the trails around the monastery. He thought it funny that here he was, able to do anything he wanted, not restrained with any kind of agenda or 'to do' list, and yet, he couldn't decide what to do. He knew he had to do something, but was at a loss as to what that 'something' was. This freedom from time felt odd and caused in him a certain amount of anxiety and frustration. His mind resisted the idea of doing nothing. To do nothing was bad, a sign of laziness and only led to unproductive results. He looked up through the tall pines that filtered the darkening sky and felt the expansive sense of timelessness instilled in the rings of the old determined trees. There was something intentional about these trees; not wanting, but allowing. Never complaining, or changing course, but only reaching, and quietly doing what they were supposed to do, created to do.

As he walked upon a carpet of dead wet leaves, an episode when he was back in California, not long ago floated up to him. Why he should think of it now, didn't really matter to him.

It was late Thursday afternoon and he had been at work in the airport hanger when a call came in. An item needed to be picked up for inventory at another warehouse and his boss shouted out for him to go. He and a new employee named Miguel were to pick up the part twenty miles away. Miguel was from a small town just outside Oaxaca, Mexico and spoke no English. Neil got in the driver's seat of the company truck as Miguel slipped in on the passenger side. Neil said hello. Miguel just nodded. Miguel wore a baseball cap, a new pair of tan boots with the laces untied and bright white socks and held himself with such a relaxed demeanor that it was as if he were simply running to the dump with his father. Neil glanced at the young boy's face and wondered at his age- sixteen, no more than seventeen. But, here he was working in America at an American job. Neil thought of all it had taken for the boy to get here, what his one road town looked like, and what his mother's last words had been before he left home and traveled North - not knowing if she would ever see him again. As Neil drove the truck, Miguel looked out the window. Neil caught the boy's reflection in the passenger side mirror. There was an old soul in this boy, a silent all knowing quality in his eyes and face as if it'd been prematurely earned from the sad and brutal land where he had seen too much, too soon. And in a strange way Neil felt inadequate and jealous of this boy who'd been branded with a stick of fire wrought from poverty and depravity- who held the entire country of Mexico in his tender arms and soft cheeks and appeared more relaxed and at home than Neil would ever feel, here, in this land called America.

223

Neil got back from his walk, read in the small library and went to dinner. He knew that he could not fight time and resigned himself to his present surroundings. Somehow, he would have to click his mind into neutral.

After dinner a small bell sounded and evening prayer was called. He went to the hall where prayer was to be held and, leaving his boots outside, walked through its ornate entrance. Saffron and maroon colored robes filled the large interior. Visitors sat back against the walls and the monks sat facing one another, forming a long alleyway between them. At the end of this human gauntlet was the altar where a large golden statue of Buddha sat with eyes closed and one hand raised. Some of the monks had sticks of burning incense, which they held with both hands as they rocked back and forth. A large padded mallet struck a gong and the monks answered with a chorus of humming, which was guttural and ancient. Neil found a spot against the wall and sat down. Everyone around him had their eyes closed and were either humming along with the monks or seemed lost in a deep meditative trance.

The Instructor popped up wearing John Lennon glasses, 'Hey, groovy,' he said, 'wanna smoke some grass, man?'

The monks hummed and chanted, keeping a kind of cyclical rhythm that went on in a seemingly endless circle. Neil closed his eyes too.

'I bet the girls here don't shave their pits,' The Instructor suggested. Minutes passed and Neil busied himself with scattered thoughts: his motorcycle, the cost of this trip, the age of the building. He imagined himself with one of these girls naked up in his room. There was an itch on his nose, an ache in his knee, and his anticipated trip to New York.

'You think they have a CD you can take home?' The Instructor quipped. 'Or maybe they go on tour, Madison Square Garden- what a hoot that'd be, huh?'

The chanting and music wasn't stopping. Neil would be here for a while. Minutes built upon minutes. It went on and on and on. It never stopped but became forever. He relaxed his forehead, eyelids, face, and entire body. But the nervous brain was still alive; spasms, backflips and cartwheels. He worried about the next moment, controlling it or protecting himself against it, but then came the idea he was worthy to deal with it. His thumbs and forefingers met, and after a long time his awareness of any physical attributes his body held dissipated. He was mowing the lawn in Connecticut, on a long humming drive on his motorcycle, lying on a raft soaking in the sun. A purple cloud against a black backdrop floated and undulated before his eyes. His thoughts no longer bounced, but became almost, almost nothing.

When the prayer had ended, Neil opened his eyes slowly as if waking from a long refreshing nap and was in need of nothing. He hadn't a clue as to how long he'd been seated, but it made no difference. His mind was soft, gentle, and clear. He wouldn't say he'd been transported or transformed by this one experience, but he did feel something. What it was he couldn't say, exactly, but he didn't care. He had no desire to talk - nothing to say, no question to ask. Silently, everyone filed out of the hall and went back to the main building.

The following morning, leaving his watch by his bedside, Neil went to the kitchen and prepared a light breakfast of toast and tea. He had only an afternoon to spend here before Mein would take him to the station. He went back to his room, grabbed a towel and walked outside to where Mark had said the hot spring was located. Behind the large hall where the prayers from the night before had been held, was a small oval steam bath dug in the ground and surrounded by perfectly placed rocks. Vapors rose from the water. There were two people sitting in the spring: one a woman, grandmotherly, but with a little more vitality and who resembled Gloria Steinem - so much so that Neil had to look twice and even then he wasn't sure. The other occupant was an enormous sumo wrestler of a man with a shaved head and Michelin man arms. As Neil began taking off his boots, the old woman began pushing herself slowly out of the hot water. She was a little more than half way out when Neil realized that she was completely naked. It was a sight he wished he hadn't seen. An awful sound deep inside his stomach begged to escape, but

Neil restrained it. He quickly looked down and began to fold the laces into his empty boots. There was plenty of space all around, but she had somehow managed to stand directly over him. There was rigidity in her stance. She dripped into his shoes without apology. She then turned bare ass and grabbed a towel resting on some rocks across the opposite side of the hot spring.

After drying herself off and grabbing a towel to twist up her hair, she placed her feet into a pair of flip-flops and trotted off. It was a relief to see her go. The heavy-set man had placed a wet, hot facecloth over his face. The back of his head rested against the edge of the hot spring as if he were listening to a glorious symphony. Neil stripped down to his boxer shorts and hesitated. He wondered at the proper hot spring etiquette, and whether or not he'd be considered a freak if he left his boxer shorts on. He left them on anyway.

The water was hot and it took a few jumpy seconds for Neil to inch his way in and submerge his entire body. It was much deeper than he had imagined. He sat with his back close to the edge of the spring. His toes found a hot stream of water that flowed beneath him. A hundred or so yards away, four deer came out into an open space and nibbled on the wet grass, taking turns raising their heads, alert for any possible signs of danger.

Neil's body adjusted to the water. He stretched his legs and felt his bones soften and realign themselves. The enormous Buddha man dragged the damp cloth down from his face and flung the wet mass over his right shoulder where it landed like a lifeless octopus on the outside rocks. He lifted himself up and, like a large hippopotamus, thundered out of the water. A torrent of water cascaded off his body. Neil felt like a guppy awash in a splash of waves. The man stood outside the hot spring and reached for a towel. He was wearing blue shorts with a Hawaiian motif. And as he finished toweling himself off, he turned and said,

"Right thought, right speech, RIGHT dress." He grabbed hold of the elastic waistband to his shorts, pulled it out, and let it snap back against his belly. He smiled, put on his sandals, and left.

Neil leaned his head back and laughed. He sank deeper in the pool. The accident was slipping, the dead man was being kind. The hot, bubbling water was siphoning much of the tension he had gathered while on the road.

Later in the day Neil and Mein moved the motorcycle wreckage from the van to a remote section on the monastery grounds next to a shed that Mein had built to store all his tools. They covered the wreck with plastic, and weighed it down with rocks. Neil offered Mein the wreck after the adjuster had come and finished the assessment for insurance purposes. Mein seemed pleased with this.

When it was time for Mein to take Neil to the train station. Neil gathered his belongings and got in the van for the drive down the mountain. In the monastery's gravel entrance a new group of people were just arriving in their shiny, expensive cars ready to strap on Buddhism as part of a weekend retreat. They all seemed anxious, fluttering about, gabbing incessantly, opening doors, slamming trunks, and answering cell phones. Mein hit his horn nearly knocking some of them over. They jumped like squirrels.

By the time Mein pulled into the train station parking lot, Neil was already preparing himself against the onslaught of emotions that usually overwhelmed him under such circumstances. He always had a hard time at airports, bus depots, train stations - any place that involved picking up or letting go of people, as though in some strange way these places acted as corridors for both, death and birth. It never failed to put a deep, aching, and hollow pit in his stomach.

Neil looked at the one room train station and thought of his father; the sandpaper kiss and quick bear hug at the train station along the shoreline of Connecticut after he had moved to New York. His father would drive him to the station and wait with him until the train arrived. The wait was the hardest part. It pained Neil. Strange, then this time was different. He felt glad, content and even filled with optimism - not because he was getting away from Mein, but because he felt that he wasn't really leaving him at all, not forever anyway. He was feeling good and felt confident that only good things lay ahead, and was excited to continue East.

As a kind of farewell gift, Mein had given Neil a unique knapsack. It was a beautiful sack made from a soft, yet dense fabric used, Mein had said, "for generations in the mountains of the Himalayas." Instead of zippers there were strong black drawstrings that formed a loop at the top of the sack. The sack wasn't one color, but many; thick bands of white, pink, yellow, orange, red and black.

Now Mein dragged the knapsack, filled with Neil's belongings, out from the back of the van and placed it on the ground between them.

"So long, Neil, no need worry, always place here, and always place here," Mein pointed to his chest.

"Don't get sweet on me, Mein," Neil said. Mein said nothing. "Thank you again for everything."

"Okay Bless Neil, bless all," Mein gave a quick, almost imperceptible bow, then disappeared behind the driver's side of the van.

Neil swung the knapsack over his right shoulder. He stepped a few feet towards the station, which was nothing more than a one room wooden structure, and turned once more back towards the van. He could see the last few scurrying steps of Mein's feet before they were pulled up into the van and heard Mein's voice call out, "Chop wood, carry water!" There was a short giggle and the driver's door slammed shut and the van took off. Neil turned and walked inside the station.

A single radiator hissed in the corner and two sets of timetables were tacked to the wall below a large faced clock. The station was old and a little worn, but spotless. There were two wooden benches with rounded corners that were connected to one another to form the shape of the letter 'L'. A few names and initials had been carved into the benches from the pocketknives of restless, lovestruck and immortal teenagers. Someone had inked with a pen the abbreviation 'TCB' on one of the bench legs. Manning the station was just the lone ticket master behind the enclosed bank teller like counter, his dark blue uniform rumbled, worn and darkly soiled around the cuffs. What was the story of this middle-aged man? Neil wondered. What did his wife look like, did their house smell of cabbage, did he collect stamps, where had he gone for his last vacation? It was quiet as hell in this station.

Neil bought a one-way ticket to Penn Station. The train wasn't due to arrive for another twenty-three minutes. He sat down on one of the benches. A woman, who looked forlorn and nervous, entered the station pushing a small stroller that held a baby.

Neil walked to the window and stared outside. The wind whistled above the empty tracks. It was hard to believe anything, let alone, a large locomotive would soon arrive here. The grey skies further darkened and the lights inside the station turned on. The days were getting shorter, and the nights longer. The anticipation of a large mechanized metal mass created a certain amount of excitement and anxiety in Neil and he thought of all the people, workers who had gotten up this morning to run the railroad in order for this specific train to arrive here, at this particular station and time. It was unbelievable and surreal to him. Even more, was the fact that this same, exact process had, not only taken place the day before and the one before that, but would happen the day after he was gone – and the day after that, season after season, year after year. And, it would happen regardless if he was or wasn't here to witness it. He contemplated the idea that any random time in his life, say, maybe a few years back in California when he might have been making his way down some grocery aisle or cleaning his apartment that at that same exact moment without him even being aware of it this train here in Pennsylvania was arriving at this station. The train, the track, the passengers; all existed without him. His mind juggled these deeper abstract thoughts and mortality; that before his conception and long after his death a train had, was and would be keeping this same schedule, down this same track, picking up people who would all eventually die. Neil looked between the iron posts of the ticket window and to the worn figure of the ticket master and felt the inherent pathos for all mankind.

The manifestation of this entire thought process resulted in a shiver that hung between Neil's shoulder blades. He raised his shoulders to his ears, turned to the rumbling sound outside on the tracks, and shook any lingering thoughts from his body.

He grabbed tight his knapsack, opened the door and walked out onto the cold platform. Coming around the wooded bend, and up ahead on the dark track, was a single, massive headlight. Whatever speed the train had gained was now being dispelled. The train came into the station at a diesel-clanging crawl. When it came to a stop a handful of people exited like ants from an anthill. A portly conductor hung from one of the metal stairwells and yelled, "Alllll aboooard!"

Neil climbed the stairs to board the train, and gave one last look to the outside platform. Down a few cars was the woman who had been waiting with her child in the station. She was now in the loving embrace of a man who had gotten off the train; all was good, all was right.

The inside of the train was plush and uncrowded. Neil found a whole row of empty seats. He unzipped his jacket, took off his boots, and sat down next to a window. "Thank God," he said. It was a relief not to think of gas mileage, maps, exit ramps, the cold weather or traffic.

The train pulled out of the station and so here it was – at last; the sweet, final leg of his journey East. This was it. Getting to New York was now out of his hands. A set of keys jingled and swayed from the belt of a conductor, who rocked between a few seats and came down the carpeted aisle to where Neil sat. Without a word, Neil handed over his ticket and, like an umpire clicking off a strike, the conductor punched the ticket, then wedged it into the top of the seat.

Neil looked up at the man, "What time ya expect we'll be in New York?"

"Bout two, two and a half hours, stalled train near Philly. Should be there round ten O'clock."

"Sounds good."

The conductor had already begun sniffing for new tickets and was moving on down the aisle, "Ye-up."

Neil settled deep in his seat. He looked out the window and stretched his legs. The cold night air rushed over the skin of the train. He stared out into the darkness and passing night, and beyond paper doll houses and toothless trees that whisked by and a sense of coming back full circle to an older life crept up inside him. He was being pulled in the direction of a city he had once called home.

'Member the way her mother eyes beamed, damn near glistened across that kitchen table thinking maybe her daughter had finally found a nice college boy after all.'

'Yeah, remember.'

'Member the promises, empty as shit.'

'Yeah, I remember that too.'

'Like snowflakes melting on an open palm, how you promised you'd call for her as soon as you got set up in New York- Mr. big shot artist, you drunk, you coward - how awful; an opened wound that'll never heal, leaving her by the way side like an ugly reminder the same way you did that child, the man out in the desert - gone, buried. But even after fifteen plus years it's all very much alive - eating you whole.'

Neil brought his fist to his mouth and dug his front teeth into his forefinger. It would be one thing if he were successful now, and could smile in hindsight at the trials and tribulations during that period of his life, but the fact was he wasn't successful and here he was forty years old, no longer in his youth, and seemed no closer to success – and, in fact, further away, he thought, than those struggling times in New York - what shame. The city that had caused him to bleed and suffer was the same city to which he was now returning and he prayed the blade that had once cut him, whittled away his faith would at best treat him with indifference.

When he left college and returned to Connecticut he had no other choice than to move in with his parents. They didn't say much. But, a conversation halted in mid sentence when he entered the room or delicate dialogue reserved more for strangers than kin, or worst of all, a smile on his mother's face that held back a whole night of tears was enough to understand how they truly felt. He found work, albeit part time, painting houses and sandblasting printing presses at a refurbishing plant. His goal was to save enough money to get out of Connecticut, find an apartment in New York and make something of his life.

There would be the smell of turpentine and paint fighting against fried filet of sole and boiled potatoes as he'd come home at night and wash up before dinner, only to find himself at a dinner table stiff with formality – a simple meal amongst strangers instead of blood and body. He never placed fault with his parents. How could he? When dinner had ended and the dishes were done, off he'd go to blind himself with drink. The hangovers were tough, but would wear off by mid-day, sweated out through the repetitive mindless manual labor. There was a tolerance breaking in his parent's eyes.

The only solace he found that summer was in a poor Irish girl named Erin with a lazy eye, tiny freckles and second hand shoes. Neil would visit her mostly on weekends, often in the late afternoon just around dusk, riding his bicycle over little, bumpy streets, zigzagging his way beneath bent telephone poles, passing close to the harbor where clapboard houses sat ablaze in the bronze glow of a setting sun whose golden rays kissed the horizon or stretched the silhouette of a feral feline slinking off with belly low and back bent, to a nocturnal sojourn where reality speaks and truth bites.

There, up on a hill overlooking the harbor and close to where the fleet of local fishing vessels used to dock, was an old whaling captain's house. With a screened in porch that had a few rips and tears, the house, its garden and yard were relaxed, not entirely what one would call messy, but lived in and worn like an old pair of jeans. There was a sense of life passing through the overturned watering can or patched up garden hose. These objects were there to serve not to be served, not to hinder or shackle the owner by the way of upkeep, driven by convention or pretense. Behind the house was a small guest cottage where Erin and her older sister, Noreen lived, but only during the warmer months. With no insulation to speak of, the cottage became an icebox when the weather turned cold.

232

The main house is where the rest of the family lived and where the engine of life ran hard. Neil spent much of his time there with Erin, her older sister, mother and younger brother Michael around the kitchen table. The mother would cook, Noreen would play the guitar and Michael, Neil and Erin would drink and tell stories. The father was a fisherman. Missing for days at a time, he was either out at sea hauling in traps or back on land at the bar, the answer to either question could be had in the absence or presence of a pair of thick rubber work boots and yellow rain slicker by the kitchen door. For Neil these were the same items that held the difference between a man and a boy. It was a glorious time, a wonderful time and yet, too, a terrible and awkward time. An earthbound albatross in search of the sea, he wasn't yet who he wanted to be.

It was a simple sentence uttered at an unexpected moment that would give Neil illumination, impetus, guidance and direction that summer. It would happen on the Fourth of July- a celebratory occasion, which had been marked the same way ever since he could remember; the family gathering on the front lawn to enjoy the pyrotechnics that were shot off in a baseball field only a mile from their home. That year it was just Neil, his father and mother. The rest of his siblings had moved away. The night was exceptionally dark and making their way across the lawn required extra care. His mother took the lead with Neil close behind. His father had yet to finish with something in the kitchen. Tender blades of grass pushed between his toes. He could feel the moisture left behind from rain showers earlier in the day. Dark clouds had pushed farther east, leaving behind bits of thin white patches that drifted beneath clear skies. His mother carried a gin and tonic. Ice cubes tinkled against the glass. Neil and his mother stopped close to the edge of the lawn and looked up at the night sky. A spray of light rippled through the darkness and a sound, like canon fire, struck the airwaves and hit his body. A large Maple tree obstructed a kaleidoscope of waterfall trails that cascaded above. They were forced to move far to one side to catch the whole display.

"I remember when that tree wasn't any higher than you are now," his mother wavered in the past.

"Really?"

"You were just a baby when your father planted it," his Mother went on, "had no idea what he was doing- uh a mess. Look at it now."

Neil realized time had moved forward and he hadn't moved with it. He was out of step. And he felt ashamed.

That Autumn, when Neil counted his money and realized he'd fallen short of his initial goal, he left anyway. He packed up his things and got on a train bound for New York. The idea seemed simple enough; to get an apartment, a part-time job and make something of himself. It might take time, a year or two or, perhaps a little more to become an established artist. But he was willing to make that sacrifice. He remembered leaving his parents, Erin and Connecticut and feeling so high, filled with a predetermined knowledge that the dream of becoming a great artist wasn't a dream at all, but a reality.

He would rarely go back to Connecticut. And had it not been for Christmas and a cousin's funeral he would never have gone back at all. Each visit back to Connecticut placed him as a courier, transporting empty promises. Whatever optimism was left in the eyes of his mother and father faded, withered like crisp dead vines.

True, a job stocking shelves at an airport hanger in sunny California seemed void of promise, but it was also void of pain.

At 10:08 the train pulled into Penn Station. Rows of track and concrete were everywhere, and looking out the train window, Neil felt as if he was pulling into the giant underbelly of an iron beast. Patches and rows of fluorescent, dull, mind-numbing light emanated from above. The train came to a stop and Neil gathered his things and exited. He stepped and weaved on the platform, walking among the nocturnal zombies and headed for an escalator. There were rag wrapped homeless men and women sitting in corners or sleeping off some horrible dream - all of them like undisciplined soldiers slumped over, broken, waiting for orders that would never come.

Neither the late night hour, nor these ghosts, held any sway over him. The excitement of being back in New York took him by surprise and held his energy high. He walked through the bowels of this mammoth structure until he reached the escalator. At the top was an immense corridor, a passageway lit with a combination of yellow, red, and orange lights sprouting from the neon signs of closed shops locked behind metal gates. The light provided a minimum amount of safety. Not much moved and as Neil walked down the corridor, it was easy to imagine himself a death row inmate, being led from his cell to the waiting electric chair... "As I walk through the valley of darkness..."

Gripping hard to his knapsack, Neil continued walking. Just a few of the shops that lined the corridor were opened. There was a newsstand, pizza counter, and a bar so pitch black inside that nothing could be seen save for several pair of eyes, peering out as though from across the river Styx.

A popular franchised donut shop was opened and Neil walked inside. Orange, pink and white and three customers and a worker and a short counter and small brightly colored tables with matching chairs, all under halogen lit lamps. The strong aroma of freshly brewed coffee, as though it were all part of an elaborate sales gimmick, seemed too good, irresistible to refuse. A dark skinned man from Pakistan or India and wearing a white uniform stood at the register, ready to take orders. Neil asked for a cup of coffee and a glazed donut and paid. The man placed the two items, along with a few creamers and a black swizzle stick on a red plastic tray and gave Neil back his change. Neil gingerly carried the tray to one of the small tables, sat down, and numbly took a bite from the glazed donut and fought the piping hot coffee with his lips.

Like new prey dropped into a cage, it wasn't long before Neil had a sense that something or someone was stalking him, he could feel predatory eyes scan his body. Sure enough, it struck.

"What kind of bike ya got?" A voice spoke as if this question was just part of an ongoing conversation between two friendly neighbors.

At first, Neil didn't even turn, but instead just looked straight ahead, bent to his coffee and donut, pretending he hadn't heard the question. At the same time, was The Instructor's panic and gobs of mortar being frantically toweled between bricks in a wall.

By ignoring this outsider's question, Neil was adhering to the first line of defense in any New Yorker's handbook; *No Eye Contact!* - It was a street-smart technique learned and utilized whether on a crowded subway or in a city park. It also meant, of course, one had to ignore whatever object with which one was to have no eye contact. And, ignoring certainly meant not responding to verbal stimuli.

But, Neil had been away from New York longer than he realized and was out of practice. He faltered. It was a second, a fraction of a second, but large enough for an open invitation. His eyes met those of a man sitting to his right, two tables away.

"An older one," he found himself saying as part of a knee jerk reaction.

The Instructor dropped the trowel, 'DAMN YOUUU!' he hollered.

A wide, political smile from having captured a vote came to the man's mouth, "That's a hell of thing, a motorcycle. Wonderful machine, nothing like it. That's a perfect jacket for riding too - boy, that's a great piece of leather, where'd ya pick that up?"

'Get up, get the hell up, run!' said The Instructor.

"Boston," Neil answered, ignoring everything and everyone except for the man before him. He knew the risks. If this man turned out to be a lunatic, a sexual deviant- so be it, no big deal; he'd simply get up and leave. The bottom line here was, that for the first time in a long while, Neil felt a certain amount of confidence in being able to handle and accept anything that came along. He was beginning to enjoy the ride.

The man wasted no time in responding, "Boston?, bean town. My alma mater, B.U., class of 59'- ain't that a hoot. Mechanical engineering, not that it's doing me much good right now...."

And, before Neil had even taken another sip of coffee, the man had moved and was sitting at the table next to him, having been executed with such natural ease, so as if to suggest he'd actually

236

been invited. The man hadn't stopped talking and in fact was moving into some fresh saga about his childhood, summers on Cape Cod, and time spent on a fishing boat hauling in lines. Neil didn't want to be rude, but the thought of telling this guy to back off and beat it, seemed a reasonable enough response. Almost simultaneously, however, was the apparently random image of Mein, the monastery, and an all-knowing smiling Buddha. He'd stay with this a little longer.

Neil let go and allowed the man to continue. The man must have sensed this letting go and affirmation from Neil, because he dug into his story with a little more vigor and enthusiasm. It was a mad story too, not just in the facts that were told, but the way in which it was conveyed, orchestrated like a wild collection of finely tuned musicians each knowing what the other's doing at any given time, the pauses, the phrasing, the choice of words-it weaved, it flowed, wrapped around the listener so tightly there was no place else to go, but into the world the man created with his words. It all took on such an important tone too, so if you were to blink, you'd think you'd have missed something vital to your very existence. His story pulled and commanded one's attention as though it were a cautionary tale, and served as a precious reminder, a favor to those who listened. Neil took a good look at this storyteller. The man's clean-shaven face was ash colored and his tinderbox grey and black hair was all brushfire. His eyes were sunk and, as far as Neil could tell, had no white in them at all. The circles around these eyes would never disappear, there just wasn't enough time left in this man's life no matter how much he slept. He wore a baseball jersey and a thick high school ring with a center gemstone that sparkled. Neil could see that this man was no two bit junkie or some low life street thug, educated only in the ways of crime and hard time, but rather, a man who had, somewhere along the line, gathered a deep literary knowledge and a good understanding of language. Here was someone who was slightly frayed around the edges, who had been through much, had seen all, done all, and as he spoke, Neil realized, had hustled all. He was someone who spent money when he had it, and had no regrets when he didn't. The man smelled of thin aftershave and brown bag scotch.

As the man continued to talk, it seemed he expected nothing from Neil, except to listen. There were a few times Neil felt obligated to respond, but the man didn't take much notice, or had already anticipated Neil's words and dismissed them as unnecessary, so that after awhile, Neil gave up, and just sat silent. The man continued on, immersed as an actor on stage or radio announcer delivering a mesmerizing monologue. At the very beginning, Neil thought about time, but knew the hotel where he was to stay was only a ten minute cab ride away, an easy ride especially at this hour. He let the man ramble, dance, weave, work and jab the hustle, which was beautiful and really magnificent. And as the man spoke, Neil could feel himself being taken, lured the way a midnight train whistle pangs your heart or a foghorn draws you down, deep and lonely. But, he didn't care. The land where the man took Neil was vivid in sight and sound. Neil could feel the cards this gambler had at one time held, smell the dreamless flophouses where the man had lodged, hear the clicking of balls around a bar room pool table, and taste the whiskey this man had drunk inside a rundown roadhouse.

He was old school, and had crafted his story through the do or die method of acting. This was no performance delivered by some chauffeur driven Hollywood star, some well known director's nephew, or public relations whore turned starlet. No, this was a performance born out of necessity, survival. The words the man spoke were so rich in color, texture, and careful preparation that Neil knew what he was witnessing here tonight was a performance of a lifetime. So impeccable was this man's performance that it seemed cut and sewn from the seamless raw unspoiled American landscape, which had spawned it. Bravo, kudos, God bless you merry man of Windsor.

If all of this hadn't been enough to illicit the strongest of praise from the staunches of critics, and it truly had been, the man reached for the coup d'etat, the bullfighter's final thrust,

"Course after the wife passed away....." He lit a *Kent* cigarette pulled from a white and blue pack, which lay flat on the table and, slowly turning a sliver POW insignia Zippo lighter that he held between his forefinger and thumb, blew a thin stream of smoke from his mouth. He seemed to be lost inside a private moment for which Neil should not have been present.

"Yeah, we sure had us some awful good times," he hiccupped a laugh and silently stared at the cigarette as though it contained the woman's image. There was a long pause. He ashed into his empty coffee cup. "We raised the two boys and they turned out alright, makes a daddy proud. Scott, the older and Chip the younger -both smart and good. No trouble getting the ladies either, that's for sure. Their mother, Rebecca passed back in 92', hard on both of the boys, especially Chip. Don't have to tell you how hard it can be when someone so close to you passes."

If Neil wanted to leave now, he couldn't, not with these emotional words being shared like wafers on a Sunday Mass. He felt trapped, and suddenly wished for the man to finish with whatever he had to say.

"You ever have someone die who's close to you?" The man's eyes narrowed, the edges creased. He was looking hard at Neil until it seemed the question really required an answer, but it didn't -

"If you have, then you know exactly what I'm talking about. Not looking for sympathy, nobody's giving that away for free, don't I know it- but well, three weeks ago I get a telephone call at my home in New Hampshire and that's why I'm here tonight."

Neil, of course, couldn't make the connection, but knew it would come. It did.

The man continued on and told how one of his sons had graduated West Point, and the other, Annapolis. What amazed Neil most of all was the detail the man had given about each school- all the facts and figures, what it took to get into each school, the curriculum, the instructors, and daily regiment. Too, words he quoted from things his two sons had said, things they did and classmates they had become fond of; all told now with such vivid recollection. After graduation the two boys went off to war. One died in a helicopter crash while serving in Afghanistan and now this man had just come back from Washington where his second son had died while serving in Iraq and been buried with the highest of honors at Arlington National Cemetery. A crumpled piece of paper that had been folded and refolded a hundred times or more he produced from his pocket to bear as proof for having made such a trip. It looked like a visitors brochure of some kind, but Neil wasn't about to question it. The attention to detail was astounding. The man spoke of his most recent trip and how a so and so four star General stood at his son's coffin and, "snapped one off," as he put it, rapping his knuckles on the donut shop table three times in a dramatic gesture before re-enacting the salute the General had given.

Making very little money on a teachers pension, the man recounted how he had decided to hitch hike back home in order to save on expenses. He grabbed a ride from a trucker and left his bag with his money in the front cab when they had stopped at a trucker station in New Jersey where he used the trucker's 'kit' to go shower and shave. When he returned from the shower, the trucker was gone and so was his bag and money.

"I come out of that damn stop, and if that S.O.B. isn't gone - well..and it's a shame too because I remember riding in that cab and looking at the I.D. number, which every trucker by law must have- and I know because I used to drive for a living. For the life of me, I can't remember those I.D. numbers only part: BZ52, which I told the police and the truck station authorities, and, ahhh," the man waved away the story and lit another cigarette. "I'm sixty seven years old, lucky if I can remember what day it is, let alone a set of I.D. numbers. Anyway, walked too many miles to count to get here and here I sit thinking of a way to get a ticket or somesuch way back home. I dunno."

The man took a drag from his cigarette and began talking about baseball or some such nonsense as though the saga he had just finished telling didn't count for much and was nothing more than a comma in a light daydream. It was at this point that Neil looked down and caught sight of the man's ankles. The grimy socks had lost their elasticity and were well past their expiration date. It was a glimpse into the devastating by product of an alcoholic's life; the man's ankles and partially exposed leg were bloated, swollen, red and purple in color with a layer of dry flaking crusted dead skin. The sight was repulsive and it turned the entire situation from slightly amusing to utterly tragic. The man was still playing his hand when Neil stood up, took out a twenty-dollar bill and placed it on the man's table.

The Instructor objected, 'What the fuck do you think you're doing?'

But it was too late, the man reacted right on cue in this beautifully scripted hustle, responding to the twenty dollar bill as though it were a pocketknife that Neil had menacingly opened,

"What's this?"

"Money to help you get back home." Then doing a little acting of his own, Neil added, "it's all I got."

The man pushed the bill across the table back towards Neil, "That's too kind of you, son -too kind, but I can't."

"Come on take it."

"No, no something will work out."

"Don't -"

"Say, I'll tell you what - why don't you write down your address and when I get back to New Hampshire, I'll mail you back the money."

"Forget it, no big deal. Besides, I don't have time right now - I'm running late. It's no big deal, honest. It's only twenty bucks."

The man took the bill, stretched it between his two hands and held it as though it were a lost pet that he hadn't seen in years, eyeing its marks to confirm its identity. "I'll be a sonbitch," he looked up at Neil, "man oh man, the world could sure use more people like you. What's your name?"

"Neil."

The man reached up and shook Neil's hand, "Thank you, Neil."

"You bet." Neil grabbed his knapsack and left the donut shop, and the golden performance sold at a matinee price behind.

As Neil walked through the remaining corridors towards Lexington Avenue, he wondered at the difference between himself and the man he had just left.

'There's no similarity, please - we're so much better than he is,' The Instructor pointed out.

Neil knew better. There really wasn't that much difference, a weakness that mattered, a paycheck or two, a traumatic event. And, all the while, the gerbil wheel constantly spinning.

11

After taking the subway and getting lost because of late night track work and rerouted trains, Neil ended up somewhere on Lexington Avenue. He hailed a cab in the misty night. Gusts of wind were starting to blow, pushing the drizzle with it. He got inside the cab and slammed the door. Eyes of a Pakistani or Indian driver stared at him from the rearview mirror.

"Good evening, where to my friend?"

"Heading downtown, 92 Front Street."

"You got it," the man said. He started the meter and pulled away from the curb, "How are you?"

"Fine."

The cab began down Lexington Avenue, but quickly came to a crawl after having gone only four blocks. People had filled the street and sidewalks, engulfing traffic.

"What's going on here?" Neil asked the driver.

"There's a big protest tomorrow, it's been like this all day - I should have known better than to take this way."

'Uhmmmm,' The Instructor groaned.

"What are they protesting?" Neil asked.

"Something to do with world banks."

"Oh, you mean the World Trade Organization," Neil had caught a newspaper headline while walking through the train station.

"This is right."

"Maybe it'd be better if we tried the East side, down Second Avenue?"

"No, no, exactly the same, worse near the U.N. ."

243

Looking out the side window, Neil took in all the different people who had congregated for the protest. Most were college kids. Some were slightly older - in their late twenties and early thirties. Sprinkled amongst these were folks who looked much, much older. These older ones were the most interesting ones of all, something in their appearance gave the suggestion they'd taken just one too many hard knocks earlier in life so as to end up here in the company of like-minded out casts or misfits on the fringes of society and, who, without any other place to call home, now found acceptance in the chaos that had spilled out into the streets. The cab started up again, but then, quickly jerked to a stop to avoid hitting an older protester who passed by the cab wearing a long overcoat and a 'Cat in the Hat' stovepipe hat. Then came another; a grey haired bespeckled schoolmarm of a woman dressed in what looked like purple pajamas. She pinched her thighs, lifted an umbrella above her head and, in a halfhearted pirouette, twirled.

A protestor wearing a scream mask walked by and slammed his fists on the hood of the cab, "Watch where you're going mother fucker!"

"You see they're all like this. Mother fucker you!" the cabbie yelled back through the window, but the protestor had moved on and was already out of earshot. Neil was thankful.

"My country my country my country," the cabbie made a clicking sound with his tongue. "What we do in my country and what is so wrong here. Where are the woman, ladies, parents and fathers? What do you say to men who have lost their way or never had a way to begin with and all for what- nothing but to perish in the end and nothing to believe in, a waste of life."

And just at that moment, an old man with long grey sideburns and a ponytail moved past the front of the cab holding a sign while chanting, "Hell no we won't go!" Behind him minions followed as if called by the pied piper.

"We call them Bhuta or BhutaVampires where I'm from," the cabbie said without turning around. The back of his head didn't move but Neil could feel the disgust in his eyes. "Feeding on the hungry minds of the young ....."

244

'And there's no plumbing where you're from,' The Instructor interrupted, 'and you openly defecate in the streets, so what's your point?'

'Would you shut up?' Neil shot back.

The cabbie's eyes now fixed on Neil through the rearview mirror, "Did you say something?"

"No," said Neil.

'Hey, ask Babbaganush if he'll save some coin and take you the right way,' The Instructor dinned in Neil's ear.

"They don't know what they want," the driver continued, "all they know is they're unhappy and someone's to blame."

'But someone is to blame,' Neil said to himself.

'Don't see your fat ass out there doing anything about it,' The Instructor said. 'You're all talk no action.'

"Had one in my cab today," the driver said, "him and his girlfriend from Brooklyn. I asked what was going on and they couldn't really tell me, not exactly. Like the rest of us I suppose. It's all a bumper sticker, a slogan."

As if to confirm what the man had just said, Neil looked to the sidewalk where large homemade cardboard signs rested on curbs and against buildings next to protestors who were covered in blankets, sleeping in lawn chairs on the sidewalk waiting for their big debut tomorrow. Scrawled on the signs were all kinds of messages including, "No War", "Say no to WTO", "Meat is Dead", "No Fur", "Police=Racism", "Save the bay", and "Silence=Death". It was a mish mash of messages, with no apparent, cohesive theme, but all were short enough to chant or place on a bumper sticker.

The cab was moving now, breaking through the soft pockets in the crowded street. The cab driver continued talking, "Spoiled. Know nothing of the realities of the world – hardship, pain or hunger." And again it seemed true what he said; most of the young people who had gathered here, looked like well to do suburban dwellers, who, at the end of the day would be driven back home by parents waiting in Volvos parked around some prearranged corner and tucked away from the eyes of any fellow protestors. And the more Neil looked the more truth could be

seen in the driver's words. There were designer tee shirts, cell
phones, and expensive fashionable tattoos; there was just
something about all of it that reeked of being disingenuous. Neil
wondered if this protest had really come out of pain or was it an
amusement, a way of taking a walk on the wild side without the
ramifications; a make believe costume party wrapped around a
safe and predictable day of social unrest? Neil imagined any one
of these kids was here because they thought it cool and hip,
earning them bragging rights on campus, a way of making a girl
or improving their reputation. And maybe Neil could understand
that. After all, he'd been young once, but what pained him most
was the thought that maybe some poor innocent kid was here
tonight, honestly believing in what they were doing all because
somewhere, somehow, somebody had convinced them that any
righteous sounding catch phrase or slogan like those used back in
the nineteen sixties must also be right and relevant today. Some
certainly were, a few at best, but basing a current belief system
on a temporary paradigm from a flash in an adolescent history,
was, in Neil's eyes, sad. Things change and change is inherent in
all things alive. The ability to adapt is one of the amazing
attributes given to human beings; the difference between living
and dying.

'What an awful sin,' Neil thought, 'to take advantage of some
young kid wanting to do right.' And yet here they were, some of
the same old renegade spokespeople from those turbulent times
of the nineteen sixties, who hadn't adapted and changed, but
instead now eked out a living by feeding outdated rhetoric to a
new generation of adolescent gerbils. These spokespeople - or
BhutaVampires as the cab driver had called them - preyed on
new blood found in the veins of inquisitive, youthful minds.
Some of these old BhutaVampires gave lectures, wrote books,
were self-proclaimed political activists, heads of organizations,
and college professors with big names and impressive resumes
who'd garnered tenure from words and thoughts that at one time
had flashed bright and poignant and even vital, but had neither
changed nor adapted to reflect present circumstances. It was
intellectual hubris playing that one hit wonder with no new

variation. Put another quarter in the jukebox and boogey to the same old beat. Baah baah black sheep ye DO go gentle into that good night.

And the most amazing part of all was the absolute hypocrisy; this was laughable. To question these BhutaVampires often placed the inquisitor into reactionary files with accusatory and demeaning names such as, ignorant, rightwing, bigot, neo-Nazi, racist, and - the most hypocritical of them all - narrow-minded.

So, sitting in the cab on this night after having traveled across the land of America, Neil felt both hope and sorrow. Hope, he felt, because of the vibrant desire seen from those who wanted, and searched to avoid sterilization - and sorrow because the old vampires held cages with different colored bars, but which still led to a spinning wheel that turned and a door that locked.

'A bitter older man, a naysayer you've become,' The Instructor noted, 'these young people are doing your dirty work. What have you ever done to help change the world? Nothing. All you do is judge and complain. You're above it all, aren't you?'

'I'm not above it all!'

"Not above what?" asked the driver.

Neil was confused, "Not above- what?"

"You said, not above something."

"I'm –sorry. Just a thought."

"Oh," the driver said. He hesitated before turning slowly back to the wheel to continue navigating through the crowd.

'You're a mess,' said The Instructor.

"Tell you what, just cross over to Times Square, we'll head down Seventh Avenue, and cross back over when we get downtown," Neil instructed the driver.

'Need to get a hold of yourself.'

"Park Avenue would be much shorter," the driver said.

"No, that's fine, really."

"Okay, no problem."

"Thanks."

Neil had to laugh at himself; when was the last time he argued for a taxi driver to take a longer, more costly route? But, the truth was, he wanted to take a good look at this city and reflect, before leaving it. Something told him he'd never be back.

Neil said, "What d' ya gonna do, right?"

"What are you going to do," the driver smiled back. "It's okay - protest. Still number one."

"Still number one?"

"Yes, yes, America, still number one."

Neil didn't respond.

"Look at me, American dream, brother," the driver said.

"Yeah, I don't know, seems to be all about the money, power, you know how it goes."

They had stopped at a red light, and the driver now turned half way around and, using his right arm against the back of the front seat for leverage, looked directly at Neil,

"Welcome to the world, all the world, it's the same, all, everywhere. In my country you wouldn't believe."

"Still."

"Still,... not in my life. I am thankful for what I have, you have got to be thankful. Just tend to your garden." Getting ready for the light to change, the driver went back to the wheel, but continued talking. "I have two beautiful children, and I am thankful. Children change everything, wait till you have children."

How this man knew Neil didn't have children was anybody's guess. The light turned green and the cab continued on.

'Almost had one-tell him about your chil-' The Instructor started. But Neil cut him off.

Times Square was different and Neil marveled at the changes. He had been away longer than he thought –nothing looked familiar. Gone were any seedy shadings of a darker underworld. Where were the broken lights, broken dreams and broken hearts? Where were the dirtbags, pimps, hookers, and heroine? All had been replaced with the gloss of an outdoor shopping mall and a prefabricated theme park. There were large, clean colored lights, high tech signs that flashed corporate logos, neat and orderly buildings, restaurants, and chain clothing stores. It looked safe and clean, but seemed to lack something, which this cold, austere, façade had covered up, but couldn't erase. Maybe it was character, or maybe, it was just Neil expecting an unrealistic complacency from a city that never halted, but instead continued to change, rebuild, and press on.

The sidewalks buzzed with people, vibrating and humming in a never-ending swirl of commotion. It was amazing to think of all the separate lives, desires, interests and personal history in each of these souls. One common thread however, which was different from when Neil was last here, and one that he now saw moving up and down sidewalks, crosswalks - was a newly attached appendage. In every direction he looked there were people who held, carried or had planted to their ears, a cell phone. At first glance, it looked as if all had gone mad - pedestrians jabbering into the air, to an invisible entity, waving their arms, laughing, yelling and even cursing. The cell phone had become a crutch; Linus' blanket. There was the sense that some of these people who were talking into their cell phones placed more importance and meaning into their cellular world than into their present reality, albeit that of simply walking down a sidewalk, alone. Apparently that wasn't good enough. No, there had to be more, and one that didn't require too much work. They would create an exciting, thrilling, intoxicating life that existed in the virtual reality on a screen or the other end of a screen or cellular connection. So, they talked, laughed, cajoled, punched in letters and numbers, and gasped into these machines with twice the importance and focus expelled in a normal face to face encounter. Neil couldn't help but think if a feeling of inadequacy prompted the use for such a device - certainly, not all these cell phone calls had been dialed out of real necessity. He wondered if a fragile connection between us all was somehow being destroyed through the use of these digital devices. And it seemed speed was part of that. It was everyone doing something, anything, moving fast, hurriedly, multitasking but never stopping and asking about the destination, moving was all, to stop was death. They had, unknowingly, exiled themselves- becoming islands of isolation. He tried to remember the last time he had sent or received a handwritten letter.

The windshield wipers slapped at a thin drizzle of rain as the cab moved through the city and headed downtown. The night was cold and the streets were wet and quiet. With the exception of other cabs, city trucks or commercial trucks delivering goods not much moved in the streets. The hour was late. White steam exhaled from manhole covers like breath from an old, slumbering, iron dragon.

He was heading to a small downtown hotel near the Fulton Fish Market and close to the South Street Seaport that he had come familiar with while living in New York. He'd used it a couple of times to house out of town friends and family who had come to visit. Soon, the cab was rumbling over cobbled stone streets and Neil's mind went to hearing the cloppity-clop of horse drawn carriages that had traversed these same streets a hundred years ago or more. This lower part of Manhattan was the oldest part of the city and as the cab made its way through a fine mist, it wasn't hard to imagine the early days of the city when large cargo laden, wooden, sailing vessels with furled sails would be pulled along docks waiting to unload both cargo and passengers. The docks would have been busy and the streets bustling with trade merchants. There were pewter mugs filled with ale inside taverns that served as both a place of business and pleasure. They'd be oak barrels, horse drawn carriages, and questionable characters all up and down these narrow streets.

The cab swung onto Front Street and stopped outside the small hotel. Neil paid the fare and the cab disappeared back into the dark misty night. Standing in the quiet desolate street, Neil took in his surroundings. A man bending his hat to the wind walked a welsh terrier. A few leaves shot past and stuck to the curb.

He looked up at the gas lamp lit sign that swung in the wet wind, *The Commodore Inn*. Large wooden framed glass windows dripped with age, distorting and rippling the passage of light. There was a large door with a brass handle, which he pulled, then pushed and opened. Three small steps covered with a thick low pile green colored carpet leveled off down a narrow hallway and opened into the lobby.

The lobby had all the characteristics of an old colonial inn; there was an enormous fireplace, leather armchairs, Mallard duck and fox hunt paintings. An oversized oriental rug covered much of the wide-planked floor. Exposed wood beams supported the low ceiling. Long curtains hung from tall windows and were tied back with ornate frilly ropes. A black and grey freckled marble top ran the entire width of the room and served as the reception desk. Behind the reception desk was an assortment of wooden cubbyholes with either paper or nothing at all inside and marked with room numbers.

A silver bell rested on the marble top. No one was around. Neil tapped the bell and seconds later a man in a green vest with a folded magazine under his arm appeared from a back room. He wore thick coke bottle glasses.

"Yes sir?"

"I'd like a room please."

"Single or double?"

"A single, just for the night."

"Two night minimum." Tiny black pupils blinked behind the eyeglasses, reminding Neil of a pair of funny Halloween glasses he'd seen a few years back – only these eyes were cold and stern like those of a Coney Island seagull on a barren beach in February.

"Hmmm." He didn't need two nights

"You *could* stay just one night, but you'd have to pay the penalty charge."

"What's the penalty charge?"

"Almost as much as the cost for the second night."

Neil still needed to make airline reservations, get in touch with his insurance company, and deal with the entire reason he was here.

"Yeah, sure that's fine, two nights."

He filled out the information card, put a deposit down, and was handed the plastic key card to his appointed room.

His room was on the third floor. He had the option of taking the wide carpeted stairs or a small, quirky freight elevator. He remembered the elevator having, as best he could describe it, a humorous side. Humorous, because of the total disregard for efficiency; with stomachs tucked and breath held, three people *might* be able to squeeze inside. Then there was the delay between pressing the old, fat typewriter buttons and the elevator actually responding to the command - about the same time needed to give detailed directions from Jersey City to Clemente's bar in East Harlem, including alternate routes. And once the elevator did start to move, the rate of ascent or descent was slow enough that each and every brick between floors could be studied as they passed the small porthole window in the elevator door. Then came the total panic: searching for topics of conversation on a long slow ride with a perfect stranger. Neil took the elevator.

He got to his room, unpacked his things and went to sleep in the four poster bed. When morning came Neil prepared himself for the day ahead and with the cold black and white tiles beneath his bare feet, he washed his face, brushed his teeth and stared into the bathroom mirror. How far he had come, this face was his, yet it felt slightly removed as though it wasn't his and his alone. He sat at the edge of the bed and pulled from his knapsack a soiled envelope and a worn roll of money held by an elastic band. On the envelope was a hand written address; Rosa Willis, 137 Maple Ave, Bethpage, Long Island. He held the thick roll of bills in his palm and played with the weight of the paper mass as he pondered the circumstances that had brought him here and the events he had encountered along the way.

"Why, why did I do it?" he asked himself, sincerely. "Always the dope, idiot, taken advantage of, not a business bone in my body, so after all these years of banal struggle, what do I have to show for it? I could have taken the money. Idiot. And why couldn't I have kept my mouth shut - be content at the hanger or.........now not even the respect of a simple job." The old mattress springs seemed to further compress from this doubt that weighed heavy on him. It was a hell of a way to start the morning.

A good breakfast might improve things. He dressed and left his room. The hallway was silent and a spongy soaking sort of feeling moved like mercury inside his head.

Neil stepped out onto the sidewalk. The gerbils were already spinning their wheels; men and women crisscrossed the street, cars moved, horns honked, tourists flapped around, trucks idled and the city hummed. He was glad to be in a place like New York, a place where no one gave a damn about who he was or how he felt or his personal story. The gerbils here primarily concerned themselves with themselves because it was the only way to survive, for them to do otherwise in a cage such as this, filled with its overloaded stimuli, and overbearing competition for every scrap of sustenance would only drive them to madness and demise.

Neil found himself walking up Fulton Street where sidewalk vendors were selling everything from baseball caps to glow in the dark yo-yos. From behind a cart someone was frying up curried chicken and onions. It was all too much for him today. He ducked down a less crowded side street only to have a driver honk and curse at him. Was there no peace in this city? He jumped out of the street and back onto the safety of the narrow sidewalk and continued walking. There was something muddy and heavy in his uneven gate. He found a sandwich shop serving breakfast and ordered a bagel with lox and the largest size coffee they had. He sat down to eat, but something wasn't right, he felt odd and disconnected. He took a bite of the bagel, threw the rest of it away, and grabbed the coffee to go. Something was going on, his equilibrium was off, or.... it was too vague to pinpoint exactly.

He figured that a quick walk might do him some good. He zigzagged through cavernous streets of lower Manhattan, which were darkened by the shadows of tall buildings. He found himself in the heart of the financial district, and economic center of the world. The sound of barking seals came from across the street where men in construction hardhats were pulling nails out of wood scaffolding. Wall Street was only a few blocks away and he felt The Instructor quiver with excitement. A small bear poked its head around the corner. He was close to Broadway when from across the street an orange glow caught his eye. He stepped off the curb and crossed the street to get a closer look. There was a large opened doorway the size of a firehouse entrance. Inside and far back against a wall, was a man wearing an apron spinning a long rod, which he held inside an orange glowing large potbellied like stove. Inside the stove coals glowed brightly and Neil, although only at the entrance, could feel a slight increase in temperature. Another man pushed a flat crate on wheels across Neil's path, and at the same time a firm, instructive voice spoke from behind,

"Now, children, I want you, all, to remember, stay in line and don't touch anything - David, I need you to stop and listen now, okay? Jeanna, I need you to look at me and stop talking."

Neil turned around and moved to one side as a woman in her mid-thirties with tight curly hair entered holding a clipboard to her chest. A large group of young school children, all in single file, followed behind her. They wore large colored paper nametags written in crayon fastened to their jackets or coats with bobby pins. The children all looked to be about six or seven years in age. He smiled at their bright shiny hair, perfect little noses, tiny shoes and nonjudgmental befuddlement. Some held hands as they entered into this strange new setting.

"Now, remember, we're here to ONLY watch, NO touching," the woman had turned to the children, but continued walking backwards until she was deep inside the structure.

The man, who had been working the fire, took off his gloves and began walking towards the group. In addition to the apron, he also wore a pair of brown overalls, a sturdy pair of workman boots and tiny spectacles, which seemed almost lost among an overgrown bushy grey beard. His hair was the same color as his beard only slightly lighter and was held back with a ponytail that extended half way down his back. A shark tooth hung around his neck. He had a rugged, but affable look to him. He approached the woman and waited by her side until she had finished addressing the children. She turned and seemed almost surprised to see him there, but quickly recovered. She shook his hand and took on a much lighter and gay, almost flirtatious tone, which differed completely than the one she had just dealt the children. After the introductions, the man walked back to his furnace and began preparing his tools. The woman, in the meantime, had turned back again to the children to give last minute instructions, which were to be strictly followed. After she spoke, and as part of the instructions she had just given, the children formed a large semi-circle around the man and furnace.

Neil, all the while, was given not the slightest of attention and was paid no mind by either the adults or the children. He was in a kind of in-between state, feeling removed like an unnoticed ghost. Apparently, the woman and school children took him to be one of the workers and the workers must have taken him for an assistant with the school children. He could feel his head floating in a dense, peaceful pool of saffron water.

The worker at the furnace had already begun to talk to the children who all silently listened. It was hard to hear what the man was saying, Neil's ears felt clogged and stuffy. The words he heard were muffled and unclear. He put his hands in his pockets and moved in closer to the semicircle of children.

The man was a glassblower, and this was to be a demonstration.

"Can anyone tell me where the main ingredient for glass comes from?" the man asked the group of small children. The children looked at the man, but none spoke.

"A cow?" a boy finally threw out.

"No, not a cow. We know that the paper we write on and cardboard boxes we make comes from trees, then where do you think the glass for a window or bottle comes from?"

Again, silence.

The man answered his own question, "It comes from sand, silica, like the same sand on a beach." And here he held up a glass test tube filled with sand and corked at the top. He then handed off the sample to the teacher for her to give the children so as they could pass it around.

Neil thought of the school trips that he had taken as a child; the excitement and mystery he had felt had been almost inexplicable. And it all came back now with unusual clarity - the smell of rubber and vinyl seats inside the school bus, the girls across the aisle, the brown bag lunches and the feeling of flying into an uncharted world free from the confines of a stale chalk classroom.

To the right of the furnace was a black, cement slab about four feet off the floor, which was used as a table. On top of this table were a variety of long handle tools resembling small spades. The man stood close to these and began talking about the time required to become a master glassblower, the history of the art and at what temperature the furnace ran. He then donned a pair of special eyeglasses and began gathering glass onto the end of a long pipe, which he called "a blowpipe".

"Like a giant spitball," one boy impressed himself with this description.

The man turned the molten blob, pulled it out of the furnace, gathered more glass, and placed it back inside, and all the while continuing to slowly spin the blowpipe. He repeated this pattern several times until he had gathered the desired amount.

A few of the children seemed not just amazed, but a little frightened too.

One girl asked almost in a whisper, "Is it hot?"

The glassblower, wearing thick gloves and now spinning the glowing glass on a metal rail, answered in a calm, uplifting manner, "Only hot enough to reshape the glass."

Neil watched the children and the glassblower and felt the subtle power of something pass between them. It was a magic show that transfixed the children's attention; had a spaceship landed and a Martian popped out, the reaction would have been the same.

"What you see is what you get, there's no faking it. There are no shortcuts. It all takes time, there's no rushing time," the glassblower explained. This man was a cheater of sorts; stealing the properties of a solid, turning them into a liquid, and then back again to a solid, but in a newly formed shape. It was like disrupting fate, the fate of the translucent blob, and like clay - shaping, bending, molding and ultimately breathing a form of life into this once stagnant mass. He continued to work the glass until eventually, the end result was a kind of winged horse, which the glassblower held high above the heads of the children. There was a collective gasp. The glass sparkled, and light danced inside and through the clear figure, flowing deep inside the children's eyes.

Neil shuffled back out towards the street. The sky had become dark and grey and a cold rain had begun to fall. The figure of a lone hooded woman holding a black umbrella glided past like something sprung from the pages of a Sherlock Holmes mystery. Neil poked his head out from below the entrance overhang and looked up at the sky. The rain was here to stay. Up the block was a black man in an oversized army jacket holding a large umbrella above his head. He stood behind a large overturned cardboard box, which was being used as a makeshift table.

There was no mistaking the strong accent for anything else but Jamaican, "Umbrellas, umbrelllaaas, five dolla, a steal now. The umbrellas are here, mon!" he shouted. He then shouted something else that Neil thought rhymed with 'wet', but the word or words were lost in the rain.

Neil thrust his body out on to the sidewalk and began walking towards the man. Normally, the rain would have been cause for Neil to hasten his pace, but he wasn't feeling, or even in the mood for 'normal,' and instead he now felt himself softly embracing the falling drops of water, welcoming them, the moist air and the cold temperature. He was wrapped in a numb blanket and nothing could do him harm. He was in no particular rush to get anywhere right now. A pungent coconut filled air -and some other fruit-papaya, coming from several sticks of burning incense partially wrapped in aluminum foil, which were laying on the cardboard box next to a row of neatly stacked umbrellas. The Jamaican man's skin had an oily reflective sheen around his nose and forehead. Neil stood calmly in front of the box and, for a second or two, this cool Jamaican man looked slightly startled, causing him to hesitate, stumble, drop his act, his bag of tricks. He appeared genuinely scared as though Neil were a dead cousin who had returned to collect what was owed. The man kept his head down and made no eye contact while Neil purchased an umbrella.

With the umbrella spread above him, Neil walked in a sort of peaceful trance up the sidewalk and crossed Broadway. His knees felt weak and shaky, but still he continued to walk. He passed white gravestones with haunting figures and cherub faces. The gravestones filled a plot behind a black, wrought iron gate, and were planted next to a brownstone church. At the highest point was a white cross, outlined against a forbidding, tempestuous sky. The gate was part of an iron fence that ran square around the church. Hanging from the fence were shirts with numbers and, banners with words. There were flowers, postcards, a white elephant and stuffed animals. At the lowest part of the fence, and covering parts of the sidewalk, were flowers; some vibrant and alive, others wilted and dead. All were messages meant for the living, and now scrawled for the dead. Neil was having a hard time making sense of it all and his head kept trying to close. His right boot dropped into a puddle, but his foot remained warm and dry.

He walked up a newly constructed ramp and onto an observation deck and stood overlooking an immense void, a pit of what used to be – three years earlier two towers fell in this spot and shook the entire world, shook the Bill of Rights, the Constitution, democracy and woke the founding fathers from their graves. September the 11th would be etched in the American psyche forever. A collective mortality would fall upon the nation. Perhaps not immediately, but it would come.

September the 11th was a day Neil remembered with such clarity: the news reports, The President in a Florida classroom, planes, fireballs, buildings, The Pentagon struck. The President had been whisked away to safety, and the country was under attack. "Under attack," Neil remembered hearing those words and knowing not how to process them, let alone respond. There didn't seem to be a place inside his head for such words, or if there were such a place, it'd be filed right alongside a Hollywood movie, or some distant paragraph in a history book. He thought of the Redcoats, Kamakazie pilots and the Vietcong. "Under attack," - what was he, or anyone supposed to do when "Under attack?" He was supposed to do something, wasn't he? The gerbils had become complacent with their protection from any threatening outside danger. Overturn the wagons.

Now standing on the platform, he stared into the lifeless hole. The only sound came from the individual drops of rain that thudded against the taut black umbrella above his head. A damp gust of wind pulled at the handle. The dark sky cradled the thoughts inside his head as he remembered the lives lost here, not all the lives - there were just too many for that, but instead, he drifted to images of those black spots falling. What had it taken to force one to jump? The terror that must have uprooted any familiar feelings, which these people had ever experienced in their lives, fed those feelings into a mulcher and spat out the rapturous face of Satan, what had it taken? And then there were the black dots holding hands as they plummeted together towards horrific death, maybe Satan hadn't taken everything. But, God, God - where was God September the 11th?

If there was to be any God that day, that God was Allah - an angry God defiled by men whose evil and corrupted minds had hijacked commercial airliners, destroying the lives of innocent beings. But, Allah, a just God, a righteous God, a vengeful God, took the men who piloted those planes from their mortal lives and threw them into the awaiting arms of virgins from whose wombs expelled waxy balls of hungry maggots to devour and consume these men's evil, fighting flesh...forever. Perdition.

Sura 44:39-41. *We created them not except for just ends: but most of them do not understand. Verily the Day of sorting out is the time appointed for all of them,- The Day when no protector can avail his client in aught, and no help can they receive,*

Sura 44:44-49. *The food of the sinner! Like molten brass, it seetheth in their bellies As the seething of boiling water. (And it will be said): Take him and drag him to the midst of hell, Then pour upon his head the torment of boiling water. (Saying): Taste! Lo! thou wast forsooth the mighty, the noble!*

On September the 11th America changed, and so the world around her. September the 11th would become important a benchmark in American history as the year 1776. What it meant, 'to be an American' held as much meaning that day in September than at any time Neil could recall. A line had been drawn, and it was time for an entire nation to shake off its complacency.

The wind pulled again at the umbrella's handle and broke Neil from his thoughts. He felt his legs shaking and his thick head sway, as though it were filled with seaweed. He was numb, but could still feel a rise in his body temperature and, as he turned to walk back down the ramp, knew cracks had opened and a shell was beginning to dislodge.

He made his way down Broadway, through the canyons of lower Manhattan. Church bells trickled behind him. There was Battery Park and tourists, a green lady with her arm stretched high above the water and a silent, tired promise in her eye. There was a Customs House, four continents, The Buddha, a Cross, skulls, an eagle, and an Indian in a full war bonnet and all the beauty and horror of mankind. This was the beginning of something, things moved and the earth opened up and the shell cracked again. Neil was in touch with something grand, larger than himself; somehow he had made it full circle back to the beginning, but with new eyes. He stopped at a Deli and felt the layer of sweat, his undergarments soaked. He hoisted the two and a half gallon plastic container of spring water up onto the counter. He troubled himself with trying to count and figure the correct change the man at the register had asked for. Neil's hands trembled. They were white and cold and he could feel the blood drain from his head as he pulled and fumbled and fought to straighten the damp *In God We Trust* bills. He needed to get back to the hotel, his room, and into bed. He paid or thought he did, then pulled, pushed at the deli door. The deli owner shouted out after him, wobbly words too blurry to recognize. Outside in the silver rain, Neil focused hard at the task of getting back to the hotel- he was at the goal line and needed to force his way into the end zone. He began towards the hotel, he was getting wet, had left his umbrella back at the deli, or somewhere, but it didn't matter now. He didn't care. He reached the hotel, climbed the soft stairs, opened his door and dropped remnants of a shattered mask heavy to the floor. There was nowhere to hide, he knew a battle would rage and he was ready.

12

A misty morning or early evening, the smell of wet leaves and rotting wood by the riverbank and hound dogs barking hard in the distance. The tugboat captain in thick cable knit wool sweater and stereotypical pipe with musty smoke pilots enormous wooden wheel, hand over hand- now in panic in his old tired face as pirates approach skeleton figures move, cockroach scurries between his feet, now skeleton feet. The Instructor is the captain now and like in movie turns head towards camera for close up and winks into lens. There's a field of purple flowers, a large field snowcapped mountain in the distance, rumbling of violent moving subway train beneath the ground. Neil is on the track running into deep, dark tunnel between stops, but the train on same track follows behind, faces, only heads, part of tunnel wall laugh at Neil, then become serious one even sad, but not wanting others to notice as though it would betray entire secret. Now on the number 4 train green color, and moving on track below cavernous city, moving into Brooklyn sees old apartment used to rent, but much nicer, quaint even open window, green leaf trees in outside private courtyard and something about carpenters redoing, fixing up entire building- beautiful three story building white, brilliant white, white, super white bedroom, spacious hallways with old familiar slanted floorboards. Brooklyn is nice, essence of life and prosperous connotations, dear old Brooklyn, like Philadelphia linked to an eternal sincere past and seeds of a nation. Heavy slabs of broken sidewalks along summer tree lined streets, red brick buildings and old literary colonial days.

Neil wakes in wet sheets and looks out to damp streets and dark sky, gray fog. He moves to bathroom splashes faces, drinks spring water and returns to bed. He's back in rollerblade California, everything light and non - serious. Moving up Pacific Coast Highway and sun drenched twisting road. He's driving bootleg whiskey truck with questionable characters in back one mean eyed looks through cab window but, boulders and rocks high up on roadside cliffs rumble, shake and crash down around truck, road and into never ending, deepest Pacific Ocean. Hard to maneuver, snakes on road too and some splat beneath tires. The Instructor high on chuck wagon urging, whipping team of horses on "Heeeehaaay!"

Shhhhh. quiet inside dignified opera house, plush velvet all around expensive jewelry and perfume sparkle among delicate white gloved ladies with collapsible fans. Neil crawling down aisle towards stage. Spotlight burns brightly on him as all heads, audience turn in his direction. The feel of raw stretched canvas, but nothing on it, all is blank and white, empty. Lobby door opens and throws light like movie projector into theatre as silhouetted figure in its stream shouts and points at Neil, "He's the one! Nothing to bring, empty promises stolen from the hearts of our youth, a thief, liar and bum!" Ladies turn old and wither until nothing but The Instructor's face is left on all their sagging bodies.

A solitary being on an empty beach, Neil clutches sand dribbles out in a fine stream like an hourglass. There's music, old ancient muse type music coming from a bluff and now caves can be seen along the cliffs and an old feeling of Tristan and Isolde. The waves ebb in small, tiny little foam patterns gently tickling the beach. A bright half moon makes complete passage in sky in less than ten seconds, something horrible approaches. Now blanket of fog descends and the sound of timed menacing beat of oars striking gunwales of boat, which emerges through this blanket. Vikings are near, and The Instructor is at the bow wearing helmet and standing one leg up in war charging pose. A sword lies in sand close to Neil and a guitar with teal pinching words, "Hello cowgirl in the sand, is this place at your command?"

Neil's laughing and throwing back another shot as he's bellied up to a bar, jazz sounds inside smoke filled nightclub. Purple places things with black centered pupils rich and murky deep centered gravity never ending hole so mysterious and deep complemented only by rich and clean, loving and daring mumbling either in the dark of night or blue and black and, once again purple, Miles Davis pierces and deep heavy riff hangs in air stopping time and in it is a knee bending supplication for God to cry and forgive. But now way too much drink and in blurry oatmeal porridge state can't move, can't think and life is wasted away on those who sleep and drink. Neil wants to wake and break but can't shout out as jaw can't move, doesn't work-nothing moves and the futility of all is held heavy in such dreams. But trying again, he struggles against the impossible and feels good in the very act of trying and suddenly a string is untied, and a rope burned, a cable unravels and his body begins to feel light, free and sunny true happiness as though the purpose of his being is strong, right and has always been.

There's a soft rolling road in green hills of Kentucky and a single RED barn sits atop one of these rolling hills filled with hay and peak of summer when work is done and rest is reward. No other car except maybe an old-fashioned clean, white milk truck with clear cold glass bottles softly clinking in simple crates and there's uniformed milkman with a 'glad to see you' genuine smile.

Neil got up from the hotel bed and heard laughter in the hallway. His room was dark and he went to the bathroom and turned on the light. He ran the bath water hot and slipped into the tub. He was weak and his mind was empty. He stared at his knobby knees and looked up at the freshly painted ceiling and thought of all the gerbils who at one time had put all this together, the bathroom, hotel, and city. He knew the city was ever changing and the gerbils would never stop. Never stop. When the bath water had cooled, he pulled the chained rubber stopper and pushed himself out of the tub. His chin trembled and his entire body shook from cold or fever, he didn't know which. There was barely enough strength in his body to grab a towel, but he somehow managed to dry himself off. With small, aching steps he walked back to the bed and sat at its edge. He poured some spring water into a small glass and looked at the clock; 8:17. He placed the empty glass on the nightstand and fell back into bed.

He wasn't sure if he was dreaming and then waking, dreaming again. It was completely white, very white In the white with white gowns and white linen and white ice the reality of death; white is pure and cold and symbolic. The colorless corpse, proverbial cadaver is a white death. And pure? And virginal? The bride comes to the wedding in white. But, life is red, crimson, scarlet and the bride bleeds for the groom and monthly flows for pregnancy. White is all color. And Christ bleeds for humanity, doesn't he? And, yet he suffers unto death on a cross stained with sacred blood so we do not have to suffer needlessly, without hope. That is the meaning of the Mass. The secret of death being thrown against the window of the church and its cries blue and crimson colored yellow sacrament making its way down the corridors and gateway to eternity fear not fear not the horrors of hell and the fires of the soul. Christ comes to us again and again around the globe, changing wine into his blood, bread into his body. Supplicate and all is well.

White again with an icy wind blowing and Neil sees two men clad only in their boxer shorts and black socks sitting next to one another on a block of ice. The men sit half facing one another and engaged in a wordy argument of some sort. He is in the Antarctic and getting closer to the two men, Neil can see it is William F. Buckley Jr. and Truman Capote, or....the white was still white but now pillars of a walkway, Washington D.C. and walking along the white pillar walkway of the White house is Henry Kissinger and a young school boy who lends an attentive ear to this man's low mumbling instructive voice. Suddenly, The Instructor appears beside them and assertively injects words into the conversation. Then, an odd thing, The Instructor looks up, and seeing Neil watching, hurries the other two along and seems

264

frightened as though part of a secret underworld had been exposed.

The race is on. Neil looks in his right hand and notices he holds a laser like flashlight, capable of burning. The Instructor ducks down a passageway and runs. Neil pursues.

The heartbeat of a fetus. "I never regret the past, I did what I did in a moment because I felt it to be right," the doctor said after the ultrasound and weeks before the abortion. Neil was back there now. "Besides she's not ready," the doctor continued, jerking his head up and in the direction of Sarah who sat next to Neil. She was crying softly through two quivering lips that wanted to stay shut. They had just finished up in the other room where Sarah had been given an ultrasound. The doctor spoke again, "I tell you she's just not ready."

They drive home in silence. At a traffic light Neil places his right hand gently cupping her left kneecap and a soft shake and gentle pat. A fish on a line fighting, fragile and sad, but nothing sadder, really - a Christmas tree left to rot or never bought, but instead left behind like an unwanted child. Holidays come, but then they go, nothing stays, nothing lasts, not even a smile and that's the saddest story ever told.

Neil wakes from the hotel bed and in the darkness can feel the soaked sheets and his wet skin. He reaches and finds the water. After drinking several glasses with water spilling on the floor he swims into a red ocean.

A Saturday morning a subway beneath New York and then fog blowing off the Pacific, snaking its way through downtown Long Beach. Too cold and wet, windy and dark for this time of year he remembers thinking. Sarah gathers her things, pocket book, jacket and keys. He wants to retch the illusion of normalcy they're trying to maintain. He's weak and disconnected. They barely look at one another on the way to the clinic. It's all too real and raw and thoughts too truthful and deep to share. He parks the car. She stops in at a convenience store for a bottle of water. A middle-aged woman is peddling pamphlets saying something about another choice. Heads bent. Too shameful. Don't stop. Don't listen. The second floor and clinic. They don't say a word.

About twenty woman and a few men sit quietly. The room is awash in regret, shame and fear. Most are minorities, poor and simple. Sarah and Neil stand out. He feels inadequate, and embarrassed, lacking the money to have the procedure performed discreetly with a private doctor. No discretion here. The poor always pay in shame. A form filled out. Eyes stifle their movements. Two Negro women are in a back corner shucking and jiving and carrying on as if on a Harlem street corner. One even claps her hands together and leans forward in her chair laughing from a remark the other has made. Her front upper teeth are missing and her jaw protrudes like an old witch with do-rag on her head and big gold loop earrings and rings flash on her fingers. One ring, the fattest of them all, is in the shape and design of a dollar sign. Sarah is called. Terrible wait. Alone with imagination. Sarah returns and the past is locked, their fate is sealed and somewhere an Angel screams.

Red rock formations of the West, The Instructor turns into a gecko, but Neil onto him, the Great Wall of China, the Nile River, the Canadian Rockies, Bilderberg Hotel in the Netherlands, the Australian Outback, Vienna, Peru, college exams, and then into Neil's third grade classroom, an old playground, a Halloween night, homemade radio, a highchair, an old house, antique trunks, an attic with a cradle, a basement door was opened and a surface of water rose from the damp and dark. The surface rose and moved, Neil looks hard and seeing it wasn't water, at all but a thick layer of rats, which scrambles and bites, gnaws at anything around them. Amidst them all, is a rat with eyes that seem to be looking, studying Neil. In this moment and at the very center of his mind, an impartial voice: telling him that in the balance of it all was a choice, he was either going to transcend this battle, this element of himself and catapult into a bright, limitless unknown future, or capitulate and go mad -stuck wrestling with a demonic companion of the past forever.

Neil grabs the laserlight and jumps into the menacing pile.

He wakes and screams out in complete darkness, "I love you mother! I miss you Father!" Angels come roaring down the hill.

The bed was hot, wet, and all that had swirled and ached was ...gone, dissolved like Alka-seltzer in a New Year's Day glass of water. There was no time and the innocent beginning of the world was in his chest. He was sure a star had exploded somewhere in the universe and began its life anew. He took a wonderful breath and fell into a deep, blessed peaceful sleep. When he woke again, it was a new morning.

13

Figures danced on the white wall. The hem of the laced curtain swayed from a gentle breeze that blew into the room with a fresh radiant morning light. Neil walked to the window, pulled back the thin white curtains, and looked out upon rooftops and the East River with its strong swirling currents and thought of George Washington one August night in 1776 and a nation's salvation and, farther still to Brooklyn, oh Brooklyn- holy holy holy, sacred art thou amongst boroughs. Today was a glorious day and Neil felt certain in it. The gift of life filled him. He showered and dressed and laughed at his own giddiness and a ridiculous but truthful and overwhelming desire to click his heels - if he only knew how. He packed his things and checked out of the hotel. It had been an exhausting night, and he was weak, but his spirits were high.

Stepping out of the hotel and on to the cobblestone street, he looked out again towards the East River and to The Brooklyn Bridge. White, fluffy clouds drifted high above the water, bridge and shipyards. The air felt clean, and pure. Possibilities like kites, and as boundless as the clouds were high, pulled at the strings of earthly imaginations.

Neil was famished. He adjusted the strap of the sack, which hugged his shoulder and walked down towards the water. At the lower east end of Manhattan, the old streets crisscrossed and angled themselves in different directions. The Wall Street brokers and business suits had been replaced with Sunday tourists who were just beginning to dot the streets. A few delivery trucks rocked along the narrow cobblestone streets. Neil continued walking and spotted a sign hanging from a building, "The Blarney Stone Rose" - it was a pub that looked old enough to be part of the original beads for land deal struck with the Indians when Manhattan was first founded. Everything had been built around, above and below this establishment, you could tell by the different colored brick and modest height of the building.

Neil took a seat in a booth towards the back and close to the bar and ordered steak and eggs. The place was as dark as a cave, and so secluded that there was no way of telling whether it was day or night, or even what the weather was like outside. Around him was old, dark paneling - wood gathered from ships and farmhouses. Sawdust speckled the floor like potpourri with a fragrance of stale ale and burnt timbers. Neil leaned back and took it all in. Sunday morning, slow and easy. An old man sat at the end of the bar. He wore a ratty old tweed topcoat that scraped along the floor beneath his bar stool, collecting bits of sawdust each time he moved.

Three workers were getting ready, prepping for a lunch/brunch crowd that was as inevitable as the rising tide. There was a young and beautiful girl; thin, pale with a long braided ponytail, but with too serious a look, Neil thought, for someone her age. She had a nervous energy about her, as though someone or something had wronged her and now she fretted with the possible aftermath from anyone discovering what that secret someone or something was. Neil took her for an actress or dancer - maybe played the cello, or violin. Whatever she did, she didn't take it lightly. She took her craft, her art, seriously. He could easily imagine her practicing for hours and hours and knew too, her art was all of her, life and death. Amazing what he gathered just sitting in his booth - yes yes yes, it might have been an assumption, but it felt true and real to him. In him was an amazing heightened sense of perception. "God, it's so awesome," he said to himself. He felt it now, all of it- encapsulated here with the complete joy and drama reflected in this girl's being; the struggle and desire to participate in the game of life - the hope and the pain. All was good, not just good, beatific. How wonderful - the opportunity, the possibility and the precious, tenuous nature of it all. He thought of the phrase, *Life is not a dress rehearsal.*

The cook came out of the kitchen; he was an older, gruff, brute of a man - a work in progress - with a long stained white apron that came down to his knees, and a short sleeve dingy tee-shirt. He was all about the ponies and Monday night football, a meat n' potatoes guy with a gut and an anchor tattooed on his forearm and if he didn't like you, he'd let you know it. In fact, from the looks of it, Neil bet there weren't too many people this guy did like. Out of the kitchen he came, grumbling and grunting like a bear coming out of hibernation, pouring himself a soda at the bar, looking up at the television hanging in the corner, fiddling with the remote, then grumbling back, soda in hand, to his den. The third worker was a young, teenaged looking clean cut Mexican kid who, although was working like a mule, still had time to make sweet little remarks to the waitress.

The old man at the bar pulled photos from a wallet and showed them to the waitress who stood behind the bar cutting limes with her long, white, determined fingers. He spoke about his family, his grandson and granddaughters; how they were promising to pay him a visit sometime around the holidays or early next spring or maybe the year after. Neil really dug the whole scene, enjoying this small slice and how it seemed to encapsulate so much of an American drama that was, is, and always would be going on. He was glad he'd come here and thought of the first generations of families who had arrived in this country in search of economic prosperity and a new life. In that regard, he supposed, little had changed.

After breakfast he walked back out to the street, and, with a feeling of revitalization, began the final conclusion of this entire trip.

He pulled out a crumbled piece of paper with a handwritten address, which he'd carried since the desert. The address was to be his last stop before returning to California. He had booked a flight while at the hotel and would be flying back to California later today.

Neil took the subway into Brooklyn, got off, walked through a connecting tunnel to Flatbush Avenue and then to the Long Island Railroad. He approached the ticket window.

"When's the next train to Bethpage?"

"There's a train track 3, leaving 10:29," responded a Puerto Rican woman with fresh, manicured nails and a snazzy, sexy hairdo. It was 10:17, just twelve minutes to wait. Neil bought his ticket and boarded the idle train. The half empty train car served as a reminder it was Sunday.

Once he had settled in his seat, he again, pulled the piece of paper from his pocket and examined the hand written address. There really wasn't a need, but he was slightly nervous and had nothing else to do while waiting for the train to pull out of the station. Satisfied, he pushed the paper back into his pocket. He then placed his knapsack on the floor between his legs, and reaching inside, fingered through the layers of clothing like a loaf of bread until he found what he was looking for - the thick roll of money and the plain, white envelope with a note inside. He pulled the items on to his lap, looked over his shoulder and to his side and made a last minute check on their condition- everything was in order. A buzzer sounded twice and the doors of the train slid shut. The train then lurched forward and began moving out of the station and down the dark track.

Within minutes, the train was out of the tunnel, moving like a reptile out of its hole and into the light of day. It ran east, out of Brooklyn and, then, into Queens. Neil peered out the window. There were clotheslines, barbed wire, blacktop roofs, cigarette billboards and vacant lots. It looked more like a prison yard than a neighborhood. It was hard and gritty and he marveled at the existence of life under such conditions. It was high top sneakers, basketball, pizza slices, tank tops, pit bulls, and bodegas. He wondered at the dreams and desires of a typical teenager living here, maybe they were the same as anywhere else in America; a nice car, stylish clothes, and a sizzling love life. Still, at any age, it had to be hard living here. He just hoped the woman he was visiting didn't live in a place like this.

271

It now started to worry him as to what exactly he'd say to this woman to whom he'd be giving the note and money. He started to formulate words, sentences in his mind, but they became twisted and convoluted, compressing into a dead mass. After a while he gave up and relaxed, reminding himself he was only acting as a messenger and his job (if it were to be called that) was only to deliver the items as instructed by the dying man. The words of instruction had been plain and simple. His mind started again. What if she wasn't at home, what then? Would he wait, or...he didn't have an answer, but knew he just had to get out there and finish this trip.

He thought too, of how this whole thing had begun, starting with him packing his things the night before his departure. Now, leaning back in his seat, the scenes of over a week ago flickered off the train's window like a silent movie. He remembered laying out the items on his bed in his small Long Beach apartment before packing them into his saddlebags. He stayed up late that night talking briefly on the phone with Sarah, taking a shower, shaving. He sipped a cold beer. Chet Baker's lamenting and melodic trumpet, aching with smoky rifts, drifted from an old turntable. He studied maps and felt the anticipation and excitement that comes before any new adventure. It was a struggle to fall asleep. Getting up just before dawn, he fumbled with the teapot and hypnotic blue flames on top the stove. He checked his tent, sleeping bag and camping supplies one last time. There wouldn't be too much stuff. After all, it was only a four-day trip into Prescott National Forest.

It wasn't until he had ridden out past the entangling freeway system of Los Angeles that he really began to feel like he was on vacation; his ride became smooth, easy and open. After crossing into Arizona, he rode along the flat desolate desert. Having the need to relieve himself, he turned off the main highway, and onto a dirt road to stop, stretch and find a spot to urinate. He was in the middle of nowhere. It didn't matter what he did out here. He had turned the bike off, pulled the ignition key and walked over to the side of the road where there was a small gulley and a ravine. Having dismounted his motorcycle and without air

272

rushing around him, the heat of the day hit hard. Neil unsnapped his helmet. Dirt and small rocks flowed under his boots like layers of snow. He hip hopped, jumped and sidestepped, slaloming like a skier down a slope. The bottom floor of the ravine was speckled with cactus and other shrub like plants. Great rock formations hung in the far distance and a small meandering river not seen from the road cut through part of this arid land. He remembered finishing, zipping up his pants - and while turning to head back up the embankment, spotting the outline of a lone, dark figure leaning against a large bundle of plants that provided shade. The figure sat in the dirt facing the small ravine and the vast landscape that stretched forever. Neil had to look twice, three times even to trust what he was seeing. He stopped, studied and then walked cautiously in the figure's direction. When he was within 200 feet, and could define the figure of a man, Neil called out,

"You okay?"

The man didn't move.

"You alright?"

The man was slumped over, his chin nearly touching his chest. Maybe he was resting or… sleeping. But, resting, sleeping out here in the middle of nowhere and the sun burning hotter and hotter? Neil made a 360 degree scan - nothing. It didn't seem right, feel right, something was wrong.

"Hey there," Neil made another attempt while moving closer to what he could now see was definitely a man, an old man: worn, wrinkled alligator skin with deep, loose canyons. What the hell was this old man doing out here with nothing around for miles and miles?

Neil remembered feeling spooked, like coming upon a sailboat in the middle of the ocean; empty and adrift, halyards clinking against a mast. Ahhooy! Anyone there? Anyone? Then the hazy, half death eyes of this man moved; the eyes turned to Neil and in a very soft, calm voice, the man spoke.

"What's your name, son?" he asked.

- And that's the thing Neil remembered more than anything, stuck with him – not the question the man had asked, but the questions the man didn't ask; "Do you have any water?" or "Can you call for help?" Instead, it was like this old man was almost expecting to meet a stranger at a prearranged spot.

"Neil, Neil Adams," Neil answered, then looked back up the ravine.

"I am glad for your arrival." The man was barely able to squeeze out.

"That's good," and someone inside his head added, 'You crazy bastard.'

"Need help?" Neil asked.

The man squinted his eyes and his body suddenly stopped. He then coughed, a deep horrendous cough and released the catch into a yellow handkerchief. He gasped in air, seemed to settle himself and shook his head 'yes'.

Neil moved closer to the man. The man wore pants that were dark brown or black - so soiled, stained and married with grease, oil and dirt it was hard to tell their original color. A corduroy jacket was tied around his waist and a torn dark blue shirt covered much of his torso. A loose bracelet made of wooden beads hung from the man's left wrist and covered much, but not all, of a dark purple bruise. The man's hair was cropped short, almost bald. In front of him and on the ground was a small pile of twigs, sticks and dried sage. A snake's skin or carcass lay close to the man's left knee. On the man's right side was a brown paper bag and a tiny, clay urn.

"I'll go for help."

The man lifted his right hand and shook a finger, 'no'. He coughed again, then after a few moments said,

"It is hot today, Neil," his words soft and sparse.

"Yes it is."

"A...... beautiful day."

"Yes."

This whole thing seemed a little crazy, but this was out in the middle of nowhere, and crazy had no meaning.

Neil squatted in the shade next to the man and said again he'd leave and go for help. The man refused, and placing a heavy hand on top of Neil's right wrist, tenderly patted it. The act was done so calmly, mindfully, knowingly that all the history ever told within the deep earth seemed to come forth and speak, infusing its rhythm into Neil's being; giving a calm, steady story of its creation, so that all that was known or ever would be known was told. Suddenly, it occurred to Neil that he had mistaken a man who was dying for a man in trouble.

"Can I ask you to sit and listen to a dying man's words?"

"Of course."

The man said his name was Jack. He was born a Sioux Indian and now he was dying. Jack had spent most of his life drinking, gambling, working and riding the rails. Neil remembered hearing that phrase, "riding the rails" come from Jack's mouth and almost smiled. He had heard the phrase before, but like words from a fairy tale, didn't believe it was something that actually existed. Jack talked slowly, parsing out air and words as though he were pulling savory treats from a bag that was almost empty. He paused now and again to cough, or just regain his strength. As he talked, his clod-like fingers worked on pulling off foul smelling leaves from a small, dried branch and crumbled them into the clay urn. He had made a mess of his life, a life in which disappointment found most anyone he ever met, including those he had not met - his ancestors. His biggest regret was for the husband and father he had not been, and the pain, which he must have caused his daughter whom he didn't know. He had been sick for several years and the last few months, especially so. He told Neil that he had come out here a few days ago to die.

"Much of my life has been wasted. Chasing a dream others had fashioned, and my mind too weak to know the difference. This world we live in a lie. All fabricated. A lie dependent.....built...on trust. I feel anger even now when I think of it, shame. But, that's behind me, I'm going to a place where my dreams will not be stepped on, a place where dreams serve no purpose."

After Jack had talked for a time, he slipped into a long silence as though he were gathering the last amount of strength he had left in his body and then quietly summoned it all up,

"This is the land where I was born, and here I've come back to die. I have made ready a shallow grave there in the gully. I have two things to ask of you. Would you give the items in this bag to my only child and return me to the earth?"

Neil looked at the crumbled brown paper bag the man had laying beside him on the ground. He would certainly honor this man's wishes by sending these items to his daughter, but wasn't about to 'return this man to the earth', burying him here in the desert. This old man didn't really expect Neil to do such a thing, did he?

Neil took the bag, and clutching the rolled wrinkled top with both hands, looked back up the ravine, and then to the distant rock formations. His head jerked back for a moment as he caught a small wiff of the retched concoction inside the clay urn. "I'll make sure your daughter gets these things, I...."

"We share... things, are one. Go now down to the riverbed .... and think on this."

Neil wanted to speak, felt the need to say something, anything, but looking at the old man, and seeing his eyes were closed - privately immersed in the last precious moments of life, knew he had no right to interrupt such a holy thing.

Neil straightened himself up and, as the man had asked, walked slowly down to the riverbed. What was he supposed to do? This old man needed help, not have someone like Neil simply walk down by the water. This would accomplish nothing. He'd give the old man a few minutes, but then, no matter what, Neil would get back on his motorcycle and go for help, this was crazy, way too crazy. He looked back towards the man and could see that the small pile of sage and twigs had been lit and thin white billows of smoke pillowed the old man's body. The old man's head moved up, and his lips made silent words as his hands cupped the smoke and made slow splashing motions towards his face. This process was repeated several times in an almost hypnotic fashion.

Neil turned back to the stream - not much of it left. It had dried up to the point that only a small current trickled. To bury someone in the ground was wrong, wasn't it? Burying a dead body required a whole set of regulations and controlled stipulations; there were taxes, embalming procedures and funeral home costs. You're not supposed to just bury someone in the ground. There had to be a law against such a thing.

"Always abide by the government," a voice waxed inside his head.

Neil pondered the word, government - what it was, what it meant. A government is an artificially imposed group of men, a body, which formulates, regulates people. So infused has government become in the daily lives of all people that to even consider life without these gatekeepers seemed ridiculous, impossible. He reminded himself that at one time there was no government, at one time.

The sun beat down on the dry desert land and the temperature continued to rise. The ancient rock formations stood like unchanging ghosts. Everything out here worked according to a set of unseen hands, unaffected by the daily lives of men, past or present.

Looking out across the land, Neil wondered at the number of dead already buried in the desert; those first wagon trains, men and woman lost and wandering, and before that, the Indians.

'Inherent to all things was birth and...death,' Neil thought as he looked into the stream. Beneath the surface of the trickling water, a small pebble dislodged from the rocky bottom. It tumbled a bit then came to rest again.

14

"Jamaica. Next stop, Jamaica!" the conductor's voice rang out as the eastbound train rocked and shadows moved.

'Five more stops and I'll be there,' Neil told himself, testing his mettle. He still had to transfer to another train here at the Jamaica stop in order to continue on. But, it wasn't a problem. The other train was waiting across the platform, and as he found a seat inside the connecting train, he could see how Sunday morning marked itself; men, smelling of weekend aftershave, had traded in their nine to five business attire for jeans, sneakers and comfortable shirts. Sunday newspapers were spread, children jostled down the aisles, footballs were tossed, and baseball bats and cleats hung on shoulders. The train buzzed with activity. Freedom shot high and loud. Two older women wearing fashionable sunglasses sat across from Neil. One was riffling through a purse on her lap while the other was staring out the window talking about what she would be getting at the mall. Neil sat somber with grave business like intentions and wondered if he had made the right decision in coming out here today. But, it was too late for second- guessing; the train moved away from the platform and into the stomach and heart of the unknown.

He tried easing his anxiety, telling himself he could get off at the next stop, any stop and try again later if he felt up to it. But then he remembered the airline ticket he'd purchased for the flight later in the day and knew he had to keep on schedule.

"Why couldn't I have just mailed the damn note and money?" Neil asked himself. "What difference would it have made? So what if the wishes of a dying man weren't kept?"

He imagined the poor Indian daughter, and, how he might find her. "No- I'm doing the right thing," he said to himself. There she'd be - at her small kitchen table with laundry hanging on a clothesline in her backyard that she'd have scrubbed by hand after having returned from Sunday Mass where novenas had been repeated over and over for a father she had lost touch with long ago. She'd be a solemn woman, who quietly held her feelings in check and kept saint like ways in her solitary life.

Fifteen minutes, and five stops later the train stopped at Bethpage. Neil descended the steps of an empty platform and stood on the sidewalk. There wasn't much to the station in this suburban setting; a small parking lot, two payphones and a tiny beige concrete structure that held postings of timetables, and public announcements.

He walked across the street where there was a donut shop and a convenience store. A florist was making deliveries. Wearing a red apron and handlebar mustache, he pulled flowers from the side door of a cargo van. Neil asked him for direction.

"Only about a mile down, follow this main road and it'll be on your right- can't miss it."

Neil was thankful for the nice weather and not having to call for a taxi or car service.

He moved off the store-lined street, and turned down a quiet block that ran parallel to the main road and began down the sidewalk. It was a beautiful Autumnal day; clear clean crisp light blue skies – leaves of burnt orange, yellows, reds scattered on the ground and on the sidewalk and some still bravely clinging to Oak and Maple trees that flanked his path. Here and there the sidewalk rippled from the roots of these trees that bespoke a New England history. A middle-aged man washed a Pontiac SUV in a driveway while his son scooted on a tricycle. A squirrel ran up a large tree, then froze close to the base in a gravity-defying act and twitched its tail. An Elmer Fudd of a man rode a mower along a small patch of grass between the sidewalk and road.

There were modest little homes with neat little driveways and perfect lawns with straight, even manicured lines and bushes cut to exact proportions. American flags were proudly displayed. Above ground Doughboy pools, looking like pregnant whales, sat covered in backyards. It was the American dream and everybody was holding on tight. The houses, with everything sewn up tight and perfectly square, were sure to include a prepackaged vacation tour brochure lying on the kitchen table and prepaid cemetery plot.

The craziest thing of all was that these 'modest' little two bedroom houses were selling for close to a million dollars and the cheapest fixer upper would sell for only slightly less than that amount. Real estate prices were ridiculously over inflated. He referenced this to the times when he was a teenager and for kicks would drive up on a Friday night with friends and a few beers and cruise the few million dollar homes and marvel at their size and extravagance which were reserved only for the extremely wealthy, all cloaked in mystery or hearsay, feeding the imagination. No one knew anything about them except the names: Getty, Rockefeller, Du pont, or CEO's of companies like Xerox and Coca-Cola. Things had changed.

Sometimes, now, Neil would grab a Sunday newspaper and scan the real estate section. The prices for homes seemed so far fetched and ludicrous that the listings proved more entertaining than factual. He'd sit with his morning coffee, look at the listings and shake his head. Had he been left in a time capsule? What he was reading didn't actually reflect his reality. It was one thing to be flabbergasted at the ridiculous prices for these properties, but what was even more astounding was the fact that these properties were actually selling like hotcakes, and sometimes even above the asking price! These outrageously priced properties were being snapped up -'Who the hell are these buyers?' he'd ask himself. 'Where's the sustainable income to afford such things?'

He knew it was just a matter of time until something very ugly would be occurring within this economic market. For the very first time, renting for one's entire lifespan was becoming more appealing than buying. Neil had always considered himself middleclass, but this real estate craze had caused him to reconsider his classification in the economic food chain. Property, the owning of property, had become a crazy golden chalice often filled with the blood of its pale owner. He'd heard stories, from older people mostly, about 'the good old days' - a time when a middle income, blue collar worker could grab a nice piece of property, take on a thirty year mortgage and still be able to provide a decent life for his family; a time when a man would spend maybe a third of his total income on his monthly mortgage payments and the rest for whatever he pleased. Now it seemed reversed: a blue-collar worker had little to no chance of acquiring something nice, let alone even a modest home. And, whatever he could buy, would cause him to spend three quarters of his total income on a monthly mortgage payment, leaving very little for anything else.

So, here it was, 137 Maple Avenue: a small, white two-story house and driveway with a single car garage. There were two small concrete steps and plain black metal railings leading up to the white aluminum front door with a glass upper portion and a solid wood door behind it. A silver colored SUV was parked in the driveway that also doubled as a small basketball court with the backboard and net attached to the upper part of the garage. Neil stepped over a hose and lifeless sprinkler, which lay in the front yard. A yellow plastic, Wiffle Ball bat leaned against the front steps. Maybe the woman he was looking for lived in the back, a guesthouse or rented room.

This was it, everything - Neil knocked on the thickest part of the aluminum door. Sharp, yipping and yapping barks came from inside and then little paws began beating the front door. Through the glass and past the opened door, Neil could see into the front hallway, gaining a partial view of a living room where black cables extended from a television set. Arcade game sounds boomed from the set and there was music, loud rap music with angry lyrics blasting from somewhere inside the house. The dog continued to bark. Neil knocked again. The dog went into a frenzy, tearing into the door with all its might and barking uncontrollably. But still no one came to the door. He then noticed the lit doorbell and pushed it.

"Danny, someone at the door, Honey!" A woman's voice hollered from inside.

A few seconds passed. Then, mixed with the music, came the sound of heels striking hard wood floors. The sound slapped the air. A woman appeared in the front hallway and approached the front door.

"Betsy, calm down, easy, sweetie!" the woman commanded the dog, but it was of no use, the dog continued barking. The woman stood right behind the glass door. The clear portion allowed a view of her from the waist up. She looked to be in her late forties, maybe a little younger, but there was hard wear on her face. She had a hairbrush and a lipstick stained tissue in one hand and a long thin cigarette that was lit in the other. She wore a leopard skin pattern, low cut blouse and her breasts looked unnaturally high.

Neil was first to speak, nearly screaming to be heard through the door and above the sound of dog and music, "I was told I could find a Rosa Willis here?"

The woman looked away and exhaled a white stream of cigarette smoke, "Shit, I haven't heard that name in a long time," she tightened slightly and pushed a thin smile to her lips, exposing a lipstick smeared tooth, "what's this about, are you polling? A fund? Census Bureau or - who are you with?"

Neil opened his mouth to speak, but she cut him off - turning over her shoulder and yelling into the living room,

"Danny, turn that Goddamn thing down!"

She turned back to Neil, and asked, "Who are you with?" She didn't wait for an answer, still not satisfied with the excessive noise, "Damn it, how many times I gotta say it - turn that frigg'in thing down!"

Again, she turned back to Neil, and with half closed eyes "Kids," she said and shrugged. "Anyway, you're gonna have to keep this short. I just don't have the time today."

As if given a verbal Heimlich maneuver, Neil coughed up a response,

"It's about your father."

"My father."

"Your father, Jack?"

"Wow," the woman said, dropping her present life and inhaling fragile soap bubbles of her past. In a mercurial voice she asked,

"How'd you come across him?"

"Oh, I knew him back in Arizona."

"So, that's where he's living now, Arizona, huh?"

"That's where I met him."

The woman grasped hold of her present life and, regaining her previous footing, opened the door just enough for her to slip out and prevent the dog from escaping. The dog jumped past her anyway, and ran out into the yard where, barking incessantly, it made a few, quick, tight circles. Faster than Neil could snap his fingers the dog had scampered its skittish body close to his ankles and in a crouching position challenged him by showing teeth and growling. It was a small foo foo of a dog with a red bow tied atop its head. The dog's coat shined and looked cleaner than Neil.

"Damn you, Betsy!" The woman bent and threw her arms out towards the dog. It immediately fled then came back. "It's alright, she doesn't bite." The woman looked up at Neil and then towards the door she'd just come out of as if making sure no one had followed. She turned to Neil and said in a clandestine whisper,

"I don't talk much of my father, their grandfather," she thumbed towards the house. "The less they know, the better off it is. Tell their friends. People's opinions change, get funny ideas when they think you're part Indian or some such nonsense. We're of Spanish descent, really more from Spain - you understand."

Neil wasn't about to argue, "Sure."

"I'm sure that's in our blood anyway -somehow or another."

The dog had gained some confidence and now sniffed at Neil's leg.

283

The woman's perfume was overpowering. She looked tired. "I'm just surprised he, you even knew my address. I haven't seen or talked with Jack in ... awhile. How's he been?"

Masking much uncertainty, Neil said, "He's been good."

All seemed to have been said. Now the woman filled an awkward gap, "That's good."

"But, see the reason I'm here, is, your father, Jack, he - he wanted me to give you this," Neil reached into his bag and pulled out the roll of money and note and handed them to her.

"What's this?"

"I really don't know - he just wanted me to give them to you."

"Money." She took the rubber band off the roll and began a quick examination. "A lot of money," she smiled at the roll of cash and said, "I don't know what the fuck. He gave this to you?"

"Gave me to give you."

"Jesus. Comes at a perfect time too. Tony - Tony's my boyfriend, him and me are going to Atlantic City today, spending the night. I can't believe this!" She suddenly stopped and looked at Neil, "But, why, wha- why the money, why the note, what's this all about- hold on a sec. Who are you again?"

"Neil. I...really don't know, he just wanted to make sure I gave them to you. He knew I was coming out this way, and well, he was sick, Jack - real sick and he-"

"He's alright?"

"He wanted me to give you these things."

"But, is-"

"He's, he ahh, No, he's not alright. I hate to be the one to tell you this, but - your father, he didn't make it. He's gone, passed away."

She waited for more to be said. A second or two passed.

"I'm sorry," Neil said

She bent her head, stared at the money and slowly tapped the envelope on her hand. "Well, what are ya gonna do? It's not like like -"

"Mom! This is such bullshit! Laurie says she won't get off the computer and I need to download some stuff now - she's being a real bitch!" A plump ten year old boy had suddenly pushed open the front door and now stood holding it open with one of his sausagelink arms.

His mother did not react in her usual way, "Danny, I'll be there in a minute."

Danny had already blown up his chest to expel more complaints, but sensing it wasn't the right time, he let it go and went back inside.

"Kid's looking at porn half the time on that thing," she said to herself, to Neil, to no one really. She smiled nervously. Then, as if this whole exchange between them had never taken place, she lightened and added, "well, listen...."

"Neil."

"Right, Neil. I have got to get ready. Tony'll be here any minute." She threw her cigarette down on the lawn, tilted her head back and blew the last bit of smoke through her laughing lips. "Here I am," she said while twisting the cigarette butt out with her right stiletto pump, "in my 'Sex and the City' shoes putting out a cig. See how you got me now - all crazy." Then, as a quick kindof afterthought she asked, "you got family around here, Neil?"

He lied, "Yes, in Westbury."

"Great. Maybe, I'll see you around then." She rubbed her arms and through shaking lips said, "God, it's frigg'in cold out here. She extended her hand, "Thanks for coming by. It was nice to meet you."

"Likewise." Neil shook her hand and walked back to the station.

15

At 4:30 in the afternoon Neil unlaced his boots and took them off. He placed his boots, belt and the bag that Mein had given him on the conveyor belt to be scanned and x-rayed for any possible contraband or weapons. The security guards said nothing. He was free to board the plane. He put his boots and belt back on, grabbed his bag and boarded the Airbus A320 aircraft bound for Long Beach, California. It was to be a nonstop flight with an estimated five hour thirty-two minute flight time. It was an unusually light flight, on this late Sunday afternoon. He found his seat next to a window and sat down. Thirty minutes passed. An easy smile crossed his lips as the powerful engines pinned him against his seat and the aircraft bolted down the runway. It was always his favorite part of any flight; the few moments right before the aircraft lifted into the air, but especially so this time. The large metal mass pulled itself from the earth's grip and ascended into sky, only sky.

The plane climbed, banked, climbed some more, banked again, and leveled off towards the West. The puffy, white clouds, which Neil had seen much earlier in the day, had broken up into smaller patches. The plane flew through these and, then, above them. The sun was beginning to set, casting long slumbering shadows inside the peaceful cabin. It was a soft amber light straight from God's eyes, making everything and anyone it touched angelic. Neil leaned back in his seat and looked out the window. His eyes blurred, filled with tears. He was neither happy nor sad, and didn't try to control, analyze, or judge, but instead just enjoy and allow - enjoy where he was, what he was doing, and for the first time in a long time, who he was.

"Way up high..," a fragment of a song floated inside his head. He didn't rush to grab the rest, but it came anyway - his silent lips barely moved, "where troubles melt like lemon drops, way above the chimney tops..."

His breath softened and a sweet feeling wrapped itself around him. He would paint again, discover Sarah in earnest, marry her and live a life filled with intention. Some would call this a new start, but America was like that on Sunday; the promise of a new beginning. The winding down of all Sundays- when supper has ended, the dishes washed, and somewhere between the melancholy of a dark changing night and the hard expectations of tomorrow comes a possibility of a better life.

And, so here again, was a Sunday, and, somewhere underneath Neil was America. He tried looking through the clouds to the land below, but it kept changing; the clouds held different patterns and formations, each glimpse of land was different. But, it was alright, he turned from the window, closed his eyes, folded his hands, and rested in the comfort of a humble silence.

END